DRIFTING SOUTH

Also by CHARLES DAVIS

ANGEL'S REST

Charles Davis

DRIFTING SOUTH

MIRA®

MIRA®

ISBN-13: 978-0-7783-2542-0
ISBN-10:   0-7783-2542-3

DRIFTING SOUTH

www.MIRABooks.com

Printed in U.S.A.

DRIFTING SOUTH

Follow the banks of the Big Walker off of old Route 11 in Winslow County, Virginia, and head the same direction as the current. But don't walk the train tracks. What you're searching for lives on the other side of the river. When the waters grow still and wide and the mountains steep, a brushy trail will lead you to a cemetery that's surrounded by a long, sloping cornfield bordered by faraway houses too big and fancy for any family to live proper in. Pay no mind to them. Stop and read the names above the sunken graves. Then make your camp at the water's edge of that cornfield and after supper you might just hear what I'm about to tell you.

If nothing else, you'll hear music. It'll come from whichever way the wind's blowing, and I doubt you'll ever find the fiddle player if you dare go looking for him. Folks will tell you there ain't nothing or nobody to find, so just sit back and listen. Close your eyes and you'll soon hear the sounds of crickets and the other critters of the dark. Pay no mind to them, either. Pay no mind to anything, except for the singing of an old fast-water river, long ago gone. And listen with most care when the breeze moves the trees.

You'll believe what I'm about to tell you then.

Prologue

I came to know that lost place the way only a select few did. I was born there, a month too early on the scrubbed pine floor of a whorehouse in the spring of 1942. Ma's first sight of me was by lantern light. She said I glowed like sunrise and I was the most beautiful thing she'd ever seen. Conceivings could naturally be expected on any given moment in Shady, but few birthings. Ma told me I came sudden and ready to meet the world on a Sunday at midnight and I wasn't about to be born in a bed where business was conducted. Especially on a Sunday.

"Bad luck," she said.

Ma was a charm-carrying believer in astrology, signs, luck, and evilness of all shapes and varieties. She believed in goodness, too, and a life after this one that was full of that goodness. And she also believed in a thing that she could feel more than she could see, that she called "the mystic." It's right there living alongside us. And sometimes among us, she said. Ma always did have a superstitious nature and peculiar beliefs about so many things compared to most. She was pretty and graceful with curly black hair, and she was a whore and had to be a hardworking one because she believed in keeping her children fed.

We all had fathers of course, but we never were sure who they were as Ma never got much help raising us. I didn't think she knew who our fathers were, either, by the way she kept trying to hang each of us around the neck of about every man who'd blow through Shady Hollow. They'd always leave for good or try to once they got wind of what her intentions were.

People who lived and worked in Shady Hollow just called it Shady. Wasn't but twelve dozen of us or so at any one time who had a bed to sleep on that wasn't being paid by the night for. Most of the faces in Shady changed quicker than day and night coming through the same window. But some took root for years and years for their own good reasons, which weren't nobody's business, Ma said. And she told me it was none of my business why we lived there, either, or why she did what she did for a living, when I asked her one time. Ma was only sixteen years older than I was, but she always seemed a lot older no matter what age I was at, even though she didn't look it.

Shady Hollow lacked a lot of things, like electricity and flushing toilets and a post office, but a person who had nothing in the world but a stretched-out hand never got too cold or too hungry.

Shady never became a real town and the name never was on any map. If you did hear about Shady Hollow in some rambling story from a man or woman you wouldn't be apt to believe anyway, you'd think the place never did exist. But it did. It was the realest place I've ever lived and, even after all of those years I spent in prison, that's saying something.

Ain't many places more real than a prison.

From the stories I heard over and over as a boy, Shady Hollow got started in a two-story barn in 1861 by a man named Luke Ebbetts. He named his place "The Establishment on the Big Walker," and he sold homemade whiskey and hired a whore from Tennessee who soon had more work than she could handle shaking the rafters in the loft.

Luke believed he could make a sizable profit providing to soldiers what the Blue and Gray armies wouldn't provide for them. Things like liquor and good cigars and women and a hot bath and photographs of them standing tall and fierce in their brushed uniforms and decent hot food and music everywhere. You could hear music in Shady day or night from the earliest times, they say. Night it was louder.

I'm not sure if Mr. Ebbetts would put the things I listed in the same order that I did per a man's necessity, but he made sure all was aplenty and more to suit any man's tastes and size of pocketbook.

Luke was a rebel through and through, but he was a businessman above all and he welcomed any uniform wandering into Shady as long as those boys didn't ask for credit and stacked their weapons when they showed up with their powder dry and ready. Those long rifles would be stacked quick or there'd be shotguns pointed at them. The soldiers who risked coming to Shady Hollow weren't shy of a fight for certain, but they'd do what Luke said, because the one thing they didn't come for was to hurl lead at one another. They'd had enough of that, and that's why they'd walk away from their guns peaceable for a day or two and sometimes even have a drink with their enemy before they'd go to killing each other again on some battlefield up on the Shenandoah.

It wasn't long before a couple of men who worked for Luke saw how he was making more Confederate and U.S. money than he could bury in canning jars. With his permission, they soon built their own leaning shacks with hand-painted signs atop them, sold whatever things were needed to keep the place running, and hired their own whores who kept more tin roofs shaking. Luke got his cut from all of it.

Before the end of the war, flatboat drivers were braving boulders and swirl holes to float pianos and piano players into Shady, and the rest is pretty much what it came to be—a haphazard outlaw settlement tucked deep into the Blue Ridge Mountains of Southwest Virginia.

Deep. Deep in those mountains.

All sorts came to Shady Hollow once word of the place started drifting out of those foggy hills. Coal miners. Timber workers. Rich northern college kids with old money rearing to depart their new pockets. Gamblers. Orchard pickers. Foreigners. Roamers. Murderers. Thieves. Forgivers. Saviors. And the unrepentant, those rarest of few who in their final dying act would find the will to hold up a shaking middle finger for whoever could see it, and take note of it, one last time.

And politicians and railroaders and mill workers and carpetbaggers and just generally people looking for a good time or those who'd lost their religion or way in some other life.

Fugitives and fortune seekers all of them were, winners and losers, adventuresome folks who'd heard about it and some who came from thousands of miles away. The strangest and the bravest and the most curious of the needy or greedy or forgotten or unwanted seemed to collect there. Good and bad they were, most often a troubled mix of the two things churning away in the same person.

And women were among them. Shady was full of women. Most didn't stay long like Ma, but they were always coming in and out. They were all sizes and shapes, showing up barefoot and hungry most of the time, a few with a dirty baby nursing on a tit and a screaming little walker in hand.

But some gals made up all fancy would come to us riding tall on a hungry horse or, later, sitting in a new shiny automobile running out of gas with a smile on their face that anybody from Shady could see right through. They had life growing in their bellies, and like everybody else, I reckon they all hoped what they needed to find was there. And one thing for sure, everybody found their true nature in Shady Hollow, because it was the sort of place where a person's true nature was bound to run into them right quick.

Anyway, Shady wouldn't have been what it was without its women—it would have been one mean miserable place for sure then—and I reckon the place probably needed children, too. It's where I grew up.

During my time there, the churchgoers scattered around that part of the Allegheny wilderness country called Shady Hollow "No Business," because they said no man nor beast had no business going near there. The faithful would proclaim in their town meetings that the government should destroy Shady because there was evilness just a day's walk from their back pasture fences. The Shady elders would send spies to their gatherings, and we'd soon get secondhand tellings of all the goings-on.

There'd be family men standing up, quoting the Holy Bible in the strongest voices they could muster after their church visits, all of them worn down from trying to save our souls.

But as I'd come to learn already, what some people would say or pray in church on a Sunday morning, and actually do in Shady Hollow on a Saturday night, were two different things.

And you could put a fair wager on that about every time, if you could find somebody foolish enough to take such a bet. Which weren't likely.

In those church meetings, some of the folks with the loudest voices would come back alone when they could get away with it unnoticed, and they wouldn't be thumping on a Bible. We figured they had butter and egg money in their pockets, and God sound asleep on one shoulder and the devil picking a five-string banjo on the other. And they'd come back again and again.

We'd welcome them with their stern or bending ways as it suited them, politics and people and religion being the way they are and always have been. So we were a tolerable lot in Shady, even with the Bible toters.

My whole world my first seventeen years, save one trip not so far by miles but a long distance by all other measures, was that curved riverbank with shacks and stick buildings lining both sides of a one-lane road that was mostly mud, tire tracks, horseshit and changing footprints.

Besides the occasional car coming in or out, people rode horses and mules and walked and even peddled bicycles through the mountain country to get there, because the law was so bad about stopping anybody coming in or out on the only dirt road that led to Shady. And some of those yahoos were lazier at thieving than we were by the way they'd hold up folks leaving and charge them for this or that crime, before telling them that if they paid their fine in cash on the spot, they'd be let go and there wouldn't be a jailhouse stay or court hearing at the county seat of Winslow.

And the fine was always however much money the law could find on them. They'd take watches and rings, even wedding bands for payment, too. When they started taking vehicles and sending people walking out of those freezing hills in the deadness of a January night, something had to be done.

A couple of those lawmen never left the outskirts of Shady Hollow once it came to light what they'd been doing. They were running off business, Ma said, and they were giving Shady the crookedest name of the very crookedest kind.

Those deputy sheriffs never even made it into the hard but forgiving dirt of Polly Hill, neither, once they ignored threats and turned down bribes and were sentenced according to a final judgment by the Shady elders. They ended up bobbing down the river with their bellies bloated and their badges pinned to their foreheads for all to take warning of downstream.

I guess Shady is where I grew up in about every way a young man could and I saw almost every kind of good and bad there is to see. Almost.

Shady Hollow is all gone now, all of it, except for the dead still buried there. I still ain't sure if the kneelers finally got their prayers tended to or it finally outlived its times. Maybe it just came down to plain bad luck that outsiders might call prosperity.

Over the years many more than a few died trying to find and get to Shady, wandering up on the wrong liquor still or copperhead at the wrong time, or just getting lost in the wilderness. If for no other reason, I still figure there must have been something decent—and maybe even special about the place—if so many folks died trying to find it. It was something in its day, and I'm sure in the last moment before it took its final breath, the diehards of the holdouts threw the party of all parties.

I missed that fine celebration that I can only imagine. But contrary to what some people still claim, it wasn't because I had six feet of clay piled over top me on Polly Hill.

Most days I'm still pretty sure I ain't dead yet. Maybe a little bit dead, maybe a whole lot more than a little bit.

But I'm still here.

I had to leave Shady in a great big hurry on September

28, 1959. September 28 fell on a cool early fall Sunday, and I was seventeen years old. And even though I've survived so many things since, I still think about it. Especially when dark falls and all gets still and quiet but the visions and ghosts of once was, and once that was never to be, who come back again and again to pay me a visit.

Almost half a century has passed since the shooting. But the sounds and sights of Ma's yelling and crying, and Amanda Lynn's screaming, and every single thing that happened on that Sunday afternoon is carved as deep into me as it is into homemade river-rock tombstones overlooking what once was a place called Shady Hollow.

Chapter 1

Harrisburg Federal Penitentiary
June 16, 1980

"You're not out yet, Henry. Well, keep that in mind, yep," he said.

The guard behind my left shoulder—the head goon who ducked through doorways and always walked behind prisoners with my kind of history—tapped me on the right shoulder with his stick. *Tapped* probably ain't the right word. He hit me with it not hard enough to leave a mark a day later but hard enough to where I'd feel it a week later, whatever that word is. I was used to him walking behind me, and had come to know his stick in a personal kind of way. My head had put a few dents in it.

Officer Dollinger always ended everything he said with the

word *"yep,"* and he was letting his stick tell me that I'd been mouthing off too much to a new guard walking in front of me.

Anyway, the head of the beef squad behind me had never called me Henry before. It seemed the whole bunch of them would come up with new words to call us every few years, same as we'd come up with new words to call them. Lately the guards called all of us convicts either Con or Vic.

Don't see that in movies, prisoners being called Vic. Don't see a lot of things in prison movies, at least the ones they'd shown us in prison, that actually make being locked up look and sound and smell like what it is, which is similar but different in an uglier, more crowded, louder, smellier way.

But mostly the guards just called me and the rest of us "you." After I'd learned to write, I'd signed so many of their forms over the years with that name.

You.

But in D Block, Pod Number Four-B of the Number Nine Building known as the Special Housing Unit of Harrisburg Federal Penitentiary, the few pards I trusted with some things but not all, and had become friends with as much as you can in a place like a prison, called me "Shady."

At some point in some lockup or lockdown, I was feeling dangerous lower than is good for a man to feel, and I decided I might need something to remember who I used to be before I had to live behind tall walls and wire, even if I couldn't feel that way no more. On my last day in prison, both of my arms were covered in fading blue ink, pictures and words. Those prison tattoos read like a book of my youth, and across my back and shoulders in big letters was the word

"Shady." It was the first thing I'd ever had scratched into me. Nobody knew what Shady meant because I never told anybody about my past or what little I knew of it, but it came to be what I was called by the other inmates.

So anyway, given a kind warning by stick standards, I decided to not say anything more to the new jug-head guard in front of me. I just kept shuffling slow and steady, wearing irons on my ankles that I'd gotten used to so much that I'd grown permanent calluses from them. I kept shuffling slow and kept my bearing about me as I tried to ignore the irksome clanking of the chains at midstep, because it wouldn't do me well to raise hell about any of it.

I'd already been through eight hours of a hurry up and wait drill, first in my empty cell with a rolled-up bed, and then sitting outside the warden's office watching the guards keeping an eye on me over top issues of *Life, Field & Stream* and *National Geographic* magazines.

An old trustee with heavy glasses on and small shoulders who seemed to have been there before time began and a man who I'd always gotten along with somewhat tolerable came in to say at long last that the head man of the Harrisburg Federal Penitentiary was busy attending to a bunch of local politicians touring the place.

All of the guards laid down their aged magazines, bored, like they'd probably done a thousand other times, and then they grabbed me up and escorted me to another waiting room. After I watched them sip on cold bottles of pop for another hour, I finally had my farewell talk with the assistant warden.

The tall shiny wooden sign sitting on top of his desk

yelled that his name was Theodore Donald O'Neil, the Third. And he was young, a good bit younger than me, and I wasn't that old. He seemed proud of himself sitting behind his long name and polished oak desk in a way a young man is until he's really tested and finds out what's really inside of him.

But like this old Chinese lady had come in to teach us once, I kept focusing on my breathing. I took in air slow like it was the gift of life and let my lungs fill up with the gift before letting it out, just as I'd done over and over from years of trying to let out what was about to make me explode, or eat my insides away to nothing.

The assistant warden told me to sit.

I sat.

He looked so serious, and then he grinned.

He leaned back carrying that grin and stared as hard as he could for what seemed a decent long time until his eyes started to get watery.

"If it were up to me, you wouldn't be leaving. I've scanned your file and sitting here looking at you, I know you're still a threat to society. It's written all over your face."

I kept staring at him because my eyes had dried up years ago when something deep down in me turned the water off, and I could now stare at anybody until I just got so bored with it that I'd decide to stare at something else. It was written all over Mr. O'Neil that he wasn't quite yet the hard man he'd need to be in this new job, as his eyes left mine and he began talking again and fiddling with a pencil that had teeth marks on it.

"Besides not making parole several times for various violations, you've been involved in several serious altercations. You even managed to kill an inmate here."

"I'm sure it's in the file what I did and why," I said.

"Actually, the file only has your version of what happened, being the other man is dead."

"I had to defend myself if I wanted to keep living is the short of it."

"Yes…you never did say why the man tried to kill you, as was your story."

"Don't know."

He looked over the papers at me. "Well, we can't ask his version of what happened, can we?"

"You could dig him up but I suspect he wouldn't say a whole lot," I said.

He kept looking at me for a good spell, then at the head guard before he eyed his watch. Then he turned his attention square back at me.

"The warden doesn't have any other recourse than to let you go. I'd like to believe that you'll begin leading a decent life, but your nature toward violence will lead you right back into incarceration, if you don't get killed first, of course. But you're a hard man to kill, aren't you, Henry Cole?"

"This damned place hasn't killed me yet."

"This institution didn't try to kill you, it tried to rehabilitate you. And we failed in that task. The taxpayer's money has been wasted in that regard. You are living, breathing proof that some men cannot change their behavior, and therefore they should be restrained and kept from society that they will naturally prey on and do harm to. It's my opinion that you should be kept here for as long as you have the capacity to continue to be a threat to others, which would be until you are either a feeble old man or until you die. But as you know, even though you still have evil in your eyes as you sit there staring at me, I lack the authority to keep you here and throw away the key, as they say. I did want you to know my feelings on the matter, however."

I couldn't hardly stand to be quiet anymore with that young man with not a scar on him judging me the way he was doing, but I kept trying to sit on my temper best I could. It was starting to catch my ass on fire.

"What're your plans?"

"Don't have any," I lied.

"None?"

"Not a single one," I lied again.

"What do people like you think about in here for...what was it...eight years?" he asked.

"I've been here a lot longer than eight years."

"Didn't you ever think about what you would do when you were released?"

"What do you think about in here when you're locked up behind the same rusty bars as I am, day after day?" I asked back.

The assistant warden tried to grow another grin but it slid away.

"I can leave here whenever I want. You can't. But to answer your question, I think about how to make sure predators like you stay here where you belong," he said. "It's very, very satisfying."

He looked like he meant what he said, and I respected him

more than I did when I'd first laid eyes on him, but still not much. He went back to scanning and flipping page after page of I guess what amounted to my life in prison, which amounted to all of my adult life. He stopped to read one section with a lot of care.

"You've been housed in protective custody most of your time here. Why?"

I didn't say anything as he kept reading. He finally looked up.

"Why the attacks?"

"If it ain't in there, I don't know," I said. "I was actually hoping you might."

"You don't know why inmates on two other occasions tried to kill you?"

"I didn't even know them."

"This is a complete waste of time." He closed my file and threw it onto a stack of other files.

I noted mine was the thickest and an old pain shot through me in a thousand old places.

"The reason we received the order to release you two days early is certainly not because of good behavior, it's because the Bureau of Prisons has red-tagged you a security risk. The unannounced change of date reduces the threat of another violent incident just before, or on, your actual court-order release date. Do you understand what I'm saying?"

I nodded.

"Your file reads that either you have a very difficult time playing with others, or someone has wanted you dead for quite a long time. If it's the latter, we would rather that not happen on our grounds, especially the moment you walk out of the gate unprotected. You will be a standing duck for anyone who may have been waiting for such an easy opportunity. It's happened before and we don't need the mess or paperwork." He started showing what looked like his first real smile. "Your safety will very soon be your own responsibility. I do wish you good luck with that."

He acted like he was waiting for me to say something. I couldn't think of anything to say besides wanting to tell him that if the guards were to leave, I'd probably try to mop the buffed floors of his office with his face to get rid of that real smile and the smirk I'd had to stare at. He was lucky because if it were just another day and I had a ton more time to pull, I'd try it even if I was chained up with guards all around me. I'd get one lick in for sure somehow that he'd carry with him for a long time, and maybe he wouldn't smirk at and talk down to the next man sitting in front of his desk who'd pulled his time. He definitely wouldn't smirk at me again.

I kept staring at young Mr. O'Neil, thinking how three months in isolation and catching another charge for assault on a federal officer and two more years on the tally is worth every minute of it, every now and then.

But not that day.

He was lucky. And I figured that I was lucky, too, because my better nature was in charge of me sitting before him. The nature I'd known as a boy. He finally asked if I had any questions.

I leaned forward as far as I could and shook my head.

He shot up all of a sudden. "You won't be out for long." He then nodded at Dollinger, and that's when I could feel being

let free. I could feel it all over me like I was standing under a
waterfall. It made me nervous, and that was a feeling I hadn't
felt since I didn't know when. It hit me at that moment how
long it had been since I'd felt anything at all except rage or
rainy-day late-morning hollowed-out lonesomeness.

The guards stood me in an elevator, facing the back of it,
and we went down to the bottom floor of that building and
when the doors opened, we all walked like a formation again
into a bright room that looked like a poured concrete box.
Wasn't anything in it that wasn't colored gray. Even the prison clerk behind the counter wore a gray uniform and he
must've been down there so long, his face had taken on the
same colors of the walls and file cabinets.

"What hand you write with?" the stump guard beside me
asked.

I raised the first finger on my left hand and he took off
the one cuff from it, and then cuffed that bracelet through
an iron ring mounted onto the top of the long counter. One
of the older guards behind me took off the leg irons, being
careful to stand clear in case I bucked.

I looked over my shoulder and made sure he was out of
the way, then I stretched and shook out the cramps in my
legs as the clerk handed me a pen and shoved paper after
paper in front of me to sign while telling me what I was sign-
ing. But I'd learned to read and write, probably the only good
things I did learn in prison, and even though I was in a hurry
to get out of there, it looked like they were in a bigger hurry
than me to finally get me out-processed. I saw on the clock
that it was shift change.

I decided to take my time reading those papers. I read careful and signed every single sheet with the name "Shady." They'd been kicking me all day long. I figured I'd get in one last kick from Henry Cole.

"Where's my belongings?" I asked.

The clerk bent down and pulled up a wire basket that held a big paper sack. He dumped the sack onto the counter. A button shirt, dungarees, old drawers, white socks and a pair of withered-up brown shoes lay in a heap. Uncle Ray's revolver wasn't there as I surely knew it wouldn't be, and the razor and whetstone and Ma's roll of money were gone, too. But it made me want to smile seeing the clothes because I could remember wearing them. It made me feel young in spirit for one of those too-fast seconds you try to grab hold of but the next second it's off on some breeze.

I didn't want the clothes to wear, knew they wouldn't fit and I figured it might be bad luck anyway to put on clothes with sewn-up bullet holes, but it was nice seeing them because they brought back a feeling of better times. I did need the shoes because I figured there was still a ten-dollar bill sewed between the sole and the bottom leather for just such a predicament, as Uncle Ray had taught me when I was a boy in Shady Hollow, just before he'd gotten killed.

I ran my one free hand through everything, checking careful and hoping with all the hope in me to find a folded piece of pretty yellow paper with her handwritten words and scent on it. Amanda Lynn's letter to me. Feeling through that pile of old things, I was afraid that it hadn't made it through all of those miles and years. But I looked and kept looking, because if by some chance it had survived such a journey, I was going to be certain right then about locating it. I kept feeling for it, not paying any mind to anything else. It was the letter she'd given me in Shady Hollow, the same one I'd never gotten to read, and the same one that was taken from me after a shoot-out years before, and before I'd even learned how to read. I could read now, but that letter and whatever was in it was as gone and still as big a mystery to me as she was. The scent of her was nowhere in that dumped basket of old things, either. All of it just smelled like the sort of dust that only collects in a prison.

"What're you looking for?" the clerk asked.

The quiet noise of his voice sounded like a slamming door to me. I gave up my search, stared down at the truth before me, grabbed the shoes and clothes and threw them back in the bag. I took hold of everything in my one uncuffed hand, then after I'd signed the last of the paperwork and it was official that I was a free man, they uncuffed my other one.

"Want to throw those clothes away?" the clerk asked.

"They're mine and I'm taking them," I said.

Just like I knew I could give that young assistant warden sass and the one green guard some serious mouth, I could surely speak to that clerk like a man would to another man and not get in a bad way about it. I felt like saying more, and I would've said more with so much battery acid still going through me, but he'd treated me fair and seemed all right.

I could've raised a lot more ruckus than I did that long day and gotten away with it. I wasn't getting out on parole. They'd denied me that three times. I knew, too, as much as

I was glad to be getting out of there, that some of those guards were glad to get rid of me, so I didn't expect any trouble from them. It'd been a long twenty-one years on both sides of the bars in the two prisons I'd been in.

Around five that evening, I walked through the yard toting my paper bag of all I owned in the world, and with no steel on me anywhere. I had on a nice suit of clothes that the prison issued me, blue pants and a white shirt, stiff black shoes and a canvas tan jacket. In my pocket was fifty dollars of state money, and a bus ticket to Wytheville, Virginia. Ma was on my mind heavy at that big moment.

She'd told me from the time I was a little boy I'd grow up to be a wealthy, powerful man, and that I had a true good nature hiding amid the boy mischief in me. She also told me that one day I'd use that wealth and power for the good, because I'd outgrow the bad and all that was left would be the good. But I never could figure why she'd say such things, except maybe that was the sorts of hopeful wishes all ma's say to their young'uns.

On my last day in prison and with so many things working in me, I knew for certain I'd turned out not to be any of those things, especially good. I'd turned out to be no good account at all…an apple knocked from a tree limb when not half-ripe, then left on the ground to do nothing but rot slow and turn dark from the inside out. I figured if I'd turned out to be anything, I was maybe just an old name in some worn-out old story told in the beer halls of Shady Hollow.

Somehow I'd aged behind gray prison walls to be almost

as old as Uncle Ray was when he died. That hit me hard on the morning of my release. I didn't know if he was a good man, but he was a far better man than I'd ever turned out to be, and he'd passed so young in such a bad, bloody way trying to protect me.

I never expected many visitors or letters or anything like that while I was locked up. Most of the people I was close to couldn't write and didn't have the means to up and travel to prisons for visits, plus most of them steered as far from them as they could anyway. But I did expect to hear from a few, like my ma and my brothers, and maybe even Amanda Lynn. Just maybe. I don't know why, but every night I hoped to hear something from her that next morning, but that next morning always was exactly like the sliver of a fast-fading golden streak on a double reinforced concrete wall morning before it. I never heard from nobody, and my worries over it grew every year, but I kept trying to tell myself things like it was because they wouldn't know the name that I'd been going by for so long, and they were having a hard time locating me.

But even trying to believe in that reason, Shady Hollow would've gotten some wind of what had happened to me. Had to. And they would've known I wouldn't have given the police my real name of Benjamin Purdue all of those years ago.

I was raised better than that.

Ma had to know where I was, I was almost sure of it, if she were okay and nothing bad had happened to her after I'd left. She'd know where I was, I kept telling myself, probably just like some of the religious prisoners I'd known believe Jesus always knows where they're at and he's listening to the prayers that they mutter asking for the same old important tired things and important worn-out blessings over and over while trying to fall asleep.

Ma wasn't some God or some God's perfect son in some fancy black book that you best never disagree or quarrel with too much, though. She was real. She was as real as the bars in my prison cell or as real as the feel and look of a sunny day long ago in a place I'd seen through young eyes, not through bars. She was real, and she'd told me that she'd find me, and that I could never ever come back home until she did, when it was safe.

At the end of serving my state and federal time, I was thirty-eight years old, tall and convict lean with a head of hair still dark as Ma's, and a ponytail fell halfway down my back.

I'd changed so much in prison that I figured quite a bit had changed in Shady Hollow. Not just the looks of me or the looks of that lost place, but the stuff inside of both of us. I hoped it wasn't all hollowed out and hadn't gotten as mean and hard as I had over those years. I wondered if even my own ma would recognize me. Almost all of Benjamin Purdue got killed a long time ago. I didn't just go by the name Henry Cole now.

I *was* Henry Cole.

My whole life was still one awful, empty mystery. On my very last day locked up, I had a lot of reasons and questions and especially darkness inside of me—old wounds that had never healed up right, and a lot of other things I couldn't even put to words—calling me back home.

But I guess the first thing calling me back was that some-times a person just needs to go to his roots and see old faces that knew you when you wore a different face...a face with a smile on it that only a young man who thinks he's got the world by the tail has. Sometimes a person just needs a thing like that in a real bad way. To go back and try to grab back hold of something you once had, and had felt the missing of it every day since. Then maybe some repairs could be made to some things.

Just maybe.

I was twenty-one years older than the day I'd gotten ar-rested, and as I was about to take my final steps toward being a free man, the last thing I cared about was whether it was safe or not to go back to Shady Hollow. I didn't have a care if I died once I got there.

I was finally heading back home.

Home.

Chapter 2

I was still inside the fence but outside the walls, and the air already tasted different. I guess most of all, it just tasted clean. The prison control room popped the first gate, and I walked through it by myself and stopped before the second gate, doing just what the loudspeaker told me to do. Once the first gate closed, the other one chugged open, and I didn't need any instructions on what to do next. I'd always figured I'd hurry at such a moment, but I didn't. I took a firm step at a time, cleared the last gate and, as I'd suspected, there wasn't nobody who I knew outside to greet me. I thought of the people who could have been there but weren't.

Remembering what that assistant warden had said about somebody wanting me dead, I took a scan at the tree line about a half mile away in case somebody with a scoped rifle who had dying business with me may have found out my release date got moved up.

"Take care of yourself, Henry, yep," the guard in charge of the beef squad said. I turned around to look at Dollinger. He was twenty yards behind the first gate, and he was nodding at me with his stick smacking into one hand that was as big as a ball glove.

"You're getting a little slow with that thing. Bad thing for a man with your responsibilities," I said.

"We'll keep the light on for you if things don't work out, yep," he said.

He didn't smile or wave or nothing like that and I didn't, either. But out of all of the guards, he always did seem fairest to me and as that goes, I didn't wish bad on any of those fellers who worked there. Well, a couple I did, but you just got tired of it all, and they were part of it all.

A van sat in front of me with the middle doors open. I knew it was my ride out of there. It felt strange getting in a vehicle without being all shackled up the way I could move so easy.

I slid into the backseat and sat my paper sack beside me. Except for looking to see if the driver had a gun on him anywhere—and I didn't see one poking out in the usual places—I never took my eyes off of his. He was a mountain of a black man, almost as tall as Dollinger and twice as wide, but he looked gimped-up in his neck and right side the way he sat off-kilter and had a hard time turning his head. I sensed he was a former guard or soldier or police officer of some kind who'd gotten out on some kind of medical. Could be a stroke or car wreck, or he almost got beat to death by a prisoner or shot up, something that messed him up bad.

He didn't say anything after we locked eyes so long in his rearview mirror. I didn't have nothing to say to him and I don't think he had much to say to me, either, at first. I was enjoying the quiet. There was always some sort of loud in prison, breaking the still. Always. Even at night, there'd be the sounds of loud ugly. Men pissed off at somebody or another, or just mad at the whole goddamned world, even in their sleep.

I rolled down my window and, besides the humming noise coming from the van and the nice sound of tires on gravel, all I could hear was the sounds of a country evening. It'd been a long time since I'd listened to such a peaceful thing.

But after we got held up for a few minutes at a train crossing, he started talking. His voice sounded nervous, but I knew sometimes folks just talk that way even when they were calm, so I noted it but didn't pay much mind to it.

"Want to hear some music?" he asked loud.

I shook my head.

"Well, good thing, 'cause the radio don't work." He laughed a little and turned toward me all bent-up looking. His grin faded and he turned back around. "Wished it did, though. Sometimes wished it did."

The train started hitting its whistle every five or ten seconds. Listening to it brought me closer to home, recalling the late-night sounds Norfolk and Southern trains made on the other side of the Big Walker across from Shady Hollow.

"How long were you in?"

I was suddenly back in that van, not sharing a bed with my brothers listening to a faraway coal train across a river.

"What?"

"I say how long were you in for?"

I liked him better before he got so windy with so many things working in me at that moment. He turned with a sack full of green apples and offered me one. I shook my head.

He pulled out a lock-blade knife careful and looked at me in his mirror quick before he grabbed one and started peeling it.

"A long time," I said.

"Big day for you then," he said, looking at me and smiling again like we were big buddies. "How long is that, if you don't mind me asking."

"I've been locked up in one place or another since I was a boy."

I figured he'd pulled out that knife and was asking questions about how much time I'd pulled to figure out how bad a person he was sitting there with in the dark, stuck at a train crossing way out in the countryside. Peeling an apple was just an excuse to have some kind of weapon out if he needed one. Never know what something wild just let out of pen was apt to do, I figured was what he was thinking. I'd probably do the same thing if I was half-crippled and driving the van and was hauling somebody who looked like me. You'd ask the time first, not the crime. You'd maybe ask that later if the conversation got off on the right foot.

"Where you heading?" he asked, after a few moments and a dozen more train cars passed by.

"Home."

"By your accent I'd guess that's down South somewhere."

I nodded, looking all around us again to see if we had any bad company. I wouldn't feel safe until I was a long way from that prison. At least I knew the driver wasn't a threat. He had the knife but not the eyes to use it.

"So where you heading?"

"Why?"

"What you say?"

"What's it to you where I'm heading?" I said.

"Just talking…"

"You talk too much."

He didn't say anything for a long moment and then said, "Always had a friendly nature, I guess. No harm meant."

I leaned back in my seat, remembering how I used to have the same easy friendly nature and used to enjoy conversation. I didn't just enjoy it, I was good at it. Ma used to tell me that talking was my one true gift of many. I was the only person she'd ever known who could "outtalk a mockingbird," she'd say on many an occasion with an ending to that always of "Let's hush now, child."

Anyway, after a while I finally said to the driver, "Gonna stay with my ma for a while. She lives in Virginia."

His head was still and then he nodded and nodded like we'd made up and he peeped at me again in his mirror. "I used to take my family to Virginia Beach until the kids got older and my wife passed. She passed last year. Emphysema took her last breath. That's when I started eating all the time and got fat. I smoked more than she did and she made me swear off of them before she died. Almost killed me quitting them. Probably eating will kill me now. Get rid of one bad thing, you just pick up another. You quit bad things but the hole the bad thing was filling never goes away is what it amounts to. Just end up filling it with something else no good."

I blew out a deep breath, wore-out with his stories already, and I looked as far down the tracks as I could. That had to be the longest train I'd ever seen.

"Heard the place is all built-up now."

"What is?"

"Virginia Beach. Probably wouldn't even know it if I saw it."

I didn't say anything, but just hoped he'd still himself or I was gonna have to tell him to. I'd never seen a beach and I didn't care to comment about it or his wife passing. I didn't want to get ugly with him being as mangled up as he was and he seemed like an all right feller, so I figured me not saying nothing back would work to let him know finally that I wasn't definitely in the mood for talk. But it didn't.

"What you gonna do with yourself once you get settled in back home? Got you a girl to go see?"

"Had one a long time ago. How far's the bus station from here?"

"Few miles. I say, what you gonna do once you get back home and settled in? Gonna go see that girl?"

I wasn't going to talk about the only girl I'd ever had that I would ever call "my girl." I wished I hadn't brought the thought of her into that van. She wasn't the kind of girl to be spoken of in such ways in such conversations in such places. But I knew he didn't mean no harm even though it bothered me in a dark way and I said, "Have quite a few things to do," louder and faster than was necessary.

"Like what?"

By that point, I figured he was one of those folks who couldn't help himself to shut up even if he really tried. If he wanted to know what I was gonna do after I got home, I'd tell him a few things for him to ponder on, because I'd been pondering on them a long time.

"First thing I'm gonna do once I get settled home is find out why a man tried to kill me when I was seventeen years old for no reason I can figure."

The driver's voice dropped. "I see. You gonna go looking for him?"

"He's dead. I got some other people I need to find and have some serious business about it. Gonna go see a preacher, too."

The driver set his sack of apples to the side careful. "The preacher help you through your trials and tribulations?" His voice had gotten shakier.

"Not quite like that. He helped get me into my trials and tribulations. I'm pretty sure I'm gonna kill him over it. Been leaning that way heavy for a long time. Gonna go see a sheriff after that. I owe him a visit, too, just like that preacher. He might survive my coming. I haven't made my mind up about him."

The driver dropped his knife on the floor and reached down to get it back in a hurry, just before he turned around to where he could barely get a wide eyeball on me. Then he turned around quick and we both sat in the stillness for a good five more minutes until the train passed. After ten more minutes, he dropped me off at the bus station, pulling right up front.

He didn't wish me good luck or offer me any more of his apples or nothing else, but he nodded after I thanked him for the ride. Both of us knew I was dead serious about the business I'd spoken of. It was the same business I'd figured that assistant warden didn't have any business knowing a few hours before when he'd asked what my plans were when I got out. Assistant Warden Theodore Donald O'Neil the Third had seen it in my eyes though, sure enough.

Her head turned sideways and then almost upside down, which made a big mop of red curls fall over her face. She was leaning so far out of her bus seat that when she took one hand to move her hair, she fell into the aisle. Her mother and baby brother didn't notice the commotion, or her holler, as they kept sleeping while she climbed back up, situating herself for more room. It worked and she got a little bit. Her ma put an arm around her again, I guess out of instinct the way she looked sound asleep when doing it. The little girl soon moved it again without much notice.

Looking out the bus window, I kept feeling a strange peacefulness trying to come on me as I stared at a landscape that went on in all directions to the sky and that had no fences, or at least they were ones a man could jump over without effort. I hoped the busy little girl would soon find something else interesting to help pass the miles…besides me. We were the only two people awake on the bus. I kept seeing her out of the corner of my eye leaning toward me, even after I cleared my throat loud to wake her momma.

She'd been studying on me for some time. Something about my hands had caught her attention not long after the last stop, and even after I moved them to where she might study on something else, she kept trying to get a good look at them.

I finally closed my eyes, and my mind was still drifting south to thoughts of home when I felt the bus seat move a little and felt a small finger touch my left hand. I pulled it away.

"You get on back to your seat now," I said.

She looked up at me and smiled. "What's that on the back of your hand?" she said.

"None of your business," I said. "Now go on back with your momma."

"My name is Grace."

I turned to look out my window.

"What's yours?"

I tried to give her a hard look and then said, "It don't matter none is what my name is."

"'It don't matter none' isn't a name, silly goose." She started to laugh at her joke but stopped. "My dad used to have an ink drawing on the back of his hand."

"Grace, leave me be like I'm telling you."

"Momma likes men with tattoos. Frank doesn't have one on his hand like Daddy did, but he has one on his arm." She grabbed one sleeve and pulled it up to her elbow and pointed at the place Frank has a tattoo. "He's meeting us at the bus station. We're moving in with him. He's got a house and a car but it doesn't run right now."

"Hopefully he'll get it running soon. Go on, now. I need some sleep."

"You haven't been sleeping like everybody else, just watching what everybody is doing and looking out your window like me."

I grabbed her by a shoulder easy as I could to move her toward her ma when she turned back toward me. "I just want to know what that picture is on your hand."

I cleared my throat again loud, this time waking the old woman up in front of me, who turned around shaky with a scared sneer, and then I decided I best show my hand to the little girl if I was to get back my quiet. I turned it the right way so she could tell what it was and said, "It's a big oak in the middle of a field."

"Why do you have it there?"

"Something nice to look at from time to time, I reckon."

"Frank is a war hero. His is an army picture of a parachute with wings. Momma said Dad was a drunk. He had Momma's name on his hand, though."

"Frank sounds like a fine feller and sorry about your daddy. Now go on. I need the rest."

She slid down and as she took a step across the aisle and jumped back on the seat beside her ma, she said, "He's not nice but Momma keeps saying he's got a job and a house with a big yard and a dog, and lots of other stuff."

I looked at her ma, who was still sleeping while trying to hold on to a baby boy on her lap through the whole conversation. She looked like a woman who could use a house and a big yard, and especially a lot of other stuff, minus

Frank most likely, as her daughter pulled out a pad of paper and coloring sticks from a sack.

For a good while the girl kept asking me questions and telling me things about her and her ma and brother and her dead daddy and Frank, and drawing pictures and wanting to show them to me. I kept playing possum with my eyes closed through all of it. I didn't want them closed, I wanted them open to see what I'd been missing all of those years out that window. But I did feel safe that I could close them without worry of harm, because I'd studied every set of eyes at every stop that bus made and never saw a threat. And I could always tell the blazing look trying to be too still, or almost always.

I did notice, watching everyone on that bus earlier that evening, that I was different in ways I hadn't figured on, even when so many seemed not to be much more prosperous than I was, like that little girl and her family. But not so different. So much had changed, but some things surely hadn't.

I guess Frank was waiting for Grace and her family in Carlisle because that's where they all got off in a hurry, but not before she laid a picture on the seat next to me. It was a nice colored drawing of a green tree in a yellow field. I ignored it at first but then gave it a good look over after they got off, and then I put it careful in the paper sack with the rest of my things.

With no more commotion beside me, I was able to not pretend I was asleep anymore. On the half-hour stops in Hagerstown and Chambersburg, I did a lot of walking around and spent over five dollars buying Coca-Colas and Zagnut candy bars. Things I hadn't tasted in quite a while and they tasted so good I couldn't get enough of them.

Between the stops and just looking out my window and trying to figure how I was gonna fit in any of it, I had a lot of time to think about Shady while watching the quiet miles of highway go by and drinking my odd-looking bottles of Coca-Cola. The pop tasted the same, maybe even better, at least to me, but the bottles and machines they came out of were a lot different.

For some reason all of the new around me made me not think about what was to come and all of the things I was gonna do; it made me do a lot of remembering on being a young'un and growing up in Shady Hollow, and the bad that happened there on a nice Sunday evening, September 28, 1959.

September 28, 1959 was the last day before my life ended, and I never saw it was coming.

Ma did, though.

Chapter 3

"What's for dinner?"

"Your momma's gonna be busy for a while," Uncle Ray had said.

"How long?"

"All-nighter."

"You eat yet?" I asked.

"Not hungry."

Uncle Ray looked thin as the shoestring tie he wore with his city clothes, him sitting there on Ma's sofa with his feet propped up on a heavy piece of glass that laid atop a chicken crate. Ma had at some moment the year before fancied that that particular crate would suit as a new coffee table, being me and my brothers had broken past repair the one she had before it…something she wasn't pleased about, being that that one was actually store-made furniture. She'd made me and my brothers scrub and sand down the new one to where it was nothing but shiny dry wood and no chicken, before she stained and lacquered it and after all the fuss, it came to sit in the middle of her living room. Her decorations and lately Uncle Ray's feet tended to take up most of the space on the glass top she was always keeping tidy for customers and company.

Uncle Ray sitting there as usual looked to me the same as he always did, pretty much. He had two suits that he'd switch wearing every so often to his preference, one brown and one black. That day must have been a black day, because that's the suit of clothes he had on.

Both suits had wide white stripes up and down them and he'd usually wear a pair of shiny tan boots that he was so particular about when he'd step off a boardwalk. But Uncle Ray hadn't been able to wear his boots for weeks because his feet were so swollen after the beating that had been put on him.

"She here or downstairs?" I asked quiet.

Uncle Ray didn't take his eyes away from a straight razor in one hand that he was pushing slow and so careful against the grain of a small white stone he had resting on a leg.

"She's in the back," he said.

He finally looked up at me because I'd been standing there looking at him, and he pulled a flask from his coat pocket. Then he took a long swig of gin as easy as a person would take a drink of lemonade.

Uncle Ray was one of those people who drank from morning to bed, always straight gin liquor, and he never seemed the least bit drunk whether he sipped or chugged. I didn't care if he drank or not, or was drunk or not, but it was bad news that he wasn't hungry. I knew I had to either make dinner myself—if I could find something to make— or rustle up something for free somehow from one of the bars in Shady.

I'd never spend my own hidden stash on food, even hungry as I was, and I knew better than to ask Uncle Ray for eating money because lately he'd always said he was broke as a three-legged polecat whenever I'd asked him.

Ma never believed Uncle Ray was as poor as an honest man, either, like he was so fond of saying at other times. He made a weekly wage from the elders for the doctoring that he did in Shady, and even though Uncle Ray always tended to gamble and drink away whatever money he'd make or win, Ma thought he squirreled away a little bit. But I guess after he got all busted up, I could see where he wasn't able to make much of a living because he had to spend so much of the day with his feet up in air.

From what folks said, the only reason Uncle Ray was back with us at all was because the Shady elders convinced him to do so. The elders were all business, and quick at convincing. Word was that every one of them was from Ol' Luke's bloodline and they ran everything. The head of the elders was Tobias Chambers, and that's who you'd go to if you were having some sort of problem you couldn't handle by yourself. Once Mr. Chambers listened and nodded, that problem got fixed. And fixed for good. But if he didn't nod, whatever problem you had was about to get dreadful worse.

Uncle Ray couldn't walk for weeks after he left Ma and broke the elders' contract with him to doctor in Shady. The elders tracked him to New Jersey and sent serious men to fetch him. Uncle Ray came back with both feet busted up, which displeased and troubled Ma, but Uncle Ray did seem to like staying with us more than before he tried to run off, or at least he acted like he did around Ma while he was hobbling around.

I walked toward the kitchen and could feel the pine planks under me moving up and down, and then I heard the muffled sound of loud music and static coming from the transistor radio in Ma's bedroom. I looked over my left shoulder at the framed picture of Jesus that Ma had hung at the entrance of the narrow hallway. The picture of him with bright lights coming from his head was bouncing back and forth against the wall a little, and when the Jesus picture was agitated, is how me and my brothers could always tell for certain that Ma was busy working. Not just working, she was busy working. We'd learned from more than a couple of times when she'd lost business to our interruptions, that we weren't to bother her until the Jesus picture calmed, unless one of us needed her for something of an emergency nature. She always said not to disturb her business at all over nothing serious if her door was closed and locked, because Ma never closed her door unless she was working. But we all knew as long as the Jesus picture was steady that we could peck on her locked door about this and that without too much fuss from one of her customers.

I pulled on one end of the twine that was hanging over a nail to level the picture of Jesus when Uncle Ray said, "Your momma made pork hash this morning, but your brothers wiped the kettle clean."

"She make any bread?"

"They finished off the johnnycake, too."

I stuck my head in the kitchen and saw the kettle and plates and forks soaking in a washtub, walked over to open the icebox, and there wasn't a scrap of food in it except for a half-empty jar of mustard and the top stub of a pickle floating in a canning jar. Same as yesterday and the day before. Looking around in that icebox put me in a worse mood than I was in already. The thought of that hash made my mouth water.

"You been at Hoke's this whole time?" Uncle Ray asked.

I walked back in the living room and nodded.

"Make any jingle manning the broom?"

Uncle Ray had put his straight razor, whetstone and flask away. He was staring at me with eyes set close together like a hawk while training his new wide mustache that went all the way down to his chin. Wasn't his business whether I made anything or not so I kept quiet, but the fact was I didn't make anything.

"Until they let you back in the poker games, that violin is what'll earn you a living. The way you fiddle on it all the time, you should be down in the saloons making it work for you."

I'd been thinking about trying my luck in the music business, being the gambling business had been going so poorly. Uncle Ray had told me I had an ear for making music the first day he'd gave me that fiddle after winning it in a knock-rummy game. I was playing "Cripple Creek" and "Don't Hit Your Granny With a Big Ol' Stick" and a bunch of other old mountain tunes before that evening was over.

Music did come easy to me, the same way Ma had always fretted that most things did to me. I wasn't as sure about that as she was, but she feared the easy, because she believed people became lazy if they don't end up venturing to where things are hard for them. And to Ma, there weren't but a hair of difference between laziness and evilness. She kept all her boys busy and I guess tried her best not to raise lazy, evil sons, but I believe it was a bigger job than one woman by herself could sometimes handle.

I just figured music came easy to me because I'd always loved to listen to it so much. But what I couldn't do was sing like good singers can, so I didn't see profit or future in making music, and my goal in life was to make money however it could be made the quickest and the easiest and the most. I wanted to be rich because I'd seen how the rich are treated so different than folks are with nothing but holes in their pockets, and I'd never owned nothing without a hole in it somewhere.

Anyway, I was still standing there in the hall next to Ma's kitchen and had just gotten back from Hoke's Billiards Emporium. I'd been there all the last night and into that morning, waiting on a new shooter I'd spotted coming into town with a loud cowboy hat and fancy cue.

Hoke had rented me a broom to lean on as a prop so I might be able to hustle up a game and not look like a real player. He told me that he'd have to eyeball the shooter I was hunting before he'd assign him to me, because the hat and cue could be a ruse.

Even though Hoke knew I was one of the better poker

players in Shady—so good it was rare anymore when I could get anybody to deal me a hand—he thought I needed more time watching the other shooters.

It was the same way I'd learned to play poker, by studying the players as much as the cards, and by abiding by the unwritten rules more than the written ones. Like I learned young that cheating's always fair, an unwritten rule, but only as long as you can get away with it.

After getting too famous for my own good at poker, I was determined to not let the same thing happen shooting pool. The one poker lesson I picked up too late was not to win as often as I could. That was one hard lesson Hoke drove into me every chance he got. I'd been trying as hard as I could to beat off the nickname I'd taken on: Luck.

Nobody wanted to play a sporting game of anything against a feller nicknamed Luck.

Hoke always got his forty percent share from the takings in his place. The bad thing for me was if I didn't make nothing, I'd have to pay him a quarter just to lean on his broom, it being part of my role as the floor sweeper who'd just like to shoot a game for a cold bottle of pop while on break. He controlled the whole place while watching eight tables at once from the window of his small upstairs office. Hoke was as round as he was tall, and he smoked two cigarettes at a time by the way he always had one lit, and he reminded me of those puppet masters who would float into Shady now and then with all of those strings dangling from their fingers. Everybody who worked for Hoke were his puppets. And the ones who came through the door just looking to shoot an hour away became his puppets, too, if they weren't mindful. One game or one drink too many, and Hoke would own them and everything they had.

But my mark never showed. I suspected he got sidetracked early by the whores and now probably didn't have a penny left on him, and that's why I was in a surly mood that late Sunday morning when I got back to Ma's apartment.

I turned my eyes away from Uncle Ray to a pair of muddy trousers stuffed with straw hanging over the kitchen door. They looked like they'd been run over by the tire tracks on them. I'd seen odder things in Ma's apartment, but couldn't figure why half of a scarecrow would be dangling in her kitchen. I figured it was a charm Ma had hung up to ward off some sort of evil.

"Want a lesson?" Uncle Ray asked. He didn't say it too loud because he only taught things when Ma was away or working. Ma frowned on the lessons he taught, except for the times he'd tried to teach me to read and write, which I never had any interest in.

"I got to find something to eat," I said, studying on those burlap pants.

"I'm about to teach you something about being able to keep a full belly. But if you think tending to your empty belly at this particular moment is more important, then we'll forget about it."

Ma always said Uncle Ray was half angel and half outlaw. He had to be the most educated man in Shady because he'd went to college and was the only person who knew what to do with all the things in a doctor bag. And he always liked to talk up a storm in his half Southern and half Yankee accent about things in the world nobody else knew much about or cared much about. I feared he was going to preach book learning to me again and pull out a pen and pad of paper like he'd do from time to time.

"Teach what?"

"You can't scare up a game of cards, aren't having much luck at the tables and you don't want to fiddle for your breakfast, so I thought you might want to learn how to use this."

Uncle Ray stood from Ma's couch and turned a half step. He pulled his straight razor from a sheath he carried in the small of his back. He put it up to the window light where it caught a glare and then he stared at me. I'd just seen him honing on it but he made a pretty big deal out of flashing it around.

He walked into the kitchen and over the next hour I soon forgot about my empty stomach as he made me practice over and over how to pull a razor and hold it. Then he had me walk up to that pair of pants a hundred times practicing how to cut the side of a back pocket without cutting in too far but far enough.

"Pair of pants like this, you don't cut the bottom, you cut the side. Not too far and it has to be done quick," he said.

Before I started the actual cutting, he took his razor from me and he cut both pockets so fast that I missed how he did it, even thought I was watching with wide eyes. I never even saw the razor in his hand.

"Goddamn, Uncle Ray," I said.

"Sew them up," he said.

After I sewed those pockets up, which he showed me how

to do, too, he gave me back the razor and then he moved my fingers around to the right position.

"Keep the handle against your wrist, and your thumb and middle knuckle of your pointing finger way down on the blade. That way no one will know what you're carrying and you'll cut only as deep as necessary. You slash a man's backside wide-open with a razor and I can assure you he'll be prone to kill you over it."

"You ever done that?"

"I never got the lesson you're getting right now, let's put it that way."

I practiced and practiced with him telling me how to approach those stuffed pants like I was just walking normal, and then go in fast with that blade until the pocket got cut without the pants moving any, and I didn't cut anything under it. When I started getting good, he gave me one of his old razors and a smooth whetstone to keep for my own, but that's when we both heard Ma's radio turn off and she walked in from the back bedroom. Uncle Ray fought the pants into an empty pantry cupboard and both of us tucked our razors away.

Ma was wearing her red shiny robe, and wrapped herself up in it tight when she saw me. She kept looking back and forth at me and Uncle Ray, but then stopped at me.

"Didn't hear you come in, sugar. You make any money last night?" she asked.

I shook my head, but I would have shook my head whether I made anything or not, because Ma was more likely to give me money when I wasn't making money.

"You lose any?" She looked at me hard and long when she asked that.

"Just the quarter."

"You eat?"

"Had a few peanuts last night is all."

Ma shook her head, dug in her robe pocket and then stuck out her hand. She gave me several bills folded in half.

"In a couple hours, bring back a steak dinner from Merle's, make sure it's hot, and with whatever's left, get yourself something but bring back a sack of biscuits and gravy and a pot of brown beans for you and your brothers. And collards, too, if they have them. I won't be doing no cooking tonight."

"Where are they?"

"They're fishing down at the falls. And they better be home before dark. If they ain't, you fetch them and tell them to hightail it back here."

I nodded and then thought about the steak dinner. I knew it wasn't for her and it wasn't for me and it wasn't for Uncle Ray. "You want anything?"

"I'll eat in the morning," she said.

Ma never ate while she was working, even if she had to work all day and all night with one customer. But she looked hungry so I figured I'd ask. She never looked at Uncle Ray and he never looked at her, he just kept looking out the window. Ma gave me a quick hug and yawned before she went to the icebox and fetched a bucket of beer, the only thing in it besides that jar of mustard, the pickle stub and a crock of spring water.

She then went back to her business and kept that bucket

steady as she walked down the hall wearing a pair of shoes with black high heels, and didn't spill a drop. When she opened her bedroom door to go back inside, I heard a man snoring.

After she locked the door, Uncle Ray pulled his razor back out and wiped it down with an oiled cloth he kept wrapped in wax paper in his front pocket.

"A man who keeps a keen razor and knows how to use it will never starve," he said. "Good thing to know if times get bad, especially if the day comes that you have kids to feed and real jobs are scarce, or you need money to get out of somewhere fast and there isn't time to hustle what you need. You're getting at the age where you need to ponder such things. It's misfortune you've passed on the real education I've tried to teach so you could make the way of an honest man, if you ever needed to or wanted to, and then you wouldn't have to worry about such things—you're not listening to a damn thing I'm saying, are you?"

I realized I wasn't, looked at him and lied, "Yeah, I am," I said.

He took a step closer. "Listen to me. Going through life ignorant is so far your choosing. You're going to have to *take* and not *give* in this world to *get,* and sometime, someday, you may need to take with more than just your wit and that grin and good luck of yours that follows you around. One day you'll grin at the world and it isn't going to grin back. Mean is going to stare you dead in the face. Understand?"

I nodded.

"You will one day, I assure you. And good luck's always too fickle to bank a future on whether you think so or not right now. You're not always going to have a woman cooking your supper, providing a roof for you and doing your wash like your momma does, tending to you hand and foot. What I'm trying to tell you is this—you don't know anything about pain.

"Real pain. Suffering kind of pain. Hard times.

"You're about to become a man, and from that day on the called side of the coin will land upside only about half the time, and that's only if you stay lucky. You don't know anything about that kind of business, yet, and there isn't a way for you to even understand such serious business. You don't know anything about being a man, is what I'm telling you. Not yet. You think you do, but you don't."

I looked at Uncle Ray to study his face because of what he'd said toward the end of his rambling about having a woman doing stuff for you. Ma was doing those exact same things for him, but I decided to let it pass because it seemed to have passed him. That's about all I got out of all whatever he'd just said.

He finished oiling down his razor, put it away and then he rummaged through the pantry. He wrestled those pants back out and hung them back up, then he got started again with his lesson and after each turn I made at the pants, he'd make me stitch up those britches so I could practice again.

"We'll practice on different pockets tomorrow," he said.

I got real good at cutting and stitching. He told me the two skills went together like cold buttermilk and cornbread.

He went on while I was slashing that if I cut a pocket right and kept walking behind a man, soon that wallet would poke out far enough to grab or plain fall out for the lazy taking. And you always took a wallet you know has something in it or you were just picking empty leather.

He told me how important it was to look for the man with a full wallet. He said it wasn't hard because men who wore fancy hats or boots or had some gold or silver showing on them generally had something worth taking. He said it didn't take much thinking or education to find where the money is, I just had to pay attention.

And he said money didn't belong to any man who isn't smart enough to keep it. The bigger wad they had on them, the more they showed it on them like decorations because most men with money like to let folks know that they have more than others do.

He said it wasn't nothing more than human nature.

"You choose your mark by watching what a man orders for a meal and how much he leaves on his plate, how much he'll bet at a gaming table, how much he tips the tavern help because the rich don't tip as much as the poor, generally. And especially take note if women are interested in him, because women can smell green on a man and they attract to it like bees to wildflowers. Always watch the women," he said.

While I'd stitch those pants up, Uncle Ray would tell me all kinds of ways to get another man's money without them knowing it and without harming him too much.

He went on to say that sometimes a razor wasn't the proper tool to rob a man with. He said if a man I'd marked for robbing had a wallet in a hard to reach place like a front pocket or breast pocket tight to him, it was best to have two people helping to make easy payday even though I'd have to split the loot three ways.

If I did it by myself, he said I'd generally have to hurt the feller too bad to get his money or worse, I might be the one getting hurt.

There were all kinds of ways to do the robbing, but the easiest and smartest was for one man to hit the feller in the nose hard and unexpected, another to help the feller hit get off the ground, and the third to carry on like crazy and chase the rascal who'd hit him and both would run out of sight.

"The man helping the mark up is always the best thief of the bunch," Uncle Ray said. "He's the one who takes the money, rings, watch, whatever he can grab without the mark knowing, as he's just acting to be helping him up."

Uncle Ray went on that after it was all over, the mark would get off the ground, find his hat and go about his way light in the pockets and jewelry but quick in step. He wouldn't know he'd been lightened of his load yet.

Uncle Ray said the most important thing was, "If you have to hit a man, hit him hard. Hard enough so that his first thought is that he'd better just get to somewhere else from wherever he's at to get his brains together before he decides to check his belongings."

I knew that already from a couple dozen fistfights and practiced that myself whenever I had to hit somebody, but he said there was a code among professional thieves like him that you never hurt anyone too bad unless it was by accident, and you always left a little. It wasn't just being charitable, he said, it was the proper way to do business.

A place like Shady Hollow needed people to mend up fairly easy with a dollar or two still left in their pockets, because we'd all want them to come back one day, and we needed them to come back without too many hard feelings. They'd just be more protective of their valuables next time, so all in all we were just teaching them an important lesson so they wouldn't get robbed again so easy by nobody else, he said.

He kept going on but at some point my hands were tired from all the slashing and stitching and I couldn't stand my empty stomach any longer, so I thanked him for the razor and whetstone, stuck both in my back pocket and the robbing lesson ended.

I took Ma's money and headed down to Merle's Diner, where I placed her order and counted what change was left. It wasn't much, so I told Miss Paulene to forget the collards and instead bring me a bowl of catfish chowder.

I could have turned up the bottle of ketchup in front of me waiting on that chowder. I was wishing they'd go ahead and bring me some soda crackers to munch on when Herbert Mullins walked in, all out of breath.

Me and Herbert were good pards and had gotten in and out of all kinds of trouble for as long as I could remember. He was two years older than me, but I'd always been bigger than him. I'd always been pretty sure that I was by a far sight the smarter one between us, but Herbert would fight anybody or anything. Ma always said I was tough as a pine knot, but Herbert was a lot tougher. He loved to fistfight like some people love to gamble or fish or be lazy. Loved it. Herbert wasn't a bully, though.

He always stood up for the runts in Shady and those who just got picked on for one peculiar reason or another, and that made him popular with those who got picked on all the time when he wasn't around. I never saw Herbert ever pick a fight with somebody smaller than him, and that's how we got to be friends because he loved to pick fights with boys bigger than him.

Herbert picked a fight with me for no good reason at all on the first day he showed up in Shady Hollow, except he wanted to rile me up to see if he could whup me. He knocked a pear out of my hand that I was eating and then grinned. We soon fought for two or twenty minutes until we were both so covered in mud and dust and plumb worn out, that neither one of us could swing anymore.

After that, we both stood and he tried to shake my hand wearing a big bloody smile, and he told me what his name was. I told him I'd shake his hand if he got my pear off the ground, cleaned it off and gave it back to me. And he did.

Anyway, Herbert was standing there all wild-eyed like he'd get over the smallest things, and he grabbed me by the arm out of breath. "Been looking all over for you. Come here."

He tried to pull me off my stool, but I jerked my arm away and told him I wasn't going anywhere until I ate my dinner. He grabbed me again but harder the second time. I saw how agitated he was and I knew if I was gonna eat in peace, I had to get up from that stool.

"You see that blue Ford parked up the street?"

I stood and nodded. You noticed cars in Shady, especially new, shiny ones. It had North Carolina plates and I wondered if it was that new pool shooter's car. But I didn't recollect seeing it the night before.

"A girl drove it in fifteen minutes ago. She's the best-looking thing I've ever seen and I mean she's the best-looking thing I've ever seen. She's been asking around...for you."

"For me?"

Herbert grinned.

I pulled my arm away again.

"I ain't lying, Ben."

"How old is she?"

"About our age, I'd reckon."

"Where's she now?" I asked.

"She's checking in at the Alton House. Had three leather bags. I carried them in for her and she tipped me three dollars before ol' Mr. Alton saw me and started running me off."

"Three dollars? Shit."

Herbert showed me the money and I couldn't figure what a good-looking rich girl with three dollars to blow was doing looking for me. It had to be for a bad reason because I couldn't come up with a good one.

"What's she look like?"

"Just wait till you see her."

"Tell me," I said.

"You know that blond dancer that came through here a while back performing at Barton's Opry Show? Me and you kept sneaking in and—"

"Yeah."

"She looks like her, but even prettier. She sorta don't belong here though like that dancer did, know what I mean?"

I nodded.

"When she first pulled up and asked me where the best place to stay is, I told her, and then I asked if she needed help with the bags because she looked so rich and everything. She looked scared, too."

"What'd you do?"

"No, I was kind to her. She was just scared looking, I don't know."

"You sure she asked for me?"

"I'm sure. She asked me if I knew Benjamin Purdue."

"You swear it."

"I swear, Ben."

"What'd you say?"

"I told her I knew you and that me and you were pals."

"What'd she say then?"

"She wanted to know where you lived but I didn't tell her. I didn't know if you'd want me saying you lived overtop a saloon to a girl like her, so I just said that I'd find you and tell you to meet her at the Alton House."

"She with anybody else?"

"I didn't see nobody."

"Get her name?"

"She told me, but I ain't sure if it's right, because she told me when she was digging in her purse handing me those bills, and I saw a lot of other bills in there, but I think she said her name is Anna or Amanda, Annie, something like that."

I felt nervous all of a sudden when he said Amanda.

I thought as hard as I could. I'd known a few gals named Ann but only one Amanda. None of the Anns would come close to the description of this girl Herbert had just given me. Not even Anna Jean Davis. But Amanda Lynn would.

But it couldn't be Amanda Lynn. Couldn't be. She lived in Durham County, North Carolina, on a plantation a thousand times the size of Shady Hollow, with tended gardens and pastures, and tobacco and soybeans and field corn growing as far as you could see. It was then that I recalled the new Ford up the street had North Carolina plates.

"Amanda Lynn Jennings?" I asked.

"That's it," Herbert said. "Amanda Jennings."

I drew back and couldn't say another word as Miss Paulene brought me my fish chowder. She always gave me a local's portion with big chunks of catfish and set it down in front of my stool with buttered crackers and the free side of barbeque slaw, but I looked at all of it, and then at Herbert, and then flew out the double doors. I didn't even think to pick up the four cents change she'd left on the napkin.

"Who is she?" Herbert yelled, as I took off out of Merle's like the place was burning down around me. I didn't know right then that it may as well have been.

I'd never see that place or any of those folks ever again.

Chapter 4

At some place outside of a dirty window that separated me from all of what I couldn't stop staring at on the Trailways bus, I found myself drifting back to Shady Hollow, back to when I was free and running with the devil at my heels. I was young and fast then, but he was about to catch up to me as I tried to holler something back at Herbert. In that old memory, I couldn't say a word, as naturally talky as I was back then, generally. I'd been quiet like that, too, around Amanda Lynn the first time I ever saw her, for a short spell anyway when she'd first cast her spell on me, and just the thought of her showing up in Shady so unexpected had knocked the wind right out of me.

I knew Herbert wasn't trying to pull one on me because I'd never told him about Amanda Lynn or where I'd been taken the year before. After the elders had hauled me back to Shady, Ma told me to never tell nobody about going to Durham County because the elders had ruled on it. I never did because the last thing I needed was to get on the wrong side of the Shady elders.

But ever since they'd brought me back home, I never told Ma or nobody else that I'd been saving up to go back to North Carolina to be with Amanda Lynn one day. I couldn't wait to get back there.

I always told folks in Shady Hollow that I didn't have nothing but a bent slug dime, but I had a canvas sack full of real money, twelve hundred and fifty-seven dollars and change, most of it poker loot from the days when nobody knew I was lucky but was only just catching on to it. I'd saved all of it and kept it hidden under a floorboard that I'd pried up in my bedroom, and I had a ten-dollar bill hidden in my shoe at all times just like Uncle Ray had told me a man should keep.

My road stake was to go back and find Amanda Lynn when I turned eighteen, because that's the day Ma had always told me I'd have my own way about things. And even though Ma wasn't firm about much, she'd always been firm about that with all her boys. My eighteenth birthday was coming around soon enough, and that's the day I'd planned to leave Shady Hollow.

A tugging part of me didn't want to leave because I loved Shady, and I knew it wouldn't be long before I'd be moving up Hoke's pool shooting ladder to play the bigger games. But I never ever figured that Amanda Lynn would come there, so I always figured I'd have to leave. It would be hard saying farewell to my ma and brothers and all my old pards, I dern knew it would, but the older I got, I felt that place shrinking around me. I was being pulled away from there a little at a time even before I met Amanda Lynn.

The biggest part of me was pulling harder to leave than the tugging part of me was to stay, is what it was. That bigger part wanted to see all the things I'd heard so much about from so many who came and went from Shady. The best thing I'd ever seen was out beyond those mountains and far from the cold river that ran shallow and fast along the rocky banks, but so deep and slow and silent in the pools.

I'd never told Amanda Lynn anything about me but a pack of lies. It wasn't that I was ashamed of me or Ma or my brothers or Shady or nothing like that, because I wasn't.

But I guess Aunt Kate was right, telling me upon my welcome to the flatland the year before, that to someone who hadn't spent time actually living on the side of the Big Walker in a whorehouse called the Last Rebel Yell, there didn't seem a way to talk about any of it right that would come out without grit and dirt and blood and other things not suitable for dinner table talk all over it.

But Amanda Lynn had come to see me.

I didn't know how she'd found me or why she'd come, but I kept hoping it was for the same reason that I wanted to go back and see her. I kept hoping that with all my might.

Running as hard as I could up the brushy banks of the river behind all of the businesses while trying to dodge cans smoldering with burning trash, and getting bit by chained-up dogs that were there to keep drunks from trespassing behind those same places, my mind was filled with Amanda Lynn and the times we'd spent together on the plantation. All of those long nights and the laziest days that went by too quick. I didn't long for nothing else when I was with her. Nothing.

I wanted to hold her again to me tight so bad that it made me hurt all over. I prayed to myself, hoping that she'd be able to forgive me for just leaving her like I did with no notice and not a word or look said between us. And I prayed more that she wouldn't ask me why I left so sudden, because I still didn't know the full answer to that.

I still didn't even know the real reason why my Aunt Kate took me away in the middle of the night to go there with Ma's permission, except Ma said her and Aunt Kate finally agreed that a summer in North Carolina would do me some good.

But it was clear to me by the forceful way Ma and the elders had brought me back before that summer was near over that she'd changed her mind about that. I'd never fought nobody so hard as I did the day the elders took me back to Shady for no good reason that they'd tell me, except the elders had ordered it was time for me to go back home and we had to be quick about it.

Since I'd been a little boy, Ma had always told me that the world outside of Shady Hollow was a dangerous one. She said I wasn't yet ready to step foot in it whenever I'd get in a wandering mood. But after she'd let me leave Shady Hollow with Aunt Kate and I spent those short months in Durham County, it didn't seem a bit dangerous to me.

She kept telling me that she'd fetched me back because she missed me and needed me around to make money to help her take care of my younger brothers, but I didn't think that was the real reason as she kept saying it was over and over. I remembered how the elders looked so serious and loaded down with guns when they came and grabbed me all in a rush.

Whatever the real reason was, Ma'd kept it to herself, as she'd do with so many other things.

As I crept up the back steps to where I lived so Amanda Lynn couldn't get a glimpse of me yet, all of those thoughts swirled in my head. The one thing I didn't think about or realize was that the terrible danger my ma had always feared and I'd never understood, had come to Shady Hollow.

And it was looking for me.

Uncle Ray jumped off of Ma's sofa just as fast as I'd thrown open the front door. If he'd been standing behind it instead of lounging with his feet up, it may have killed him.

By the time he said something, I was already in the bathroom pouring a basin of water.

I grabbed the cake of soap from the rim of the bathing tub and I rubbed and rubbed on it and finally got some suds going even though the water was cold. After I finished and dried off, I still thought I didn't look as good as I could. So I reached into Uncle Ray's shaving kit that he kept on the second shelf and I searched and found his bottle of fancy hair-oil treatment. I squirted a bunch of it in my hands, rubbed it through my black hair in a big fury and then slicked it all back away from my face and over my ears like he carried his hair.

I studied my new look for a bit from the front and then side to side, and noted how it made me look older. I thought I looked better, too. I figured if I ran into my brothers, they were sure to give me some sass about my hair all shiny, but I'd shut that up right quick.

I was more pleased with my new look than I could have even hoped for, especially at that important moment, so I took one long last look before I wiped my hands on my dungarees and went into me and my brothers' bedroom. I searched the closet and dresser for the best shirt I could find.

I found my favorite shirt, which was a little past a little dirty. A person would have to get close to notice though, I figured. I'd just tell Amanda that I'd been working hard all day to make traveling money to come to see her, that's what I'd tell her if I saw her looking too close at the shirt.

I was buttoning it up when I heard Ma's footsteps. I tried to grab my stash hidden in the floorboards so I'd have money to treat Amanda Lynn to a nice evening, if she'd be agreeable to it. She was the only person in the whole world I'd spend that money on, but Ma peeked around the door too soon, still wearing her shiny red robe but she had on her old slippers now. There was no way I was gonna let her know I had a sack of money, so I kept a foot on the board.

"Did you get the food?"

"You won't believe it, Ma. You know that—"

"Sugar, did you bring back the food?"

I shook my head. "You know that girl I told you about last year, the one I got to know in North Carolina?"

Ma stepped into the bedroom and her face looked like it

froze on her. I wondered if it was over me not bringing back the steak dinner, but it was even a more serious look than she'd given me the couple of times that I'd gambled away her supper money.

I backed up from her look and the excitement fell out of my voice, but just a little. "Remember, the girl who lived on that—"

"I remember."

"She's here. She checked into the Alton House and I'm going down there."

Ma walked across the squeaking pine floor for a moment and both her hands started grabbing at the robe where it draped her legs. She now just looked spooked.

"You mad I didn't bring up the steak dinner yet?" I asked.

Ma rolled up her hair to the top of her head. She pulled a pin from somewhere in her robe and stuck it into the ball.

"I put the order in. I paid for it already, Ma. I'll bring it back from Merle's in a—"

She shut the bedroom door and stood between it and me. "Have you seen her?"

"Not yet. But Herbert saw her and said she was looking for me. It's her. It's Amanda Lynn. She told Herbert her name."

"So she knows you're here?"

"Yeah, Ma. He told her I lived here."

"You can't go see her."

A long ugly quiet passed between us. Ma's eyes were watery but never blinked.

"What?"

She started pacing again and wiped under one eye. "Find

your brothers, right now. They should still be down at the falls…you tell them to stay until I come for them. Tell them not to come back here. Don't you come back here neither until I find you. Do not come back. For any reason. Now go. Right now, Benjamin. And do not go to see this girl." Ma tried to turn me toward the door with one hand on my shoulder, but I didn't move.

"What's going on?"

She started pushing harder. "I'll tell you when I meet you at the river."

"I wanna know now."

Ma let go of me and starting pacing again, but this time a lot faster. She went to take a seat on the double mattresses that me and my brothers slept on, then she looked at me all of a sudden like she'd forgotten I was standing there. She shot back up.

"Go! And if you see any men you don't know, don't get near them. Run. Don't speak to anybody, not even your friends. Now find your brothers. I'll be there soon. And go through the woods to get there, don't take the river trail. I have to go talk to the—"

"I'm gonna see Amanda Lynn."

Ma took one long step and slapped me hard across the face. I mean real hard. "I said no," she said.

I turned back to her. I was a lot bigger than Ma and had been for a couple of years. I'd never gotten so mad at her as I got the second after she laid a hand across my face for no reason. Before, she'd always had a decent reason for some-thing I'd done. Not this time. I hadn't seen Ma with the moonlight in her eyes in ages, and wondered if she was off in the head and that man she was with had given her something bad to drink or sniff or smoke like had happened before one time.

I stepped up full in front of her and she backed up from me. I tasted the blood in my mouth and wanted to hit back and hit back hard, but I didn't. It was the first time I'd ever wanted to hit my own ma like I'd hit a man, being riled up as I was, and it shook me up even more feeling like that because I'd never felt such a dark thing before.

"Don't ever hit me again," I finally said.

When I went to leave my bedroom, Ma tried to grab hold of me. She pulled my shirt out from where I'd just tucked it, but I was walking fast toward the front door.

"Don't let him leave!" she screamed at Uncle Ray.

I looked back at Ma knowing she was acting crazy now. I think Uncle Ray thought the same thing by the way he watched her. But he rose from the sofa, looking back and forth at us with his quick eyes. Ma was still screaming right behind me, trying to slow me down.

"Stop him!"

Uncle Ray went to grab me same as Ma did, and at first I tried to get his hand off me easy-like, but he wasn't letting go. He was taller than me, but so thin and with his feet busted up, I just turned fast and shoved him back down onto the sofa as hard as I could.

He rolled onto the floor and I felt bad about what I'd done the moment I did it, because I knew Uncle Ray wasn't expecting what I'd just done to him. He'd always been good to me and I knew from then on we'd always be different toward each other. Besides that, I was always a little leery of Uncle Ray the way he was so book smart and good with a gun and a razor. But I had to see Amanda and he was in my way of doing it. And now I just felt like I had to get away from Ma, too.

I yanked open the door and ran out with Ma still trying to hold on to me and yelling. When I looked back, an old man with hair sticking up everywhere was peeking out her bedroom. I stopped at the bottom of the back steps when she said all out of breath and shaky, "You can't go." She was holding on to the top railing with both hands when I turned to leave. "She may've brought trouble here!"

I walked back up one step and leaned forward, staring at Ma as hard as I could. "You don't even know her. She's the best thing that—"

"Danger may have followed her."

"What danger?"

"We have to leave until I can find out if—"

"You're talking crazy, Momma. I'm going to see her."

"I forbid it!"

Ma drew a line in the dirt right there with those words and with her hands now all fisted at her sides. A line I'd never crossed that she'd ever found out about. She looked plain shook-up, standing up above me and staring down. I felt sorry for her all of a sudden for whatever was wrong with her with the shape she was in, but I had to go. I figured we'd work it out somehow when I got home. We'd probably worked out worse before.

"Come here," she said, finally lowering her voice and trying to cover up more with the chill in the air.

I didn't say anything else and took off around the side of the saloon to head up to the Alton House. Ma didn't say or scream anything else, but I could hear her running through our apartment, yelling at Uncle Ray.

Just before I was out of earshot of her kitchen window, opened a crack, it sounded like she said, "They're gonna kill my baby."

I slowed, wondering if I'd heard her right. I did hear "kill" and "baby" clear enough. Ma tended to call all of her boys "baby" sometimes, even though none of us were babies anymore. But it wasn't just what she said, it was the way she said it that sent a sharp chill through me. My legs were still trembling. It was the first time I'd stood up to her in such a way and flat disobeyed her like I just did. Something big had changed between us.

I stood on the boardwalk outside the open door of the Last Rebel Yell and tried to get my breathing back to normal and my legs still as all sorts of folks started to funnel into that place laughing and having a big time.

I paid no attention to them, even the ones bumping into me, and wished I'd have grabbed my green corduroy coat before I left, because the wind was starting to kick up cold off of the river. I shivered and tensed myself all over a few times and then leaned over an old rotten horse trough to see if my hair still looked all right in the reflection, but I couldn't see nothing in the black water.

Then I looked up the street past the shacks and businesses as people were starting to go here and there, walking toward the gaming parlors and bawdy houses and restaurants and taverns. The sun was way over the mountains now, and Shady always came alive in the evening hours like the whole place was a bunch of vampires in a comic book.

The Shady keepers stuck out from all of them in their white bowler hats and black bow ties, making their rounds like they always did an hour or two before dusk, lighting all of the lanterns and turning on gaslights, and spotting potential trouble to report to the elders.

Amanda Lynn's car was what I was looking for, and it was still parked in a dried mud lot off the side of the Alton House, right next to an empty lean-to with a tin roof where farmers would bring in country hams and homemade sausage and bushel baskets of things that come from the dirt to sell during the spring through summer months. In the fall and winter, those with nowhere else to go, drunks mostly, tended to find refuge under it.

After a minute or two, my legs were shaking a little less but still wobbly. I'd warmed up some but wished I'd snuck in a long drink of Ma's beer earlier, or at least got a little of that chowder or a few crackers down in me.

I thought for a minute about going back to ask Ma about what had gotten into her. But if she was on a bad high, I didn't want to be around her until she came back down from her visions. I was going over all of that in my mind when a blue dress caught the corner of my eye.

My full gaze turned toward the blue dress coming down

the boardwalk on the other side of Alton's. Even though I hadn't seen her in months and months and she was a good fifty yards away, I knew it was her at first glance.

Amanda Lynn looked just like a dream I'd had over and over, always knowing deep down inside when I'd wake up that it would never come true.

But it had. She'd come to Shady, and I felt like I was in that dream.

I turned my body full toward her and, even so far away and with all of the other folks milling around, I saw her smile.

I wanted to run or walk to her or jump up and down or do anything but what I did there for a few moments—I just stood not able to move and kept watching her walk, getting closer and closer.

Finally, I raised a hand to wave after she waved at me, and I realized she really had recognized me, and I couldn't believe how she was even more beautiful than I remembered. She'd changed in her face and body since I'd seen her last, fuller in places but just a little, and they were all real good changes by the looks of it.

I noticed, too, that I wasn't the only one looking at her in her blue dress that fit tight against her in all the best places.

Something finally happened in me, and my legs moved a step at a time as I began walking past Phelps's Grocery and The Oasis Lounge. Then all of a sudden, yelling and name-calling and some sort of ruckus spilled out of Chappy McGee's Public House across the street. I took my eyes off of Amanda Lynn when it turned into a full-blown fistfight between two men as people from all directions swarmed in to watch it.

I had to look, too, because I needed to see if any in the fight were my brothers or pards, but they weren't, so I kept walking. When I started to turn back toward Amanda Lynn, I saw a man less than twelve feet from that fight. Unlike all of the other folks gathering, he wasn't watching the fight. He was staring at me.

Staring hard, too.

He wasn't a big man but not small, either, and he wore a long overcoat and had a fedora pulled low on his head. When I stared back at him, he turned around and walked through the open doors of Chappy's. He'd looked at me like he knew me, but he was a stranger. I'd remember a man with cold eyes like that stranger had. But then I thought I did know him. It was hard to tell who he was by the way he was all covered up in coat and hat, but he couldn't hide those cold eyes. They looked just like the eyes of a man I'd met the summer before, a man who worked for Aunt Kate. I wondered if it was him, and if he'd driven Amanda Lynn to Shady.

I then turned and saw Amanda glance at the fighting, too, and it embarrassed me that she'd have to see such a thing on her first day in Shady. She veered away from it as far as she could on the boardwalk, and I figured it was probably the first fight she'd ever seen.

I sucked in what little stomach I had to raise my chest and look tall as I could when we got near, but then when we got close, the air went out of me like I was a leaky tire. I couldn't say a word or touch her or anything, and that was a strange feeling after all of the touching and talking we'd done in the past.

I don't know what came over me but I guess my arms just couldn't stand it anymore, so they pulled her to me. I hugged her with both hands that ended up around her waist, and I felt all of her against me from my chest to way down my legs.

I soon had to back myself away from the feel of her a little bit, and when she pulled away from me, her eyes were wet and she was smiling. I just kept taking in the smell and look of her blue eyes and all of that blond hair. I went to kiss her and that's when she put a folded piece of yellow paper in my breast pocket, and then she smacked me across the face harder than Ma even did. It was the second time in ten minutes that I'd been hit by a girl.

Then she grabbed me and pressed her face into me. I kept holding her, feeling the sting on my face and hoping her mood was changing and wishing I had on a cleaner shirt. After a long time, she pulled from me and said, "You promised you'd never leave without me."

I didn't know what to say back because it would take a whole day to explain, so I just wanted to say I was sorry for everything.

"I didn't want to," finally came out of me quiet.

She looked at me for a long time like she was really studying my face in a good sort of way, like I was doing to her, and then she looked past me at all the loud goings-on around us. Shady Hollow was definitely different looking and acting than the place I'd made up that I told her I was from.

I looked down at the fancy paper poking up out of my pocket and saw there was handwriting on it. I hoped that later she wouldn't want me to read it out loud with her around because I couldn't read and she didn't know that.

"How'd you find—" I said.

I couldn't finish my question because the fight across the street headed in our direction and the crowd was about to run us over. So I grabbed Amanda Lynn by the hand, looked around for somewhere to take her inside so we could talk and hopefully patch up. I led her up the street back to the Alton House, which was a fairly decent place to be at that time of the evening.

"Ben!"

I turned around and Ma was running toward me wearing her robe and old furry slippers, and Uncle Ray was trying to keep up, limping behind her. He didn't even have his boots or socks on.

I gritted my teeth and wanted to yell or cuss or something but didn't with my company. Amanda Lynn turned around, but I just kept hold of her hand and starting walking faster in the other direction as she started saying she had to tell me something.

Ma's hollering cut off whatever that something was. She was carrying on like she'd completely gone off nutty and I just thought about the pure bad luck of it having Ma high as a hootie owl on the one day that Amanda Lynn showed up in Shady.

I finally went to turn around to yell at her, hoping Amanda Lynn wouldn't catch on that she was my ma. That's when I saw that man with the cold eyes again, his eyes staring into mine like they had earlier, but this time he was walking toward me determined and fast. He had a newspaper over one hand.

Ma saw him right after I did. I watched her grab Uncle Ray and point at that man, and Uncle Ray pulled out a revolver from his waistband and directed it at him.

I pulled Amanda behind me and felt like my heart had quit beating. When it started again, it pounded in my ears and was the only thing I could hear until Uncle Ray yelled.

"Stop where you're standing, mister!" he said.

I'd never heard Uncle Ray say anything over a normal talking voice. He'd yelled so loud that most of the people watching the fight just down the street turned to look. And then a Shady elder who was watching the fight to make sure it didn't get too out of hand saw Uncle Ray holding that black revolver, and he came running up the street, pulling two guns from hip holsters.

Uncle Ray kept hurrying until he got about ten feet from me, trying to get between me and the man I was almost sure was the same man who worked for Aunt Kate. That close to those eyes, there was now little doubt.

I even remembered his name. It was Mr. Charles. I didn't know if Charles was his first name or last name, but that's what Aunt Kate called him.

"Empty your hands!" Uncle Ray yelled at him.

I raised one of my hands to try to say something to stop whatever was about to happen from happening, and tell Uncle Ray everything was all right and to simmer down whatever it was that was boiling up in him.

"Drop that gun, Ray!" the Shady elder ordered.

Uncle Ray paid no attention to Elder Butch Sarver but kept his gun leveled on Mr. Charles. The odd thing was,

Charles didn't even act like he'd heard a thing or knew a gun was pointed at him.

I was turning to Amanda Lynn to see if she could figure out what was going on and do something to settle everybody down. I figured her and Mr. Charles had traveled up together. But out of the corner of my eye, I saw him walking toward me now even faster, so I turned back and in one quick motion, he raised the front of the newspaper he was toting a couple of inches, and two explosions came out of that paper so loud it sounded like cannons had shot from it, and the paper caught on fire.

Uncle Ray flew backward toward me and Amanda Lynn, and Ma screamed.

Charles dropped the newspaper and started leveling a silver pistol in my direction and I froze still like I was dead already. I was sure I was, looking down the barrel of that big gun. Then a shot came from behind him.

He turned and fired three quick shots and one of the elders, Butch Sarver, fell forward, dropping one of his guns. Butch tried to raise his other revolver from where he was lying and the man with the ice-water eyes, who I'd known the year before but only a little more than I could claim knowing a complete stranger, took a careful long aim with both hands and shot him again.

Butch's face, or what was left of it, dropped into a mud hole and didn't come back up.

When Charles turned back to kill me, I'd picked up Uncle Ray's gun and I was already squeezing the trigger slow and steady, just like he'd taught me as I kept the front sight in the middle of Mr. Charles's chest.

Chapter 5

It was early morning now, and as orange colors started taking over the sky and the bus made its way through the bottom end of the Shenandoah Valley, I kept wondering again like I'd had a thousand times if Uncle Ray was following his own nature that terrible evening.

Uncle Ray had always told me that the time would probably come when I might need to fight for my life or run for my life, and I'd have to choose quick and wise or I might never leave those mountains whether I wanted to or not. That was the sort of thing that made me think of the choice he made that day so long ago. I remembered how he told me once that I wasn't born with two feet to just stand on and get killed.

And he told me that cowardice was a much misunderstood thing by most—those of the weaker stock. The same bunch who may talk loud around like weak ears, but stand to the side and become quiet men and steer clear of actual situations where they may have to come face-to-face with such a thing.

As the bus headed south toward Roanoke and then Shawsville, I couldn't think of a single lesson of Uncle Ray's that didn't come in handy at some time or another. Looking around at the children keeping their mommas awake and having a time of things on that bus at such an early hour, I wondered if most boys from other places got lessons on fighting and running so young, and do so much of it, like boys in Shady Hollow did. I reckoned they probably didn't.

When the bus neared Christiansburg and started having a hard time going up those rugged old mountains, I felt like I was home already and I wished I had a window that would roll down so I could smell it. It's hard to describe such a feeling that I had that early June morning as the sun was just starting to blaze up the hills and ridges. It was one of those full, peaceful feelings that comes so seldom and sits way deep down inside a person. It made me hopeful, like there was more going on than just another day had come. I wondered if maybe my long spell of bad luck had finally come to an end.

My anger wasn't gone from me, I knew that, but it was being stilled the closer I got to home. I'd never figured that would happen, but I was starting to feel good and young again in ways you only get when it comes natural like it was doing.

I knew I couldn't ever get back the years I'd lost and that fact still set in a fiery bad place in me like it always had, but now it looked to me that maybe some answers and a sunny day or two were ahead of me. I didn't feel like I was just taking a breath to take another one maybe, to only then be able to take another one. It felt real good inside is what I'm saying, and that was a new thing for me. I didn't feel so dead inside anymore. I felt alive in all ways, many of them I'd forgotten that I even could or ever had felt before. My stop was coming up soon, and I'd never been so dang anxious about anything.

I kept wondering what I'd say after being gone for so long, if Ma still had my old fiddle and other things I'd known as a boy, what I'd holler walking into Hoke's, and especially, all of the things I needed to say and ask Ma and my brothers when I first saw them after we'd had a chance to fellowship and get to know one another again, if I could do that without facing the most serious of things with them first. Truth was I didn't know what I'd do or how I'd act when I stepped foot there. As loud as the things were inside me, the years had grown me silent on the outside and I might not be able to say nothing.

I'd been either worried about or had been mad at Ma for a long time. But the closer I got to her, I just wanted to see her and hoped to find some peace between us somehow because I needed to feel something like that in a terrible way. I wondered about her for a long time on that trip and then somewhere on the road, my thoughts went to my brothers and where the winds may have taken them.

I thought about each one of them, and was curious to find out if they'd stayed in Shady, and how many of them now had families of their own, and if over time they'd left to find their own places and fortunes somewhere else, which I figured they all did.

I hoped luck had been good to them because, besides being my brothers, they were a good bunch of boys even if none of them ever came to visit me. I'd missed each of them more than they'd ever know, and I tried to figure like I'd done countless times what they'd aged to look like and such things because the last time I had seen them, most were just half-grown or less.

We were the closest of close growing up, sharing that one bedroom and generally one mattress, unless one or more were too young and slept in a bureau drawer or a pasteboard box beside Ma's bed.

I was the oldest, and then there was Milton, James, Bernard, Franklin, Theodore and little Virgil. We were all kinds of different colors but we all carried the same last name Ma had, which was Purdue. Her first name was Rebecca, even though almost everybody in Shady called her Violet, which was her working name. Her closest friends called her Becca, which is the name I guessed she favored most to be called. Ma didn't carry a middle name back then that I knew of.

Me, Frank and little Virgil were white-looking, mostly. Jimmy was shaded just like Ma, Milton was a red-brown color and Bernie was dark with slanted eyes. But Teddy was the one who stuck out the most from the rest of us, like the time when Ma let a photographer pay for her services with a sit-down photo of us. Teddy had green eyes, blond-red wiry hair and skin dark as a midnight with no moon. It was a black-and-white photo, but you could sense the different colors on him if you studied the picture where it hung in our living room.

Me and my brothers didn't look much like brothers but we got along as brothers do, beating the tar out of each other one minute but not letting no one else put a hand on any of us the next. Local folks called us the Mutt Gang, and we didn't look for trouble much, just mischief, but few boys or even grown men dared cross us after wronging us once.

Little Virgil was the only one of us who ever had a real dad in Shady because for some reason, a short feller with a small round curly head named Arthur Hoskins decided to face up to his responsibility about it.

I was so young then that my memory of Arthur Hoskins was fuzzy but I remember Ma wanting to get married quick to Arthur before he tried to get away. Arthur couldn't go to the outhouse or take a walk by himself for a week before the nuptials without a man hired by the elders keeping an eye on him if Ma wasn't around.

She told us that she'd finally found a decent man who could tolerate children and her occupation, so her and Arthur up and got hitched one hot Saturday afternoon under a walnut tree beside the Big Walker River. They even hauled in a real preacher from Abington on the back of a hay truck to do the ceremony. Ma insisted on a legal wedding.

Everybody in Shady Hollow went to it dressed up in the finest they owned as we all stood on the grassy riverbank.

Once it was over and dark set in, there was general high living and raucous behavior of all sorts. The elders paid for all of it.

But that short loud feller Ma had got hitched to got himself shot outside of McCauley's Pavilion just before little

Virgil was even crawling. Got shot square in the face. By a woman. Ma found out later that her dead husband was married to about a dozen other women besides her. One of them tracked him to Shady Hollow and killed him over it because he'd taken a good bit of her fortunes before he left.

The elders questioned Ma afterward over and over why a true professional con man like Arthur Hoskins, whose trade turned out to be robbing wealthy women, would want to marry a whore in Shady Hollow who didn't have nothing but a bunch of hungry young'uns. Arthur's other wives were all rich or within spitting distance of it. Ma kept telling the elders that she didn't know, maybe Arthur just felt love for her and little Virgil.

They never bought into her explanation, I don't think. Even grieving over her dead husband, Ma was summoned to a lot of elder meetings that year. Looking back, I believe that's why they started getting suspicious of her.

Anyway, growing up, me and my brothers never called any man Dad or Papa or anything like that, but Ma told us to call some of the men who spent time around our second-floor apartment our "uncles," so we did.

We had lots of uncles in Shady Hollow, and they came and went like leaves ride the river current.

They'd be there for a spell, giving Ma as much money as she could talk out of them and they'd eat her good Southern cooking and bounce a baby on a knee. They shared her bed, too, when she wasn't working or when one of us wasn't in it sick, and then one day we'd wake up and all sight and smell of them would be gone.

We'd stand quiet in our three-room apartment, looking out an open window, feeling the chill, watching the way the curtain would blow in and out. Ma had a cowbell nailed above the squeaky door to our apartment to keep better track of us. I guess that's why they always left out a window—to keep from ringing that bell, same as we did when we'd sneak out.

Ma would shut the window tight all of a sudden and tell us that Uncle Pete or Uncle Shelby or Uncle Carl or Uncle whoever wasn't bringing back breakfast because he wasn't coming back. And that's the last time any of us could speak their name as Ma would go to making grits on top of the coal stove.

She always made grits when we lost an uncle, not sure why because Ma hated grits and I was never fond of them, either. But we'd salt and pepper them and put butter or cheese in them and sit and eat quiet. Times were gonna be hard for a while. Grits signaled such times and we ate a lot of them between uncles.

Uncle Ray was my favorite uncle out of all of them.

Ma had told me the first day he moved in with us that he wasn't my real uncle when I asked her, which meant he wasn't my real father. But he could have been one to one of my brothers I guess—even though he didn't look like none of us that I could see, except Teddy, because Teddy sort of looked like everybody.

Uncle Ray was getting a head start on being an old man in those times. But when he was younger, he'd went to a big college in Connecticut learning to be a doctor, Ma said. He got in some bad trouble not being able to pay off gambling and schooling debts to a bunch of serious fellers in New York City. Uncle Ray took off and I don't know if he was ever a real doctor. But he could cut and stitch like no one else and he doctored in Shady whenever needed, even if he had to leave a card game to do it. And even if he was winning big or losing big, which he was admired for by some and not for by some others. I figured, too, sometimes that was the reason why Uncle Ray tended to be such a poor gambler.

He'd taught Ma and a couple of other gals to be his nurses for whenever he needed help, and he always told me that Ma was the best of all of them and it was a shame she never got an education. I remember both of them going off together in a rush at all times of the day or night once summoned for help from somebody, most usually for a woman in trouble. I guess I can best say that as far as making a living, Ma tended to the wants of men and the needs of women, all who came to Shady for such different reasons.

But before they worked together as doctor and nurse, it was clear from the first day Uncle Ray stepped foot in Shady that he liked Ma, because he was her best-paying customer. He doted on her more than most men ever did, buying her fancy garments or a hat or even flowers, stuff he didn't need to buy because he always paid his turn with her in advance. I guess he just wanted to spend more money on her.

I didn't think back then that Ma deep-down loved Uncle Ray like some folks you see do in movies. He didn't love her in that way, either, but she seemed to care for him in a more than tolerable way. He stuck around long enough even when he wasn't forced to, to show me how to do things like use that razor and how to load and shoot a gun—by not paying mind to what's going on around you or the stirrings in you at that moment, but to just keep eyeballing the front sight and make sure it stayed in the middle of what you wanted to hit, and then keep squeezing that trigger nice and slow no matter if your hands were shaking because they were gonna be shaking if someone was shooting back at you.

"Nice and slow," he said over and over.

I must have squeezed the trigger on his empty wheel gun a hundred or more times in Ma's apartment as he'd lay a dime on the barrel. He told me I could keep the dime when I aimed in and squeezed the trigger and the dime was still balancing.

I eventually got to keep that ten cents, and got to pocket about a dollar's worth more change over the weeks as we'd keep practicing. One day when we walked to the edge of Shady, he finally gave me a real bullet to put in his gun.

I hit an old chicken-pecked pie tin from thirty paces away that he'd hung from a locust tree branch.

Dead center.

He took his revolver from me and said, "You don't need any more shooting lessons."

The gun bucked up and backward and I brought it down to squeeze the trigger again, but when I did Mr. Charles was flat on his back in the middle of Main Street. His hat had fallen off, and looking at his thin white hair laying in the muddy street, I now knew for certain that it was him. Ma was crying hysterical and she ran over and kicked the pistol out of his hand even though he wasn't moving.

I looked down at Uncle Ray and he wasn't moving, either. Not even his quick eyes, which were wide-open, staring at the sky.

Then Amanda Lynn screamed to the top of her lungs.

I'd just fallen down, almost like my legs were yanked out from under me. I believe it was her scream that helped me to get my head back together and shake off whatever had gotten hold of me. I came to and then stood so I could get a good look at her to make sure she hadn't got shot, too. When I did, I could hardly stand up so I looked down at myself, wondering if I'd been shot. I didn't see blood coming out of me anywhere, and I looked back at Amanda Lynn. She had both hands up to her face, still screaming, and when I went to touch her, she put her arms around herself and backed away from me all of a sudden like I was something bad she didn't want to be near.

I just stood there shaking. Everything had happened so fast that I wasn't sure what had just happened. I wasn't even sure what I'd done until I felt a heavy weight in my left hand. I looked down at the revolver and dropped it into the dirt and felt even more dizzy when I saw smoke drift out of the barrel. I was sure I was gonna fall over so I went down to both knees as a foul taste came up in my throat. I saw Ma was now laying across Uncle Ray.

Some kind of wailing I'd never heard before came from inside her, then she looked around scared to death and ran a couple of steps over to me. Ma grabbed Uncle Ray's gun and it seemed like she didn't know what to do with it, but needed to keep it as she kept looking at the crowds. She finally eased it into a robe pocket just before she pulled me up gentle and looked me over. It looked like she wanted to say something but couldn't get nothing out. Then she looked again at all of the faces staring at us. There wasn't a sound in Shady Hollow but for the sounds of our breathing.

Ma turned back to me and then looked over Amanda Lynn while trying to take in quick deep breaths. Then she pointed at an old Chevrolet sitting about twenty yards from us in a weedy field between Goldie's Pawn and the old burned-down horse livery.

"Take. Take. That car. Now."

The way Ma couldn't talk right made me shake even more than I was doing. Then I wondered if maybe she was talking right but I just wasn't hearing things right. I looked over my shoulder at Amanda Lynn and she flew toward me and grabbed me around the waist from behind. I could feel her shaking, too.

"Why'd Mr. Charles—" I started to ask Amanda Lynn.

Ma got right up close to my face and talked in a rush like her mouth worked right again but she was still all out of breath. "There may be more of them here and they're gonna try to kill you. You have to leave. Now!"

I stared at Ma and then pulled Amanda Lynn around where I could see her. Her eyes looked wide as quart jars. She'd quit screaming but her face had gone a sick-looking shade and she didn't even look like the girl she just was a minute or two before. "Why'd he do such a thing? Why'd he—?" I asked her.

She couldn't speak so I tried to read her wide eyes, but

I'd never seen them like that and couldn't make a word out of them. I couldn't tell nothing about her except she was terrified.

I turned back to Ma when Ma said, "She can't go."

I got all choked up and fought back the bad tastes in my throat and my eyes filled up with water. "What's happening, Ma?"

Ma turned from me and kept scanning the crowds. She turned back. "You have to go. Right now, Ben. Right now."

"It just don't make no—"

Ma grabbed my hands and barely got out, "They found us and more will come. You have to go!"

"We been hiding from somebody?"

She peered down and then stared straight into my eyes as best she could even though it looked like she was falling apart. "I've been hiding you," she said.

"From who?"

"I have to get your brothers."

"I ain't leaving without you all."

She squeezed my wrists hard. "You're gonna do exactly what I say."

"But why do I have to… What ain't you saying?"

Ma shook her head and the far edges of her eyebrows sunk down like there were lead sinkers tied to them. Then all of us turned to look when we heard men yelling coming from down the street. Their voices broke the dead quiet of the crowds.

Ma turned back to me. "I'll find you and explain things. I'll find you when—"

"I can't leave—"

"We all may be in danger. You have to—"

"Can't the elders protect us?"

"Not from this," she said.

As I was trying to make sense of what she'd just said, we all noticed how the people were starting to mill closer to us. Ma pulled out a roll of money from her bosom, shoved it as far down into my back pocket as it would go, and then grabbed my hand and put a car key in my palm with her fingers cold and wet as a drip from an icicle.

She turned me toward the old rusted-out Chevrolet. It didn't have any plates on it. "Take it," she said, pushing me toward the car.

"Whose is it?"

"Take it!"

Ma started pushing and pulling me harder and I figured it was her customer's as Ma and Uncle Ray didn't have a car.

I had Amanda Lynn's hand in mine and was pulling her with me. Ma stopped and grabbed both of our arms and jerked us apart.

All of a sudden a shotgun blast came from a block away that made us jump and sent my heart racing even more. People were trying to run but it looked like none of them knew which direction to head. I just stared at Ma because I didn't know what to do.

She grabbed me hard by the arm and with her other hand, she pulled the revolver out of her robe, holding it by the very end of the checkered grip. It was then that I noted the blood on it. Ma looked as scared of that gun as she did at whatever frightened her in the crowd. She tried to hand it to me but I wouldn't take it. She finally pushed the barrel of it way down into my front pant's pocket. It was clear to me that she thought I was gonna need that gun again. I was so scared at that point that I didn't think I could even hold on to it, and I didn't never ever want to have to fire a gun again. That made me scared even worse. Ma giving me that gun had told me whatever was happening wasn't over.

Another shotgun blast echoed off the buildings and mountains and this time it sounded closer.

"Go!" Ma started pulling me again to the car as we all started running with our heads way down in our shoulders.

I had Amanda Lynn in one hand again and the car key in the other. I was all tensed up and it felt like my legs were so heavy that I was trying to run upstream through rapids.

"Go to where?" I yelled.

"Head toward the mines. Don't tell nobody your real name. And don't come back until I find you. I'll find you. You can't ever come back here unless I tell you it's safe. Not ever."

"Ma…"

We were almost to the car when I stopped. All of us were trembling from the head down to the ground.

Ma grabbed me hard by both shoulders and stood up as tall as she could, then she kissed my cheek real fast and put an arm around Amanda Lynn, who now didn't even look like she was breathing.

"I'll make sure she gets home. I'll take care of her. You know I'll take care of her. Now go!"

"But why was he looking to just kill—"

I was looking at Amanda Lynn, begging for some answer,

for her to just say something, and then at Ma, when another blast came. This time I found out that the yelling and the gunshots had come from three elders who were trying to part the crowds. Elder Bertrand Puckett had stuck his shotgun straight up in the air and fired it. The other two elders were carrying their double-barrels at the ready.

I looked over at Uncle Ray still laying there in a heap with his legs tangled up underneath him. His eyes were still wide-open, the front of his white shirt was red and the dirt around him had turned into a dark maroon color.

Ma let go of Amanda Lynn, then half dragged and half pushed me the last few feet to the car, flung open the door and I jumped in it or I'd of fell into it with Ma pushing me so hard. "I'll find you, baby," she said. "I promise I'll find you. Don't get off the dirt roads."

She slammed the door.

I looked at Amanda Lynn, dropped the key on the floorboard, found it and then couldn't hardly get it into the ignition with my fingers not working. So Ma grabbed the key back from me, fired that car up and started yelling "go" over and over and over, as I just held on to the steering wheel.

"Get out of that car!" Elder Warren Ratcliffe ordered. He'd taken cover behind the corner of Steiner's Fine Men's Clothier and had his shotgun pointed right at my head. Ma ran and put herself between him and me, waving her hands in the air and screaming for nobody to shoot because it was her boy in that car.

She then turned back toward me, pleading with her eyes for me to get out of there.

My leg was barely able to hold in the clutch as I jammed the shift straight up the column into Reverse and spun the car around until it was in the road. That's when Ma grabbed Amanda Lynn's hand and they ran nearer the elders as she begged them again not to shoot.

I watched in the rearview mirror as Amanda Lynn pulled away from Ma and ran back toward me before she fell in the street right where we'd just stood. She went to her knees and screamed my name as the elders kept ordering me to get out of the car as they slowly circled Amanda Lynn and Ma, waving away the crowds with their shotguns when they weren't pointed at me.

I started crying like I hadn't cried since I was a little kid, and I didn't know what else to do, so I did what Ma said. I slumped down in the seat, popped the clutch and stomped the gas pedal to the floor, praying those elders weren't gonna shoot. I never let my foot off until I'd climbed the first hill that led out of Shady Hollow.

I wasn't planning on running all the way to the coal towns just over the border in West Virginia like Ma'd said. I was just gonna go far enough where I couldn't hear Amanda Lynn's screaming or Ma's yelling no more. I pulled the revolver out of my pocket and laid it on the seat beside me because the long barrel was pushing into my leg and the butt of it was jammed into my stomach, making me sit almost sideways. I then sat up straight once I was out of the elders' shotgun range and I drove that old car as hard as it would go up the steep hill out of Shady, and almost tore the bottom out of it bouncing over ruts.

After topping the knoll, the road got muddy and I about drowned through the washed-out places that I hit thirty miles an hour going down the other side.

The windshield was covered with water and mud and only one wiper worked. I eased up on the gas pedal some and just needed time to get my breath so I might be able to make some sense out of what had just happened.

I couldn't believe Uncle Ray was dead as I leaned my head out the window to see and fought the steering wheel around curve after curve.

And I couldn't believe most that I'd just killed a man and for what reason I didn't know except he was about to kill me.

Coming up fast on a sharp bend below, I remembered an old logging road less than a mile away from where I was at. I could take that road as far as I could go before the road became too rough. I could hide the car there and even camp in it for a couple of days if I needed to. I could walk back to Shady that next morning before daylight when few would be awake and the ones who were wouldn't be able to notice.

I'd wake Herbert Mullins and he would know or could find out whatever was going on. I was sure Herbert would help me. He'd know what happened with Amanda Lynn and Ma and my brothers after I left. And why a man with cold eyes from North Carolina had come there to kill me. Herbert would have gotten wind of everything.

But I never was gonna make it to that old logging road. I thought I was driving out of trouble, but I was headed into the deadest, thickest kind of it. And I didn't know yet that a big part of me had just died, too, on that street in Shady Hollow.

Chapter 6

My nose was almost against his.

"Why're you following me?" I asked again.

He didn't say anything. I stood upright and hit him again.

He yelled in a high voice and the gash at his hairline spread and sent more blood pouring as it started to pool on the restroom floor. He raised a shaky, lost hand to try and wipe it all away and I hit him again, aiming for the same place, but this time the metal landed just under his ear. Unlike the other blows, there was no sound after of begging or hollering or screaming.

Only the thud.

Both of his arms dropped like cut-down trees.

His face was now covered in blood. He was slumped on the floor with his legs out from him and the back of his neck and head were against the tile wall. I was standing in front of him with the metal paper towel holder still in my hand. It was colored white when it was on the wall. Not now.

He started to tip over and that's when I saw that the bathroom door didn't have a lock, but there was a wooden scotch lying near the corner next to the door. I ran and jammed it under the door and kept kicking it until it held tight. I noticed the blood drops hitting the floor while I was kicking, looked at my left hand and that's when I realized I had a deep cut across my palm from the edge of the metal digging into it when I was hitting him.

I moved the paper towel holder into my other hand, looked over and he hadn't moved since I'd left him. He was still breathing. The doorknob shaped like a wing suddenly turned but not much, and the slight noise it made broke the silence like a far-off siren, and then there was a knock, then a louder one. I walked back fast and looked down at the man I'd thought had followed me into the bathroom to kill me. Standing back from him now but still holding the piece of metal I'd torn from the wall only less than a minute before, I watched as he suddenly moved and tried to find his face with both hands. He opened one eye and saw me standing in front of him, then tried to crawl away. I dropped my weapon, pushed him all the way down onto his stomach and gave him another quick search for a gun or knife. He still didn't have one.

"I wasn't following you," he said weak.

Whoever was at the door was now pounding on it.

"You followed me through the station and then into here," I said.

He shook his head. I stood and kicked him hard in the ribs.

"I thought you might have some dope," he said, coughing. "I wanted to buy a joint. That's all I—"

"What were you doing sitting on the bench when the bus pulled in? You looked to be waiting on somebody."

"I wasn't waiting on you. I was waiting on my bus. I got a ticket to Charlotte," he said.

He went to grab something out of his inside jacket pocket and I knocked his hand away and pulled it out. It was a ticket to Charlotte. He was telling the truth about that. I was starting to feel sick knowing he'd been trying to tell me the truth about everything.

"You were eyeing me," I said.

"I thought you might have some weed. That's all. I was just looking for some weed. I swear. I swear it." He rolled from his stomach to his side and moved his hands from his head to his ribs.

"You don't know me?" I asked.

He tried to shake his head but stopped. "I ain't never seen you before. I wish I never did."

"Open it right now!" came from the other side of the door. It moved in a couple more inches, then a couple more. Whoever was out there was now pushing hard on it.

"Be out in a minute!" I yelled.

I reached down and grabbed the collar of his leather jacket. He looked like a biker by the looks of him and had a hard time trying to open his eyes, but I saw the fear still in them.

"You've pulled time?" I asked.

He nodded.

"Where at?" I asked.

"When?"

"Whenever," I said.

"Lot of places."

"Where, goddamn it?"

"Petersburg. Nottingham. Powatan. Green—"

"For what?"

"Lot of things," he said. "I don't know what's going on but you got me pegged wrong, mister. I just got out from the prison camp in Pulaski and am heading home to Charlotte. Just got out today."

The loud bang that only a stick makes against a door made me jump. "Police. Open the door! Now!"

"You on parole?" I asked.

He nodded.

"Then you don't need no trouble from this. You don't need no trouble. When they come in, you tell them you fell when the holder pulled from the wall. You were just trying to get something to clean up with on your trip home. This was an accident. You understand? You don't need no trouble on parole, and you don't need no more trouble from me. Understand?"

He nodded again.

The stick was pounding on the door louder now.

"Hold your damn horses, I'm coming!" I yelled.

I saw where my shoes were leaving bloody footprints across the floor, took off my shoes and was careful where I stepped as I ran toward a line of windows but stopped long enough to run one sink full blast and throw handfuls of water on the floor to muddy my prints near the man I'd just almost killed. I threw my bag outside and my sock feet were barely out one of those windows when I heard the door crash open.

I ran as fast as I could until I had to bend over about three blocks away and choke down what was in my gut trying to come up. I'd only been out of the can for less than twelve hours, and I'd already almost killed a man who I thought was gonna kill me. And all he wanted was a joint.

I knew he wouldn't say anything with his circumstances, and I now was sure what he'd told me was the truth. He had the look for sure from the get-go, but not a weapon to do it with.

I had to get farther from that bus station. Found an outside spigot at a nearby house with no cars in the driveway and washed the blood off my hands and the gash out in my palm, and the spots I saw on my jacket and pants. I pulled out the bottom of my shirt and tore off a piece for a bandage and got my hand fixed up, then washed my face off good in case there was blood on it. I then rinsed my shoes, put them back on and was quick about it, and then made my way from that house and that small, crowded depot in downtown Wytheville as fast as I could. A taxicab drove by as I was going down a side street. I yelled it down and asked how much it would cost to get to Hillsville. I thought it best now to get out of that town altogether but didn't have money to go far. Hillsville wasn't far but I hoped far enough. I got in and it was a quiet ride. The driver didn't look but once in his rearview mirror at me because I guess my eyes told his that once was enough. He let me out where I'd asked, did a U-turn pulling away, and when he was out of eyesight I left the road and ran down to the riverbanks of the Big Walker, making my way toward Saltville.

Just being beside the waters of my old river was aiding me already. I'd missed it so much and here it was trying to help lead me home.

Saltville was a good-size town and it was on the way to Shady. Even though I hurried, it was a couple hours before I got to where I was going. I climbed back up the banks to Main Street and just enough time had passed for my innards and brains to get settled and get my situation sorted out to where I didn't feel like a man running, but a man just walking.

Once in the thick of town, there were people and vehicles going in every direction, busy as a hive of honeybees and way too many eyes to study proper. It hit me then that I wasn't going to go through the rest of my trip home like I'd just done. I maybe could do it, but I wasn't going to, and I decided instead to hope I'd changed enough on the outside that if somebody was still after me for whatever reason, they'd have a hard time making out who I was, and they wouldn't know I was heading home yet being I was released from prison early.

I gave it quite a bit of serious thought and ended up deciding to just try and enjoy being a free man, because after my last stop it was hard to tell how long that would last. I figured if trouble was just around the corner, I'd probably never be able to recognize it in time with so many people and so many new things and the big mistake I'd just made. It was right there while sitting on a bench in front of the

Saltville theater that I made all the effort I could to let down my guard and feel like a free man.

After I got that all sorted out in me, I walked down a bunch of sidewalks, trying to take in what walking down a sidewalk in a real town is like. I got more than a little bewildered by it all and decided to just sit on another bench and collect myself. A lot of people looked in my direction while walking by or driving by, but none seemed to mind me sitting on a bench in their town.

I sat for about an hour, occasionally checking myself for any bloodstains before I spotted a hardware store across the street. I soon headed over there where I bought a small pocketknife they had sitting in a display case near the cash register.

It was the first thing I'd ever bought that I didn't buy in a prison canteen or from one of the businesses in Shady Hollow. I paid three dollars and ten cents for the knife. I didn't know if it was a good price or not, but the two blades were sharp and it had a can opener on it and it basically seemed pretty sturdy for its size and a man needs a pocketknife, so I got it.

They gave me two packs of matches, too, for free after I asked if they sold them, right after I'd wondered if I may need to camp a night on my way home.

I was feeling pretty good about myself, but wished I wasn't toting that paper bag stuffed with my old clothes and shoes. So within a few minutes, I walked out of another store that sold clothes and stuff you'd buy for a house and about any kind of thing you could wish for or need.

They had a black bag with a long strap selling for just

under six dollars. That was a lot of money but it looked just the right size, so I bought it and, once outside the store, put all my things in it. I kept the paper bag, too, just in case I might need it for something down the road.

I reckoned that I rolled into town at the busiest time because the streets had started to slow down. I looked up and could tell where the sun was that dinnertime would be coming soon, and I knew I'd be hungry. So I found a grocery that sold foods of all kinds and some things to eat that I'd never even heard of.

After going down a few aisles and looking at the prices of things, I ended up at the meat counter where I rung a bell and asked the meat man to cut me a hunk of bologna and a similar sized hunk of cheese. He asked what kind of cheese I wanted and I said the kind people usually ate, and he seemed to understand what I was saying.

It wasn't but a couple of minutes before I was at the checkout with my bologna and cheese, and I'd also picked up a loaf of sliced bread, two oranges, a few more Zagnut bars, two bottles of Coca-Cola and a quart of Miller beer.

I hadn't had a drink of real alcohol since I was too young to buy it anywhere but in Shady, where if you had the money, you could buy about anything there no matter how old you were.

All I'd had to drink with kick to it the last twenty years was prison hooch concocted with stuff you didn't never investigate too much. So anyway, I just liked the looks of that big cold bottle of beer. I was careful with it and took all of my groceries and put them in my black bag, and soon took

off walking southwest until I found old Route 11. I knew
about where it should be, I just wasn't sure where it was, but
I eventually found it. It would be a lot quicker taking the
road than trying to follow the Big Walker, so that's the path
I chose to get home.

It was such a nice day that I didn't stick out my thumb
for miles. I just kept walking and walking and walking, eating
my oranges along the way and I stopped worrying about
being hunted or the police and just was thinking about
Shady while carrying my new satchel, and I felt for a long
time that I could walk right across the whole country if I
had a mind to, but those new state shoes I was wearing put
a stop to those thoughts after about ten miles.

I started slowing down and pulled out the money in my
front pocket. I had a few dollars left and still the ten in my
old shoe that I was carrying with me, and I knew I wouldn't
have to spend a dime more of any of it before I got home,
and it made me feel assured getting there carrying a nice bag
with my things in it and wearing some nice clothes and
something in my pockets that in the event a couple of old
pards bought me a round, that I'd be able to do likewise, if
they'd let me.

Around noon, my hand was killing me and my left sock
at my heel was turning wet and red and I saw a creek way
down a steep embankment with a cow pasture bordering it.
I wasn't sure what creek it was but figured it fed into the Big
Walker River. The sun was getting hot on my shoulders by
then and I'd long since stripped off my canvas state jacket,
and with my heel giving me such a fit with each step, I de-

cided to go down off the side of the road and find a shade tree to have dinner.

It didn't take long to reach a nice spot.

Once I sat, I cleaned the wound on my hand with sand, gravel and creek water, redressed it with some more of my shirt tail that I'd scrubbed, too, took my new socks and shoes off, and I lowered my legs into that stream up to my knees and I made two bologna and cheese sandwiches and topped that grand meal off with a Zagnut bar and washed it all down with a Coca-Cola.

After I finished, I eyed my bottle of beer that I had cooling in the creek, but knew I'd eaten too much to enjoy it proper, so I decided to save it for later. The sun and shade and full belly and the sounds of the water and my few cares that afternoon were putting me to sleep. I knew I'd wake there way after dark with skeeter bites all over me if I gave in to such a nice feeling, and I couldn't wait to get back to Shady. So I got my things together and trudged back up the steep hill.

I soon found a flat spot on the top of a bashed-in guardrail. When I'd see a car or truck, I'd stand tall and stick out my good thumb in the direction of Shady Hollow.

But after about an hour, it was looking like people around those parts may not be as charitable as they once were or as I'd once thought they were, so I started walking south again.

It surprised me late that evening when a silver Buick pulled off of the road in front of me. That car must have been one out of a thousand that had passed me by…seemed like poor odds for hitchhiking.

So I hurried as best I could with my blister and everything else, hoping the sight of me wouldn't change their mind. When I got close, I saw two old people's heads with white hair sticking up not very far above the front bench seat of that Buick.

Once I got to the car, I pulled on the back door but it was locked, and that's when the tiny codger in the driver's seat rolled down his window an inch and peered at me through bifocals.

"Where you heading, young feller?" he asked.

Just by the sight of him, I thought he might leave me standing there if I told him I was heading toward Shady, so I told him I was heading to Winslow. Shady was before Winslow, so I figured I'd just ask him to let me out before we got there.

"Why you walking?" he asked.

He'd caught me off guard with that one. I thought for a second or two and said, "Having some hard times and trying to get home," I said, which was all pretty much true.

He rolled down his window just a little more. "Where's home?"

"Winslow," I said.

"You done said that," he said. "Where'bouts?"

I felt for sure then that that sharp old man was never gonna give me a ride as bad as I needed one. I fumbled around for something to say and finally said, "I'd appreciate it if you'd drop me off just before the Winslow town limits."

"We live in Winslow. Where you trying to get to exactly?"

I put down my shiny bag of belongings on the ground and he rolled his window back up a little when I put my eyes just on the other side of the glass as his. I noted his wife was studying me hard, too, and she looked a lot more uneasy than he was getting.

"What happened to your hand?" the old woman asked.

I realized she didn't miss much, either. Maybe between the two of them they didn't miss nothing in the whole dern world, I feared. I thought for a second. "Caught it on a blackberry bush back up the road."

There was more quiet. They were good people through and through for stopping to pick up a stranger, I didn't doubt that a bit, and I don't know, but for some reason I just grabbed my bag, thanked them for pulling over and wished them, "Good fortunes in your travels," which was always a popular farewell in Shady. It came out awkward but I meant it.

I just figured being so different, we weren't meant to be traveling companions and I'd have to find me another ride. It looked like the only way I'd ever get to ride in their car was if I stole it, which would be easy enough for sure, but I wasn't in a nature to do nothing like that right then even though the thought did briefly pass my mind.

I walked about twenty yards from them when the old man honked his horn and waved me back. About the time I got to his window, it was rolled all of the way down and he said, "Get in."

I nodded, seeing the back door wasn't locked anymore and I did what he said, and slowly the old man got his huge car back on the highway so very careful. We rode for a time with no conversation, and I just kept wishing he'd put his foot down to at least drive the speed limit.

We passed sign after sign of towns ahead and like I figured, I never saw one that had Shady Hollow on it.

"What's your name?" the old man hollered loud all of a sudden.

I quit looking at the high ridges running on both sides of us and saw him peering at me hard in his rearview mirror. "Ben Purdue," I said, before I'd even realized what I'd said. I guess thinking about old times made my old name come out of me like it was shot out of a gun. I just couldn't believe I'd called myself by my real name. I figured I was starting to feel a little like Ben Purdue again, and that was the best feeling.

"So who you going to visit in Winslow?" he asked.

I took a deep breath and pondered on it as long as I could. "I'm trying to get back to visit with my old ma who used to live on a dirt road in Winslow County. I ain't seen her in years, and I ain't even sure exactly where she did live, but I'll recognize it when I lay eyes on it."

He looked me again in his mirror and said, "What's your momma's name?"

"Rebecca Purdue," I said.

He looked over at his wife. "Don't know a Rebecca Purdue, do you, Hazel?" She scrunched up her nose and then shook her head before she turned around.

"Is she kin to the Hundley Purdues or the Gillespie Purdues?"

"I don't know, ma'am," I said.

"Who's she related to?" the husband asked.

"I ain't sure, beyond me."

"Well, you don't seem to be sure about much of anything," the old man said, and not joking. His eyes kept looking at me and he finally said, "You look like you seen some trouble in your life."

I didn't say anything and looked out the window. It looked like my ride was about to end a few more blisters shy of Shady Hollow.

"You look like you been in some trouble, that's what I'm saying to you."

Even with my new bag and nice state clothes, it was clear I was already having a dang hard time just trying to be a regular person. I decided just to tell him what he seemed to know already.

"I have, but I can assure you I've paid for it. I just appreciate the ride and I'm gonna help you out on the gas money."

"You a churchgoing man?"

"I ain't never been in a church but I've prayed on occasion," I said.

"What you do for a living?"

"Carpenter," I said.

"Around here?"

"No, up in Pennsylvania." I wasn't lying because before I had all that trouble finding me and got locked down into protective custody, I did work as a carpenter making bunk beds and wall lockers and desks in the prison wood shop for the military people to use.

He started jawing about that he'd worked construction for years back in the Depression and he was lucky to have a job at all when he was a man about my age, then he started going on about sports and how the football team up at VPI looked to be doing.

I told him I'd been interested in sports as a young'un, but hadn't kept up with any of them for a good while.

About the time we got twenty miles from Winslow, I asked that they slow down as we were about to crest a mountain I knew so well. Then I asked them to drop me off at the edge of a road that was once dirt but was now paved two lanes. At first I wasn't sure it was even the right road it had changed so much, but I knew from where it was sitting on the side of the notch of Hellbender Mountain that it had to be.

Had to be.

I'd walked that road a thousand times, and more than that, where that Buick sat seemed to be in my memory the exact spot the sheriff of Winslow County had pulled off the road and given me a beating after I tried to run from Shady Hollow like Ma had made me do twenty-one years before.

What a long road it had been leaving Shady, and then so many years and years later, trying to make my way back home. I remembered like it was yesterday the last time I'd been sitting in a car on the side of Hellbender Mountain. I suddenly felt handcuffed and shot to pieces.

Chapter 7

I'd gunned and fought that beat-up moonshiner's car to go as hard as it would tear ass out of Shady. But I hadn't gotten a half mile when the state and federal officers I ran into on the other side of a sharp bend started shooting just as I slammed into their roadblock. I didn't mean to run into them, because I didn't know the car I'd stolen from Ma's customer was so light on brakes, but if I didn't do what I did, I would have went off of the side of Hellbender Mountain into the Big Walker River.

I stuck both hands out the busted windshield sure I was done for, and to be honest about it, I don't think I cared much if nothing whether I was alive or dead at that point. I guess instinct is the only thing that made me raise my hands.

They rushed me as I was trying to shake glass off of my face and out of my hair, and they didn't know what my name was as they called me about every name you could think of ordering me to get out of that car. They had a picture of me, though. One state trooper held it upside my face, and with his other hand, he held a pistol that he'd screwed into my right ear.

I'd been hit by two bullets, one that was stopped by my right shoulder, and the other had went clean through my leg just an inch below where no man would ever want to get shot. I closed my eyes and ducked my chin into my chest as hands started grabbing me in different places, all of them trying to pull me out of the car in different directions.

I thought they were about to tear me to pieces.

"He's got a razor on him," one officer yelled. It was then that most stopped pulling on me and instead piled on top of me.

I felt the razor and whetstone being yanked out of one back pocket and then Ma's roll of money out of the other. I tried to get a gulp of air to yell out that my name was Henry Cole, the first name I could make up. Henry being the name of a dog of mine that had gotten run over by a logger who was in too big a hurry to get to Shady. Cole was the first name of my best friend who'd gotten accidentally killed by a drunk who thought he was shooting at a ghost after staggering out of Shady Al's Bar on a foggy Halloween night. Cole was just standing in the mist with a lantern, looking for dropped pocket change like kids do in Shady before the street sweepers would find it the next morning.

Anyway, those officers didn't believe my name was Henry Cole, and after they got off me and searched me all over, one of them yanked Amanda Lynn's letter out of my shirt. I reached to get it back just as a couple of them started taking turns pounding on me after they dragged me out into the road. They broke three of my fingers on one hand and my thumb on the other getting handcuffs on me, and the last thing I was doing was trying to give them a hard time even before I felt the first bone snap. It may sound crazy, but through all of everything going on, I just kept wanting that letter back.

I was crying and yelling scared and mad the way they were treating me, and then I got just plain scared the more it went on. I kept swearing to them over and over that my name was Henry, and that I didn't do whatever they'd shot me over, but they didn't believe me.

After one of them taped thick white bandages across my shoulder and around my leg, they hogtied me up in chains and dumped me headfirst into the caged backseat of a sheriff car.

I lay there on my stomach for what seemed like hours but it may've only been a couple of minutes. Officers gathered around, and every now and then one of them would look again in the open trunk of the car I'd been driving, or bend down to take a look at me. Some of them grinned looking me over. Some of them didn't. I feared more the ones who did.

Finally, two armed men wearing the same brown county sheriff uniforms, one with a blond crew cut and one with a gray crew cut, got in the front seat and they took me on a long, slow, bumpy ride. I couldn't believe I didn't bleed to death on that ride.

I prayed we were heading to a hospital and I was quiet except for my crying which just kept pouring out of me when I couldn't keep it all inside. Instead of thinking about the mess with the law I was in, I kept trying to think about Amanda Lynn between bumps, and Ma and Uncle Ray, and what had just happened in Shady Hollow.

Lying there soaking in my cold sweat and blood, I didn't think I'd probably have another day to think about anything. I was almost sure of it.

Everything had come upon me so quick and unexpected. I felt like I was in a nightmare, the kind that would wake you up grabbing for a window to open for air and would then keep you awake the rest of the night because you'd fear if you closed your eyes, you'd fall right back into the middle of the terrors.

None of it seemed real and I couldn't make sense of nothing that had happened being that, only an hour before, I'd been sitting at the counter of Merle's just feeling my normal self on a Sunday and waiting on a meal.

I was having a hard time with my confused thoughts and the things on my heart, and I got worried all of a sudden about Amanda Lynn and Ma and my brothers, because Ma had said there may be more danger in Shady. I started thinking if I were braver, I never would've run like Ma had told me to do.

I wasn't a boy no more. I should've stayed and fought again if I had to, and not hightailed it out of there crying like a coward and leaving Amanda Lynn and Ma and my younger brothers to fend for themselves or depend on the elders to protect them.

But then I recalled what Ma'd said, that all of them would

be in danger if I stayed. Mr. Charles had come to kill me. That made me shiver the worst, because I still had no idea why.

Ma said it was all from something that made us hide in Shady. I just didn't know what to think about any of it because none of it made any sense.

I always thought we lived in Shady Hollow because it was a pretty good place to live. Ma didn't have much else and she liked the place and none of us minded any of it, and business was always good in her trade, so I figured that's where we lived because it suited her and me and my brothers, basically.

While I kept bleeding all over my favorite shirt, I just prayed Ma and my brothers and Amanda Lynn were safe, and I hoped the elders were on Ma's side and I couldn't figure any reason why they wouldn't be so that was at least one good thing. While I was wondering about everything a hundred miles an hour is about the time the county officers in the front seat begun asking me questions. The longer I didn't answer them, the louder they got. I started talking eventually.

Once I had a story put together, I started rattling on best I could between trying to get my breath and trying not to cry anymore. I said that I was the son of a sheep farmer in Ballard, West Virginia, who'd died fighting the Germans in World War II, and my ma had died giving birth to me. Anyhow, I'd just been float-fishing the river trying to catch my dinner like I did on most evenings. When I pulled up to Shady Hollow to camp, a man had asked me to take his car over the mountain to fetch a case of orange pop because the grocery in Shady was sold out of it.

I said, "The man was gonna pay me a dollar to do it, and that's how I come to run into you fellers, because he never did tell me his wipers and brakes weren't any good. I ain't a good driver anyway because I've only drove a car a couple of—"

The younger deputy sheriff driving the car cut me off with a big laugh, and then his eyes got serious in the rearview mirror. "I guess he gave you the gun, too, to fetch the…Orange Nehi."

"I don't know nothing about no gun, Officer."

"You don't know anything about the gun we found in the driver's side floorboard?"

"No, sir," I said.

"I guess you probably don't know nothing about the razor we pulled off you, either."

"I own the razor. I shave with it," I said.

"I doubt you got a real whisker to shave, boy. How much money did that man give you to buy the pop?"

"He was gonna pay me a dollar when I got back," I said.

"Well, where'd you get the five hundred dollars we found in your back pocket?"

I don't think I took a breath for a full minute realizing how much money Ma'd given me, unless they were lying about it. But it was a heavy, tight roll and I'd seen the outside bill had a twenty mark on it. I just couldn't believe Ma had that much money, but something told me they weren't telling me a tale.

My story was starting to spring leaks like a rusty old bucket. I was trying to figure out something to come back with about the money, but that's when the older officer beside him reached into a paper bag and pulled out Uncle Ray's revolver by the bloody checkered grip. He held it up high over the seat back for me to see.

My stomach went up into my brains just looking at it.

"Boy, I'd bet a dollar to a dead goddamn mule that we're gonna find your fingerprints all over this gun," he said loud. He spoke a lot less but talked much louder than the younger officer.

I didn't say anything back because I was just thinking I wished that bullet that was in my shoulder had hit me more dead center. I tried to turn my head away from where they could see my face but it hurt so bad doing it, I just closed my eyes instead.

"How old are you?"

"I ain't sure."

"I'm growing weary of your lying," the older officer said.

All of a sudden, I felt like I was getting worse by the second. Something bad shot from my shoulder way down through me. It made me hold my breath and I thought I was gonna get sick. "When we getting to a doctor?" I asked when I had to let my wind out.

Nobody answered so I opened one eye and saw the driver staring at me hard in the rearview mirror. "That black hair…you know what, you look like you might have some nigger in you. You got nigger in you, boy? Lot of niggers come out of Shady Hollow."

I shook my head.

"Well, you're a Puerto Rican or Arabian or Indian or something."

I wasn't sure what a Puerto Rican or Arabian was but

thought I might be one and hoped I was, if it would help me out. "Might be," I said.

"You don't know what you are?"

Ma had always told me and my brothers that we had colors in us besides just white. Ma looked a mix of black and white. She said she had a grandmother who was part Cherokee and part Negro. She said all of those colors and bloodlines is why all of her sons were so handsome and we were growing up so tall and sturdy.

"You don't know what you are," he said again, but louder.

"I'm American is about all I know for sure," I said.

"No, you're fucked is what you are for sure. Now I ain't asking again, how old are you?"

The driver hit his brakes hard and I flew forward into the metal cage. I yelled and found myself all in a knot in the floor. I was trying to twist myself where I could breathe better when the driver sat up high and swiveled his head to look down at me.

"Squirrel ran across the road. Hate to hurt the little varmint. Probably have the same thing happen again and again on the way out of here unless you might decide to change your mind about telling us—"

"Seventeen," I blurted out.

"What's your birth date?"

"I don't know the day or month, I swear it," I lied to him. "I was born in 1943, think it was in the summertime but I ain't sure," I lied again.

I was trying to work myself back into the seat when the older officer asked, "Where'd you get the load of moonshine?"

I closed my eyes again but tighter this time when I heard "load of moonshine," because each question they asked made it clear I was getting in worse trouble by the second.

I'd been lying about most everything else, but I didn't know there was 'shine in the car.

"Running liquor while carrying five hundred dollars, a razor and a loaded gun with one empty casing in it... umm...umm...umm. You don't know who I am, do you?" he asked.

I opened both eyes and shook my head just a little as the older officer sniffed the end of the barrel real careful. Then he put his smallest finger down into the end of it and sniffed that finger some more.

He turned his big head sitting atop his big neck and stared right at me.

"This gun's just been fired. You tried to kill one of my deputies. I'm a pretty goddamn easygoing feller when it comes to most, but I take killing personal. Real personal. That and the way you been lying shows you ain't got no respect for me or the law, but you're about to, because I am the law around here. You're about to meet your sheriff. Did you know I'm the sheriff of Winslow County?"

I didn't know whether to nod yes or shake no.

"Pull over, Franklin," he said.

I thought I was gonna mess my drawers right there if I hadn't messed them already, which I was beginning to think I'd already done. The heavyset sheriff got out of the car. When there weren't any other cars coming or going, he opened the back door, pulled me up out of the floor by my collar and I let out a yell because I thought my shoulder was ripping in half.

He drew back one huge fist, and with all he had, let it go.

When I woke, I was in the hospital. I was there for over a month with stitches all over me and leg irons chaining me to a bed. That sheriff had broken my jaw, too.

I kept laying there all casted up with my jaw wired shut day and night after day and night. I wondered what happened to Amanda Lynn and if she were okay and if she knew why Mr. Charles had come to kill me. I knew Ma would take care of Amanda Lynn as best she could, but her and Ma were as different as morning and evening. And with her being witness to such a thing, I didn't think she'd ever get over it, being the gentle person she was.

I was pretty sure of one thing, though. I figured she'd gotten over me right quick after that terrible sight and she probably couldn't get out of Shady Hollow and back to North Carolina fast enough. I just hoped the elders didn't have her in meetings too long, warning her to never ever speak of that day again before letting her go. I couldn't stand the thought of her having to sit before such hard men after seeing such a bloody thing.

I thought about Uncle Ray a lot, too, and how brave he'd been for me. I wondered if he knew the same things that Ma knew that I didn't, things about Amanda Lynn and the man who'd followed her, and things about me from the past.

Anyway, those nurses and doctors were good to me mostly and got me back in walking health. I finally got to where I could use my fingers and thumb again pretty good. The thing that hurt worst was my jaw.

My top and bottom teeth still didn't ride right together when I'd try to chew, and I started hoping I'd get the chance to trade licks with the sheriff of Winslow County one day for doing that to me. That was the time I started losing the fear of that man and a hate started growing in me. The kind of hate I'd never felt before for nobody.

I'd hit him first next time.

Once they released me from the hospital, they locked me up by myself in a cinder block walled holding cell the size of a toilet closet in the Winslow County Jail. The next few weeks the police would pull me out every day and put me in rooms with no windows. They tried to stick about fifty names on me to match a hundred different crimes of all description.

Some were mean crimes but most of them were just little things. Some of them the same little things I'd actually done before that never really hurt nobody. I didn't let on to them that I'd ever done anything but walk the straight and narrow.

I kept glued to my leaky story and it aggravated them plenty as I waited on Ma and the elders to come bust me out of there and take me back to Shady Hollow, just like I'd heard they'd done back in the old times when a Shady local needed such help. I kept waiting and waiting.

I'd look at those officers quizzical and tell them I must look like a bunch of other young fellers, but unlike me, they must've steered from the good. I was raised a Christian farm boy who didn't have no schooling or no living kin, I told them.

They never believed any of it. They didn't believe me when

they showed me pictures of people who lived or had lived in Shady and I told them I didn't know none of them. They asked me all kinds of things like who was moving the liquor in and out of Shady and how they were doing it. They said if I helped them, it would put them in a mind to help me. I was gonna need a lot of help when the day came I'd be standing in front of the federal judge over in Roanoke, they said.

I just kept shaking my head to all of it.

The name Henry Cole stuck to me for a long time after they finally got fed up questioning me. As hard as they tried, they couldn't pin any other names to me, even the name, Ben Purdue, that I saw on a couple of those warrants.

I couldn't read, but I could read and write my own name.

But some of the misdemeanor papers they had did stick to me, even if the names on them didn't match what I'd given them.

I'd been using different names for as long as I could remember in Shady. I found out that it didn't matter what my real name was if they had witnesses to point at me in court saying I was the one who did whatever it was that they claimed I did.

But that's where I had my first bit of good luck since getting shot, as witnesses turned out to be few for most of those warrants. The biggest piece of good fortune that blew my way was I was to stand before Circuit Judge James Fletcher for the state charges, and he was one of the best old friends Shady had.

Back when Judge Fletcher was a younger man, but not even that much younger than he was then, he was known to visit Shady Hollow, enjoying the place in the ways a feller would. A couple of the elders were even on a first-name basis with him and didn't call him Judge, they called him Jimbo. That's the name he was called growing up in Winslow before he got educated at the College of William and Mary and became a top defense lawyer and then a state judge.

From what I'd always heard, too, Jimbo liked his moonshine. Even after everybody started calling him Judge instead of Jimbo, he still liked his homemade liquor with a hard spearmint candy dropped in it while rocking in a chair on his front porch.

So I wanted to holler out happy when I found out it was Judge Fletcher who I was to stand before. And just as I'd prayed, he dismissed almost all of my charges over a lack of direct evidence, even though the commonwealth attorney was objecting loud and bold to his declarations.

"I see hope in your eyes," Judge Fletcher said, after I got to talking to him in chambers with a young lawyer at my side that the taxpayers were paying for. I swore as hard as I could over and over to him that the gun they found in the car wasn't mine, and I didn't know the car had moonshine in it, and I never meant to ram into those police officers.

All of that was true, and I don't know if he believed me, but he nodded like he did. Then he told me that the liquor and gun charges would be taken up with the federal court, not his, so his opinion on those crimes didn't matter a bit, he said, winking at me.

After Judge Fletcher shooed us out of his private chambers, my lawyer told me I was getting a good deal and I needed to plead guilty to the couple of things that the judge didn't throw out. So that next evening at my sentencing, Judge Fletcher stated loud after talking for so long that he'd about put everybody to sleep but me that, "I believe this young man deserves a second chance since they're as scarce as sunshine in Shady Hollow."

Even though the judge was a bad weather friend of those who lived in Shady Hollow, it was clear to me at that point that he didn't know I'd shot a man and stole a car, or if he did, he surely wasn't letting on.

I was pretty sure that I was the only one in that courtroom who knew about any of it.

Shady Hollow tended to be like one of those swirl holes in the Big Walker River when it came to life and death things that would happen ever so often. Some things were let to float downstream, and some things weren't. Big things tended to stay there. The folks who lived and worked in Shady surely weren't going to say anything because whatever happened in Shady, stayed in Shady. I figured the elders gave clear, stern warning to all of the visitors that they weren't to take any memory of that day with them when they left. As those folks had to look into the eyes of Tobias Chambers one at a time, I'm sure they believed there'd be future trouble following them if they did.

So I was hopeful but still worried as I sat in court facing my petty theft and driving charges all quiet and still, sweating but cold and having a hard time swallowing. And the truth is, I'm not sure if I'd even done any of the things they were claiming in particular when I'd pleaded guilty. I'd done so many small things that I had a harder time than the police wondering if I'd done exactly what they'd claimed I did.

All of a sudden, Judge Fletcher pounded his gavel and a big tuft of his gray hair flew up in the air and then it landed back over his forehead.

He ordered me to be put on three years' probation like he'd just thrown me under the jail.

His decision didn't seem to surprise my lawyer, but it surprised me. For weeks all kinds of police officers had been telling me I was a menace to good folks, and I was starting to believe them.

I just sat stunned as he made his rulings. He ordered me to be sent off to the home of a preacher and his wife who'd both showed up at the hearing, telling him that they could get the devil out me if the state reimbursed them twenty-five dollars a month to do the Lord's work.

I noticed how the judge and the preacher favored one another and even spoke alike in the same booming voice. I just hoped the preacher was gonna be as good and fair to me as the judge had been, or at least tolerable.

Looking back and forth at the judge and the preacher and the tiny lady with a huge head of hair who kept pecking on a machine between them, I couldn't help but keep noticing how the two seemed so similar but a little different like a right and left shoe would from the same pair.

The judge was heavier in his face and neck and kept a much longer head of peppered hair compared to the preacher, and he was the sterner one up there covered in his robes looking down on everybody over top his reading glasses. But in his private chambers as he talked to me and my lawyer before the guilt hearing, he'd had his feet up on his desk while eating on a peach, and he didn't seem to have a care in the world except for a drop of juice that might miss the handkerchief he'd tucked in over his collar.

The preacher turned out to be just the opposite of the judge once he took his hand off my shoulder. He'd been so nice and respectful to me and everybody in the courtroom while so many folks were in there for whatever reason, but once the bailiff yelled for all to stand up as the judge left the courtroom, the preacher squeezed my bad shoulder harder than you'd ever do to a friend, especially if that friend had a bad shoulder. Then he took his hand off of me and looked behind us to make sure no one else could hear what he was about to say.

He leaned into my ear and said, "I'm not here to bring you to Jesus, son. I don't have the time to tend to such a weedy garden. You know what you are to me?"

I shook my head.

"You're twenty-five dollars a month I'll use in my ministry to help those in need. Folks who want to be helped. Folks who can be saved. My calling is to look after the sheep, not the wolves, but I've given an oath to make sure you have a roof to sleep under and I'll keep you fed. But that's where it ends. If you cross me, if you don't abide, if you stir up a thimbleful of trouble, I'll see to it for your own good that you're right back in here quicker than you could—"

"Afternoon, Pastor."

He turned from me with a sudden smile to look over behind him at the lady who'd just been pecking on the machine in front of the judge. She'd spoken and smiled at him as she made her way down the aisle struggling with her dress bunched up around her big bosom and trying to tote the pecking machine and a thick stack of paper she had in a cloth bag.

"Let me help you with that, Mrs. Kendall," he said.

He hung her bag of papers in the crook of one elbow and then grabbed the machine by the legs letting the heavy-looking part rest on one shoulder. He then turned toward me and his eyes laid heavy on me again and the smile was gone.

"If we have an understanding, it's time to go to the parsonage," he said.

I didn't know what a parsonage was but it sounded a lot like an orphanage, so I figured it was pretty much the same thing. Mrs. Kendall was about to go through the thick wooden doors to leave the courtroom when she stopped to look back at the two of us. The preacher held up a finger to her and smiled, and she smiled back and went through the doors.

"Do we have an understanding?" he asked again, and by his hushed tone it sounded like I was getting myself into some kind of solemn agreement.

I wasn't sure what all he was trying to tell me or all I was supposed to understand, except that I was to mind his wishes and go to a parsonage. I knew exactly where I was standing, and that he was my way out of being in handcuffs and more jail time.

The last thing I wanted was trouble with that serious

preacher who seemed to be so popular and in good stead with God and the judge and everybody else but me.

I nodded my head to him and meant it, even though he'd called me a weedy garden and he could smile on and off like his mouth was hooked to a pull string. Ma had always told me to never ever trust such people with such smiles. She never cared for preachers for some reason, either, as that goes.

In fact, as much as Ma seemed to like the Bible, she couldn't stand the sight of a preacher.

But Ma wasn't there to take care of me or try to help me out with the law like she should have and I always figured she would. It just wasn't like her not to stand up and show up and do all she could for one of her boys when we'd get in trouble, and especially with me being in the terrible serious sort of trouble I was in.

I remembered as I was about to walk out of that courthouse, I had a real bad feeling in my stomach that something bad must've happened in Shady Hollow after I left. More bad than what had already happened there.

Something so bad I tried to push it out of my mind.

Chapter 8

"Sure this is where you want let out?"

The old man's voice brought me out of those times when I was young and in a lot of trouble as I realized he and his wife had both been staring at me over the bench seat.

I nodded.

"Aren't any houses within a half mile of here."

"I think this is it," I said.

"Well, you don't look like you think it is."

I took a deep breath and looked out the window, and saw the place fade back in time. Everything blurred together and I felt dizzy all of a sudden.

"You okay, son?" the man asked.

I rubbed my eyes and tried to get my focus and mind back in the right places, then looked again at all the hardtop.

"I ain't real sure about a lot right now to be honest, but

some places are hard to forget. This don't look like it, but it's got to be it, if that makes any sense."

"But how do you know it's it, if it doesn't look like it?" his wife asked. She eyeballed me pretty hard and then looked at her husband.

"I guess I can feel this place, ma'am," I said quiet.

"What'd he say?" the old man asked his wife.

"He says he can feel it," she said loud.

"Feel it?" He turned to look at me but couldn't get his head all the way around to do it, then started rattling off at me with only one eye gazing at me heavy.

"That don't make no sense much at all," he said. "This is either it or it isn't. Listen, if I was you, lost as you seem to be, I'd go to the post office and then the county courthouse in Winslow before you go searching aimless around here for your mother when you seem so unsure about things. Post office and the clerk's office will have records on everybody around here and will know where she lives. Point you in the right direction, see."

I nodded at his trying to help, he was trying to help, but then I told him directly where both of his eyes could see mine, "Ma never got no mail, and I'll find her without having to step one foot again into the Winslow County Courthouse."

After the preacher and his pretty young wife stopped at the clerk's office to get their twenty-five dollar check, I was taken out of the Winslow County Courthouse by them, not in handcuffs or leg irons or any sort of restraint, but I was still wearing the clothes I'd got shot up in and wished that they'd get me some new clothes when I brought up the fact that I needed a coat, too.

The hospital had washed most of the stains out of my shirt and britches and I figured the matron at the jail I was kept in sewed up the holes. She was real good to me during my stay and I'd seen her sewing and knitting on other things like socks for babies and quilts while guarding other prisoners.

Anyway, once we got outside the sky was mean and gray with the clouds hiding the mountains. It was spitting snow and I watched the flakes twirl around not going anywhere, and I wished again that I'd grabbed my green corduroy coat before I'd left Ma's apartment to see Amanda Lynn. It wasn't September now, it was almost Thanksgiving, and I lacked a lot of things but right then at that moment, I really needed a coat.

I gazed at the preacher and his wife in their long coats as she kept her hands in her pockets, and I figured one of them might be kind enough to find me a coat soon even though neither said nothing when I mentioned, shivering in my short sleeves, that it looked like winter had done set in early.

I walked on my crutches behind the preacher's wife and with him behind me. It was a lot easier working those crutches now that I didn't have to do it with both hands in cuffs hooked to rings welded to a waist chain. Now and then I'd look back at the preacher as his wife kept getting farther ahead of me, and he'd just nod for me to pick up my step.

We finally got to Mrs. Kendall's car where the preacher loaded her things up for her. It was parked off the sidewalk on Main Street, and it seemed like those old brick buildings on both sides of the road were funneling in a cold wind coming from the northeast.

I kept tensing up my chest and stomach trying to get warm, and did get some blood going and it helped with the weather but not enough. I hoped the preacher's vehicle was close by and it had a good heater.

I moved those crutches as fast as I could once we were on our way again, and tried to put the cold and my Shady worries and fears aside in hopes all was good back home. Fretful as I was about a lot of things, I still felt lucky being put on probation, because I knew it was good luck that I wasn't heading back to the jailhouse.

But my lawyer had told me in a hurry as the preacher was taking me away that I wouldn't be out on probation for long, because the federal prosecutor in Roanoke was getting ready to bring the liquor and gun charges on me. They'd probably set bail on those charges too high for me to make. I figured I couldn't post more than ten dollars hidden in my shoe for bail, so anything higher than that and I was gonna be short.

My lawyer was a little befuddled they didn't already put a holding paper on me with the state court so they wouldn't let me out of jail. But then he said they probably weren't familiar with Judge Fletcher's administering of justice.

He went on to say that the law worked a lot different in a big city like Roanoke than it did in a small town like Winslow. A lot different. People in small places know a lot about each other is the difference, he said, and you're more careful about throwing rocks at one another.

Even being new to the big kind of mess I was in, it was

obvious to me what I had to do with those big charges coming after me soon. I had enough sense and good raising to
see that there was no fork in the road that I had to ponder
on about what to do next.

I had to run.

I had nowhere to run to but back to Shady Hollow, and
I just hoped all was back to normal and the danger to me
wasn't there anymore. I needed a place like Shady to hide
out from the revenuers and federal prosecutors and whoever
else I might need to.

It seemed like we walked and walked as people that we
passed waved and chatted with the preacher. We went by a
small patch of dead grass with an iron fence around it where
a tall statue of a rebel soldier stood on guard, then we finally
got to an empty theater lot where a real old-looking short
bus painted blue as a summer sky sat by itself.

Across the side of the bus was a bunch of white letters,
one line of them atop the other. Once we got right up to
it, I asked the preacher what those letters said because the
bus sort of looked like the vehicle the jail driver hauled me
over to the courthouse in, except this one didn't have bars
across the windows.

The preacher looked at me and then I leaned on one
crutch and pointed at the words with the other.

"Groundhog Valley Holiness Church of the Trinity.
Spreading Seeds of Eternal Salvation Wherever the Road of
Life Takes Us," he said.

"What's *salvation* mean?" I asked.

He studied me and said, "It means you're ignorant because you don't have a proper education and have never been to church."

"What's *trinity* mean?"

He sniffed a couple of times before he wiped his red nose with a handkerchief. "Have you ever seen a Bible?"

"I've seen a bunch of them," I said, which was true. I owned one a missionary woman had given me telling me to read it cover to cover. Uncle Ray read his worn one quite a bit and Ma even kept one in the bottom drawer of her night table. She never read it, but she'd hold it sometimes during hard times like it had powers or it would warm her up on a cold night or something. It had pictures in it that we'd looked at every so often when I was younger and she'd tell me the names of the people dressed in robes and wearing sandals.

The preacher didn't ask no more about Bibles, but held out a hand in front of open double doors on his bus, and I kept thinking on the meaning of salvation he'd given me. I hadn't known him for more than fifteen minutes, and he'd already called me an ignorant weedy garden.

"Get in," he said.

I climbed up the three stairs one at a time with my crutches and looked to the very rear of the sawed-off bus. I started heading back there when the preacher said loud but without hollering, "You'll sit behind me."

I got myself turned around and did what he said, plopping directly behind him on a cold bench as he got behind the wheel and lowered a long mirror over his head where I could see him, and I knew, too, that he could see me at all times.

His wife sat in the seat on the other side of the walkway

directly across from me, and I glanced at her a few times not-ing again how she was a lot closer to my age than his, and she was pretty in a real good clean kind of springtime way. I was eyeing her coat, too.

Once the preacher got that bus moving, which I wasn't sure whether he would or not by the way it started out bucking forward and backward, we rolled slow and mostly steady to the local bank where he went inside to cash his check. About the time we got there, is when I finally quit shivering.

I saw him look over his shoulder several times at me as he was walking across the lot, and I reckon he saw me watching him in my window.

When he finally got inside, me and his young missus had an easy, nice conversation about the weather and other smallish things like how much she liked to sip hot cider with cinnamon when the leaves turned and fell from the trees.

I didn't start the talking, she did. Even though she was pretty and nice, I was more interested in all of the people going here and there and the tall buildings and fancy cars. All of a sudden when I was trying to figure out how I could get back to Shady, she said, "It's been awfully warm for fall this season, don't ya think? Awfully warm and colorful, until today."

I'd missed most of fall chained to a hospital bed or sitting in a jail cell. I'd been on that bus thinking about running with the preacher being in the bank, but I saw him take the bus keys with him and I was so wore out and worn down and hungry, and with my one leg still giving me so much trouble, I just felt like I had to have at least one day of rest and a good coat before trying to take off. So I eased back in my seat and laid down my crutches.

It was nice to be in that warm bus with the preacher's wife in a town and everything, and going somewhere besides back to jail. For all of those reasons, I put my running plans to the side for the time, and nodded that it was a cold day and it had been a warm colorful fall even though I'd missed it, and that I liked hot cider. I didn't tell her I liked it even better with some liquor in it. When the conversation went quiet, I asked what her name was.

"Mrs. Fletcher," she said.

I then asked her if she was kin by marriage to Judge Fletcher, and she nodded and said the judge and her husband were brothers. Even more than that, she said they were twins.

I felt even better about my situation.

I hoped the preacher was gonna start being friendlier to me soon and treat me like Jimbo did, and I realized how the probation deal worked out good for the preacher with the judge basically handing his brother a twenty-five dollar check to feed me and give me a bed to sleep on, with the preacher keeping the change. I didn't find fault with any of it.

"What's your first name?" I asked.

We were about the same age and she may have even been younger than me, and the name Mrs. Fletcher just seemed so formal and stiff a name to call her as kind and smiley as she was being to me.

She didn't care to say for a few moments for whatever reason. Then she said her first name was Louisa, and that she was from the Hoge family over in Tazewell in Tazewell County, the same family who owned the dairy farm off of Route 43 near the army munitions factory, and her family's farm was easy to tell apart from the other farms in Tazewell County because her mom raised peacocks that strutted around the place.

I'd never heard of such a thing as a peacock and had never been to Tazewell County and told her so. She said Tazewell was an even bigger town than Winslow, but as she was going on with all of that, Preacher Fletcher walked toward us with his court money and her story drifted to silence. Soon we all got on our way again just after he gave me a hard look, much harder than the judge ever gave me.

That preacher definitely wasn't warming to me, yet.

Once out of town, I could tell that we were heading south, but I wasn't familiar with the countryside we were in. We traveled a dirt road with some gravel on it through rare land in that part of Virginia, because it was flat but it wasn't lying along the banks of a big river. It was a real peaceful valley with small creeks running this way and that way. I'd never seen such a peaceful place besides the countryside I saw around Durham County with Amanda Lynn. I thought how that valley would be a nice place to go settle one day and do something honest for a living like so many other folks did, if I could make a lot of money at it and not work too hard.

I wasn't in a hurry at all to get to the parsonage. I was just generally feeling good feeling decent again, and was enjoying seeing the fields and farmland everywhere.

But after turning up a hill past a small white church with windows painted a bunch of colors with its steeple that looked so big it might cave in the small box building it sat on, we eventually got to the parsonage late that afternoon. It turned out to be just a great big farmhouse lacking shingles here and there, and a crooked porch that went all the way around it.

When I stepped out of the bus, I saw a bunch of other young'uns I figured they'd taken in, little ones to big ones. But I was the biggest and probably the meanest of them by the looks on their faces and by the way they steered clear of me.

I tried to add up how much money that preacher was making raising kids at twenty-five dollars a head every month, but it got too high to count. I did notice that they all had coats.

Going inside, I shook the chill off me and it looked like there wasn't an empty bed in that farmhouse, even with all the beds they had in each room. I didn't care because I'd be having my way around there and had to be leaving as soon as my leg healed a little more.

Even if I didn't have to leave, I didn't feel at home living under a preacher's roof in that pretty valley. I knew my place and was heading back to Shady Hollow as soon as I could whether Ma said I could or not.

Running from Shady and trying to hide hadn't worked out and it never did set well with me from the get-go.

That first evening Louisa showed me around. She looked at me the whole time like she was starting to like me a lot more than she liked her husband. She got closer to me in every room, and each time she'd smile, I'd smile back even though little in me felt like smiling most of the time.

I was glad to be around a girl so nice and pretty, but I just kept hoping for a car full of elders and shotguns to take me back home like they'd done in North Carolina.

It was a hard time in many ways that first day at the farm-house, and I don't think I slept a wink in such a strange place with so many young'uns all around me. One of them laid there and cried the longest time for some reason until one of the older boys yelled at him to shut up about it all. I told the boy who'd told the crying kid to shut up, to shut up, and he did and then it got mostly quiet the rest of the night except for the constant snoring and coughing and fidgeting around.

As much as I wanted to leave the morning of the second day, I still knew I just wasn't in good enough shape to go yet. My lawyer had speculated that it would probably be a couple of days to maybe even a couple of weeks before federal mar-shals showed up to haul me to Roanoke over the gun and lightning charges.

He said the local sheriff or state police would surely be calling them to let them know I'd been let out on proba-tion, but even then they'd be slow to get their papers in order before arresting me.

"The federal government is slow doing about anything except cashing a tax check," he'd said.

My biggest predicament was how to get home. I just knew I'd get caught or freeze to death sure enough trying to limp my way out of that valley. I figured the only way I'd make it was to steal the preacher's coat and borrow his bus, and the only problem with that was, he carried the keys in his front pocket hooked to a chain that went around his belt.

I kept thinking on how I was gonna get those keys and

he even caught me staring at the chain a couple of times. I soon could tell that the preacher wasn't never gonna be as good to me as he'd let on in court when he'd put a hand on my shoulder in front of his brother, but I found out that second day right after dinnertime, that Louisa was a lot more fond of me than I'd realized.

"Maybe it'd be best if you get on out of the car, then. Get on to where you're trying to head to."

The old man's voice in the Buick pulled me again slow out of those old rememberings, right after we'd had our eye to eye understanding of things, and only a moment after I'd leaned back in my seat. In my mind I was just about to hold a preacher's young wife.

I looked at the old man who was nodding and his missus who wasn't, and could tell they'd gotten wary of me again, even more than they were before they'd decided to give me a ride.

I nodded to his nod, and collected my bag beside me.

I had no idea how long we'd been sitting there on the side of the road or how long they'd been staring at me. I figured it wasn't a long amount of time. Getting so close to home and already seeing the changes mixed with all those good but mostly bad memories had rattled me in a way I'd never figured would happen.

Just before I got out, I asked just to make sure, "This road still leads down to Shady Hollow, don't it?"

"Used to," he said.

"Used to?"

"Used to, don't now."

"Well, where's it lead to now?"

He raised one finger and pointed around in little circles. "It goes on down to the lake."

That made me even more confused because there weren't any lakes around there, and that was the only road that would go down to Shady, and he was saying it didn't go there anymore.

"Then how does a man get to Shady Hollow from right here?"

"There ain't no Shady Hollow no more. That where you trying to head? Son, the state dammed the Big Walker about fifteen or twenty years ago. Shady Hollow now sits at the bottom of Big Walker Lake. Folks say one of the reasons the state built the dam was to get rid of Shady Hollow for good. Bunch of rich people from up north now have vacation homes down there. You go around that curve a couple hundred yards and you'll see it for yourself. Lake goes from here clear into Tennessee. Shady Hollow is gone. Been gone a long time."

Chapter 9

I thought I was gonna get sick, or have to bust up something to get the sick, busted up feeling inside me out of me with the news of what I'd just heard. I got out of the car in a hurry but walked around it in a daze a couple of times. I just couldn't believe what the old man had said even though I knew he was telling the truth.

Nice car after nicer car after boat after bigger boat was either heading down to where Shady used to be, or leaving there. I looked over at the street sign that said "Bender Mountain Road." It was a shinier sign than the one I remembered, and they'd dropped the "Hell" that used to be in front of "Bender."

I felt like I had rocks in my stomach, realized I hadn't been breathing, and then it felt like someone had lit a fire under me. I looked over my shoulder and noticed I'd been leaning against the old couple's car and it was the heat of the engine on that hot day that was burning up my backside. I took a quick step to the back door then my heel blister spoke loud to me, so I slowed and got out my bag and stood outside the driver-side window. I dug down in my pocket, pulled out the money I had left and tried to hand the man a dollar for the gas money I'd promised him. He looked at the bill shaking in my hand and then shook his head.

"You want us to take you somewhere else, somewhere else near here?" he asked really slow, like I didn't hear good.

I tried to say something but couldn't, and after I got my bag situated across a shoulder, I crossed Route 11 and started walking down the side of that busy two-lane road.

It was getting near sunset now and when I got about half-way down Hellbender Mountain, I saw that the old man definitely wasn't telling me a lie. There was a lake below me to my southern side that went for miles and miles in every direction, with coves that looked like skinny broken fingers coming off a hand.

The sight of that lake tore me to pieces as my eyes filled up with water.

I sat down right in the gravel as more cars that only rich folks drive and the boats that only they would haul passed by. A couple people gawked at me and some others glanced in my direction, but most didn't pay any attention to me at all. I was trying to see if I could recognize a familiar face or see a killing face among them, but didn't. I stayed quite a long time eyeballing everybody coming and going, and studying that lake and the people out on it skiing and fishing.

Then it hit me that surely Shady would've moved somewhere near there, higher up. It couldn't just be gone. A place like Shady couldn't just not exist anymore. It just moved. I got up and started walking a little quicker in step. I got to the spot where I'd hit that roadblock in the dead-man's curve and saw where they'd dynamited a side of the mountain away to straighten it out. A horn honked coming up behind me, and I moved off the shoulder when I saw those old folks pulling over.

I waited patient like I'd learned already for the old man to roll down his window, one inch at a time.

"Wife made me come check on you, you looked so fiery shook up."

I looked at her and she did have worry on her face.

"Where'd the folks in Shady go once they dammed the river?" I asked.

The old man looked at his wife but she didn't do nothing but look back at him with the same look.

"Police arrested a bunch of them and there weren't many left down there once it started flooding." He put both hands up like they were birds and said, "Those few just left."

"They didn't start up Shady Hollow somewhere else, maybe higher up on one of the mountains around here or over on John's Creek?" I looked around but when I looked back at him, he was shaking his head.

"Ain't never heard of nothing like that. John's Creek is part of the lake now, too. This whole area has changed, son, and not just the water. Money in here now and big money. Folks around here wouldn't put up with a place like Shady Hollow anymore, most of them anyway. Shady Hollow and the people who lived there are gone. Only thing left is the old Polly Hill cemetery. It's still down there I believe unless the water claimed it, too. The man who owns most of the property around here owns the cemetery."

"Is he from Shady?"

"No. He's a developer from up around the capital. Came down and gobbled up the land when it wasn't worth nothing and nobody could figure why and now a bunch of rich city people and politicians summer down there. He's been trying to get permission to move the graves somewhere else as they're in the middle of prime real estate, is what the newspaper said a while back. He may have moved those old graves already somewhere else, I'm not sure. You want a ride into town?"

I shook my head and looked around me at so much that I recognized, and so much that didn't belong there. I told him I appreciated his offer, but I needed to walk on down there to see it all myself. I hoped at least Polly Hill was still there but it scared me bad knowing what I may find if it was.

"We'll ride you down," he said.

I figured I needed to see it alone, so that's what I did after I shook the old man's hand.

I walked away from that old couple for the last time and passed long bricked or stone driveways and home after home. The closer I got to the water, the bigger the homes got and the more spread out and tended the yards were. I slowed down walking up the last hill that used to be a brushy ridge, and it led to a steep grade that dumped right into Shady Hollow, at least it used to.

As I stood on the rise, the lake was now spread out in front of me flat and calm, and when I looked down the road, it veered an easy right only about fifty yards from where I was standing. The road couldn't go any farther, because that's where the lake started.

Judging how I remembered the long, steep grade that was still steep but not very long, the old man was right when he told me Shady Hollow now sat at the bottom of the lake.

Ma's old apartment overtop the Last Rebel Yell, Hoke's, Merle's, all the taverns and outhouses and merchant shops and shacks and good things and bad things...my sack of money I never got to spend...it was all sitting way out under that still green water.

I leaned against a poplar tree and watched a man and his son paddle a silver canoe over what I figured would have been Barton's Opry. They kept paddling and eventually dropped anchor about thirty feet off the bank and cast to shore. I just kept watching them as they threw in all directions, but they never caught nothing. I kept wondering if one of them was gonna get their line hung on something I grew up standing on or under.

They pulled up anchor after a spell and paddled down to where what we used to call Ginseng Ridge, which got its name because people used to claim to be hunting ginseng there, but what they were really doing was hunting for buried jars of Luke's U.S. and Confederate money.

It was rumored serious that an old hand-drawn map was found in an iron canister laying in the ashes after the fire that burned down Luke's Establishment on the Big Walker, the same fire that killed Luke back in the early 1870s, because he was so drunk he slept through the whole thing, and in that canister was a map of the mountains with grease pencil X marks all over that ridge.

I remembered stories from Ma that several men back in the old times had found jars and jars of Confederate money, but no real money. When folks wondered what they were doing with shovels on that ridge, they claimed to be digging for ginseng.

What surprised me most looking at Ginseng Ridge and trying to get my bearings, was that it was all cleared off now. There were a few trees, but the pines I'd grown up seeing everywhere were mostly gone. Oaks and hickories and maples were everywhere, even willow trees and some trees I didn't recognize, and they all looked to be taking good root on Ginseng Ridge.

The thing that drew my attention most was a long, sloping cornfield that went all the way to the water's edge. The corn was about half-grown and the field followed the bottom of the ridge into a hollow on the other side, and then back up the next ridge where it stopped halfway before it turned into a cut hayfield. From there, the hayfield dropped off into a cove that went deep into a hollow that I'd been in many times turning over rocks to catch lizards for bass and red-eye bait. I imagined that water went way up into that hollow, because it was so deep I could remember walking down into it and feeling the temperature drop.

That cornfield looked strange being bordered by big houses and yards the size of small farms with their rock walls

piled so tidy. The sight I saw which finally made me move
from where I'd been sitting was a square of land cut right in
the middle of the corn. It was tiny compared to the field
around it and had a wire fence around it and was grown-up
looking. I knew what I was seeing even though nothing
looked like it used to.

But it was Polly Hill, sure enough.

Polly Hill was the only cemetery plot we had in Shady
Hollow, and we'd have never let it get into such a disrepair.

Polly Hill was named after a big city stage singer named
Polly Madrid Paris. They named the hill in her honor sometime during the 1860s because she was the first person to get
a formal burial in Shady, as far as I know. Polly had got some
bad powders up in her or some bad liquor down in her, or
too much of one or both is the best thing anybody could
figure out. People said she'd just given her best performance
at the old Muddy Water House and it was standing room only
that night, and they believed with such a fine voice she was
lead singer in the angel choir now, even if she did always have
quite the devil in her offstage, according to old tales I heard.

Polly and Polly Hill both now looked to only be about
fifty yards from the waterline.

I felt my legs trembling beneath me when I took a step
toward the cornfield. It was all too much seeing water covering where I'd been born and raised. I'd finally got back
home after all these years, and here it was all so clean and
bright looking, and all so gone, except for the graveyard.

I went from trembly to scared to death and feared the new
names I might find carved into the homemade stones, but I

had to look. I had to hurry to get there before dark set in. As I made my way to it, I grabbed a long stick to swat the corn and shoo away any copperheads and blacksnakes. Working my way through the stalks growing up to my belly, I slowed when I got to the fence and saw how Polly Hill had gotten crowded since I'd left.

My eyes went to the far corner near a small boulder that I'd sat on many times back when all around that graveyard was just thick woods and more boulders.

Underneath that boulder laid two of my brothers, both who'd died before I left Shady. There was mountain laurel and other things growing wild between where they lay and where I was standing, but I could see that there were more slabs poking up on either side of them, places Ma had reserved with the elders for our family plot.

I couldn't find a gate to the fence, just barbed wire nailed and looped around old locust logs that had been driven into the ground without much care. I found a low spot in the wire, climbed over and looked down to see if I was stepping on anybody, but I wasn't.

I kept my eyes away from the ground underneath the boulder because I just wasn't ready to go there yet. I looked all around at the houses dotting the mountain. They were farther away than birdshot could reach but they still felt too close. I saw a few folks looking to be tending to their yards and washing cars and playing with their young'uns, and just enjoying summer evening sorts of thing for people who have so much of everything.

None of them seemed to be paying attention to me or had even seen me, so I sat where I'd been standing and pulled out my quart bottle of beer. Even though I knew it was warm and it was gonna spew from the bouncing it'd been taking, I pointed it away from me and used my pocketknife to uncap the top.

I lost a little of it in foam, but not much.

I remembered the good smell of an open beer and it made me more homesick for what wasn't here anymore. I turned the bottle up and took a long chug and kept chugging. It made my eyes water as I stopped to get my breath. After the bottle was empty, I wrapped it up in my old shirt and stuck it back in my bag.

I stood and put my coat back on as the sun was almost gone now. I figured I had about fifteen minutes of daylight left, so I took a deep breath and walked the ten or twenty steps through brush and weeds trying to steer clear of poison oak as I looked down to read the markers I came across, at least the ones that were still readable. I saw the names of a lot of people I'd once known.

Some of the grave markers were made of wood or the names had been scratched too light into river rock. I studied all of them close, and when I found Polly's grave, I really had my bearings about where folks used to lay. Hers was easy to recognize, because it had musical notes carved into it.

I wasn't looking for old graves though, I was looking and paying attention to the newer ones, the ones where there was more care put into the engravings and the ground wasn't so sunk in.

At the furthest corner beside the boulder was a small stone under a blooming white rhododendron. I got my courage up with the help of that beer, then got down on my hands and knees and after clearing away the moss, read what I found:

Doctor Raymond Michael Pike. Born December 2, 1918. Died September 28, 1959.

It was Uncle Ray.

I swallowed down a bad taste that came up, but to be honest I was relieved to see it was his name on that stone, and not the other names I feared seeing.

After I brushed off more of the caked dirt and mud and tried to scrub off some of the moss growing over his rock, I finally backed myself from under the bush. I moved to my right, and stayed on my hands and knees to make out the names on the other rocks near him.

I knew who lay right beside Uncle Ray. Little Virgil and Teddy. Both of them had died before I'd left for prison.

Virgil didn't make it through his third winter in Shady. He was born sickly and his heart never did work right and never would. That was what the heart doctor that Ma had took him to see in Bluefield told her, and Teddy had waded out too far in the Big Walker one day to get a fishing line unhung. He went under and that's the last anybody ever seen of him. Last I saw of him, too, because I was on the bank watching him. I remembered seeing his lucky straw hat floating down the river current. We all thought Teddy was pulling one on us because Teddy always had the best sense of humor doing such things, but after a couple of minutes, we knew he wasn't joking.

A month later Ma made the Shady elders make him a grave right next to Virgil even though there was nothing to put in Teddy's hole, but we had to believe by then that he was gone for good. My brothers and me trudged the riverbanks for weeks to try and find him so he could get buried proper, but we never found nothing but his hat. We sat it on top of his gravestone and it stayed there for a long time until one day it was just gone. Ma said somebody probably wandered up there and was in need of a hat, and that's what became of it.

Seeing their old markers made me miss Virgil and Teddy like I hadn't in a long time.

Studying Teddy's name, I could see out of the corner of my eye, over my right shoulder, the rock sitting only four feet away. I couldn't make myself look at it until I got myself through a tangle of honeysuckle and got directly before it. Once I did, it hit me hard and tears filled my eyes reading that Bernard had also died the same day I'd fled out of Shady.

I hated to think what terrible thing had happened to him because Bernie was the best one of us. His death had to do with me in some way that I didn't know, and the thought of me running from Shady when I should've stayed just made me shake so much I had to sit down with my legs crossed and try to get myself together. I knew there were more graves yet to see, and I just couldn't believe Bernie was gone.

Ma gave all of her boys the best she could, but she always treated Bernie more tender than the rest of us, because I guess he was tender.

I just never figured he'd be dead and it made me feel even

more that I had this big hole right in the middle of me and my insides hadn't hurt in a long time like they started hurting right then. Seeing Shady was gone was bad enough, seeing Bernie was gone was even worse than that. He wasn't but a little more than two years younger than me, and Bernie was the sort who never belonged in a rough place like Shady Hollow, and I hated knowing he was gonna have to lay there forever.

That only left Milton, Jimmy and Frank still above ground, unless they were in it here, too, or in it somewhere else.

"Can I help you?" came a voice from behind me.

I turned and saw a man who looked like he had a good education and was dressed like a banker standing at the edge of the fence. I stood and the combination of the beer and that graveyard made me have a hard time getting my balance for a second. I knew one thing, if he was a man out to kill me, he'd have already done it. It shook me how easy he could've, too.

"What do you want?" I said back.

The man looked me over and then started fingering on a stalk of corn. "This property belongs to Jacob Gagnon. It's private property. Maybe you missed the No Trespassing signs."

"I saw them. I'm visiting with my kin and then I'll be on my way soon enough."

He looked straight at me. "Be gone before dark or I'll call the sheriff's office."

"I said I'll be on my way soon enough."

He went to walk away. "Before dark," he said again.

"What's your name?" I asked.

He stopped and turned and went to hitch up his britches.

When he did I saw the gun and holster on his hip, which is what he wanted me to see. "I work for Mr. Gagnon."

"Doing what?"

"I take care of things that need taking care of for him."

"So he's the one who owns the graveyard?"

"He owns the entire mountain except for the homes and businesses and sold parcels in the subdivisions he's built."

I looked over the man's head who'd come at a real bad time and was trying to run me off. I saw the huge house sitting high up on the mountain. It was three times bigger than the biggest church I'd ever seen. And just as tall. It didn't belong where it was sitting, trying to compete with the mountain the way it was.

"You from around here?" I asked.

"No. Again, I have to order you to leave. Now," the man said.

"As soon as I finish my business, I'm telling you I'll be on my way."

"I expect you'll keep your word, then. We've had problems with people coming to the graveyard, drinking and littering and doing God knows what. The residents on Bender Mountain want this problem to stop, and one of the things I get paid to do is make things stop. We've even had people come and dig new graves in the middle of the night."

"Gagnon ain't kin to nobody in here?" I asked.

"No, the graveyard came with the property, unfortunately."

It hit me that the man was burning up what was left of my daylight. "I ain't gonna be long," I said, turning away from him.

"Best not."

I was surprised I hadn't heard him walk up on me as noisy

as he was walking out of there. I waited until he was all of the way out of the field before I sat again beside where I'd just been sitting.

That's when I saw Ma's name, right in front of me.

Reading it and then reading that she'd died the same day as Uncle Ray and Bernie made me want to dig down into the cold dirt and crawl in right beside her. I stretched out and rolled onto my back. When I finally opened my eyes, a sliver of the moon was making its way across the sky.

When I turned my head to the side and saw what I was lying next to, it felt like somebody drove a tent stake right through the middle of me, pinning me to the ground so I couldn't move.

My name was on a thin rounded slab of river stone right next to Ma. I died on September 28, 1959, too, it said. That rock said I'd gotten what I'd just wished.

Chapter 10

Whatever was left of me was a spirit who'd been trapped in some kind of in-between hell I'd heard tall stories about as a kid around campfires. I squeezed my hands together and ran one hand across my face to see if I could feel any of it but all I felt was cold. I was still covered in bumps all over when I came to a knee to be sure again of what I'd seen. I read and reread what was in front of me and finally got the courage to bend forward and touch it, like it might electrocute me if I did.

But a fear as deep as the one that had just gone through made me look again to my right, because there was one more stone beside mine, and as dark as it had now gotten, I couldn't read it.

I felt the deepest dread and terror that Amanda Lynn may be laying there.

I crawled across my grave, struck a match but I couldn't read the name. After some time trying to read it and feel the letters and dates with my fingers, I finally figured out that beside me was somebody who'd died back in the 1800s.

I tried to get my breath, and it was like I drifted into and got stuck in a place not run by time or memories or sun or dark or yesterdays or tomorrows, as the whole world stopped for a few moments. I came out of it though knowing she wasn't gone, at least by the sign on that rock, and then in a fury I was alive again as I got up to try and read the names on all of the other graves, praying Amanda Lynn's name wouldn't be on one.

But then after a minute or two I thought that surely, even if she had gotten killed on that day, she would've been taken back to North Carolina to be buried according to her family's wishes.

The elders wouldn't have stuck her in a pine box to be lowered into Polly Hill with a small ceremony of local mourners. They'd have kept her under the barber's care until somebody would have come looking for her and took her home.

I then crawled my way back over to where Ma and the rest of my brothers were buried to make sure I hadn't missed a grave, and after I gave it all a good check rooting around through the briars and weeds, is about the time a car pulled up to the edge of the cornfield and a spotlight worked its way toward me.

"You in there, don't move!"

I was being called "you" again and knew that wasn't a good

sign, but the man who'd yelled couldn't see me with the corn so high. I crawled my way to the farthest side of the cemetery from him, grabbed my bag, dove over the fence and started making my way through the dirt rows heading toward Ginseng Ridge.

Once I broke free of the corn hiding me, I knew I was exposed to gun sights. But I figured the law wouldn't shoot a man in the back who was just visiting an old graveyard. So I kept hightailing it up that ridge like I hadn't run since I was a kid trying to outrace trouble.

As I was feeling right then, there was no way I was going back behind bars on my first full day out of prison. He would have to shoot me and shoot me dead. I didn't care if I did die right then, but I wasn't going back.

The deputy sheriff got his light on me and it stayed on me once I was out in the open. He yelled for me to stop a few more times, but I just kept making it as hard as I could trying to chase my own shadow made by his light.

I kept running as far from Polly Hill as I could.

I cleared the ridge with tears running down my face and I kept my head low in my shoulders. When I got to the other side, I got down close to the ground and saw lights coming from a marina with all kinds of big boats and sailboats, most of them hooked to lines that led to docks stretching out this way and that way from the concrete banks.

I tried to get my wind and after looking all around because there wasn't a good place to go, I figured that the best place for me to be was somewhere in the mountains, being there still had to be some real wild backcountry around because there was just so much of it that it would be slow to fill with rich Yankees.

So I made my way around the marina and ran like a rabbit with a beagle biting its hind end, and I headed up into the mountain through a hollow I'd remembered being called Lost Hollow. I turned and saw another sheriff car or the same one I'd seen a few minutes before, as it drove slow through the big circle lot shining a spotlight under the boats and vehicles parked there.

It was clear to me that I wasn't welcome in Shady Hollow anymore as I slowed and then fell down once I was hidden deep in the forest. It hit me how the last time I'd been in Shady, I'd left running, too.

I felt like I had kerosene in my throat and sat up to wring the blood out of one sock. While doing that, I tried to get my thoughts together and get hold of myself about what I'd seen and found out on my first day as a free man. I started calming enough that I looked around in the dark and felt like it was swallowing me up, and I wondered where in the whole world I would head from there. I knew I had to go somewhere else, even though I didn't think I belonged no-where else, but I couldn't just keep sitting in the woods and crying over it all. So I took one last long look at the ugly lake way down the steep slope in front of me with the marina lights twinkling off the water like lightning bugs.

When the sheriff car left and there wasn't nothing else to do but sit and stare at that lake, I grabbed my bag and left Shady. I figured I was never coming back because it was all gone—if I were alive at all—which I was still wondering about.

I just kept walking and fighting my way through the woods in the dark. All night. I kept walking and stumbling and finding my way up through higher and higher ground until there was nowhere else to go but down to somewhere else. I headed toward the rougher country where I believed I belonged most. I needed the quiet there. At least I thought it would help me take stock of such worrisome things.

Those first couple of days, I didn't care which direction the breeze was blowing or what critter trail I took hiking through those mountains. And I soon got to feeling so low and lonesome that I didn't care if I did get put back in jail or under the cold wet ground. Nothing mattered much, no more, because there weren't much that mattered.

There wasn't anything left of me at all to even show I'd lived a life at all, but a prison record under another name and a homemade tombstone.

I went into the wild for days, where it seemed no man had ever wandered, until my provisions ran out. I was thinking on miserable things the whole miserable time and feeling sorry for myself. The more I thought about my life, the more I had to blame somebody because there were people to blame for what all had happened to me. The biggest part of my gut still blamed that preacher who'd got me locked up when I'd told him I'd be leaving and he'd better not call the law. I'd let him up when I could have beat him more or have done a whole lot worse than that to him.

The son-of-a-bitch should have let me go.

I started thinking about that preacher a whole lot.

It was he and nobody else who'd gotten me arrested again

right before I'd got sent off over twenty-one years ago. In the bad shape I was in, I was now sure I was gonna kill him over it. Then after we'd had our business, I was gonna go see the old sheriff of Winslow County. I owed him something from a long time ago, too. My jaw all the way up to my right ear still ached most of the time, when there wasn't another ache somewhere else to make me ignore it.

Visiting with both of them had been a ways down on my list of things to do once I got back to Shady and just before setting out to find Amanda Lynn. But with so many good things suddenly washed off that list in my head that I'd slept with and hoped on for years with one blanket on a steel prison cot, visiting those two were now at the top of it.

I'd swore to Preacher Fletcher that I'd come back one day if he ever gave me up to the police for what me and his wife had done. I figured he'd been looking over his shoulder for a long time on nights he might have to go outside after hearing a rustling somewhere. And I'd been on his mind many a time when there would be a strange noise in that great big farmhouse. I knew that he'd be expecting me, the way we'd looked at each other before the deputy sheriffs hauled me away.

I'd never have pulled any of the time I did if he hadn't called the law on me. I knew now that I couldn't have gotten back in time to save Ma or Bernie or change nothing that happened on that terrible Sunday evening in Shady. But I could've found out what happened. I could've led some kind of normal life afterward, not one in a cage not even knowing my own past, and now not even knowing if Ma and Bernie were really dead like their stones said. As far as I could tell, I wasn't, when my stone said I was.

It hurt me so bad to think about what my life could have been like if he'd have let me go on my way, that I'd tried for years not to let my thoughts settle there. All I knew was, I wouldn't be almost forty years old with nothing in the world and walking and living in the woods like a crazy man if it weren't for that preacher.

Thinking about him was like throwing gasoline on a fire in my gut that just kept smoldering year after year no matter how many times I'd tried to put it out. The only time I hadn't felt it was a couple of days before when I'd just got out of prison and took that long hopeful bus ride back home.

I was definitely gonna go visit with that preacher. He was about to come face-to-face with the thing he'd been fearing in the dark. I'd learned while locked up that some things don't go away until you do something about them. I had to do something to put out that burning hole in my belly if I did nothing else in this world.

And then I'd find the sheriff and, armed or not, he would get a real fight this time, not like the one when he'd laid me out with my hands cuffed up behind my back when I was nothing but a scared boy. This time, I was gonna be the one throwing the first lick, right after I'd ask if he remembered me. If needed, I was gonna jar his recollection.

We'd be even, then, and there would finally be some justice between us. Just like there would be some justice with me and the preacher.

All I'd heard about while walking a cold concrete floor,

where I could take six steps in one direction and four the other before running into a wall, was that I was locked up because justice had been served on me.

I was about to serve some justice back.

I'd thought and wrestled myself on it over and over and over. I needed some way to try and start my life over because I didn't have a life, but it wasn't just like I could start over at thirty-eight years old all marked up with ink and hard inside and out trying to fake some big smile. I had to find a way to clean the slate of my life. Erase the ugly. I wasn't even sure who I was anymore.

I didn't know how bad a man I'd turned into, but at one time, I could still remember being a pretty good boy. A decent person and probably even more than that. Good was still in me a little bit, sort of like a lantern going dim that don't quite go out.

I still had the good in me somewhere that Ma always talked about, but for my lantern to glow strong again, I had to tend to the emptiness and the wrongs others had done to me. There wasn't a way I could ever walk out of those mountains and hope to find Amanda Lynn or feel like I could start over while feeling the hurting in me like I was. I needed somehow to get Shady Hollow and what happened there put where it belonged—in the past and into the ground. All of it.

As I sat on top of a cliff where I could look for miles in all directions without seeing nothing but green and whittled rock and sky, I made up my mind to get my bearings and make my way out of those mountains. My first stop would be at a parsonage next to a country church, all of it sitting in that pretty valley of my memory.

Benjamin Purdue, aka Henry Cole, wasn't going there to do no praying. I was gonna hold court for crimes committed against me twenty-one years before. And I was gonna do it the old Shady Hollow way.

I didn't start any of it with his wife and that's the truth, because seeing her just made me miss Amanda Lynn even more. But Amanda Lynn surely wasn't there, the preacher's wife was, and anyway, he'd found out about what me and his beloved were doing while he was practicing his sermons that next evening near dinnertime when she started hollering and carrying on louder than he was in the basement where he'd gone to work on his upcoming Sunday preachings.

I stopped what I was doing so she'd get hold of herself, but he walked upstairs and in on us all quick and quiet with her bent over grabbing the headboard. He got meanness in him all of a sudden and pulled her off the bed and started beating on her with a lamp as she was trying to get her dress and undergarments from where I'd flung them a couple minutes before.

I would have let him hit her once with an open hand because I wouldn't want my wife behaving like that, either, with another if I ever did have a wife. Plus I needed time to get my pants and drawers up from around my ankles. But he grabbed that lamp and got to swinging it and I put a hand around the back of his neck, threw him down and started stomping a mud hole in him with my good leg because he was hitting her way too hard.

I stopped when Louisa started pounding me on the back.

"You're killing him," she screamed. He was on the floor and had quit moving except for his hands trying to cover his face.

I looked at her and could tell how scared she was and it bothered me in a real bad sort of way. I decided right then to leave her husband with his teeth and nose in good enough order to still preach so them other kids would have plenty to eat, and the fact was they were decent folks for taking me in even if they were paid to do it. Another thing I felt at that moment was that it made me feel bad beating on a holy man.

But then I kicked him one last time to make sure he was gonna deal with me in a serious manner from then on.

I leaned down, put a finger in his face and said, "I'll kill you if you ever lay another hand on her for what she's done, even though you're one of God's favorites and he works through you to help folks get to heaven. I'll hunt you down one day if you try to get me locked up for what we was doing. I'll hunt you down so you don't dare do it.

"And I'll be coming back one day to check on her, too. I ain't a good person just like you said, Preacher. I am a weedy garden. You understand what I'm saying to you? I'm letting you up, but you best let me go on my way. You don't, and you'll have to answer to me one day just before you meet Jesus."

I thought by the way he was looking at me with a lot of white showing around his eyeballs that he knew I was telling him the truth—even though I was just all worked up and carrying on saying stuff I'd heard men say to other men in Shady over this and that scrap.

I didn't really mean a word of it because I wasn't the bad

person he thought I was. I just wanted to scare the vinegar out of that preacher.

When I was younger, I'd seen Ma bloody and covered in cuts and blue and purple marks after she'd got beaten a couple of times, and from then on the sight of a woman getting beat always was something I had a terrible hard time tolerating.

I told the preacher I'd be leaving that evening, and it might be in a year, might be ten years, but he'd see me again. I thought I was lying to him about that, because I was sure I'd never have no reason to come back, but that preacher looked to believe me.

"You forgive her," I told him.

He didn't do it, so I grabbed him by the hair on the top of his head and he said, "I forgive you, Louisa," with his powerful voice now all quiet and trembly.

I felt real bad about the whole dang thing but sometimes even a preacher needs the devil to make him do right. Ma had told me that a long time ago. And it wasn't my fault that Louisa liked me as much as she did. The way I figured it she was as lonesome as I was and she was nice looking and more forward than some of the working gals in Shady were.

I finally walked out and left them alone to make amends, I'd finished my business pretty much with her anyway and by her hollering, she must have finished her business with me. I reckoned after beating on the preacher that the arrangements the judge set weren't going to work out so I was fixing to leave directly after supper like I'd told him.

He didn't know yet that I was gonna need his coat and

borrow his short bus to get back to Shady. I wasn't planning on out and out stealing the bus. I just needed it for a day or two, and I'd leave it where it could be found.

I thought I had my escape to Shady Hollow all planned out. Later on I was gonna take the coat and keys from him, figuring he'd hand them over without no trouble, and I was even gonna ask to borrow five dollars for gas money, but as I was washing up to eat, four county sheriff cars roared up the driveway and the men in them took positions all around the house.

I was soon in the backseat of one of those sheriff cars.

That preacher had a bigger sack on him than I'd realized. It was my fault for not beating him to where he'd get even more white showing around his eyes so he'd believe what I'd said about coming back one day.

I kicked the windows and doors of the police car but they were sturdy and it pained me so bad doing it because of my puny leg and I stopped. All I could think of right then was it was just plain bad luck because nothing else made any sense. The kind of luck Ma had warned me is ready to descend on a person if they weren't mindful and doing the necessaries to keep it warded off. I wouldn't be in steel bracelets again to begin with if I wasn't trying to mend up from being shot. I wouldn't be in that car if a lot of bad things hadn't happened one after another.

All of the bad started when Amanda Lynn came to Shady Hollow, but I knew it wasn't bad going against Ma's wishes seeing her. And I knew she wasn't bad and she didn't bring me bad luck.

The way I figured it, if she was bad or brought bad luck,

then there just wasn't any good. I'd known good so that wasn't true. Bad and bad luck may have followed her to Shady Hollow, but I knew she didn't invite it or know nothing about it.

I sat there in that backseat long enough to calm down and try to get comfortable. I figured my biggest mistake was stealing that 'shine runner's car.

At the time, I figured probably like Ma did that I could outrun them, but what I didn't know was they'd set up a new roadblock so close to Shady in that dead man's curve.

And they'd never been crazy enough to block the whole road before.

We'd harassed those state and federal men for weeks, but the more we tried to run them off, the more of them showed up. They were serious about their work this time as I came to find out, not a bit like the locals who used to do all of the shakedowns.

It was nothing like the old days when the law would come in like a small army every couple of years, mostly before some election according to Ma, but the tree watchers would see them and then jack rocks would be spread all over the roads and guns would blast from the hills and rattlesnakes would be thrown through car windows and boulders would block the only way to get in.

Then if they were still being troublesome, sticks of lit dynamite would start slinging through the air.

The law would do what they always did, get only so far and then point their rifles and pistols all around at what they couldn't see. Men with bullhorns would threaten us with the National Guard, but it would get quiet except for the dynamite going off and then we'd whoop and holler and light up the place with guns firing like the Fourth of July.

That's when they'd bolt out of there and the elders would rain birdshot down on their running behinds. The next day we'd pull their cars with shot out tires around the bend so they could fetch them with tow trucks.

The tow-truck drivers would always spend a few hours enjoying Shady Hollow, before they'd leave with their hauls.

We never did actually try to kill lawmen who were just trying to do their job, because in Shady it's respected that a man's got to do something for a living, and even Shady had its laws enforced by the elders. But it would've been easy as picking daisies to not let one of them walk out of those mountains with so many sharp eyes looking down the iron sights of deer rifles.

A couple of the harder men in Shady suggested it, but Tobias Chambers ruled that a battle like that would start a war we'd lose eventually.

"No profit in it," Mr. Chambers said.

Anyway, I'd messed up bad by listening to Ma and running in the first place, and in my big hurry taking that car instead of heading out on one of the trails through the mountains to wait things out if I needed to, and then having relations with that preacher's wife even though she's the one who closed the door of that room and touched me, at first like she'd never been touched before but really wanted to be.

I knew I'd done wrong by that preacher, and especially to Amanda Lynn, for being with another when all I wanted in the whole world was to be with her, but the truth was nothing felt wrong about it when it happened between us. It just felt good.

It felt so good and I think sometimes a person just needs to feel some good when they ain't felt nothing but bad in so long. The way I looked at it the whole thing was an accident meant to be for whatever reason. Good luck and bad luck ramming into each other at the same time, bad luck coming out on top, like it had been since that bloody Sunday evening in Shady. All of it led me back handcuffed in another car with a cage in it.

I would've outrun those sheriff deputies before I ended up shackled so easy and pitiful. I almost did get away even with the bum leg and crutches, but once they yanked those guns from their holsters and I saw the tight look on their faces, I laid down in a stand of black cherry trees on my stomach.

I just kept thinking about bad luck and how Ma always said once you get it on you, it takes a long time to wear off because there ain't no soap made a person can wash it off with.

I kept thinking about that for a long time.

So just toward dark, they drove me away from the preacher's house. I looked for the preacher's wife just before we pulled away to try and wave at her or look at her or something to let her know that I didn't mean to bring hard times and my bad luck to her, but all I saw was that preacher standing and staring at me. I stared back as hard as I could and something told me we would meet again one day. He could've let me go, like I told him to do. I kept thinking about that over and over and over.

That's why I yelled cuffed up turning around as far as I

could to keep my eyes on his. "I'll be back," I yelled as loud as I could. "I'll be coming back!"

It was less than an hour before I found myself in my old cell in the local jail in Winslow. They rolled my fingers in ink again even though they had a bunch of prints of mine already, and then they logged me in as a juvenile to be kept separate from the other prisoners, just like before.

Over the coming weeks they got all of my old charges and court hearings sorted out before a new judge who wasn't nothing like Judge Fletcher. Two short trials and three plea hearings and a few months later on my eighteenth birthday, I became an inmate at the Virginia State Correctional Unit Number Six in Lynchburg, Virginia.

As it turned out, I got away with the things I'd actually done before—none of them worth all of the fuss I was going through. But they'd nailed me to a tree on the things I didn't.

The state warden told me on my first day in prison that if I behaved and learned from my bad ways, that I'd be released in seven years to integrate back into society for all the stealing and fighting and ruckuses I'd caused.

But even after his talk, I got in more trouble behind those tall walls though I wasn't looking for it. It found me even when I tried my very best to steer clear of it, and I tried to hide or run away from it for a long time.

Then the day came when I had to face it.

I ended up being there almost ten years, not seven. And when I was released, I still wasn't free because the state handed me over to U.S. Marshals who hauled me to the federal penitentiary in Harrisburg, Pennsylvania, for the charges the revenuers had put on me.

The law had kept their claim and swore to it that I'd shot at a federal officer before I surrendered, but I know I didn't.

But the jury believed the witness who held up Uncle Ray's revolver found in the car, and he said it was the same one I'd shot at them with and that I was a dangerous young man.

But I wasn't dangerous back then like they said. I was just generally having fun like boys do at that age, and getting into things and backing out of them when the ground got shaky. When it came down to it, I was just trying to make my way in Shady and make enough money so one day I could make my way out of there.

A good part of me did turn dangerous and mean once a few years of prison life got inside of me. But I never shot at those officers.

On the long ride going from Virginia through Maryland and West Virginia and the Pennsylvania farm country to the penitentiary, I remembered how that federal judge in Roanoke sentenced me in a long and steady tone. At the end, he told me how lucky I was that the car and me hadn't went sky-high to the moon with so much liquor inside and so much lead flying around.

I didn't feel too lucky all chained up with so much time left to pull. Ten more years. More misery than I'd just finished up with the state.

But those marshals were kind to me on that ride. They bought me a foot-long chili dog, a cheeseburger and a large chocolate shake for lunch at a Tastee-Freez in Winchester,

Virginia. Same meal as they had, as we all ate quiet in the parking lot listening to country music and the news on the war over in Vietnam on their AM radio.

I sat there, trying to eat that dog while cramped up in the back of their caged car with my hands cuffed close to a chain around my waist. I kept thinking about how the state time had went by one tick after a slow tick, and I didn't know if I could pull all of that federal time they'd added to it or not.

And I came to find out like I'd feared that the federal time went by even slower than my state time. So I had plenty of minutes and hours and days to think about Amanda Lynn, and try to feel young and free as I kept aging in a box. Many, many nights. It got harder each night to think about any of that, but I figured if I ever stopped trying my heart, and then probably what mind I had left, would just go away for good.

And now thinking about those long-ago things and sitting high on a mountaintop by myself watching the sun and clouds, I felt free for sure. I felt more free in a way I'd never known a person could.

The kind of free nobody would ever want to feel.

It was a reckless, dangerous, lost feeling, and it was all pointed at a preacher who'd be seeing me very soon.

Chapter 11

On my fourth morning trying to find my way out of the wilderness to kill a preacher, I was about to find out that I was lost. I stopped walking when a limestone overhang along the rim of a cliff and the remains of a campfire caught my eye. It looked like a place I'd slept a couple of days before. On closer look, it was the place I'd just slept a couple of days before. I was sure of it, as I picked up off the ground an oak limb I'd whittled on for no reason except to do something to pass part of the long night alone by that fire.

I looked all around and knew I wasn't just turned around. I'd gone in a big circle somehow.

I'd spent a lot of my childhood in the woods with my brothers and pards, and even camped on my own on occasion and had felt the fear of being lost many times, but this was different. I knew the backcountry I was in or at least I thought I did and now I was a grown man. I knew I was in trouble.

I scrambled around looking high and low for some clue as to what direction I should head, and I decided that instead of trying to find my way to the preacher's valley, I'd better get to anywhere and soon with my provisions run out. So after taking a good rest to clear my head and shake the fear that was crawling all over me, I decided to go downhill and keep going until I hit a house where I could find something to eat and get the chill out.

But I soon found the trouble with my new method of getting un-lost by going downhill. It was that the little stream I'd been following disappeared into a sinkhole, and from there the grade would go up and down in so many directions. I couldn't go just down.

And then a fog set in.

It wasn't one of those Shady fogs that would come up from the Big Walker to be burned off in a few hours. This was a bad one that came down from the heavens to stay a good while.

Not able to see more than a step or two ahead of me, I made an early camp that evening to warm myself, but I still shivered through that cold June night. Then the next morning the drizzle turned into a steady rain which then turned into a downpour that seemed to come from every direction. I was waterlogged, the last of my matches were gone, and I had to walk and kept walking. I lost one shoe somewhere and toward that evening lost the other, and with everything I had on me wet and cold, I figured I was about to meet my end.

With my arms tight around myself while sitting in the small dugout of an old rotten tree trunk, I had to use the little girl's drawing from the bus for a makeshift hat. I felt bad about using it in such a way but I could feel my thumbs and fingers and toes going past numb on me, and it wasn't even night yet. I closed my eyes and my teeth chattered to the thundering, and not long after it got darker than a night should ever get if you're alone out in it, I got myself some serious religion about things.

It wasn't like the lightning bolt that hits a feller on his knees that I'd heard so much about from the churchgoers, but something moved through me that one miserable lonesome night where I was sure I was about to die and nobody would ever find me and nobody would probably care if they did or didn't.

It wasn't nothing out of the Bible I was sure of, because I didn't believe some of the things in that book the way preachers read it aloud claiming they know what God is saying about this and that. Things like how God once let a man named Abraham almost kill his own son to prove his love for the Almighty.

I'd read all about it in prison once I'd learned to read.

I was never gonna pray to any god who'd sit by as a man was about to do such a thing because it seemed so bad to me, and I'd turned into a man capable of doing bad. I never knew a man even in Shady—and I knew some treacherous ones—who'd stand by as another man went to do such a terrible thing. So I figured most of the book was like most things, made up here with truth scattered there, and it aggravated me trying to figure out which was which.

If there was a god and he had a son and there was a heaven

where they lived, like Ma always told me when I was a boy, he and all of it was a sight different than the feller in the white robe and white beard resting on a cloud those pounding churchgoers kept talking about in the black book. I never had any formal church schooling, but that's how I saw it.

And those stories about his one son Jesus doing things like feeding a whole crowd of folks with a couple loaves of bread and a few fish while he was telling his stories. While I was sitting in that old rotten tree trunk hungry, I figured what he should have done before he left was to tell the crowd how to do that trick with the bread and fish because a fair sum of people I'd ever known had spent a good bit of their life starving.

And people have been starving to death since before he came and long since he left. A person didn't need an education to know that.

It would've been nice of Jesus to share that magic trick with the fish and bread with a few folks who could then show it to other people instead of just leaving a story for everybody. Feeding a hundred people with one fish is a trick worth passing on, just like he said if you teach a man to fish he'd never go hungry. Well if you teach a man to feed his hungry neighbors with one fish he'd caught, we'd all get along better than we do and with full bellies. But most of the times when a bunch goes fishing, you don't catch enough to feed everybody and a man who can't work up nothing to eat will soon be up to no good.

Ain't but so many fish and so many loaves of bread sometimes and people in some places have to fight and steal for what they can get.

He kept that walking on troubled waters trick to himself, too. Teddy wouldn't have drowned if he'd of shared that.

So for a bunch of reasons, I didn't believe much in that book as hard as I'd tried a few times in my good and needing moments.

But the whole reason I learned to read in prison wasn't to read that holy book, it was to read letters even though I never got any from anybody. I knew Ma couldn't write but hoped she might have somebody write down a few things to send me. That's why I started reading the Bible, to learn more about writing and because they let us keep that book in our cells without turning it in after a few days. I did keep hoping it would help me pass the nights one after another locked up in the penitentiary waiting on a letter.

I started reading other books, too. I read every book the prison library had by the time I was released, and I got so caught up in some of them and learned things about other places and some of the stories stayed with me for a long time. But when I closed all of those books, I knew whatever was in them could be boiled down to stories I'd heard and the things I'd seen with my own eyes growing up in Shady Hollow as a boy.

Every dang one of them.

I kept at that Bible and tried to understand it even though the pages were so flimsy and what was printed on them seemed so flimsy, too, at times. To me it seemed like religious books just maybe made people not get along with each other like they'd probably do if they never read them. They wouldn't split up into groups with each group feeling so good about their place with the Almighty and calling the other group evil or looking down on them. I didn't figure a real god would be for all that choosing sides and hurling names and the violence that came from all of it when everybody everywhere is pretty much the same.

The holy writings I could get a hold of had a lot of killing and men being enemies of one another, and even God being an enemy of some folks and sometimes he'd do the killing and in great numbers with the wave of an angry powerful hand. A vengeful hand.

But I guess the reason I read the Bible more than any other book was because it was the only book my ma had ever owned. Uncle Ray seemed fond of it, too, so I tried to like it, too, even though so much of it seemed to tangle with itself depending on who was doing the talking about right and wrong and living forever.

Maybe that was the draw of it, I figured.

The tangling and trying to live forever.

But at the end of closing that book on most nights, all it did was make me more ornery, I think. Bad kind of ornery, too. The god in that book seemed to have a mean streak in him depending on his mood, much like me and the men in the other prison cells around me. It did say in it, that he made us just like him, except we being just not as smart and prosperous and not in charge of the money and the weather and whatnot.

I never could figure why he'd throw a man into a fire for eternity when that man would do the same things he seemed to do on occasion, and sometimes for things not as bad.

It was a cantankerous book and made me cantankerous trying to understand it and his way of thinking.

I always thought a real god would teach real good things like keeping people fed and he'd never watch as a man was about to kill his own son and then call it off at the last minute. If you ask me, Abraham was about 400 or 800 years old or more by that time. I can't remember, they lived so long back then, but maybe he wasn't real clear in the head at such an old age or maybe he had some bad homemade wine, dreamed the whole dern crazy thing and then told his dream to somebody and they wrote it down like it was the truth from God's own lips.

That's how big things get started generally with just a pea of truth in them. Even real big things.

I believed in a maker some of the time and especially needed to that scary night while I was hunkered down in what was left of the old tree that looked to have seen much worse than I had over its time. But God's doings and pleasures ain't never been written about right, I didn't think. Seemed to me all those books were full of words written by men, not a god. Maybe written by men who were trying their best to think like a god would, which to me was sort of an odd idea anyway, with men generally being such a misfit knucklehead bunch to begin with. I reckoned it was the same thing I was doing lost in those woods…trying to think like a god would think, and probably not having much luck at it.

I figured even the smartest man of the best nature would probably have better odds trying to think like a dog would, than how a god would. And that figuring ain't saying nothing bad about dogs. It's just the way I had it figured.

Anyway, I figured God may not have written one single word in any of those books, or maybe just a few. Which words he agreed on was up to speculation and he was so far keeping that to himself.

To me, nobody had such a feller figured out yet, and especially maybe the ones who claim that they have.

So even though it wasn't no lightning bolt that hit me out of the Good Book, because for the life of me I just couldn't become one of those true believers hard as I'd tried now and again, I did feel something strong that shook me that one bad, long night.

Felt it go straight through every bit of me like a winter wind that wouldn't quit blowing and there was no hiding or shelter from it. Storm clouds had followed me since I was seventeen years old for some reason I didn't know.

The weather that night almost killed me and I still don't know how I survived it, but it left me whole. When it blew out of there that next morning, I knew I had something I needed to do. I'd had visions during the storm, bad visions mostly. I knew when I came out of them that I had to change, and it wasn't a change to push me more to the dark side of me. It had came more and more to me when I was so hungry and cold and lost and alone in all that weather knowing that taking my next breath may be the final thing I ever did. The most terrible thing about it was that it would be a fitting end for me, I figured.

After a while even the kindest people give up on people

like me and maybe God had, too, like even that preacher did right off the go. I'd heard people tell me that before and it was starting to make sense.

It takes a lot out of a person to care, and there just ain't enough to care about when they look close at a person like me, and nothing but bad or empty or at best tolerable looks back.

I'd been the feller learning to cut the side of your pocket or who would cheat you in cards. Or sometimes worse than that. And that's what a person would see if they looked hard into me because, except for doing a good thing now and then that's about all I ever was.

I didn't like being the person I was no more, but I didn't know who to be at all if I didn't be me. I just knew, though I'd never really done much bad to nobody unless I had to, I'd never done nothing real good for nobody, either. I wondered if bad luck had followed me, or if luck followed me and I always shaded it dark because I couldn't help but rub off on it.

I had all of those temperaments tearing up my insides and that's when I knew if given one more chance, I had to find Amanda Lynn or I was gonna just go away like one of those castles me and my brothers would build out of river sand and mud on the banks of the Big Walker.

I was good around her.

I felt good just being with her. I was my very best when I was around Amanda Lynn. She'd always mattered to me more than I mattered to myself.

Sitting in the storm of rain and bad memories, and wanting so much and having so little, and mostly wanting years back that were gone forever and leaving me in such a mess, the loud gusts and rain somehow blew visions of her down from some misty lost ridge. She was still alive, I just knew it. She was my last hope at finding out what happened, and she was my best hope of maybe feeling that true feeling of being a good person again.

I wasn't in the ground beside Ma. Or maybe part of me was but not all. I might be all in the ground soon but I couldn't be in it yet. The only way I could figure why a stone said I was there was just like how Teddy had a grave—maybe they figured I'd died on that day when I took off out of Shady and never came back. I'm sure they'd heard all the gunfire echoing off the hills. Maybe the law finally put up a blockade around the place that nobody could get in or get out for a long time. I didn't know. I hoped Ma and Bernie weren't in that ground, either. I hoped that the most.

I kept thinking about that terrible day and names on rocks and especially Amanda Lynn. I still loved her. She was the only pure good thing in the whole world I could even remember. She was even as good as Ma. I never did have to try hard to be a good person when I was around her. I don't know what kind of magic she had to make such a thing happen without effort, but she did.

Toward the end of my suffering that long night when my shivering got the worst, my mind started drifting into making me do crazy things, like wonder if I was Jesus because he was in the wilderness for quite some time and he said he'd be back someday, and maybe I was him or he was me or we were the same and he wasn't letting me on to who I was just yet because I hadn't suffered enough yet to carry such a name, even though I should know already if I was really Jesus.

I gave a good think about all of that and tried to do a few miracles like get the rain to stop and make the mud puddles around me turn to Coca-Cola and turn sticks into Zagnut bars, but it just rained harder and I got colder and hungrier. I knew I wasn't Jesus because he could change the weather by just raising an arm to the heavens. I didn't know what to do then, and so I stood out in what I had no control of and screamed Amanda Lynn's name.

I don't think I had much control out of doing that, either.

I was about to die and knew it, and she was all I could think of at the very end, soaked and cold and lost to the inside of the bones of me where I couldn't see a good path or bad path if it laid in front of me. I came to no longer fear death in any way during the peak of that storm, because it had already come upon me, and it weren't as bad as I'd always figured. It was a feeling that had grown on me ever since that bloody day in Shady, and it was actually comforting to me that the troubles and bad fortunes upon me were finally coming to an end. It was in that fierce storm that the troubles inside of me started washing away, too. I even quit shivering for a time. I was just gonna disappear for good and become part of the mountain, and at least I had made it back home, and it felt like a part of Amanda Lynn was with me through that passing.

Just before I felt death take complete hold of me, I didn't feel alone.

I wasn't alone.

★ ★ ★

A big drop of rain woke me the next morning. It had been puddled in a wide green leaf above my head and bounced off of one of my cheeks. The sun had somehow followed that wonderful storm, and I came to feeling awake like I'd been born again. Even still feeling so frozen outside, inside I felt different.

I didn't feel warm. I felt clean. Something had washed away the bad and meanness I'd felt inside me for so long.

I laid in that feeling a long time and finally decided if I didn't get up that I never would. So I did, and I pulled off my clothes all the way past my drawers and socks and I wrung them out while shaking all over. I spread them on sapling branches and let them dry best they could in the streaks of sunshine I could find. The woods looked different to me for some reason like I'd earned the respect of being among the trees and other animals or something, and I wasn't tramping on them or just tramping through them no more. I was one with all of it, and they'd sheltered me and took care of me. All of those critters and trees around me had to weather the same storm and were let to live just like I had been. It was a strange feeling, like we'd all survived it together, not just me. Those may seem like crazy thoughts, but they weren't. My mind had never been so clear as it was early that morning.

I stood up as tall as I could and naked as the day I was born with my arms out from me.

I hollered up with thanks and then asked if anybody was listening up there in the blue sky, that I needed a second chance with things and if I got it, I wouldn't know how to go about being a different man, so I'd need a point or even another kick in the right direction.

I then got quiet except for hearing my own heart beating. I kept standing for I don't know how long but it must have been an hour or more. Even with the sun out, I still felt so cold and damp that I had to give up on standing naked. I ended up squatting on a warm rock with my arms around myself, moving ever so often to stay in the sun.

I'd asked, anyway. And I still felt like a man doing it. Maybe even a bigger man than I'd ever been.

Whoever or whatever had made me and everything that was and everything that had ever been, had spared me and got me to bare my weaknesses and ask a favor, if anybody was up there and happened to be listening.

I figured maybe the Maker might just pay notice to a new voice hollering up from the wilderness. In my whole life, I hadn't asked for much from him being that I never figured he liked me much anyway.

That's all that I figured I could do that morning to help myself being wrung out, so hungry and buck naked, and maybe it would fare well in my favor down the road. But I figured maybe it wouldn't, too. I was okay with all of that, though.

I looked around me while chewing on anything I could find, not sure at all where I was and if I was even still in Virginia. I'd gotten so lost in those mountains, but Amanda Lynn's memory had come to me from a strong wind blowing south.

She was calling me and had saved my life the night before. I was now sure of both of those things. And I needed to know what was in the letter that I never got to read, and why she'd come to Shady to find me. Why that man had come to shoot me down. What happened to Ma and my brothers. I had to find her for so many reasons. Most of all, my insides craved to feel that pure feeling of good again I got from her.

I'd already decided late in the storm that I was gonna let that preacher grow old and in peace if he weren't dead already. I let my hate and quarrel go with him and the sheriff and every other person I'd wanted harm to come to. I knew, unlike many other times, this time those hard feelings had gone out of me for good and wouldn't come back to haunt me and drive me into the bad.

I needed to steer myself in the directions of good things from now on, starting with my own self, and Amanda Lynn was the only true good thing I knew, so in my dried clothes, I started heading out of those hills drifting south.

I wondered if she still lived on that beautiful plantation in Durham County, North Carolina. My mind had gotten so hazy I wondered if I'd have enough memory of that flatland to find her.

But before I could do any of that, I had to get out of the wilderness. I was dry and warm again, but I was weak and feeling sick way past being just hungry. Besides losing both shoes somewhere in the storm, I had lost my bag and everything in it, too, even that old shoe with the lucky ten dollar bill in it. I had to sit and rest a lot that day being shaky as I was, finding whatever I could to keep my feet moving one in front of the other, and sipping water from springs I'd cross or where the rain had collected in spots.

After walking another day or maybe another week, I

trudged down a long, easy hill and the trees got more spread out. I heard a car far away and then I saw sunlight coating a field way below me.

I couldn't believe the first thing I saw when I finally took a step out of the forest and had to shield my eyes from the brightness. I was in a pretty valley I knew from my memory, and a half mile across a dirt road dead in front of me was a small white church with a big steeple and a farmhouse.

I wondered if I'd been brought there on purpose, led to that place and for a reason, after being put through so much that it made me change before I'd gotten there. If so that must mean I had a purpose. A real purpose, and not a bad one, either. It was the first time I'd ever felt like I had a purpose at all, whatever that may be.

If I could make it that last half mile, cross two barbed-wire fences, a small creek, that dirt road and not fall down dead within sight of his church, I was gonna go visit that preacher after all.

Chapter 12

The man was plowing rows or trying to where there'd once been cherry trees alongside a winding grassy creek. He was in the exact same place, give or take twenty-some years, that I'd gotten arrested after trying to run on a pair of crutches from the preacher's house. He wasn't the man I was expecting to see, him being wiry and short, with sweat running down a face that was dark as good dirt. He looked to be trying to act like he was paying no mind to me, but not doing a good job at it.

He was bouncing on a tractor with a parlor pillow between him and the seat. Even with his hat down so low it was touching his ears, I could tell he and his chained yard dogs didn't like the looks of me as I wandered up on him where he was working.

I waved at him twice as I limped across the road, but he

just stared with one eye on me, and kept one hand fighting the tractor wheel and the other fighting what looked to be a homemade tiller blade.

When I made my way up to the church, I slowed once I saw how most of the old painted glass had been broken and the windows were boarded up. Spray-painted words and drawings on the clapboard that looked to be spray-painted over only to be spray-painted again and over and again marked up the side that faced the road. There were burn marks here and there and it looked like the steeple wasn't in good order, either, as some kind of birds had set up roost in the place where a Sunday ringing bell had been.

I squinted, looking up the rutted drive at the old farm-house on the hill. What paint and shingles it used to have on it were all about gone. It was pretty much just gray looking. From the rotting boards that sided it to the faded tarpaper on the roof.

I didn't see any vehicles near but a farm truck that was older than I was. After giving the whole place a look around, I saw there weren't any children running around or toys or rope swings hanging from trees, or nothing like that in the yard like there had been the last time I'd been there.

Times had changed it, too, sure enough.

I waved again at the feller on the tractor and figured he might tend the farmland the house sat on for the preacher. I thought it may do well to have him go with me to the front door to ease the preacher's mind that I wasn't out to harm him, as all that had washed clean out of me in the big storm.

"Can you stop your tractor for a minute," I yelled to him

when he made a pass near me. I coughed and was worried bad about myself when I heard how weak and high my voice was.

I tried to swallow but it didn't do much good as he pulled up right in front of me looking down. He pushed up the brim of a hat that at one time was probably a nice church-going hat, before he'd cut the top off of it for whatever reason, I guess to cool his head.

"What you say?" he yelled.

"Would you turn your tractor off a minute," I tried to yell back.

He shook his head. "Turn it off, might not turn back on."

"Is the preacher up yonder?" I said, pointing at the farmhouse.

"You're looking at him," he said.

I shook my head figuring he hadn't heard me right. "I'm looking for the preacher," I yelled as loud as I could.

"I'm Preacher Washington. Who're you?"

I stood confused. "I'm looking for another preacher. Used to live here."

"Been quite a few who lived here at one time or another. Which one you looking for?"

I took a deep breath while trying to remember his name. It wasn't like it was a name I'd forgotten, because of the serious nature of things that had passed between us years ago, but I was just so fuzzy in the head about everything. It finally came to me. "Preacher Fletcher," I said.

"Preacher Simon Fletcher?"

I nodded.

"He don't preach here. Don't think he preaches no more,

either. That's my church down there now. Simon Fletcher works at the old motel off Route 11 last I heard. Ain't seen him lately. I know a bunch of poor white folk stays by the week and some riffraff keeps there that he used to try to keep an eye on."

I got up closer to the man on the tractor and I saw him pull the end of a big stick of hickory close to his lap.

"He still preaching?" I yelled.

"Don't think so. No, sir."

I started getting wobbly standing so empty in my stomach and my throat all swolled up and smelling the fumes belching out of that tractor.

"My name's Benjamin Purdue. I wonder if you could spare me something to eat, don't matter what. I got a couple dollars and would pay you for anything you could give me."

He kept looking me over. "What happened to you?" was the best I could make out of what he said over the loud of his tractor.

"You sure you can't step off there for a minute. I can't hardly hear you talking and I'm about to fall down. I need to sit for a minute under a shade tree and could use a cool drink of water."

He had to work to turn off the tractor as it took a while to die. He stayed in the seat. "You ain't bringing no trouble here, are you?"

"No, sir," I said.

"I got enough of that around here."

I felt myself getting more dizzy, and I put one hand on the front tire of his tractor but it was so hot I had to pull it away. I went to sit right there where if he didn't do something to help me, he'd have to back up, run me over, or pull me off to the side to get back to work.

"I reckon I couldn't let another man go hungry," he said.

That put a little life back in me as I tried to stand upright. I nodded. "So you're a preacher?"

"That's right. Been preaching since I was old enough to put two words together. My momma told me the first word to ever come out of me was *hallelujah*."

"You preach down there?" I said, pointing down at the boarded up church.

"It don't look like much now, but me and my wife are building us a ministry. Bank owns the house and the church that they foreclosed on old Reverend Fletcher. A couple other preachers have come through here—some of them no good account at all—but the bank's letting me work on the note when I can and keep up the place."

I looked around at the poor condition of everything and the way he and his tractor seemed so tuckered out just trying to dig a row, and I figured he'd be leaving there soon enough, too. But I didn't say nothing about that. It looked more than any one poor man could handle and I figured it would dawn on him hard one day.

But then it was almost like he'd heard aloud what I was thinking because he said, "I ain't going nowhere, and with the Lord's help and that's all the help I need, that will be my church one day full and proper. White folks started moving out of this valley once the black folks started moving in, and that church is gonna come alive again with music and praising. A miracle is coming here, see."

He was nodding his head as I wiped the sweat off of my forehead with my sleeve. When I pulled it away, it looked like I'd just made mud on my cuff.

He finally stepped off his tractor and looked kind at me until he got close. He stopped before he got within swinging distance and he stared me over and then turned and got back on his tractor.

"What happened to you?" he asked again.

"If you could just provide me water and a meal. I'll give you the money for it right here."

I started to pull out my money and some of it fluttered to the ground, but he didn't pay no mind to it or me falling down trying to chase it down, as he started tinkering with the tractor pulling on levers and at the end, used a screwdriver to get the thing going somehow because it sounded like it didn't want to. The tractor threw out a big puff of black smoke that just hung over us but it didn't seem to bother him any.

He nodded at me and said, "I got a brother-in-law who's a deputy sheriff over in Harlow, gonna be stopping by this evening for supper. That bother you any?"

"No, sir," I said.

"He'll be pulling in here about anytime."

"Okeydoke," I said.

"Police ain't looking for you for nothing?"

"No."

"Should they be?"

"No, sir."

"You ain't coming in the house." He reached back and

grabbed the limb of hickory again. "You don't even step foot on my porch, you hear?"

I nodded.

"How long's it been since you ate?"

"Preacher, I gotta go sit down somewheres or I'm gonna fall down dead right here. You got a water hose I can get me a drink of water and cool my head?"

He motioned for me to follow him. It wasn't a far walk but it was that day, the fifty yards it took to get to the old farmhouse walking behind his tractor.

He pointed at an old water pump sticking out of the ground and then told me to wait under a huge oak they had out in the front yard. I liked the looks of that oak, but I feared I'd never be able to make it over there to sit.

"I'll be keeping an eye on you, now. I got work to finish and will be back directly."

I was already pumping out water that I took down in gulps before I stuck my whole head under it to wash off the dried stuff I didn't even know what all it was that I had all over me. After I wrung out my hair until the water wasn't brown no more, I braided it and tied what I could grab hold of into a knot at the bottom and rolled up my shirtsleeves and washed my arms. When I was doing that, I looked up and saw him sitting there studying the tattoos covering both forearms. I realized he'd been studying on me the whole time.

He turned off the tractor again, climbed down and, with that chunk of wood in his hand, said, "I'll get you something to eat, but you're gonna have to be on your way and eat it on the road."

Something old and ornery flamed up inside me, him with that weapon when I hadn't done a thing to him but ask for food, and wanting to pay for it.

I thought even in my poor condition, I could take that stick from him without hardly trying, but instead, I swallowed all that down because I wasn't a man who'd do such a thing anymore and just said, "I'd appreciate it if you'd just let me rest my feet for a spell. Been walking for some time."

That preacher looked at my feet, swollen up with cuts and bruises all over them. He looked at me just like he was thinking how does a man with money in his pockets have no shoes.

"You wait right here," he said.

He turned and walked in a hurry, shooing his guineas and yelling at his dogs to hush up, and he pulled a blue bandanna from his back pocket to wipe the back of his neck when he looked back at me. I was scared he was gonna call the law—even though I hadn't done nothing wrong. Doing nothing wrong in the past had tended to get me in plenty of trouble with the law. I thought on what I should do, but couldn't do nothing but limp over to the shady side of an outbuilding several feet from me. I took a quick look that there wasn't a snake laying there before I slid my back down the side of the building. I looked all around and way off to the mountains I'd just come out of and at some point I reckon I closed my eyes.

"Let's go now," he said.

I wasn't sure where I was and I couldn't place the face I was looking at even though I'd seen it before. I felt a nudge again and saw it was that preacher and he was still toting that dern skinned tree limb.

"I'm gonna take you on down to see Simon Fletcher. Only about four miles from here. My wife fixed you a sack lunch, but you eat it in the truck. I'm driving you over there."

I saw the heavy bag of food and reached up for it just as he pulled it away from me.

"You eat on the way away from here," he said.

I don't remember anything about the ride but tearing into the big bag of food as soon as he'd laid it beside me. He may've said something or preached to me the whole time riding alongside him, but I don't recall nothing like that. I only remember eating, trying to finish off two hard-boiled eggs and a peanut butter sandwich with bacon and mayonnaise on it, two apples, a hunk of cheese, and downing a mason jar of lemonade to say nothing. I couldn't catch my wind I was eating so fast. He may've said a lot of things, I just don't know.

When Preacher Washington pulled off the side of the road before a brick motel and nodded at my door handle after I looked at him, I got out and left two dollars on his truck seat, like I told him I'd do. I did wish that besides the food, I wished I'd have asked if he had any old shoes he could see to give me, too. My feet and ankles were so tender I couldn't hardly put weight on either of them when I stepped out.

He pulled away and did a big circle throwing gravel like he was late to get more plowing done before a Sunday meeting and, standing there, it hit me that I didn't even know what day of the week it was. I was pretty sure it was still the month of June, though, but not positive about that, either.

I put my back to the cloud he'd kicked up, and was still working on one of the apple cores as I peered around at the motel ahead of me. It looked to be a pretty nice place in its day, all one floor that went into an L-shape and probably over thirty rooms, and there were a few cars parked in front of the room doors, but once I looked a little closer, it seemed most of those cars were broken-down, in some sort of poor condition just like that motel looked to be. I figured hobbling closer that I fit right in with the whole look of it.

I walked around the front that sat facing the highway, and saw the office to it had large windows but all of the blinds were closed, I guess to keep out the sun or to hide the duct tape that was holding some of the panes together.

The faded sign above the motel said, "Groundhog Valley Motel and Restaurant," and it had holes in it from bullets and buckshot.

Reading the word *restaurant* made my mouth water.

I still had a couple dollars left and even though I'd just downed a big sack of food, I felt like I was still starving. I looked around for the restaurant and saw a rotting sign above a restaurant building not attached to the rest, and it was boarded up with a chain across the double front doors.

When I got through the weeds in front of the motel, being careful not to step on the broken glass everywhere, I saw an old man sitting in a rocker in the shade outside the office door. He had on glasses that made his eyes bug out even though they were closed. I recognized him. He'd aged rough and had gone bald except for the long hair over his ears and down his collar, but it was Preacher Fletcher, or what was left of him.

I walked up close and started to say something but his eyes never opened, even though I wasn't being quiet standing beside him. I went ahead and opened the motel office door to see if anybody else was around there, but there was nothing or nobody to see or hear but an electric fan blowing and a plugged-in radio playing a Conway Twitty tune, some toys for a baby here and there and a mess of different things that looked to collect over the years and not ever get moved.

I walked back out the door, and there was another rocking chair beside the preacher so I just sat in it, because I didn't know what to say and I needed to sit, even though I'd thought about what I'd say to him a thousand times. But that was before the weather had took the meanness out of me and I'd found him looking so puny.

After I'd been sitting for a minute or two, he said loud, "You escape or did they finally let you out?"

Him talking so sudden startled me and I looked over at him quick. He may've aged bad, but his voice was strong as ever.

He still had his eyes closed with his head back against the rest. I sat straight, leaning over to look at him close for a long time until he finally opened his eyes and turned his head to look at me.

"Can you not speak?" he asked.

I was surprised the bold way he was behaving toward me, not a tremor of fear in his voice or his hands as they sat still on the arms of the rocker. He was even smiling. It was then that I wondered how pitiful I might just look after being lost in the mountain for so many days. Then it hit me that at first glance, he might not even know who I was.

"You don't remember me?" I asked.

I was looking dead at him, but he was now looking straight out in front of us where a crow was pecking around a big green dump box.

"I certainly remember you," he said in a flat voice.

"You gotten old and crazy?" I asked.

He nodded. "Old. But I'm saner than ever, sometimes I feel, unfortunately. Did you come all the way here to apologize?"

What he said made me rear back from him. I stood up and got right in front of him and while I hadn't come there to do any violence to that preacher, I wasn't about to let him make light of all the bad he'd caused on me.

I didn't know what to say for a moment. He finally laid his big buggy eyes on mine. "Son, I forgave you a long time ago," he said.

I didn't like being called "son" by him and guessed he figured all that time in prison I'd spent because of him, I'd sat in my hole wanting to tell him I was sorry for messing with his wife after she started messing with me and then beating on him after he'd beat on her.

He'd figured wrong.

I wasn't sure now why I'd come to see him except I ended up at his place after being lost and figured it was a sign like the kind Ma always talked about, that I should be there and I needed to see him, plus I didn't have nowhere else to go and needed to be somewhere. I sure enough couldn't go calling on Amanda Lynn the way I was.

"I didn't come here to say I was sorry for nothing," I said.

"I see. So why did you come?"

I thought about it and decided to speak the truth to him because I was trying to change my ways.

"There was a time, a short time ago, a few days ago even, that I was coming to kill you over you calling the law on me and getting me locked up all those years. You took my life away from me when you could've let me go. You could have let me go, Preacher. I let you up. I let you go. I was just wanting to get back home."

"You were going to find me to come and finish off the job you started. I see."

"Stand up," I said. Something bad was building in me with the disrespect he was showing toward me, but I was trying hard to keep both swolled up feet on top of it.

He stayed still. "I'll keep sitting, thank you. Looks like you could use the rest yourself. Sit back down."

I was sure a few days ago when I still had so much ugly inside me, that if he'd talked to me like he was talking to me now, by that point he'd not be saying nothing no more to nobody. Ever.

He looked back up. "If you're going to do something, please get on with it. I'm not going to try to stop you. If you're not, sit down."

I paced slow for a minute up the cracked walk and then took another seat. I thought the old man had definitely turned swampy between the ears, and standing up was killing my feet.

"You should be fearing me right now, Preacher."

"Probably so."

"You don't fear me?" I asked.

He shook his head.

"You did. I saw it in your eyes."

"Yes, for a very short time."

"You think I'd be coming back one day?"

"I thought you may. I quit concerning myself about it a long time ago."

I knew the bad of what I was capable of before the storm, and from what I could tell about any of it, he was the luckiest preacher to ever live.

"I feared you back when I had quite a lot you could take away from me. And I haven't preached in almost twenty years, so call me Mr. Fletcher or you can call me Simon. Either will do."

I studied the condition he looked to be in. He reminded me of some once preaching folks who'd gotten in a bad way that I'd known in Shady.

"You lost the calling," I said.

"Oh, no."

I kept looking him over. "You seem…different."

"I've just been led to a different path."

"To where?"

"Well, right now I'm resting on this porch."

"What after that?"

"Actually, let me correct… I wasn't led to a different path, it's just the one I was on didn't go where I thought it would. I never saw it leading here, certainly."

"So where you think you're heading now?"

"I don't concern myself with tomorrows anymore."

"Why not?" I asked.

"Why so curious?"

He glanced at me and then stared ahead.

I rocked a while and thought about it and then said, "I don't really know."

"To wherever my path ends is where I'm heading. That's a nice, short answer. Not a good one, but…these are comfortable chairs, don't you think?"

He nodded to his own question.

"Where's your wife?"

He suddenly looked dead at me and put a hand on mine. "Do you wish to sit and talk old times with her? Reminisce?"

He kept staring at me and I kept staring at him. I pulled my hand away from his. He began talking louder than he ever had.

"So you came to visit Louisa?"

"That ain't why I'm here."

"Well, that's good because Louisa ran off to California about the time you went off to prison."

"Ran off. Why?"

"You'd need to ask her that, but she told me that she wanted to become an actress, like Marilyn Monroe. She always looked up to, almost worshipped Marilyn. But unfortunately for Louisa, she was never offered any real roles to play, but she did end up starring in a few movies where she took off all of her clothes and had intercourse with men, lots of men in a couple of the films, is what I've heard. I haven't seen them. She left early one morning a few weeks after your arrest. She informed me of her intentions in a letter of becoming a movie star."

He turned back to stare at the Dumpster and I couldn't say a word for the longest time.

"So how'd all of that work out for her?"

"She started shooting drugs into herself, got in quite a bit of trouble over money and different things and she ended up spending three years in a women's prison out there. She's moved back home to her parents' farm over in Tazewell County now. Been there since the early seventies."

I blew out a big breath of air. It seemed like another month passed between us before I said, "What's she doing now?"

"She lives in a bedroom with the shades drawn, when she's not in the mental institution in Daleville. I don't know the last time she's actually spoken. Louisa is incapable of taking care of herself. The disorders she's afflicted with seem to change with each new doctor and advance in psychiatry. I don't think they're helping her any."

"What do you figure's wrong with her?"

He shook his head. "I believe only God knows the answer to that."

I glanced at him to study on him some more because there still was little emotion at all in his voice telling me such a story. A car filled with people passed the motel and the preacher waved after it honked. I noticed he didn't smile anymore so quick at other folks like he used to, but what smile he did have seemed natural, like it didn't before.

"So I take it you ain't married no more."

He turned to me. "We divorced. I haven't spoken to her since you made me apologize to her, what was that, twenty-two years ago or so? I do keep in touch with her parents."

I turned my head away from those big bug eyes drilling a hole through me. "Is all that what made you stop preaching?"

"One of the older kids saw you and Louisa together through the window, and then what happened when I walked in the room. And he told others what he saw. And they told others. Once Louisa left, rumors began floating through the valley… Let's just say, according to them you weren't the first young man she found company with in our bed. And anyway, it's a long story but the state ended up taking back the children. I began losing my congregation and my ability to pay the mortgage on the church and farm. In the end I guess it can be best summed up that I needed to find a new occupation very soon after you came into our lives."

"So you've been blaming me for you losing your faith and all your troubles?"

"I've quit trying to find blame or reason for anything, son. It's really such a terrible waste of time. And I never said I lost faith."

"You lost your calling though."

"I lost one church and found another."

"Where'd that be?"

"Wherever I am. I now tend the wolves and the sheep. Just not from a pulpit. I feel so much more useful with dirty hands. That has been a blessing."

I remembered how he'd told me once his calling was to tend the sheep, not the wolves, which he said I was. "So you've been here ever since?"

"For a while I tried to find Louisa in California. I did eventually find her, but she had friends who made sure that I couldn't get near her. In fact, I ended up in a hospital out there, their clear message being that I never get near her again. I came back, and with everything in such a mess I soon had to work at different places like many do to simply get by. I was employed as a short-order cook for several years at a truck stop just up the road. I enjoyed the work. Dreadful on the feet and back, though."

"Your brother help you out any through all this?"

"Which brother?"

"Your brother, the judge."

"Oh, yes," he said, nodding. "He did until the FBI arrested him on a long list of obstruction of justice and bribery charges."

I leaned forward, spit, and just shook my head with all he was telling me.

"Did he go to jail?"

"He's in prison now. The federal penitentiary in Petersburg. I go see him once a month."

"Damn, Preacher," I said.

"You curse however much you please in my presence, but stop calling me 'preacher.' It's a title I no longer feel fits properly."

I glanced down the empty-looking motel and the mostly empty weedy lot.

"You live here or work here?"

"Both. This oasis for the troubled and poor is owned by a man named Dominic Calbono. Wealthy man, but a good man. He uses it as a tax shelter and it shelters and feeds and clothes those who need it."

He suddenly turned and looked me over up and down. "You look to be doing well for yourself since being released from prison. Or like I asked before, did you escape?"

"I paid a lot of time I should've never had to pay. Every

long second of it. You think you know me, you always did, but you didn't know me then and you don't know me now."

"I may know more about you than you would like to admit."

"You may not know much at all about anything."

He nodded. "That's certainly a fact," he said.

I was starting to get raw again with so many old wounds and his smart-ass, well-educated ways, but then something in me broke as I looked at my bare feet and the ends of my trousers all torn and ratty, and I started chuckling for some reason, and that chuckle turned into a belly laugh for a couple of minutes.

I kept trying to keep it inside me through it all because the preacher never cut a smile, but it felt so good to laugh. I hadn't laughed loud like that since I was a teenager. Wasn't nothing to laugh about for sure, but it seemed right then by the way it came on me that sometimes, those are the times when, somewhere inside, a person really needs to just plain laugh until whatever really caused it is all out of you.

I was still trying to keep it all in me when a small rusty car with no hubcaps and a broken antenna pulled up in front of us.

A young woman got out of the car, ran around the other side, and got a baby out that she situated up near one shoulder, then she grabbed a sack full of groceries and kicked the door closed, breezing by us. She looked to have the energy of forty of me.

"You're home early," the preacher said as she went by so full of life.

"Have to go right back out," she yelled from inside the office. "I'll change her."

I looked at the preacher's hand and didn't see a wedding band, just like I hadn't seen one on her and figured the preacher didn't have the good and bad luck of marrying too young for him again. She was pretty, and looked a lot like his ex-wife.

"She work here with you?" I asked.

"She helps out when she can between her two jobs and I babysit for her when she needs it."

The woman blew back out the door, kissed him on top of the head and, glancing at me with a cautious look, said, "Be home before ten, Pappy. Faith is in her playpen and will need a bottle soon."

The preacher nodded as the baby started crying inside and the woman rushed to her car. She looked at me again as she started it up then looked back at the preacher and gave a quick wave before she drove away.

"She your daughter?" I asked.

He stared off in the distance for a long time, watching the occasional car go by, and I wasn't sure whether he'd heard what I asked or he didn't want to answer me.

"I'm not sure why I'm going to tell you this, but I've just prayed on it and I believe I will. She's actually your daughter," he finally finished saying.

I now was standing in front of him.

He looked up. "And that beautiful little baby you hear crying inside is your granddaughter."

Chapter 13

"Such a thing can't be," I said.

All I heard was the noises coming from the baby girl in the office, and the sounds that came from her were as deafening as prison loudspeakers.

I kept hearing her and hearing her, as the preacher kept staring at me. He finally leaned back in his rocker, raised one hand up behind him and pecked on the window with his knuckles, before waving and doing things with his hand and fingers like the window was a movie screen, and he was putting on some sort of show for her. He kept staring at me as he did it, his face blank as an iced-over pond. I turned a step to leave.

"Children and grandchildren change your life in an instant, so I've heard."

"Uh-huh…" I took another step backward.

"And 'uh-huh' would mean what."

I didn't answer as he took his hand from the window and placed it back on the armrest. Then he began shaking his head slow back and forth and I didn't know what he was doing until I figured out how our eyes were moving like he was on the other side of a mirror from me. He was mocking what I'd been doing.

"You can shake your head all you want," he said after he stopped shaking his head, "but I feel certain that it won't change anything. I've tried it myself to no avail."

I'd been all out of breath and pointing at him the whole time, and I quit shaking my head and lowered my finger that I had aiming dead at his chest.

He crossed one leg easy over the other and closed his eyes again for a few moments in ease and peacefulness as I was looking there at him. He never even gave notice to a gnat buzzing around one big ear. He started humming some old song I didn't know. It sounded like something a church organ would play. There was no doubt that he was the strangest preacher and one of the oddest fellers I'd ever run across, because only the hard cold truth ever seemed to come out of him, among the other odd things about him.

I knew by his whole expression that he was telling me the truth. And even if he didn't speak and behave in that stern honest way of his all of the time, there still just wasn't a reason why he wouldn't be saying nothing other than the truth to me about such a thing. That's what scared me the very most taking in what all he'd just said.

Preacher Simon Fletcher was peculiar for certain, but he

seemed like he was anything but crazy after talking to him for that last few minutes. He was one of those people too right in the head to ever get along good in this world with anybody or anything, is what he was.

I was still studying him and what he'd told me when I had a sudden flash in my mind of the young woman who'd just drove away. And be damned, I remembered right then that when I'd watched her, there was something about her, whether in how she moved or spoke, or both, that reminded me…of me.

The baby inside squalled loud all of a sudden. I leaned past the preacher just as he turned to look, too, and both of us peered through the window and I saw her on her tiptoes, looking right at me with her little hands holding on to the top of a big cardboard TV box that didn't have a top and she was peeping over and confined in. She didn't have nothing on but a diaper and had curly hair the dark color of mine.

"Such a precious little thing. So precious," the preacher said, sort of talking to himself, at least I thought he was. Then he turned to me. "You would have to be amazed, I would think."

The fear that had quaked through me a couple of minutes before started growing even more, a sort of fear I'd never felt before. I didn't know what to do, but I had to do something, so I did what came to me first and I started hurrying away from the motel and when I say hurrying, I mean I was running. I was running and hobbling as fast as I could go and was about halfway across the lot when the preacher yelled.

"I figured as much! You should run and run fast, and find another place like Shady Hollow where you can live the rest of what short life you have left lawless and reckless and drunk, and die without a care or consequence, having a big laugh about everything to the very worthless end," he said. "Worthless."

I turned and he was standing facing me but I kept going even faster.

"I didn't fear you because you are weak. You can be strong but you don't choose it. You're not a man to be feared. Look at you…you're nothing more than a common coward is what you are."

I'd never been called a coward in my whole life by nobody. Nobody.

I stopped and turned to look again, but he had his back to me going inside. Even though I knew I hadn't been a coward but only in a couple of tight situations in my whole life where being a coward was a wise and maybe the only bet to make, and just like I knew that even the bravest ain't strong in every single situation, I felt like a coward sure enough right then.

I went down to one knee all of a sudden, I guess overcome by a lot of things but mostly from just being me. I didn't want a daughter or granddaughter. I didn't deserve or know what to do with them is why, and I knew I wouldn't bring nothing but heartache and trouble to them. They were both so beautiful and pure in the eyes that I knew they didn't get much of what they were made of from me.

I went from a knee to a sit and even a good fifty yards away, I could still hear the baby crying ever so often, and then I heard the screen door bouncing to a close.

When I looked up, the preacher was walking toward me and I checked his hands to make sure he wasn't toting nothing like a baseball bat or anything that launched bullets.

I went to stand just as he stopped a dozen yards away. He glared at me and then threw a pair of old leather shoes that landed near me, one hitting the ground before it bounced off my chest.

"Man who spends his life taking advantage of others and running from responsibility needs a pair of decent shoes," he said. "Now leave before I call the sheriff's office to have you hauled away again."

He walked back toward the motel when I yelled, "I didn't mean to do wrong to you or your wife, Preacher. And you can't be judging me like you're doing because you don't know nothing about me. I ain't worthless!"

I couldn't believe I'd just yelled what I did because nothing so pitiful and weak had ever come out of me before except in the storm when I was talking to God himself.

The preacher didn't turn but said walking farther from me, "You go quickly now and take your self-misery down the road to somewhere else. I don't have the time or energy to waste on an adult child anymore. I have a hungry baby to feed."

Once he got back to the office, he closed the screen door and then the wooden one. I stayed still and looked for a little bit to see if he was watching me out the windows, but he wasn't, and I wondered if he was calling up the law on me even though I couldn't figure what in the world they'd ever arrest me over being that the preacher wouldn't make up some story about me, being he told nothing but the truth, as he saw and judged it anyway.

I sat there and hoped if there really was a god, that he wasn't nowhere as strict as that preacher. I figured that even the preacher himself wouldn't make out too good on judgment day, if he was. Things might get right hot for him, too.

Remembering back years right then, when I first had to be under the custody of the preacher as ordered by his twin brother when we all looked quite a bit younger, he had called me an ignorant weedy garden of a person, and now as a grown man...I hadn't been around him but for a few minutes and he'd already called me a worthless coward adult child.

I don't know why I even cared what he thought of me or anything else at all, but I did. I guess because mostly I didn't know nobody else to find and talk to who knew me when I was somebody else. Outside of maybe trying to look up a couple of old prison pards, I reckon he was right then about the closest thing I had in way of a friend—even though he'd called in the boat that took me downriver for my whole adult life, and that just a few days before, I was going to kill him over it.

I was a mess with it all, pulled on the shoes he'd thrown, and they fit fair enough. I tried to tie the laces, but my fingers were shaking so bad I just ended up making a knot in each shoe and stuck the ends down into the heels. I stood and started walking best I could toward the highway, and looked back every so often at the motel but didn't see the preacher no more. After a time, I couldn't hear the little beautiful baby hollering, either, no matter how hard I tried.

I talked to myself about I don't know what all to get myself together, and tried to tuck in what was left of my shirt that the wilderness hadn't eaten or I hadn't torn off for hand bandages, and was getting ready to stick my thumb out to get as far as I could from that place, but when I took a good look up and down myself as dirty and beat-up as I looked, I knew I was burning daylight trying to bum a ride being that I'd just had a terrible time a few days or few weeks before when I was wearing new clothes with decent money in my pocket and toting a nice new traveling bag.

I dropped my arm and took off walking, feeling numb like if life were a game as Uncle Ray had once told me, the game was over a long time ago and I'd done came in dead last when my nickname was "Luck," before I'd ever played my first real hand in a big game. I remembered how Uncle Ray had told me I didn't know nothing about the business of being a man back then, about real pain.

He was sure right about that.

The more I walked, the more the numbness left me and I just started feeling sick. I felt the terrible sick feeling I figured only a coward would know, because I'd only gotten a whiff of it a couple of times during my weakest moments. It became like a heavy wet blanket all over me, twisting me around the throat. I was choking on it, and that's when I turned around. Of all the hurting and mean and sad things I'd had to shave with and sleep with all of those years, I couldn't spend another minute feeling what I was feeling on the side of that highway with that baby girl pulling me back.

I figured that moment right there, I was carrying a feeling on me that my own dad carried or had carried with him, running off on me and Ma like I always figured he did, even though she'd never say anything about him.

As I turned around and limped back to the motel, I guessed my own dad must've been a stronger or meaner man than me to carry such a load. But I doubt he ever got too far in life with it as heavy as it was. I suspect if he had any decent in him at all, it'd probably killed him by now.

It took me at least three times as long to walk my way back to the motel as to leave it. When I went to open the office door, I found it locked. So I peeped through a faded window curtain and saw the preacher nursing the baby with a bottle. He looked up at me once, but then his eyes went back to his business like I wasn't even standing there.

I took a seat in the same chair I'd been sitting in an hour or so before, but moved it to a shadier area as the day had gotten so hot and the air so still and dry that I was about to wither up to nothing. I closed my eyes still feeling sore to my bones and the numbness in my insides. Mostly I just felt the glory and dread of it all like I'd felt when he'd first told me the big news. I rocked and rocked in that chair, put my head back and hoped for a breeze. I didn't feel nothing close to good, but at least I didn't feel like a coward no more. I'd walked back to have a sit-down with that hard preacher.

It was dark when I woke.

I didn't know what time it was, whether it was late at night or early in the morning. I didn't feel the hollow numbness anymore and I wasn't feeling confused or scared out of my dirty clothes like I was before. I knew the minute I opened my eyes where I was and what had happened, and the only reason I'd opened them was that I'd gotten cold and was so stiff when I went to move, that I couldn't.

Across my shoulders and over my lap and legs was a quilt that smelled like something a dog had been laying on for a bed. I guess that or the smell of me had kept the bugs off, because I only had a few bites.

I came awake clear and calm as an easy late morning and for a good while I stared at the highway and it was seldom when a set of headlights would pass.

The young woman's car I'd seen earlier was now parked next to the motel office. Seeing it is when I started feeling so little and puny inside again because a man who'd turned out like me didn't deserve children and definitely wasn't up to the huge task of living a family life.

I craned my head to look over my right shoulder and saw a yellow bulb burning in the motel office. Looking down the row of rooms, I didn't see any other lights except for the dim occasional bulb burning under the overhang to the doors, or the orange color the inside lamps made on curtains in a couple of rooms.

I went to stand and it took a while feeling like every part of me creaked or was put together wrong. There wasn't nothing that didn't throb.

I moved the old quilt from off my front and instead wrapped it around my back and pulled the edges to my chest. I took careful steps to the office door, dragging a good bit of it behind me. Looking inside, I saw the clock on the wall said it was after two in the morning, but the preacher was sitting in a stuffed chair awake reading the Good Book. I figured he was in there trying to get his calling back to tend to his sheep like preachers I'd heard about in Shady would do forever once they lost the stirring in them or couldn't find their way back to Jesus.

I was gonna tell him that I'd come to realize some things and I wanted to talk with him about the visions I'd had in my dreams and the ones that had changed me in the wilderness.

I guess he finally felt me standing there staring at him because he looked up at me and closed the book careful after he marked where he was reading with a long red paper cross. He stepped over to me, looking like he was trying to keep quiet, opened the two doors, and by the way he came out quick, I could see I wasn't gonna get invited in so I got out of his way.

He walked past me without a look or word, then walked down past several rooms, pulled a key from his sweater pocket and opened a door. He pushed it all of the way open and waved me down with a finger.

When I got to where he'd been standing, I peeped in and he'd turned on two lamps in the room. I could see the whole place was filled with clothes and shoes and coats of all kinds for adults and young'uns.

I went to speak but he raised a hand and shook his head. Then he said, "This door will be open in the morning at daylight. You come in here, get what you need, and then be gone. You will leave here before 7:00 a.m. I'll see to it one way or another, I assure you."

I tried again to tell him what I'd been thinking on when he walked toward me fast as I was standing in the doorway, so I backed up as he closed and locked the door. He walked down to the next door and I followed him as he unlocked it. Once he turned on a light, I saw everything looked old and worn-out and there wasn't a TV set or phone or nothing like that in the room, but it looked to have a good bed and it smelled clean and, overall, it was about a thousand times nicer than where I'd lived my whole life. Looking at the bed made me want to stretch out full in it right then just for the feel of laying in such a nice big bed.

He pulled money out of a pocket that was folded in half and kept together with a paper clip. He laid it on the desk, right next to a Bible. "Take both when you leave or neither. There's a truck stop two miles down the highway in the direction you were running earlier, and a bus station in Harlow another couple of miles farther down. If you don't want to keep the Bible, give it to someone else. You leave and never come back. Ever."

He stuck the key he'd opened the door with back in his pocket and closed the door behind him as he left.

I never got to have the talk I wanted to have with him as I went to the window and pulled back the curtain and saw he was gone. I looked over the room a little more, saw the bathroom, so I walked that way in a big hurry to relieve myself because I was in a bad way to do it. Then I turned the sink faucet on full blast and scooped cup after cup of water into my hands, drinking it down in gulps.

When I felt like I couldn't hold any more, I looked up and

saw a mirror but my reflection was dim in it with only the one light the preacher had turned on near the bed. I saw a switch on the wall, flipped it, and when I turned back to look at myself, all I could do was to turn that light off again.

I didn't even recognize the filthy ghost looking back at me. I'd never seen that man before in my whole life. The eyes didn't even belong to me.

Chapter 14

I stumbled to the bed and fell on it, and as much as my back and legs and my sore head were loving that big soft bed, my mind wasn't in the mood for sleep, laying there with so many troublesome thoughts. I was feeling so much better with the sleep I'd had in the chair and the food Preacher Washington had given me, but that only made my real worries worse and the more real to me, because when you're plain starving and about to die, those are the things that rule a man's mind above other things, not the stuff that will kill you slow and without no mercy at night when you have a full belly and a bed to suffer in.

So after I'd took off all my clothes and got under the sheets for a long time, I couldn't stand being there by myself in the dark no more, so I went and took a hot shower, and it was the longest shower of my whole life.

I used the small cake of soap until it was gone and when I got out and dried off, the stink in my room coming from the clothes I'd just been wearing hit me, and it was so bad that instead of trying to wash them out, I wrapped myself in the quilt I'd had around me before which I hadn't damaged too bad, and I took the clothes to the dump box and threw them in.

I was embarrassed for myself to have smelled as bad as I did and didn't even know it. I knew I was a little strong with such an effort to get out of those hills without a proper bath for so many days, but I didn't know the full extent of it until that long washing I took which reminded me immediately of what I should smell like under more hospitable conditions.

I don't know how either preacher I'd talked to had been able to not mention it, and more than that, I don't know how they'd been able to get within wind of me at all. I now knew though why that nice black preacher kept his face pointing out the open window of his truck pretty much the whole time.

So I threw out all I'd worn. The night was so quiet outside— a real country kind of quiet with no sounds of steel on steel or snoring from every direction or guard keys clanging—and I wished there was another chair to sit outside my room. I didn't want to be inside by myself anymore with the things I was gonna be thinking on and walls around me so close.

But there wasn't a chair except the two by the office, and I was buck naked under that quilt anyway. I went back in my room, flipped the sheets over from where I'd been laying under them earlier, and I grabbed the Bible from the desk after I looked again at the money the preacher had left for me. I counted it and it was fifty dollars. Same amount of money the state had given me just six or eight or fourteen days before being that I'd lost count of a day or week somewhere.

I put the money down and wondered what my next six or nine days might bring. More trouble and another fifty dollars to leave from somewhere. I hoped not. Even though I was getting cash handed to me, I was getting poorer and worse off each time it happened. As bad as the thought was, it seemed like I was better off behind bars thinking about Shady Hollow when Ma and Bernie were still alive in my mind than out in the world my ma had always told me was dangerous and a place I wasn't ready for and finding her and all of it gone.

Anyway, I laid in that nice bed for a couple of hours reading things here and there about different important Bible people, flipping the book open and putting my finger down on a passage I thought God might want me to read. I was trying my earnest best to come around to his kind of thinking. If nothing else, something in those thin pages might come in handy to me in the position I was in, if God happened to be keeping up with me on that night in that motel for whatever reason he would do such a thing.

I wasn't even sure another man living before had ever been in the position that I was in, laying there clean but bare and poor as there is, and with nothing except what charity I'd been given, and with no old family I knew of but a new young one all of a sudden. A new family who I didn't know and couldn't do nothing for. So I thought he might find the whole thing interesting if nothing else.

I was sure he'd seen much worse things, much worse, and much worse off folks, but maybe not the particular ups and downs, most downs it seemed for so long, of my life.

I started reading about a man named Saul who changed his name to Paul, or Paul to Saul, I can't never remember which. That's when I heard the sound of a key working a door lock two rooms up from mine.

I peeped out the curtain to look at the sky and it looked to be five or six in the morning.

I opened my room door a crack and saw the preacher wearing a robe, with skinny legs and bare feet poking out the bottom, and he had a knit hat on his head. He never looked back down the row toward me. When he went back in the office, I went up to the room he'd unlocked wearing my quilt, opened the door, turned on just one light and locked the door from the inside. I found a good set of drawers and socks and got myself outfitted in the best clothes I could find.

When I walked out of there a good half hour later, I had on a nice suit of clothes similar to what Uncle Ray used to wear. I'd traded in the shoes the preacher had thrown at me with a pair of broken-in black boots that looked better and were roomier and didn't rile my sore heel too bad.

I picked a red tie and handkerchief to go with it but folded both up and stuck them in a pocket and then picked out an empty wallet which I put my cash in. I found another bag not as nice as the one I'd bought new, but it was all right. In it I put in another set of clean drawers and black socks, another white button shirt, a white T-shirt cut off around the arms, and a baseball cap that had a racing car on the front of it and a thin jacket, the cap and jacket to keep off bad weather I was sure I'd run into sooner than later.

The last thing I threw in was a shaving kit of toilet items just like they'd issue in prison, and with all of it, I turned off the light, closed the door and went back to my room. Once there I brushed my teeth, combed my hair out real good and got out my pocketknife, about the only thing besides a couple of dollars that survived the week in the mountains.

I twisted my hair all the way down to the bottom where I held it with one hand, and with the other I took the knife and cut my hair straight across the back so now it fell just at my neck. It was the first real haircut I'd had in over ten years. I wet my new comb and combed what I had left back and over my ears, and then I heated my scratchy beard with a washrag for a good five minutes before I shaved it off careful, because the razor that I'd found beside the sink with the toothbrush and paste and soap had a bad bite to it if I went too fast.

When I was done with it all, I didn't feel like a new man but I surely looked like one. I looked better, but saying I looked better than I'd looked just an hour before wasn't saying much.

I got my things together, went to the window and the sky was starting to turn from black to a dark gray. I had a strong feeling the preacher, being such a man of his word, was gonna call the law on me quick if I weren't out of there soon like he'd told me to do. I figured he had one eye watching the highway.

I took a last look at my room and the bed that I hadn't slept a wink in, locked the door behind me and pulled it closed.

By the time the sun did come up, I was at a truck stop two miles away in a booth by myself sipping on a hot cup of coffee. An hour later, I had a glass of tomato juice and two more cups of coffee in me and three orders of sausage gravy and biscuits. The gravy wasn't as good as Ma's, not even close, but it was better than the gravy they served in prison over dried-out toast that could pass for paving bricks.

I was thankful for the meal whether it tasted good or not, and cleaned all three plates. But the gravy did remind me of Ma and old mornings.

By nine o'clock, the place was busy as a kicked anthill and I was ready for my check to get on out of there as far as I could go. I'd sat the whole time wondering where to head to, knowing I wasn't ready in mind or spirit to go searching for Amanda Lynn just yet. I'd never want her to see me in such a way. And I knew for sure I wasn't ready and maybe never would be ready to take on a grown young'un and a granddaughter. It would be more like they'd have to take me on, and as sorry as I was, that was something that even I couldn't do to them.

I thought about heading up to Atlantic City for a vacation. I'd never took a vacation but had heard about them and how fun they were, and Atlantic City was a place I'd heard so many good things about from men who tended to have the same appetites as I'd always had as a younger person. But I didn't have enough loot to get there and I wasn't gonna steal to get there. So I just figured I'd take a bus down to Raleigh, North Carolina, and drift around a while being it was close to where Amanda Lynn may still live. I decided I'd try to think of it as a vacation, being I'd heard it was a fair-sized city and I'd never spent time in a big city. I basically figured I might be able to rustle up some kind of vacation there because I needed one.

Raleigh was only an hour from Durham County. I'd be bound to be able to find a card game or pool hall and make enough to live on somehow until the day I got myself and my situation sorted out and improved upon. I seriously doubted I could still play a fiddle good enough to make any quarters. But my hopes were a little high that morning with my new look and money and being able to sit and drink coffee around normal people who were a lot unlike me but didn't look like they'd taken note of it yet.

It was getting late in the morning and I started looking around for my waitress, not wanting to miss the bus and unsure of when it would run. I saw a couple of the other gals pulling off their aprons all happy and I figured it was shift change around there. I pushed up on a set of aluminum blinds by my window and was checking out the big rigs parked everywhere and thought I may even be able to hitch a ride south for cheap.

"You finished with this?"

I turned to the voice and looked up past the apron to the smile, and it was a smile coming from someone I'd just saw the evening before.

It was my daughter.

I sat stunned and scared, not knowing what to do, being I was in that place running from her, and here she was suddenly waiting on me.

I nodded and she started taking away my dishes. When she turned to walk away, "I ain't finished yet!" flew out of me in a deep voice. I don't know why I said it but I did. And it came out awkward and way too loud.

She had my plate resting on an arm as she smiled again, almost with a laugh. "Well, what else can I get you, honey?" she said.

I looked at her for a long time and I could tell she didn't recognize me from the day before. I got control of my vocals and said slow and careful, "Cold glass of water, please, ma'am."

"Be right back," she said.

By the time she'd got back with my water, all she would find at my table was the fifty dollars I'd left, and I hoped she'd get to pocket all of it. At least I might be able to give her something, even though I hadn't earned it. It made me feel a little better about things as I walked out of that truck stop.

I walked and walked down that highway and it was a busy road but I didn't pay any mind to the cars and trucks rumbling by, I just kept walking. I'd done the best I could for my daughter and granddaughter, I was sure of it, leaving them all the money I had but nothing else bad, like leaving them me. I figured sometimes it took courage in a man to walk away, and figured if the preacher thought long on it, he might even come to the same reasoning.

But each step I took, I kept thinking about my pretty blond-haired daughter and her little baby girl with the dark curly hair who was yelling in that cardboard box. I wished I could have held both of them for a long time, at least once. One long holding that I could take with me.

I figured if I were to try to all of a sudden be a part of my daughter's life somehow, it would take years for her to ever want to hug a man like me who'd been such an empty place in her heart for her and who'd turned out to be so little, if she'd ever want to hug me at all. I knew all about those feelings, 'cause they were the same ones I'd carried for my own father, whoever he was and wherever he was at. It would take her years to forgive me, I figured, if she ever could.

My daughter looked to be struggling with her life but doing as good with it all as most good folks do with their normal sorts of difficult and serious struggles. She was doing much better than I ever did for sure with all of it, and she had a good steady honest man in the preacher helping her and being a real father to her. When I was thinking about all that, I realized I didn't even find out my daughter's name. I did remember hearing the precious little angel was named Faith.

I just hoped if I ever did find a way to make even a little something of myself, I could at least figure on a way to get money to them. It looked that they could use it. Maybe when I was of some use then I could even tell them who I was and tell them how sorry I was for not being around much, and I was trying to change from the empty angry person I'd grown up to be.

I kept walking and walking, trying my best to pull away from them and get closer to Amanda Lynn with each step. I didn't have any business in messing up her life, either, I'd already done plenty of that, though not on purpose, but I did need her help to un-mess mine. My life wasn't much, but it had been growing on me that it had to be worth something. Even as low and uncertain as I felt about some things, something in me said it was at least worth a try because it was my best bet, if not my only play. I just had to see her for so many reasons.

So right there at mile marker eighty-five on Route 325 going through Lee County, Virginia, is the point in my life where I started drifting south and then I headed east once I hit the North Carolina line near Jackson County in the Smoky Mountains.

It took me three months to get all the way to Raleigh. I stopped in towns along the way to pick up pocket money in pool halls. Though I did a little hustling—but only as much as I had to—I didn't outright steal nothing like I could have. I even pushed a broom sometimes like the old days for a place to sleep out of the weather.

I got picked up five or six times in different places for vagrancy or having an open beer in public, little crimes like that, even had to dang beg to get arrested once by taking a leak on a policeman's shoe. But each time I got handcuffed and hauled in I wanted to be, because I could get a shower and a few hot meals and a decent bed to sleep in before they'd kick me to the curb about the same time the walls started giving me the night shakes. It was starting to get cold, too. Summer had ended, so I'd usually get myself arrested on the coldest rainiest days if I couldn't find shelter somewhere else.

I was pretty much just a man who didn't have nothing and didn't really know who I was inside. I was trying to become something decent. I hoped that's what a person saw if they'd look at me, but most tended not to look at me, like I didn't even exist a lot of the time. They'd look sometimes like they could look right through me if they didn't look around me.

I was a drifter in all senses of the word, except I was drifting to a certain somebody as fast as the current I found myself in would take me.

But all of that was about to change the day I left my cot at a downtown homeless shelter where I'd been living in Raleigh on my vacation, and got a ride with a man who'd showed up, going down the long line of bunks looking for workers.

Laying on my back, reading the preacher's Bible he'd made me take with the fifty dollars, I was wondering at the same time what my daughter was doing that day being all so busy like she was, when a man stopped at my cot and eyed me over before I stood up and he asked if I wanted work. I asked him what kind of work he was looking for me to do, and he told me he needed day laborers for a hog farm over in Durham County.

I heard the words Durham County and a strongness stirred inside me and I didn't ask him the pay or the hours or nothing about the job. I just grabbed my bag and took off walking to where he pointed—an old army truck with a canvas tarp over the long back that was parked out front. I stood in line for my turn and then climbed up into it with about two dozen other men who he'd picked or helped stand up. Nobody tended to look at one another, we just all looked out the back of the tarp at the daylight once we sat down.

Hog farming was nothing I ever figured would suit me as an occupation, and I didn't know nothing about it and never did want to. But I felt pretty good in my place on a bench seat with the others. I told the man I'd work, and I'd lately been trying to tell the truth as much as I could, even if it pained me doing it, so I figured I'd give him a good eight-hour day. I'd never worked an eight-hour day before. But all I really wanted, and needed, was a ride to get closer to Amanda Lynn.

I wasn't sure, but I finally thought I might be ready to see her. Looking in the mirror that same morning, my eyes looked clear and my face had a calm look about it. My circumstances weren't ideal, but I was as ready as I ever would be.

I never did realize the day I got let out of prison that it would be months before I'd feel ready to see her. I always figured locked up that I'd be more than ready to see her as dern soon as I could once I was a free man. But that ain't the way it was once out. The things that happened peeled off the husk of me and changed the insides of me like they did for the good.

Things I'd never ever figured on but Ma had once predicted when I was a boy as she was studying the lines on my palms.

I was ready getting on that hog farmer's truck, hitching a ride to work for a day and hopefully see her soon. No good reason to feel such a way really, but I did. All those years I'd never figured that's the way I'd be traveling to see her, and never knew I'd be the man I was that would show up. But it was what it was and I was who I had become. For some reason even it being so different than the dreams I'd had, I was all right with all of it.

I wasn't prosperous and those were hard times in some hard ways and I carried that on me. But I felt a lot more like the person she'd known a long time ago than the man I'd been for those years since. Everything about me was rough but my eyes, which had changed back to what they once looked like.

I just prayed she'd look at them first.

Chapter 15

I'd never seen or smelled so much hog shit in my life and changed my mind about day laboring for that man the minute the truck stopped. I decided instead to give him two dollars for the ride. He already had plenty of help I figured and he wouldn't mind me leaving too much. I tried to walk away as soon as the stink hit me and we were all being corralled inside a fence that was about as tall as what I'd known in prison.

But there were a half-dozen serious working men waiting on us as we jumped down from the truck bed. They didn't waste any time not listening to whatever anybody was saying, while pushing and walking the gang of us to a huge building with short cinder block walls and the rest open above.

Whatever I said, trying to go the other direction, one of them just nodded or ignored what I was saying and kept pushing me forward.

Inside of that huge building, there weren't any hogs, but there had been a thousand of them in there it looked like because the whole place stank like only a thousand hogs and what they'd left behind would. A man got on a bullhorn and told us how they'd had machinery go down that usually did what we were about to do, and that was why we were there.

We had to put on plastic suits that made us look like astronauts on TV, and we pulled on high rubber boots. Then they assigned us all jobs and I don't know why, I guess just my usual good luck, but I ended up holding a long broom handle and on the end was a hard piece of rubber three feet across and a foot high. One side of the rubber was smooth, and the other side had knots all over it like a car tire.

After a whole morning of scrubbing and pushing crap with my rubber broom behind what a bulldozer missed, along a huge concrete floor that stretched as long and as wide as a football field, they called dinner break and let us go outside to where a pickup truck had parked. I couldn't get that suit off of me quick enough because I was soaked with sweat and stuff not worth going on about.

There were a bunch of shiny tall pots sitting beside the truck, and the feller driving got out and told us to grab a tray and a fork and get in a line. We all did as told once we had our suits off as he took off the lids.

He dished out some kind of meat I figured was barbequed pork onto my tray from one of the big pots, then a pile of rice with some kind of pork gravy on it, and a couple of slices of loaf bread. The drink was the same kind of green-colored sugar water I'd drank my fill of while in prison.

As much as I didn't want to eat a meal of pork right then and especially the gravy, I was hungry and I ate all they gave me. They did give each man a fair share of food, and I noticed the other fellers working with me had a good appetite, too.

There wasn't a lot of talking going on between any of us sitting near the truck in a mowed field, except for three men who seemed to know each other as friends and kept to themselves laughing a lot as friends do. But basically the Mexicans sat with the Mexicans, the blacks with the blacks, and the whites sat with the whites. I wasn't sure who to sit with so I just sat by myself like a few others did, and I figured if we all started going out there every day, the loners would end up in a group, too, eating in the quiet.

The lunch break ended quick, about ten minutes after we all got to sit, but I found out the afternoon shift was a sight better than the morning one, because they switched what we'd been doing and I got to man a hose instead of a rubber broom.

I tried my best not to spray hog shit on the man working in front of me, but I couldn't help it sometimes as I'd lose track of what I was doing, or go to scratch somewhere that itched at the wrong time, or he'd stop or get too far ahead and I didn't realize it. Same thing he'd done to me earlier by accident as he'd yelled loud apologizing to me once I'd ripped off my hood and goggles, me upset with the hog crap all over me like a man naturally would be.

It was at the end of the day when we got out of those suits, got to shower off and they herded us back to the big truck, when I told the man standing at the downed tailgate that I had business in Durham County and I didn't need a ride back to Raleigh. He was the same one who'd brought all of us there and he shook his head and told me it wasn't a one-way trip and told me to climb up.

"I said I'm leaving," I said.

"You're right. You're leaving. You're leaving in the truck with the rest of them."

"No, sir, I ain't," I said.

"Get in the truck."

"I'm a free man and I'll go where I want to go," I told him.

He took a step toward me and as he did it I took a bigger one toward him I guess out of nothing else but pure instinct. He looked up at me for a good while and then took a half step back.

"You leave now, you won't get paid. We pay when we get you back to the shelter."

"I'll take my money now. I earned it," I said.

"Get on the truck. Now."

I jumped up into the truck bed and grabbed my bag that they had told us earlier in the day they'd have a man keep an eye on, protecting everybody's belongings. The truck started loud and the man I'd been arguing with was chaining up the tailgate when I jumped back off. I'd never worked an honest day in my life and I wanted to feel that honest money in my pocket.

"I'll take my wages," I said.

"Get back on or I'm gonna see you get back on," the man said, before he turned around and walked away toward a small pickup truck parked about a dozen yards away.

I didn't know what he had in that truck, probably something to persuade me to do what he was telling me to do, so right then I figured I wasn't gonna be getting any honest pay. I saw the big fence gate wide-open for the army truck to go through in front of me, and I figured I'd just mark that day off as one spent on this earth being around shit for nothing. I'd had plenty of worse days—much worse—and one more wouldn't change the balance of nothing, and at least I was finally near Amanda Lynn, I hoped anyway.

I was hoofing it out the gate when I heard that little man's pickup start up. I turned and looked behind me and saw it roaring down the road in my direction. I slowed and finally stopped, and when the truck got almost alongside me, I saw the man had his left hand on the steering wheel, and his right hand was holding a sawed-off pump shotgun that he had pointed at me.

"We seeing eye to eye now," he said.

I looked him dead in the eye. "Let me be," I said. I turned to walk.

"Folks 'round here don't want your type walking around here after dark. You're going back to where you came from."

"You can't stop a free man from walking where he wants to," I said as I started off down the road again.

He gunned the truck, steered it at me and cut the tires so it was blocking the road. And he still had his gun leveled on me.

I looked back at the army truck and old times welled up in me because I'd done had it with the way he was treating me. I walked toward him fast. There was a time when staring down the barrel of a shotgun was a scary thing, but I saw he had no intention of actually shooting nobody.

I took the last few steps and watched his finger playing around the trigger. He tried to pull the gun back when I got too close and then he yelled for me to stop. That's when I ducked, grabbed the barrel and yanked it and half of him out of the truck window. I took the whole thing away from him without trouble and then whacked him on the back of the head with the stock, not near hard enough to hurt him much, but just hard enough where he'd be seeing eye to eye with me now.

He fought to drive away but I still had one hand holding him by the hair, and I pulled him the rest of the way out the window.

He looked back behind him at the man driving the army truck with a look on his face like he was about to die. That's when I let go of him and threw the shotgun way out into some weeds near a swampy tree line. Then I grabbed him by the collar to where he was on his tiptoes.

"You jackass, I'm trying hard as I can to be a good man and didn't want no trouble," I said. "I just wanted to leave, and all I asked for was to get what I earned which you wouldn't give me."

He was shaking so I let him go and he went to reach behind him and I made sure he wasn't pulling out a handgun. He pulled out a bunch of money out of a bank sack and handed it to me.

"What're those other fellers getting?" I asked.

"Just take it."

"I'm gonna take what you owe me."

"Twenty-four dollars," he said all fast and wobbly.

I took out twenty-four dollars from the wad he'd handed to me and shoved the rest down the front of his button shirt.

"You ain't treating people right around here doing things like you just done. You pull what you just pulled on me with the wrong man and you ain't gonna be around much longer. You're all bark. Now I'm leaving here and you need to let me. Let's do right by one another. Do what I'm asking. I'm asking you to do the good by us. You was asking for that knot on your head so I gave it to you, see. Now it's time for us to patch up."

We both turned at the same time as the man in the army truck was now outside of it talking in a walkie-talkie and pointing at us. A whole gang of men running from the farm in different directions started heading for the gate.

Seeing that, I took off at a full sprint toward the wood line. When I looked back, I saw the man I'd just put a little knot on his head searching for his shotgun in the weeds, and there was shooting in my general direction from way off in the distance. I didn't know if they were trying to actually hit me or not or just scare me into stop running, but there was dirt being thrown around me. I felt something fly by my head that was going a lot faster than a bug could fly.

I ran and ran for a long spell and thought I'd put that set of troubles behind me. But the bad luck of it all was there was a state maximum security prison about five miles from that hog farm, and they had two sets of bloodhounds that got after my scent near dark. They stayed on it even through the swamp I swam, and those dogs must've been able to swim, too, because they finally treed me in a scraggly tangle of trees surrounded by six feet of skunk water around mid-night. Soon all I could see looking down was the clouds of skeeters that were driving me into a crazy man and a dozen or two men with flashlights and guns pointed at me, their barrels shining in that light.

One feller, the one who said the least but seemed to be in charge of everybody even though he didn't have a law officer uniform on, looked familiar to me in a real old sort of way. Just before one of the men grabbed me by one leg and jerked me down, I wondered if I may have met him in Shady or prison or the last time I was in Durham County as a kid, but then I knew it was more than that. I remembered Amanda Lynn had an older brother, because we always hid from him just like we did with everyone so none of them would see us together. Amanda Lynn always had told me so serious that me and her were a secret not to be told to nobody.

Ever.

"Stand him up and search him," that man in charge said as I still kept trying to place who he was.

About ten of them wearing sheriff uniforms did what he said, pulling and pushing on me like men do during such times being all out of breath and ready for anything. I was the calmest among them for some reason. I guess I was used to such situations and just so tuckered out on top of that. By that point I didn't know what was worse, the law or those skeeters.

"He don't have but twenty-some dollars on him," one of the deputies said, turning his eyes to the head man who hadn't taken his eyes off of mine.

He walked up to me close and I felt everybody's grip on

me tighten and then handcuffs go around my wrists way too tight like they always do at first.

"Where's the money?" he asked.

"What money?" I said back.

"The money you stole."

"I took my wages."

"Where's the rest of the payroll?" he said quite a bit more serious.

"That feller who I took my share from still has the rest, I reckon," I said.

"I'll ask you once more where it is," he yelled.

"I took what you all owed me for the day's work is all. Ask that dern skinny man over there," I said, trying to point at the jackass who I'd put a knot on his head earlier.

"He's lying," the jackass said, getting closer to me.

"I'm not, either," I said. "He's got the rest of it. If he says he doesn't, check his pockets and his truck. He's hid it somewhere."

The man in charge turned to the twitchy jackass who must've found his shotgun because he had hold of one and it was pointed in my direction. There was a quiet and then I said, "I didn't steal a dang thing from you hog farmers. I gave you all a good day's work and then wanted to just get on my way. I'm telling you that man right there—"

About that time it seemed like everybody started talking at the same time, mostly telling me to shut up and that skinny man came at me quick and I felt something hard crack me against the back of the head, then it felt like I was floating in space.

It was the most peaceful, wonderful feeling, and my mind

and body floated right out of that swamp and back in time twenty-some years to the most peaceful of places and the most wonderful of times and to the prettiest thing I'd ever seen.

I'd been in Durham County only one night and it was my only night ever away from Shady Hollow. By midmorning of the next day, I was ready to sneak off and hitchhike back to Virginia. So far plantation life wasn't anything like I'd hoped, plain dull formal quiet is what it was, and the only thing I liked about that big house and farm was the meals and the fancy bed I'd gotten to sleep on.

While I didn't like all the rules that went along with feeding and I especially didn't like being told how to eat, I'd never had such food. At supper and then at breakfast, it all tasted so good in ways food hadn't tasted good before, and it kept coming plate after shiny white heavy plate and I didn't want it to end. I figured I'd have to put up with the rules about where to put a napkin and not hover over my plate, as Aunt Kate kept reminding me, saying hovering wasn't a proper way to sit at the table. She'd obviously never eaten at a table with my brothers or pards, where at any time you might have to defend your dinner. I figured in Durham County I'd eat the way a person does there, and I'd give her some eating lessons if she ever sat down for a meal in Shady.

She'd laid out brand-new clothes for me to wear that morning right after she'd asked if I'd like to bathe, but I reminded her I'd just done it the day before like she'd told me to do. I'd never worn suspenders before or shoes with soles that were put on them from a factory, and even had never worn a shirt that hadn't been worn a bunch of times by somebody else before I got hold of it.

So after breakfast on this porch overlooking fields and gardens, and watching black folks working while we sat and enjoyed the breeze, I asked what we were going to do with the rest of the day as the hot sun was still covered in dew and low on the horizon. Aunt Kate told me to explore and enjoy the grounds, and then she rang a bell and a white feller who looked to be about fifty and wore a white suit not nearly as white as his skin, came through a couple of glass doors, and he stood beside us after taking his time getting there.

"Mr. Charles will be your escort for the day and show you around," she said.

I stood from the table, said howdy to Charles, told him my name was Ben and shook his hand. He said it was a pleasure to meet me and then said he was at my service, as I noted his grip was dry and like a vise, similar to a handshake you'd expect from a blacksmith or somebody who turned a wrench for a living, not a distinguished-looking old feller in a white suit.

Then he moved to stand behind my seat and all got quiet, and I sat back down but I did turn to look at him now and then as he just kept looking out straight ahead.

I figured I'd try to get Charles to find a deck of cards first and we'd find a place to play a few hands, in case he had money that I could coax from his suit pocket to mine. Then I thought that house had to have a pool table with so many rooms. And if none of that worked out, at the least I figured there had to be some gals about my age working around there who might take to a new face toward the end of the day. Or maybe I could find a fishing pole and something hard to sip on while watching my line because I saw a creek off in the distance winding through a tobacco field.

I still wasn't sure why I was at that plantation and staying with Aunt Kate. She just kept saying the same thing Ma had told me after their big ruckus about me traveling south with her, telling me that spending time in another place besides Shady Hollow would be good for a boy who was about to become a man.

But besides that creek and soft bed and the good food that never ran out, it was way too quiet and slow. I didn't see much to do that I liked, and looking back at Mr. Charles again, I didn't figure him to be the sort to want to spend the day playing poker. A man with his icy blue eyes and vise grip looked to live too much on the serious side of things to enjoy a sporting game of any kind.

It was then that I started wondering if I'd be told soon to work with the rest of those folks sweating in the gardens and fields. Maybe Aunt Kate and Ma thought it would be good for a boy who was about to become a man to get a bitter taste of real work. I didn't want any part of that.

I looked over at Aunt Kate who seemed to just be enjoying watching me by the easy smile on her face. "Would you like anything else?" she asked.

"I couldn't fit in another spoonful of anything no matter how good it was," I said.

Her smile grew even more, but sort of in an alarming way. With just a look from her at Mr. Charles, he took a couple of steps toward her and pulled back her chair. As she went to stand, I said, "You're not my real aunt, just like my uncles ain't never my real uncles, is what I figured a good while back…you and Ma looking so different and all."

She got comfortable again in her chair and with another look, Mr. Charles went back inside and closed the glass doors behind him.

"Your mother and I are good friends. We've known each other since we were little girls. And as we talked about on the ride down last evening, I think it would be best if you didn't speak about where you're from and things of that nature while you're here. This place is so different from where you're from, and I wouldn't want people to get the wrong impression about you and your family. I thought you understood this last night."

"So what am I supposed to tell people who ask things about where I'm from?"

"Tell them you're from Virginia and that your mother and I are old friends, and you're here for a visit and leave it at that. There's no need for anyone to know you live in Shady Hollow or anything about Shady Hollow. It's none of their business."

What she was saying was bothering me. Bad. "Ma always told me being from Shady Hollow wasn't nothing to be ashamed of."

"It's not."

"Then why don't you want me talking about it?"

"Because some people may not understand what you and your mother and I understand…that being from Shady

Hollow or from anywhere else, for that matter, is nothing to be ashamed of. Just please do this for me and if you'd like to talk about it more later, we will."

I was sure we would be speaking on it later because from what I could tell, it was Aunt Kate who was the one who was ashamed about having me there, even though she was the one who invited and brought me there, trying to change me in so many ways to be somebody I wasn't and so quick. I didn't think I needed changing at all. And I thought it most curious that Ma and her were good friends, as different as the two of them were.

"Did you know Ma from Shady?"

"No. Your mom lived here a long time ago."

I looked out at all the colored folks working but couldn't see Ma right in there with them. Nothing about her ever seemed like the farmer type to me. "She worked here?"

"Yes."

"She work out in the sun and got dirty?"

"She worked inside mostly. She helped with things."

"Like Charlie helps you now?"

"Like Mr. Charles? Something like that."

"Not doing what she does in Shady?"

"No. No."

"And she lived in this house?"

"She lived on the estate, in another house."

"Ma never told me any of this," I said.

"We really had the best times. She was and still is one of my closest and dearest friends."

"Why'd she never tell me about living here? She always told

me she bumped around the bottom for a time trying to find her place but never took root nowhere until she got to Shady."

"Sometimes parents tell things about their past to their children when they believe they're old enough to understand them, maybe. You'll have to ask her."

I looked around. "I don't see the harm in letting on about this place. I heard you arguing in her bedroom when you wanted to bring me down here. She didn't want me to come at first. Something bad happened to Ma here, didn't it."

"Well, life can take people in many directions for many reasons. She liked living here but ended up making her home in Shady Hollow. She hopes and believes you'll have a wonderful summer. We both think you'll have a wonderful time here."

"Doing what?"

"Take a day or so to get settled in and look around. I have lots of plans for you. Things I believe you'll enjoy, new things, but for now I'd like for you to relax and meet everyone. Mr. Charles will show you around."

"I'd like to go to a city. I've never seen a big city. Is there one near here?"

"Not far," she said.

"I've never been curious about farming, to be real honest about it."

"You won't be farming."

With another ring of the bell, Mr. Charles came back outside and I got up from the table, and he nodded and called me "sir" for some reason. Then I followed him through the house as he explained and told me things about each room

and then outside to some other buildings. It wasn't long before one time when he turned around, I wasn't behind him
nodding, trying to act like I was interested in any of it.

It was in a huge stable full of horses that I ditched Mr.
Charles so he could keep talking to himself like he seemed
to be doing. I'd spotted a gal about my age and she looked
a ton more pretty and hopefully a lot more fun than he was.
She was across a field and a fence, walking in front of a horse
but even so far away, I could tell she'd spotted me, too, and
found something interesting about me.

I walked by people stooped over and working in the fields,
and I grinned and said howdy to them as I passed but nobody
said much back. Didn't seem to me that there were very
many happy people on that rich plantation besides Aunt
Kate, and she didn't seem that happy, either, when I thought
about it some more. You'd never see so many long tired faces
in Shady, for sure. And you'd definitely never see people
working so hard. I wondered if that whole place was boring
people to death with nobody trying to have any fun. I didn't
know if even some homemade liquor and teardown fiddle
music could wake the place up.

I kept walking and getting nearer, and she and her horse
would walk from me a little bit every so often but not much.
I was almost at hollering distance when I could see her face
clear for the first time, and it was the prettiest face I'd ever
seen. She was wearing cutoff dungarees and a button shirt
was tied around her middle. The collar on her shirt was open
and for a long minute or more I couldn't take my eyes off
of the tan soft skin under it, except when I was looking at

her legs and bare feet as she led and stroked that horse so gentle like she was doing.

I kept trying to come up with something good to say but the closer I got to her the more my mind wasn't working right. So when I finally got to the fence, all I did was lean on it and try not to stare at her too much. She was staring at me, though, and then laughed a little.

"You look lost," she said.

"Sort of."

She started petting her horse on the head while still looking me over. "Are you a new worker?"

"I'm staying for a visit at the plantation house back over yonder with Kate."

She grinned. "Back over yonder with Kate?"

I nodded.

"You're a guest of Mrs. Kathleen Sherwood?"

I nodded again.

"I was told there'd be a guest arriving. Where are you from?"

"I live up in Virginia."

"Up in Virginia?"

I could tell by her grin and the cut of her words that she was having a good time picking at my accent and the way I talked, but I didn't care as long as she kept smiling at me.

"Do you know Kate?" I asked.

"Yes, I know her but I don't address her as Kate. I believe you're probably the only person in the entire state who does." She tried to move the blond hair blowing across her face but stopped for a moment, looking across the fields at a man standing alone, facing us. "Are you a friend of the family?" she asked. She was still looking away at the man I figured was Mr. Charles, and not at me.

I nodded. "Her and my ma are old friends. Are you and Kate friends?" I asked.

"What's your name?" she asked.

"Benjamin Purdue."

She turned her eyes back across the fields and I did, too. "Well, my name is Amanda Lynn Jennings, Benjamin Purdue. I must say it's certainly interesting to meet you."

"Not as interesting as the feller near the house, though, evidently," I said.

"I'm not used to being watched out here," she said, turning around all the way to look directly at me.

Chapter 16

I woke not in a swamp, staring into flashlights; I was lying on my stomach on gravel, and there were blue and red lights turning the night sky all kinds of colors. I was woozy, thought I smelled hog shit and figured I was back where I'd started that morning. I noted a man on his knees beside me cleaning up what looked like vomit. I wasn't sure if it was mine or not or sure about anything, but I figured it was mine because I did feel sick bad. Trying to get my bearings in those red and blue lights and the headlights blinding me, I recognized the man I thought I'd recognized before.

"Keep still," he said.

I turned my head up a little and saw a gaggle of deputy sheriffs staring down at me. It was an ugly sight to me and I tried to come to a sitting position, but my head stopped that quick, and I had to lay back when my arms wouldn't hold me up. I was shaking all over and my neck and back felt sticky warm. There was a blanket on top of me even though my head felt like it was on fire.

"Rescue squad's on the way. We found the money."

I tried to say something so they'd get the blanket off of me, but the words seemed to come out of me backward and in pieces.

"We found it hidden in a hubcap of his truck. He's sitting in the county jail right now."

I tried to nod, but now I couldn't even do that.

"Lay still. We're taking you to a hospital and then we have some serious things to talk about."

I closed my eyes as he and his words were starting to get fuzzy and all those lights going slowed down to look like a strange sunset.

"Do you remember me?"

I moved my eyes from the gravel just under my face with the many bright colors dancing on them to his eyes, which were almost on the ground next to mine.

"You've been talking…calling out a name over and over. You've been asking for my sister. I remember you and the trouble that came with you. Your name is Benjamin Purdue, and I'm going to find out why you're here."

I looked at the changing colors in his eyes and all the colors began fading to darkness. Things went dark for a long time, but I didn't know that for a long time. The visions going through my head were of a sunny bright world, young and clean and alive, and I was young and clean and alive in it.

I was without a scar or wrinkle or bloodied up in any way.

* * *

I still couldn't think of something interesting to say to her that I hoped would say what I wanted to, so I decided to say the obvious just to say something, because I figured she'd already pegged me as backward and shy, and I'd never been shy in my life that I knew of. Backward in some things, maybe, and already expert in things most folks know little about, but as far as being shy…she'd just knocked the sauce out of me.

For a minute. And I didn't have a care if some old man had been staring at us a quarter mile away.

"You out for a ride this morning?" I finally asked.

"I used to love to ride Dusty in the mornings…I've had him since I was a little girl. We just walk now. He's too old to ride but still enjoys our walks."

I admired Dusty. He did look like a good old horse and had a good name that suited him for a good horse, but I was still admiring her more and trying to get away with it when I could. Even with her proper manners and proper way of talking, she looked about my age and I figured she'd just grown up a lot different than I did. I was gonna try to find the similar in us but was having a hard time. I still couldn't hardly catch my breath.

"I was about to give him a rest when I saw you wandering through the fields. This is our spot," she said, pointing at a big sweeping tree that looked out of place among all the flatland. I thought right then that she liked me, because I'd seen her looking at me when I was still standing at the stables, long before I was in the fields.

She led Dusty over slow to the tree and went to wrap the reins around a branch but dropped them by accident. I saw my opportunity to get nearer to her. But when I started climbing the fence, I got one of my fancy new shoes hung up in the barbed wire and ended up on my head and hands trying to shake myself loose. I was praying she wasn't seeing what was going on, but I heard her laugh when my pants ripped at a bottom cuff.

Before I knew it, she was standing next to me looking down and I almost passed right out cold looking up at her as she told me to stop moving and then got my leg un-hung. I just wanted to keep laying there with her over top of me. I could not get my eyes off of every inch of her.

I'd never been so shook up and when I went to stand, she helped me up. It was all I could do to not keep holding her hand after we were so close and looking at one another. She finally started looking uncomfortable and I asked, "What do you and Dusty do at your spot?"

"I come mostly for the quiet, to read. Have time to myself," she said.

I nodded and then backed up a step. But I wasn't going to go unless I knew she really wanted me to leave. In fact, right then I wasn't gonna leave unless Dusty dragged me off.

"It's nice. The shade," I said. "This whole place for miles seems quiet to me, though."

"Oh, it gets busy. Mr. Sherwood and his entourage are away in Europe and Asia for the summer. It's somewhat of a break for everyone. It may not look like it this morning, but you're standing in the middle of the social and political hotspot of North Carolina. You could call this the Southern watering hole of the rich and famous."

By her description, the place sounded like Shady in an odd and different but similar way. "Do you work for Mr. Sherwood?" I asked.

"I help take care of the horses. Ride them, mostly, keep them trained for his guests. It's really just something to do during the summers and I get to meet interesting people. I start at Duke this fall...."

The way her words trailed off, I could tell she'd caught me looking too hard once too often.

"My boyfriend works for Mr. Sherwood," she said.

I nodded but had no idea what Duke was, and then I realized she said she had a boyfriend when I hadn't even asked and it didn't come up in a natural sort of way. I'd had bad luck before, but hearing that news and the way she yelled it out in a plain talking voice so early in meeting her made this luck even worse. She was pushing me away when I hadn't really even tried to get close yet.

"So are you enjoying yourself here?" she asked after the long pause between us.

"Are you getting married soon?" I asked. I wanted to kick myself just after saying something so stupid.

"That's a strange question. I said I had a boyfriend, not that I'm engaged. But we are very serious," she added. "John is also in Europe. He helps run the business affairs of Mr. Sherwood. I'll be flying over in a few weeks."

"I've heard Europe is a nice place. Heard quite a few tales

about it from soldiers who fought over there. John sounds like a smart feller. Lucky, too."

She nodded just barely. I didn't know much of anything about Europe or John, but I didn't like him for the simple reason that she did, and I think it was showing on me. I was just getting my feet under me a little bit when I got that bad news, but then I figured John wasn't there and I was and that was his bad luck.

"Is John handsome like me or just smart and lucky like me?"

"I didn't say he was lucky."

I smiled. "You didn't say I'm not handsome, either."

She gave me a longer look than she ever had and then turned to her horse.

"Yes, ma'am, he's lucky," I said.

She turned back around. "I'm not sure if I liked you better shy or forward," she said all of a sudden. "I think shy."

"Well, my ma always told me life's too short a trip to ride through it trembly. I just got off to a shaky start with the fence."

"Shaky start to do what?" she asked.

I didn't say what I was thinking but instead said, "To talk to a pretty girl under a tree in a big field. Maybe make a new pard. I'm going to be here for a few months and don't know nobody yet."

"A pard?"

"Buddy…a new friend is what I'm saying."

"You're making friends with a girl who's already spoken for, though."

I nodded. "That don't mean we can't enjoy conversation. I don't figure a fine feller like John would mind. I might be spoken for, too, but just haven't spoken up about it yet because we haven't talked long enough to get to things like that on the my side of things."

"I believe I did like you better shy, Benjamin Purdue. Was the earlier an act or is this an act?"

"Neither is an act. Ever try to get your nerve up to just talk to a pretty girl? Just to talk. It ain't the easiest thing, see."

"You were doing fine. And we were making friends."

"I guess I'm the shy forward type if that makes sense. What type are you?"

"I don't know. I would say the perplexed type at the moment."

"I figure you're the type who likes to walk an old horse in the mornings to a spot where you like the quiet and to read books, but don't mind now and then having a conversation with a handsome young feller you've never met before."

"You walked all the way over here."

"You invited me over."

She laughed. "That's not true."

"Your eyes did. I've had that problem my whole life with pretty girls. I was just wandering over here to have a sit under this nice shady tree when you gravitated to the same nice spot is what happened. It pulled on the both of us at the same time."

"So do you have a girl?"

I tried to think of something more to say, but my confidence was fading on me the more I was around her. It started hitting me hard that a girl like her would never have much to do with a shined-up penny like me, whether she was serious with another feller or not. She was so pretty and had put such a spell on me that I didn't see any way I could just be friends with her. It would hurt way too bad. It was starting to hurt way too bad already.

"You're nice. But maybe you just try too hard sometimes. Do you mind if I ask…I don't believe I've ever seen such dark hair. Are you Italian or—"

"I'm American, my ma told me."

"Well, I assumed that."

A small gust of confidence blew back in me with her question, as she moved her blond hair across her face again. "I am nice like you said, but you keep forgetting to mention that I'm handsome," I said.

"And you're funny," she said.

"A girl can admit when she spots a handsome young man," I said. "Spoken for or not, it's just an observation about a feller's looks. And I hate to say this, but because we're now friends I think I should. See I'm sure John is a fine feller but I think you may be making a big mistake being all tied together with another so young like you are," I said.

"You do."

"It's a big world out there. Lots of others to choose from and meet, which is what young folks are supposed to do. No need in hurrying all those dern weighty things that turn a person old so soon."

"I've actually spent two summers abroad experiencing the big world, as you say. Have you traveled much?"

"No. I've met a lot of travelers, though. Lot of them. Heard a lot of stories about different places I'd like to see someday."

"Like where?"

"Where would you like to see?"

"I asked first," she said.

"I'd like to see an ocean," I said.

"You've never seen an ocean?"

I shook my head.

"Which one would you like to see?"

"I don't know. A pretty one like you see in picture books," I said.

"Well, the Atlantic Ocean is only a couple of hours east. The Outer Banks. My family owns a summer home in Kill Devil Hills. It's a beautiful, wild spot."

"I like the name of that place. That's where I'd like to go first," I said.

She started laughing but then stopped pretty sudden. "I don't know if you're kidding with me or serious when you talk."

"I'm doing a little of both, I guess, can't help it probably. I'd like to see an ocean someday and I'd like to see one with you."

"I'd better go now," she said.

I knew I'd stepped over a moving fuzzy line and figured I'd better change the subject to something other than me or her. It was something I was curious about after hearing all she said about Aunt Kate's husband.

"So what's Mr. Sherwood do for a living to have so much?"

She looked at me with a strange look. "You don't know what he does?"

I shook my head.

She began getting even more uneasy and walked closer to her horse while looking back across the fields. "Are you sure you're a friend of the Sherwood family?"

"My ma is friends with Aunt Kate, like I said. I've never met Mr. Sherwood and don't know anything about him."

"You've never even heard of him?"

"No."

"He runs a worldwide Christian ministry. He's a very powerful man. He's written books and is on the radio and is interviewed on the news all the… He's pastor of the biggest church in the whole country. I find it amazing that you're staying at his home and have never even heard of him. Everyone knows Sam Sherwood."

I didn't know what to say standing there feeling so out of place and evidently so stupid, too. I wished all of a sudden that I could back up time to where my foot was hung in the fence and I was looking up at those beautiful tan legs. If we could start over from there, she'd never say she was tied all up in a knot with anybody else but me.

It looked like I'd ruined things, but she was already spoken for anyway, even if her eyes were trying to tie up a little bit with me. I was down all of a sudden and I mean way down, and she still seemed agitated with me being in her quiet spot. I did feel like I was bothering her now, and that bothered me in a dreadful way.

"Well, I'd best get back. An old feller named Charlie is probably looking for me to show me around some more. I believe he's the feller you keep looking around to see. Nice talking to you and good luck with all you told me about. I'll let you and Dusty get back to your quiet."

I walked toward the fence and started to climb it again.

"There's a gate down there," she said, pointing and smiling.

I put a hand on the wire, pushed it down and jumped over with no trouble, then started walking back to the plantation house. I didn't look back and just kept walking. A full minute—the longest time of my whole life—must have passed before I heard in the distance behind me, "Dusty and I are here most mornings, Benjamin Purdue, if you'd ever like to talk again. It was nice meeting you."

I grinned to myself and spun around happy, but Dusty was heading off behind her lead.

"I'm not gonna crowd your quiet spot in the mornings, but I'll be back here after supper," I yelled. "I like that tree and I'm gonna try to learn to get along with the quiet you like so much, tend more to the quiet in me you seem to enjoy more than the noisy."

She and her horse kept walking and I stopped and kept watching them until the haze on the horizon made them disappear. Just before they did, I'm pretty sure I saw her turn, but I couldn't be sure about it. I kept telling myself she did, though.

Trying to think in terms of poker, because I generally tried to look at everything, at least everything important, in terms of a poker game, I'd already decided it was probably not my best hand to go to her spot anymore in the mornings, as much as I wanted to every single morning, at least until I couldn't stand not doing it. But I did go to her and Dusty's spot after supper that evening like I'd said, and the next and next and every night that week.

I'd lay back under that tree that she liked so much and go over in my head our talk and the look of her until the stars started shining through the branches. Then one night, just as

I was about to walk back to that huge house full of rules and echoes, Dusty walked up to me quiet in the dark, not even disturbing the crickets. Amanda Lynn tied his reins around a branch just like when I'd met her, then she got down and lay on her back beside me under the tree. She'd been crying. As the night turned cold we moved closer together, I never said a word and she didn't, either, until morning came.

"You're not a dream."

She leaned closer and then I felt her hand grab mine.

"I'm here. I'm here with you, Ben. You've been trying to wake for hours. Can you hear me?"

I had no idea where I was or what year it was or anything except for the eyes I was looking into, the eyes that I'd searched inside of so many long nights for so many things. They now had small lines around them, as they began to fill with water.

The lines were what told me I wasn't dreaming.

She squeezed my hand and I tried to focus on what was around those wonderful blue eyes and even in my blurred vision, she was still so beautiful, but she was no longer the young girl of my memories. Time had changed her, too. But so much more gentle. She leaned closer to me.

"Can you hear me?"

I nodded.

"You've been unconscious for two weeks. They thought you may never wake but I knew you would. I've been talking with you about many things. Do you remember?"

I tried to move my head to get a better idea of where I was and what was going on, and felt something very tender and scratchy on the back of my head. I moved my hand from hers to touch there and noticed the tubes running into my arm. Amanda Lynn grabbed my hand again and moved it to the place where it had just been and she squeezed harder.

"You've been injured," she said, using her other hand to pat at the back of her head.

I squinted and blinked hard to arrange things in my vision. I could hear, but the room was moving. She finally steadied and just the look of her face warmed and crushed me at the same time. I had to say what I'd wanted to say for too long.

"I'm so dang sorry for everything," I said.

I don't know if she heard me it came out so weak, but she wiped her eyes and brought a cup and straw to my mouth and I took hard gulps of what tasted like orange juice. It stung my throat and she went to pull the cup away, but I grabbed it from her and it spilled down my front.

"More," I said.

"I have to get the doctor," she said.

I shook my head.

"More."

She took a deep breath, grabbed a towel and patted my neck and chest. "The hospital let us bring you home. You've been here for a week and you're safe here. We've had doctors and nurses around-the-clock by your bed."

"What bed?" I asked.

She smiled. "You're near the plantation where you stayed before."

I couldn't come up with the name of the county or state or plantation where we'd met.

"Near our tree?" I asked.

She nodded. "It's still there, across a few fences." She looked toward a window and then back at me. "As soon as you can stand, you'll be able to see it."

As much as I wanted to try to stand and look out the window with her, I knew I probably couldn't move. If I could, I could tell I had probably better not. It was hard enough to keep from getting sick just laying there.

She sat and I laid there for a long time and I started squeezing her hand gentle but harder than she was squeezing mine. I closed my eyes for a time and then opened them again to make sure of what I was seeing.

"I need to bring the doctor in."

"You still walk Dusty, out to our spot?" I asked. My voice had started so weak but I could hear it getting stronger.

She shook her head.

"Long time ago…"

She nodded and smiled.

I pulled away the hand that she was holding, and with the other pointed at the picture of the tree on my hand. She outlined the tree with her finger and that's when I noticed the diamond and wedding band.

"I always said John was a lucky feller."

"You need to rest," she said, covering her wedding hand with her other.

It got quiet and she stood up to open the windows. The breeze felt good and I still couldn't take my eyes off of her as her hair moved with it. It was different than in my memories, shorter, a little darker in color, but still the same in other ways and I wanted to touch it. She stood with her back to me, barefoot and wearing a heavy cotton robe that couldn't help but show the curve of her. I was flooding with memories when it looked like she'd taken a sudden chill.

"Morning or evening?" I asked.

"It's early morning," she said. "It's going to be a beautiful day. I've been praying that you'd—"

"It's good to see you again."

She turned and looked like she was searching for something to keep her hands busy. She couldn't find anything and stood to my side and put a hand on my shoulder before pulling it away as quickly as she'd touched me.

"I'm going to bring in the doctor. They've insisted that I alert them the minute you…"

I reached for her hand and she took it. Even with my head swimming, I couldn't believe how young and clean I felt and how easy words came to me to say. Good words, and so easy. It was like that hit on the head and then seeing her had jarred loose things I'd thought I'd lost. It was like I could talk again and say nice things, without thinking or any effort.

"It's so good to see you, Amanda Lynn."

"I haven't been called that since—"

"It's a dang shame we had to grow up."

"You and all of your derns and dangs…I'd forgotten." She smiled. "I'm just glad you're alive," she said.

"I hit bad weather for a time. This ain't the way I wanted it."

Her hand was starting to shake in mine.

"I swear, you're still pretty as the day we met. Do you still find me as handsome?"

She smiled full this time, started to cry, started to laugh, sat, and then started crying a lot and laughing a little at the same time. I'm not sure when it ended, but I remember at some point I was crying with her so hard that it hurt too bad inside and out to do it anymore. I tried to say some things I always figured I'd say to her but nothing else would come out. It was a time for quiet.

It was the very best and the very worst I'd ever felt, and after all of those years with so much bottled up in me with nowhere to go, all of that came out all at once and it flooded the both of us. The last thing I remembered was Amanda holding me and me holding her and me trying to get myself together to ask about Ma and what happened in Shady and other painful things.

But I couldn't quit holding her and I took in the good quiet between us as she kept holding me. Those were the last things I felt before seeing white coats all around me as something exploded behind my eyes.

Chapter 17

After rising from the room aimless as a feather, and then picking up speed and riding along a current through clouds and deep blue, and then into the light blue and then the dark nothing of the night sky like I was a rocket ship, I went into a white mist that grew and grew and became so bright that I had to close my eyes the closer I got to it. But I was at peace through all of the trip, enjoying myself completely the whole way, until I was suddenly standing in a line with what looked like thousands of other people, maybe millions of them. In the distance as far as I could see, there was a gate the size of a mountain. A lone man stood before it.

I turned now and then to look at the others in line as they in turn looked at me and everyone else, but nobody spoke. There were signs posted every few yards with words printed on them in different languages and the English signs said,

"Please, no talking." I figured the foreign signs did, too, because the place was quiet and loud at the same time, like the
sounds a heavy sleet makes in no wind.

So we all just kept shuffling forward as the line moved,
urging the next step but no more, and I still felt this over-
whelming feeling of peace and comfort like I'd never
known. It may have been a few minutes or it may have been
ten thousand years later, but after a time, I was at the head
of the line and stood before the lone man at the great gate.

Something warming about the whole experience told me
I was in heaven, even though there were no pearls on the
gate and it was so big that if it would fall over, it would smash
the whole lot of us.

A tall, bearded man, who looked rough as a readied pine
before it went headfirst through a sawmill, had a clipboard
in hand. Attached to the white cloak across his chest was a
sign that said, "My name is Bill, not Saint Peter."

I was studying him and the sign curiously and he must
have noted my look.

"It's the first thing so many ask. We decided recently to clear
it up right off the bat. Should have done it centuries ago."

"Is Saint Peter here?"

He sighed and I couldn't believe I had the nerve to speak
to such a man in such a strange place as bewildered as I was
by all of it, but the thing was, standing there I felt like I had
the nerve to say or do anything. I was in a place a man didn't
need nerve, or something like that. Unlike in the line, if I
now had something to say, I just said it.

Bill kept flipping through paperwork and said without

looking at me, "He goes by Pete up here, and yes, I'm sure he's around somewhere. Maybe on the golf course or fly fishing." He looked a little annoyed with my question and kept reading and shaking his head.

"Is this heaven?" I asked.

He stared more annoyed at me before looking over his shoulder, then he shifted sideways so I could see a sign welded to the gate behind him, which also had many languages on it. The English part read, "You're not in heaven. This is in-processing into the hereafter."

"Are you an angel?"

"No. I'm only the doorman," he said.

"I'm dead, right?"

"You're dead except for the part of you that is here."

"Which part is that?"

"The part that's still alive and never dies."

"So I'm dead but still alive?"

"Correct."

"Am I going to heaven?" I asked.

He looked up from the paperwork. "I was just about to ask you the same question. What do you think?"

He stared at me for a long time without blinking.

"I don't know," I said.

He nodded, his head bent down and he checked a box on the form in his hand. "'I don't knows' go that way," he said, pointing with his right hand at a hole the size of a door that went through the middle of a cloud.

As I turned, I heard Bill the doorman say, "Next."

I'd barely walked into the cloud when I saw another man,

dressed, too, all in white, but this feller didn't have a beard and looked like a businessman without the suit. He was sitting behind a white desk that had an adding machine on it and he was adding or subtracting away at something. He never looked up at me but motioned me to sit with a finger.

I looked around for a chair, didn't see one so I kept standing when he looked up at me. "Have a seat," he said.

With still no chair in sight besides the one he was sitting on, I decided just to sit on the floor of the cloud. But when I bent at the waist, I felt a soft chair of some sort under me, even though I couldn't see it.

"You'll see things like the furniture once you become acclimated," he said. "Just do as you're directed for now and everything will proceed more smoothly." He kept adding and adding, his fingers going a hundred miles an hour on that machine when he peered at me and said, "I see we have some faith to build."

"Am I going to heaven?" I asked the second man.

With his fingers still going so fast that the machine sounded like a machine gun, he said, "I don't decide those matters, but I can tell you… Well, I best not speculate. One never knows until you get to the room."

"The room?"

He didn't respond, his focus still on the numbers flying from his fingers.

"I've tried, especially lately to do the right thing and be more—"

He held up a hand. "I'm just the accountant."

He stopped adding and tore off the long sheet with a rip.

And when I say long, it was a couple miles long, and when I say rip, the crack of the paper about ripped my ears off. He rolled it up with little effort and with blazing speed put it into a large envelope. He stamped the outside with something I tried my best to read, but it was in a language I'd never seen before. He stuffed the envelope into the cloud behind him and it disappeared. And then he yawned, checked his watch and he and his desk disappeared, too.

Just like that, it was only me sitting in a cloud, and it was then that I noticed I was naked as the day I was born but warm and snug with it all like a baby in the womb might feel, I reckoned. I was alone but didn't feel alone. I felt like I was inside of something greater than myself.

I was surrounded all over by something good and things began getting noisy from the voices of a dozen people or more, louder and louder. It came from all around me and after I'd looked behind me to see nothing at all, I turned to my front again and found myself sitting in the same invisible chair, but this time I was at a long oblong table that looked to be made of glass. After I tried to put a hand on it, I found out it was made of water. Around the water table were men and women, a few I recognized from pictures in books I'd seen before.

Some of them looked like Bible-type people and some didn't. Abe Lincoln stuck out from the rest and two people sat to his right, laughing about something he'd said. Down three seats from him was a man who I swore was the same man I'd thought was a bum who drifted into Shady one time out of the blue and left a short time thereafter during one of

Shady's harder, darker times. He was talking with an old woman beside him I didn't know, but he stopped long enough to look my way and nod and wink at me like he knew me.

I nodded to him but decided not to wink back.

I was trying to take it all in and it looked like I was at some kind of meeting and everybody there looked to be important except for me. Along the cloud walls everywhere were television screens and on them were movies and pictures it looked like of people in different sorts of dire predicaments. Lot of crying and screaming on those screens. Nobody seemed to be paying much attention to the pain and suffering going on, except for a man sitting at one of two chairs at the very head of the table. He was scanning everything and writing notes down onto a tablet. I figured he was God, even though he was punier looking than I'd have ever imagined God to be. He did look like one smart feller, though.

All of a sudden, a short, stout, bald-headed man who reminded me of ol' Hoke a whole lot walked in, and he was clothed in the same white drapes as the rest of them. When he entered, all got quiet and stood. He raised a hand and took a drink from a coffee cup and all got seated again with their attention turned toward him. I looked at him, too, and it looked like he was counting heads, skipped by my head, but he did notice two empty spaces, one of them next to me. I figured right then I was wrong about the puny feller and I was now looking at God himself. He looked like God would look to me, anyway.

"Where's Moses?" he said in a voice that shook me from top to bottom, but not in any sort of fearful way.

The man who was taking notes turned, and that's when I saw the golden wings on his back. He said, "Last I saw, he and Noah were at it again…about something in Genesis… again. Want him summoned?"

"No, I'll do it," the short, bald-headed, big man who I thought was God said. He snapped his fingers. "And Jesus?"

"He said he'd be here shortly."

Everyone at the table looked at each other out of the corner of their eyes, some with a grimace and some looked to be trying to keep back a snicker.

"Our Monday-morning staff meetings are getting longer and longer because of this tardiness," the man in charge said. "If this keeps up, you all will be receiving a memorandum about it. Let's not forget evaluations are at the end of the month."

Hearing that, everybody scooted their chairs up and looked alert, and all the grins disappeared from their faces.

"Has everyone met Benjamin Purdue?" he said.

Everyone looked at me and said or mumbled something, waved, that sort of thing. I didn't get their names, though.

The head man took another long sip of whatever was in the cup and said, "Okay, down to business… We're not going to wait this morning… What do we have on our plate to-day?"

Down the line, each stood and took their turn, giving out information about wars and droughts and famine and people in need of everything people could possibly be in need of. There was a shipwreck off of South America and there was grave concern about the leaders of a country or two. Two of the men and one of the women didn't talk about people;

they talked about animals that were having a hard time. Another man started talking about some trouble on some other planet when the head man said—

"Let's keep the discussion to Earth, please."

At the end of the period where people were standing up talking, which seemed to speed by me mostly in fast-forward time, the last person, who looked old as time itself, gave a slide show so fast that I couldn't keep up with the faces or the calamities and horrible things the faces in those slides were facing. He didn't say anything, but just kept flashing those slides and everybody watched with intense interest.

Then he did the same with a bunch of fast slides that showed people happy and having a big time, and pictures of tender moments of people caring for one another and helping each other, that sort of thing.

At the end of the slides, the head man cleared his throat and said, "Thoughts?" I was surprised God asked for such things, him being God.

Then down the line each of them stood again and said what should be done in each case of the disasters of all sorts and whatnot, not suggesting winds that should turn at a certain time or rains that should stop and so on but what men living on Earth might do to help out with each situation. Help one another. Mostly how to comfort those with no comfort left.

The man who presented the huge shipwreck talk said that perhaps it would be best to let "Receiving" know that Tuesday through Thursday would probably be unusually heavy days with so many catastrophes going on at the same time.

After everyone was done, the man who I thought was God up to that point stood and everyone else did, too, so I did. Then a woman with long blond hair rolled up on her head walked in wearing the same garb as everybody else, and she had the strangest look of being so old and so young at the same time on the same beautiful face.

She never sat but instead walked behind each at the table. They all smiled and nodded to her as she passed. All the while she kept her eyes on the television screens that were everywhere—now some even played above us like there were a thousand or more TVs in the room.

When she got to me, she stopped behind my chair and placed her hands on my shoulders, and suddenly the table disappeared. I couldn't see a thing but had the sense that I was flying with her holding on to me. My ears were filled with the hopes and prayers and songs and laughs and pleas and cries and screams of happiness and horror from those I passed over but who I could not see. When I finally slowed and stopped, I was back in the cloud room, but all of the men and women who were there and even the table were gone…except for the beautiful young-old woman who was late to the meeting.

She now sat across from me.

"My name is Helen," she said in a kind, soft voice. "I'd say it's nice to meet you but I've known you for a long time. I'm here to help answer questions you may have, and just so you'll know, the true hearts of all are known here, so don't be surprised when you speak only the truth as you know it, for otherwise it's only to waste time…and as you're beginning to learn...time, though endless, is a very valuable thing, here, as well as from where you just came from."

"Where am I?" I asked.

"There is really no 'where,'" she said. "You've moved into a different space of being. You're no longer bound by the things you were bound by on Earth. You are entering a different phase of life. It will be challenging and complex in many ways, but in different ways than what you've known. What was challenging for you before, even mystifying beyond possible understanding, will soon not be. You are about to gain great knowledge, and with it great responsibility. But you're not quite ready to receive it. Soon."

"Is this heaven?"

"Yes, newborns here call it that. But it's not what you have been taught."

"Do I get to meet my dead kin and some of my old pards who've passed?"

"In time, but that will also be different from what you could only imagine now."

"My mother?"

"She's not here."

"Where is she?"

"She's still where you've just left."

"You sure?"

She smiled.

"She's still alive...down there?"

"Yes. And that's all I can tell you now."

"Can you tell me if she's okay?"

"She's okay."

"What about my brothers and Uncle Ray?"

"There will be lots of time later for you to ask and receive answers to these questions."

"I never got to meet my dad. Is he here?"

Her smile eased away. "Yes."

I tried to take everything in I was hearing. "So I'm not going to hell?"

She smiled again. "There is no hell."

I sat and felt free to say anything I wanted like I never had before to anyone. "It can be hell down there, ma'am," I said.

She nodded. "You will also feel that feeling here, as well from time to time, and sometimes for great lengths of time, just as 'down there.'"

"I thought heaven was supposed to be a place without pain," I said.

"You will not feel individual pain. You'll feel only the pain of other people and other creatures, which is far greater than any pain you've so far experienced. You will also feel great happiness, like you could never even imagine."

"But why is there pain at all? Why not have a world without any of it?"

"The same storm that brings rain that floods a country, feeds another one. The same rain that sinks a boat in one body of water provides for a fish harvest in another one. The pain from one lost love provides the appreciation to understand love in a deeper meaning. The pain of having and raising a child bonds the child and mother forever in a way not possible without that pain. Your education will continue on to study things such as these, while being part of them, just

as before. One cannot learn deeply by only being an ob-
server. You will have to experience it yourself, as you actually
have been doing for some time."

She kept the pleasant smile on her face after her pause.

"But there's pain that's just pain. Suffering that shouldn't
be. Suffering for no reason. Shouldn't never need to be at all.
For nothing. Terrible, awful things."

"You believe you have suffered for nothing," she said.

I nodded.

"Your individual suffering is over."

"I still feel like I'm suffering now," I said.

"No. You now are feeling lingering past suffering and the
suffering of others, not any current suffering, which has ended.
What you seek now is the understanding of that suffering?"

"Yes, ma'am. That's exactly what I've been trying to seek.
And I still just don't see the need in any of it," I said. "If I
were God, I'd make the world a big party, a good place to
live and not just some of the time."

"But as a teenager you wanted to leave a place that in many
ways was a big party." Her smile grew more as she placed her
chin in one hand looking at me. I felt like I was in a trance all
of a sudden. "One day you'll have a better understanding. Life
can't be a big party and it would be a terrible thing if it were."

"Are you my angel?"

She shook her head. "I'm the one you've prayed to, cursed,
feared, shouted at, hated, argued with and loved. I was with
you the night you were born and I'm here now to welcome
you. It will be a long time before we'll speak again like this,
though like always, I'm listening."

"You're God?" I asked.

"You may call me Helen from now on."

I'd never figured God would have the name Helen or be pretty. Just never figured it.

"Let me ask you...you are now 'up here,' as you put it...would you do something about all the suffering, if you could?"

"Of course I would, Miss Helen," I said. "Anybody would. What I don't get is why you all ain't doing more to help and save folks, like saving all those people that were on that ship. Why aren't they being saved right now? Why'd the boat have to sink in the first place?"

"Some will survive," she said.

"Some are drowning right now."

"Yes."

"You all just sit around a table and pick and choose who will live and who won't depending on what you think about a person or whatnot, if you think they're good or not or worship you in the right way? That don't sound right. It sounds like something a man would do, not a god would do."

"That's not what was happening in that meeting."

"Save one person and let the other person beside them drown. Why don't you pull them all out of the water right dang now?"

I stopped and couldn't believe the words that were coming out of me, even almost a cuss word, but they just were.

"Would you save this ship if doing so meant you would die?"

"But I'm already pretty much dead, aren't I?"

"You have just begun to see, to live fully. You are very

young. I ask again, would you save this ship if it meant you would die. Die forever."

"But people don't die forever, right?"

"The question is—would you, if it meant you would die forever?"

Suddenly a TV screen on the wall showed people floating on the water, some already with eyes that had stopped moving, and some still struggling to keep their heads above water. Their prayers and choking screams for help and them sinking, with eyes wide-open, dead, to the bottom of the ocean filled the room. I had to turn my eyes and close them from the pure terror and horror of it.

"Would you?"

"Turn that off," I said. "Turn it off, ma'am."

When all got quiet, I opened my eyes and I was lying in a bed and the back of my head was killing me, throbbing and my skin was no longer clean but covered with prison tattoos. I looked under my sheet and I was half-naked and suddenly felt like it. I looked all around for Helen in the dim light of my room, but God was gone. Amanda Lynn wasn't there, either. I kept closing my eyes and opening them back up, wondering if I was going to go back to that wonderful strange place, but nothing more ever came of it right then. I felt such a strong pulling to go back up there, but a bigger tug to stay where I was. Helen had kicked me back from where I'd come whether I wanted to or not for her own good reasons, which at that point God herself only knew why, which to me was a fitting way of thinking for a woman anyway, God or not.

That's the best I could figure about the whole disturbing, wondrous thing, exciting as it was, and I laid there figuring on it for some wide-eyed, haunted in a good way, time afterward.

I had both feet over the side of the bed when I heard the knock. The doctor who was checking my vision and balance and putting me through all kinds of different tests yelled "yes," and I turned to see Amanda peep her head in. I could tell by her eyes and smile what she was about to say.

"You're looking better," she said.

I nodded to her as the young doctor put two hands on my shoulders just like Helen had and said, "Slow and steady, remember."

"Slow and steady," I said back.

"And the dreams?"

"I think I'm back with you full time," I said.

"You know which is which..."

"I believe so," I lied a little.

"Do you still feel steady sitting?"

I nodded as she stared at me hard to make her slow and steady order sink in, and then she gathered her things. On the way out the door I heard her say, "He can stand but only with help. And only for a few moments. The last thing he needs is another head injury."

I felt embarrassed wearing the hospital dress and tried to cover up my backside better because it was in Amanda's line of sight. She hadn't seen it in quite a few years and I'm sure it had changed some from when she did. I knew I was too late when she asked, "Would you like a pair of pajamas?"

I grinned to myself and then wondered if she'd also seen all the tattoos on my back. I already knew she'd seen the ones up and down my arms. It made me stop grinning and I turned toward her. She wasn't wearing cutoff shorts or a shirt tied around her middle like I thought she might for some crazy reason. She was wearing a summer dress and sandals and the whole look of her would level any man young or old. And like so long ago, it didn't look like she was trying to look beautiful, she just was. She was the closest thing I'd ever seen that looked like God.

"How's your head?" she asked.

I rubbed the shaved part of my head where it met my neckline. "She took the stitches out. Doc said the good news is a hard lick like that will sometimes knock some sense into a feller who needs it."

She didn't smile. "How are you?"

"I'm still wobbly but perking better."

"Your color is almost back," she said.

She kept standing at the door and I had my head turned around looking at her, but soon the pain of that made me look straight ahead. I wanted to stand but I wasn't sure about it right then. I reached with one leg and pulled a chair over, then stood myself up using it.

"So I've been here for some time," I said.

When she didn't say anything I turned to her. She was now at my side with her hands out like she was ready to catch me. I was road-worn thin but still tall, and as small as she was, I figured all she'd do trying to catch me if I tipped over, was land on the bottom of the pile, which would be just fine with me. When she saw I was okay, she took a seat in a chair across from me.

"Do you remember our talk a few days ago?"

"I don't know. Happy and sad reunion, is what I do remember."

She smiled. "Yes, that's what it was." It looked like she was searching for the right words. "I thought we could talk about some other things, if you feel up to it?" she said.

"I've missed our talks."

"I think it may be a good idea if you sit down."

"I'm all right," I said.

"Well, I don't know what you know or don't know…I'm not sure where to start."

"Do you know what happened to Ma and my brothers?" I asked.

"I'm sorry to tell you this, but I'm just going to tell you. Your ma died."

For some reason I was surprised, because in my vision Helen had said that she was alive…and for some crazy reason I just had had a feeling and hope that Ma was still alive. I felt weak up and down all of me, pulled the chair to the bed, then worked my way down into it.

"I saw her gravestone in Shady. I went there before I got to here. Read where she died the day of the shooting."

"She didn't die then or there, Ben. She and one of your brothers, Bernie, and I left Shady Hollow that night on a raft…a bunch of the security men there floated us across the river. We walked the train tracks until we met a car that was waiting for us. Your other brothers wouldn't go. There was talk about an upcoming fight with the police. Your ma tried to get all of them to go with us, but they wouldn't. They ran from her and as hard as she tried, she couldn't find them. She ended up leaving instructions and money for them to follow behind us, but I don't know if they ever did. Your ma didn't die on that day or in Shady Hollow."

"So when did she die?"

"It's been a few years. She was sick for a long time. Kate knows more than I do. She'll—"

"Is Bernie alive?"

"I don't know. I'm sorry."

"Why the gravestones? I had a gravestone, too. It says I died that day you came to Shady."

"I don't know the answers to all the things you're going to ask."

"What about my other brothers. Are they still alive? I haven't heard from any of them in over twenty years."

"I don't know about your other brothers. I'm not sure how much Kate knows about them. I'm so sorry."

"Why wasn't I told about Ma? About any of this?"

"Kate will be able to help you."

"Where is she?"

"She'll be here tonight, if you're strong enough to see her."

"I'll be strong enough. Did the man I shot follow you to Shady Hollow?"

"He did, Ben, but I didn't know that. I swear to you that I didn't."

"His name was Mr. Charles and he worked for Aunt Kate, right?"

"He actually worked for her husband, not Kate. She only thought he worked for her. His name was Charles Windham Douglas."

"Why did he try to kill me?"

"He was sent there by someone."

"Who?"

"He's the reason there are guards outside your door right now."

"Who?"

"Kate's husband tried to have you murdered. He also tried to have you killed in prison. Ben, it's a miracle you're alive and once you leave here, you'll still be in great danger. What started a long time ago isn't over yet."

Chapter 18

Wet concrete started to fill my legs, and my head was pounding and beginning to spin. I feared I was about to feel another huge explosion behind my eyes, reached for the bed, and when I tried to maneuver myself into it, I began pulling all the bedding off. Amanda yelled for help in a frantic voice and a man who looked like an off-duty police officer followed by a nurse ran in.

"Get him back in bed," Amanda told them, as they struggled to do what she said.

After I was settled, I tried to slow my breathing and then told them to leave. They didn't do as I said, so I yelled loud as I could for them to leave. Amanda walked them out and talked to them outside for a minute before she came back in. She was crying and looked more shaken up than I was.

I started to ask her something and she said, "We'll talk more after you rest but no more for now. No more now."

Something in me made me try to sit up, and when I got halfway, I hugged whatever I could grab hold of, which was the middle of her, a soft warm place I remembered and knew so well. She soon laid me back onto the pillow and turned to leave in a hurry.

"How've you been all these years?" I asked.

Her eyes and face were a mess. She didn't answer so I asked again. "I'm happy now. It took a long time."

"You have children?" I asked.

She smiled easy and held up three fingers. "A girl and two boys. Sheri Lane is fourteen and Thomas and Kenneth are nine and four."

I took a deep breath with the great and terrible of hearing such news.

"Busy house," she said, followed by another sad but real smile. The real of her smiles were killing me.

"Your husband?"

"His name is Daniel."

"So he's the lucky man."

She didn't smile or say anything to that as time passed slow between us.

"What's he do for a living?"

"He runs the history department at the University of North Carolina. I also work there. I'm an English professor."

I knew how much that job would suit her with her love of books and was happy for her. I was happy for her about everything she'd just told me, except that she was telling me with all of it that the times we had were part of her past, and wouldn't be part of my future. She didn't just have a life, she had a good life, and it showed on her. I was glad for her about that, but only as much as I possibly could.

"I need to know something, before you leave," I said.

She put her arms around herself.

"Where I was all those years...did you know that I was in..."

Her face broke again as she began nodding.

"Did Ma, before she got sick?"

"Yes."

Suddenly the door flew open.

"Daddy's here!"

I turned to the young voice and looked at her nine-year-old son. He didn't look a lot like her but he was a nice-looking boy, and he started studying on me serious when Amanda wiped her eyes and said, "I'll be down in a minute, baby."

"You okay, Mom?" her son asked.

"Tommy, this is Mr. Purdue."

"Hello, Tommy," I said.

He walked a little closer before he said again, "Daddy's here, Momma."

"Tell Dad I'll be down in a minute."

After he left the room as fast as he'd entered it, she looked at her watch and said, "After the doctor comes in, I'm going to have lunch brought up. And maybe this afternoon you'll feel up to going outside. I'll ask a nurse to take you outside in a wheelchair, to get some fresh air. I remember how much you always loved to be outside."

"Will I see you later?" I asked.

She moved my hair away from my face. I went to reach for her hand but she pulled away from me. "This is hard, Ben," she said.

"But we'll talk again, right?"

"If you still want to, we'll talk more after you talk to Kate."

"If I still want to?" I could hear her son and husband calling her. "Why wouldn't I want to talk with you again?"

She made sure the door was closed, locked it and then looked at me. I could tell her legs were shaking because her dress was shaking.

"Ben, I lied to you. There was a man named John who worked for Sam Sherwood, but I wasn't his girlfriend. He was one of Sam's underlings, hired to act like we were a couple. It made things easier, made it seem like to others that…"

My heart felt like it had quit beating seeing the things in her that were eating her up, and that she was afraid to tell me. I'd never had such a sad vision or dream of her while walking the cement floor of a prison cell.

"You can tell the truth now," I said.

"I didn't have a boyfriend. I was a nineteen-year-old girl going on forty that summer. And my whole life was a lie. Everything. I told you so many lies that I'd rehearsed and recited hundreds of times, maybe thousands of times, before I ever met you. My whole life had become that lie and I was lost in it. I was so lost, until you came along. I felt like I was dying, unless I was with you. You made me feel like a real person again and the world was a hopeful place with all of your talk about luck, and you trying to show off all the time. I wanted to feel like you did. I wanted to be happy and free like you.

I craved and needed what was inside of you, the things you gave me. You were so full of life. My God, you were so full of everything." She started to smile and looked like she was about to laugh, but then her face went serious again. "I'm trying to say that you didn't really know me then, and you don't know me now, and I just don't know how to—"

"I lied, too."

"You're not hearing me."

"I did know you," I said.

"No. You knew the person I wanted to be, not the person I was."

"You turned out to be that person, that person you are now though, that person you wanted to be, so I did know the real you."

She pulled a towel from where it was draped over a chair and then started kneading it in her hands.

"I needed you then. I needed everything about you. You were still so young then compared to me. But it turned into such a horrible thing, and times have changed. The years crept on and my life changed. I changed. I'm not the girl you thought you knew then. Can you understand that?"

"You loved me. I know that."

"I did. A long time ago. And I still care for you and always will. Maybe I still love you and always will, but I need for you to forgive me now. I need for you to forgive me. And if you can do that, I then need for you to let me go."

Her eyes looked like they were pleading with me to understand a lot of things I didn't know, but especially what I knew already. I'd figured it out the first time I ever laid eyes on her, and that didn't hold me back then, but times had changed lots of things for sure. I knew finally and with certainty that we would never again have what we had for such a short time.

"What we had was real," I said. "You have to tell me that."

"That was the only thing that was real. I need for you to forgive me," she said again.

Two of her sons started banging on the door and turning the knob, yelling for her. I heard heavy footsteps getting louder and a man's voice say loud, "Honey?"

"You best go," I said.

"I found out where you were. I wanted to see you so badly. I wrote you a thousand letters over a thousand nights. I wanted to send them, but..."

That hurt ran sharp and deep in an old dark, longing, empty place inside me. A place I knew I had to fight to get out of quick because once there the dark would want me to stay.

"If I didn't know who you really were then, who were you?" I asked.

Her eyes were watery, but she looked at me without blinking and in a direct way that she hadn't before. I could feel something powerful coming and I waited for it to come out of her.

"I was the lover of the man who tried to have you murdered. A very powerful man. I was Sam Sherwood's mistress. And that's why I always told you we had to stay such a secret."

She turned and I tried as fast as I could to think of something to stop her from leaving, but I could tell there was little

I could do or say that would bring her back at that moment. My thoughts flew back years and I remembered hearing her say Sam Sherwood's name over and over during those times. He didn't seem like just a man to hear her speak of him then. He sounded like he was better than any man I'd ever known. A god, almost, and better than I was, for sure.

I wondered if I should tell her how I'd read all of his self-help books that he'd written, at least the ones that the prison kept in the library. I'd read them just like all of the other books they had, but read them first because she'd always talked so much about the man and seemed to look up to him so much, worship him almost. Something about reading those books made me want to be more like him so she might think of me in the same way, someday.

I watched her pretty hand that I'd held so many nights turn the knob on the door.

"Does Kate know?" I asked loud.

She stopped and leaned her head against the door before she turned and nodded, her face streaked in black below her eyes.

"Come here," I said.

"I can't. But I want you to know, really know how sorry I am for—"

"I remember you used to talk about him."

"I've been trying to tell you…I was not the person I told you then. I wasn't from money, and I wasn't well educated, well traveled…so much of what I knew, I knew from him. How to dress, how to act, how to speak, when to speak, how to do…everything. Before him, I was a country girl who fed chickens every morning and cleaned the houses of rich people after I walked home from school, and I wanted so much more than I had, not realizing what I did have then and, to me, Sam Sherwood had everything. He was my dream. And the dream I had then started to become true when I went to work for the Sherwoods when I was sixteen, and soon all he seemed to want more than anything was me. This man who had everything, and could have everything, wanted me. He was smart and famous and rich and powerful, and he wanted me. I wanted to be his wife more than anything."

"It's all right," I said.

"No. It's not all right. I prayed and prayed that he'd divorce Kate and I could live the life that she lived. I hated her then. At one time I hated her so much I even fantasized about killing her to have him to myself, and to have all that she had. The life she had. It was all so wrong, Ben. I was one messed-up girl. I was young and naive… It was just wrong. All of it. I'm so ashamed of that time and who I was trying to become. And I never knew how wrong it was until you came along." She sniffed and turned square toward me. "He's dangerous. I know you've lived a very hard life and I'm sure you've had to deal with dangerous men, but he's dangerous in ways you've never met or known."

"And he's been after me all this time for being with you?" I asked.

There was another bang on the door that made both of us jump. "Hon, can I come in?" I heard.

Amanda turned from me, looked around for what I guessed was the towel she'd thrown a few minutes before or for a tissue that she couldn't find, then she bent at the knees and pulled the bottom of the front of her dress to her face and wiped her eyes with the inside of it. When she stood she said, "I'll be out in a second," in a shaking loud voice, and then she turned to me and said, "No, that's not the reason. He just found you by following me."

"So he followed you to Shady Hollow, too?"

"No. Sam would never get his hands dirty with something like that. He had me followed. Ben, this is really hard to say but I'm going to just say it, and then I have to leave and Kate will help you understand the rest. He had me followed to find you, but it wasn't because of me. I was actually nothing to him during that time. I was only another of his possessions that he used like he used and still uses everyone. And in the end, he used me to find you."

"But you didn't know that."

"No. But…he'd asked me to help make sure you didn't leave until he returned from his tour in Europe. He found out who you were and that you were there just a day before you were taken away back to Shady Hollow, exactly what he wanted to make sure didn't happen. He wanted for me to make friends with you, to get to know you…gain your trust. And then I was to pass on whatever I could find out about you when he returned. Of course by that time I was already in love with you. He had no idea about that, and I had no idea why he was asking me to do these things, but it scared me."

"You never told me."

"I'm sorry. I should have but I was afraid to. He'd never asked me to do anything like that before. But I never told him anything about you, other than we'd spoken briefly a couple of times in passing. I had no idea why you were so important to him, and why I was to try to make sure you stayed there until he returned, and he did return early. He canceled the rest of his tour once he found out you were there. It was odd and in an odd way very scary to me, but I had no idea that in the end he was planning on killing you. I swear to you that I didn't know."

"Why..."

"The rest Kate has to tell you. Ben, what you'll hear is going to be painful and difficult to understand, but you need to trust that what she tells you is the truth, and you need to do what she's going to ask you to do. You have to trust Kate. Trust her."

Amanda reached in a hurry to open the door. It opened for her, and I watched as a man's hand grabbed her arm as she took a step to leave the room.

"You have to tell me what was in the letter!" I yelled as she was already halfway gone from me.

She seemed as confused as I was, stunned by how and what I'd just said.

"What letter?"

"The letter you gave me in Shady Hollow."

She turned so she could look at me and slowly shook her head. "I'm sorry. I don't remember giving you a letter. We were just kids. You have to move on, now." Her face dissolved into tears. "Goodbye, Ben" was the last thing she said before walking away.

I heard the same voice of the man I'd heard just outside say, "You okay," over her crying, and before his hand shut the door behind her, he put his head in the opening and looked at me for a few moments. Nothing was spoken between us, I guess he just wanted to see the man who in the end of things had caused so much pain to his wife. The door shut, and I closed my eyes after the sight of her husband, and hearing her teary final goodbye. But I couldn't do that for very long. It made my insides hurt so bad missing her forever like that, which I knew is what it was, so I tried instead to put together the broken pieces of old things she'd told me, and prepare myself for what I was about to learn. I kept trying my best just to think of those things, not a terrible goodbye. I just couldn't think about that right then. My insides kept doing it, but like in prison, I focused as hard as I could on not thinking on what I just couldn't think about.

I took a deep breath, wanted to get the hell out of that bed even though it was my only place to be in right then. I knew that whatever I was about to learn from Aunt Kate looked to scare Amanda Lynn to death.

I wasn't scared of whatever that was. I should have been, but I just couldn't believe I'd never see her again after such a time and time of things. I tried my best to just be glad I'd ever got to see her again at all. I tried real hard at doing that, to just be thankful for such an important thing. To be happy for her that she'd made a good life for herself. That made my insides hurt worse, though, but I figured a person's insides are supposed to hurt like that sometimes when the hurt inside just ain't to be stopped, until the day and hour and minute comes when it just don't hurt no more, if such a time should ever come.

She couldn't remember that letter.

Chapter 19

I was carried downstairs, and then led by a nurse and two men with pistols strapped to their belts to a back door off the kitchen. Once outside, the screen door opened to a long, covered white porch. I saw Aunt Kate standing at the very end of it. She'd stood from a wicker chair upon seeing me, and a glass table and another chair and a half-dozen rockers was what was between me and her.

It hit me immediately that she'd aged, but I figured she wouldn't even recognize me from the teenager she'd known. She was very thin and her hair was now gray, but she did have the same pleasant look about the whole of her that she always did have. If there was one word to describe Kate, inside and out from what I knew of her, it would be the word *pleasant.* I smiled seeing her and she smiled back, and then I asked for a cane or stick to lean on once one of the guards tried to slide a wheelchair under me. I was feeling better, and I didn't want it. I pushed it away, wanting my feet under me. I needed to walk.

As the nurse and guards looked at one another for what I'd asked, I went ahead and made my way across the porch, pulling myself along at times by the lattice that had vines and flowers growing on it that concealed the porch on all sides.

As I got closer to her, she walked toward me and we hugged, and hugged for a long time. She had the same clean and fresh right out of the laundry smell as she always did, and it was so good to see her. She'd always looked old to me when I was young, even though she was still a young woman then, but now I thought we probably looked about the same age or me even older, the way I'd caught up so hard in the aging.

"You look good, Benjamin," she said.

I kept patting her on the back easy like I had been doing, and knew then she hadn't lost her good manners that she always had. I probably looked about as good as a sack of rusty nails.

"You've changed a little bit but I'm sure I look a good bit older," I said. "Not sure how that happened."

She kissed me on the cheek and pulled away but held me by my shoulders looking up at me. "You're taller than the last time I saw you."

"Late bloomer," I said. I believe I was smiling when I said it.

After a time she quit squeezing my shoulders and arms, and she tried not to stare at my tattoos but couldn't help it some. My legs were starting to tremble and that moved all the way up on me and I figure she felt it.

"Sit down. Please. Sit. It's been so long."

I sat where she pointed and was disappointed to be glad to be off my feet so soon, and then a man who behaved a lot like Mr. Charles did years ago, but was a lot younger than him, brought out a tray of iced tea. Kate's glass was already filled. He filled mine and she thanked him in her formal manner and then handed me the glass. I noted the name she called him, Mr. Hollins, and I gave him a pretty good look over now wary of her help as I was. The last man who'd waited on the both of us killed Uncle Ray.

I took a sip of my drink and it tasted better than any iced tea I'd ever had, and I couldn't help but down all of it. She filled it to the top again from a glass pitcher.

"I see you haven't changed," she said.

I wondered why she said that for a second, but then got what she was saying. I was a difficult one to fill up, she'd said one time after one of our meals at her fancy table. It got quiet for a time as we both took in each other and I tried to get my head to sit as comfortable and steady as it would on top of my shoulders. It just couldn't find the right spot.

"Amanda told me a little about Ma. That she passed on."

"She was living on Ocracoke Island, just off the coast near Wilmington. She had a beautiful little house and ran a flower stand there for years. She was doing so well before she got sick and the doctors found cancer. I didn't know she'd been sick until just before she died."

"Did she ever marry?"

Kate shook her head.

I felt sorry for Ma, knowing how much she'd always wanted to find a good husband. It made me real sorry for

her now no matter how good a life she'd made after Shady.
I was glad to hear about the flower stand. Ma always did love
flowers, particularly wild ones.

"When did she die?"

"October 10, 1977. She's buried in Shady Hollow. That's
where she wanted to be laid to rest."

"In the old Polly Hill cemetery?"

She nodded. "She wanted to be buried near her boys
there, and near Ray. She loved him. She made me promise
I'd take her back there."

"Is she where the marker is that says she died so many
years earlier?"

"Yes. That's where she is. I was afraid that if we changed
anything about that spot other than laying her to rest under
her gravestone, that the people who own that property may
take some sort of action to disturb her. I tried every way I
could using every mean to have her buried there with a
proper service…the owner of the cemetery would not agree
to it. I'm sorry, but just taking her back and having her
buried where she wished was…a very difficult final request
to fulfill. I owed her that, though."

"So she didn't have a funeral?"

"They had a small service on the island before she was
taken to Virginia. I was there. She'd made a nice—"

"Any of my brothers there?"

"No. Benjamin, I'm sorry but I don't know what's happened to your brothers, except for Bernard. Your mom told
me he joined the army and was killed in Vietnam. He's
buried in Arlington Cemetery."

I suddenly felt the same I'd felt when I'd read their grave markers in Shady. Very alone.

"He was a hero."

I nodded. Bernie a soldier. I never would've figured it, but he would have been a brave one for sure. He would've made a fine soldier. It got quiet for I'm not sure how long.

"Your mother was very proud of him."

My eyes got messed up and I was still thinking about Bernie and wondering how he died, hoping it wasn't from some suffering wound. Buried in a place like Arlington suited him better than in Shady, I hoped, and at least I was glad for him for that. Then thinking about him made me wonder about the rest of my brothers.

"Did Ma ever find out what happened to the rest of them?"

Kate shook her head. "If she did, she never said."

"Did she try to find them after everything went bad in Shady?"

"Yes. But it was a terrible time. I'm sorry. I'm really, really sorry to tell you these things."

"Why the empty graves in Shady?"

"Your mother told me that state and federal law enforcement surrounded the whole area. The National Guard was called in to help serve arrest warrants and search warrants on the people living in and running Shady Hollow. Your mother paid the elders a large sum of money before she and Bernie left to make the empty graves, hoping that the person after you would think that you all had died. She hoped that people would think that you had been shot and killed trying to leave there…to protect you. She said it was a very chaotic time, and there wasn't time to plan or think. She did the best she could to help protect you from what she knew and could do, and try to protect herself and Bernie."

"I reckon that didn't work."

"What?"

"The grave to protect me." I suddenly felt that on top of all I was feeling, I was in danger, and that awoke a deep anger in me.

"Where is he?"

"Who?"

"Sam Sherwood."

Kate took a long drink. From the good sweet smell of her breath afterward, I could tell that her tea had something extra in it besides lemon and sugar.

"I assume you all ain't still married."

Kate pulled out a handkerchief. She wiped her eyes with it, got herself back in order and sat up straight. She was slight, but it was the first time I'd ever seen her look weak.

"I tried to divorce him."

I looked away from her eyes to the vines growing on all sides of the porch and saw two guards, one trying to cup the glow of a cigarette and the other leaning against a tree, facing a dirt road that was down a quarter mile easy slope.

"Where am I?" I asked.

"You're safe here. I've arranged all of this very carefully."

"Where?"

"You're staying in my grandparents' home. My old home-place, where your mother and I sometimes played as young girls. It's several miles from the plantation where you came that one summer. It's just behind you. If we turned off the lights, you'd see the glow on the horizon. He has no reason to think you may be here."

"Your grandfolks live here now?"

"No. No one has lived here for years. Benjamin, I'm sorry for so much, so much you've gone through. I was at the prison. I had people there with me to pick you up when you were supposed to be released. I didn't know you were released early or I would've been there then to make sure you left there safely, but I believe it may have been a blessing that your release was—"

"Where's your husband?"

"Please don't call him that anymore."

"Where is he?"

"Tonight he's in Boston, and he's booked in other cities every other night for the next two weeks until the finale of his sold-out 'The World Isn't Big Enough' tour at Madison Square Garden. It's going to be broadcast live on television."

"What does he do at these shows he puts on?"

"He speaks. And when Sam Sherwood speaks, people will pay a lot of money to hear him."

"Preaches?"

"No, no," she said, almost laughing at the end. "He hasn't preached in years. That's just where he honed his craft."

I started thinking about all of the salesmen who'd come into Shady, standing and selling whatever it was they had for all they were worth. "What's he say or selling that all these people come to hear him?"

"Well, lots of things, but basically he sells people the idea that they can be happy. It's made him a billionaire, one of the most famous and respected men in the world. He ignited the whole self-help industry. People worship him."

"A billionaire?"

She nodded.

"From selling happiness...now if that ain't something."

"Yes. Happiness, how to be successful in life, improving your self-esteem...things like that. When I first met Sam, he was a young country pastor who never even graduated high school. He quickly gained a huge following traveling the revival circuit. That was back in the late thirties and early forties. He was a faith healer in those days, too, quite the magician and showman." She started to smile again. "Sam always thought the best salesmen in the world were those that didn't sell physical things. They sold ideas, like politicians and preachers do, selling things like the idea of living forever. Hope. You can change who you are to become the person you'd like to be. But he thought the 'product' of happiness was the one of pure genius, and there is no baggage, like guilt, attached to the happiness he sells—he made sure of that. Happiness with no guilt. He sells it like popcorn.

"Anyway, the last few years he's made most of his fortunes using radio, and now television. His cash registers get busy mostly around two in the morning when those who can't sleep use credit cards and a telephone to order his secrets. He's the very best in the business. Sam Sherwood is the best salesman in the world. If he ran for president, he'd win easily, against anyone, as long he covered up his past before people started digging too deeply into it."

"Maybe he will run one day. Sounds like he could sell a drowning man a bucket of water."

"He is going to run for president one day. Both parties are pushing him now and have been for a long time. It has been his plan as a very young man. First wealth, then fame and then power. Power has always been his true ambition."

"What after that?" I asked.

"That's the scary part," she said. "History books are full of men like Sam."

"I read two of his books in prison. I remember what he looked like from the pictures of him on the covers."

"Oh, he's beautiful," she said. "He has the entire package and he knows it more than anyone."

I looked at Kate, so different in so many ways from this man I'd been having to learn about from her and Amanda.

"How did you all get together?"

"Well, let's just say Sam didn't have a very hard time sweeping me off my feet." She had a strange smile on her face that faded into a very sad look. "My family had money and status...old money and old status, things his family did not have. Sam came from poverty. His father was a thief...he had a very difficult childhood. Anyway, my family didn't have nearly the money Sam has now or the status he now has, but he needed what I had at that time to fuel his ambitions. He courted and married the richest girl in the state, but he never did love me. He did love some things about me—the money of course, the social circles I introduced him to. In many ways I was the perfect woman to be hanging on his arm then, but it ended there and didn't carry home.

Looking back, it was all so exciting but terrible at the same time. It didn't take very long to find out what kind of person he really is, but when I did, it was already too late."

"You all can't be still living together."

"Good heavens no. I see him occasionally when he demands it, and when he demands it, I have to…for special appearances, occasions, that sort of thing. But that's it. He hasn't been here in I would guess ten years, now. He lives all over the world. I love it here. He doesn't come back to the plantation. I've made it clear he isn't welcome back here. But that won't stop him if he wants to come back. He just doesn't want or need to come back, so he doesn't."

"I've known some great con men, but even not counting the real bad things he's done, I don't believe I've ever met a man like the man you're describing to me."

"He's a genius. He understands people inside and out, but how he uses that knowledge, that great gift he has… He is an extremely dangerous man. He used to tell me that he could detect the 'hidden frailties and sources of terror' as he'd call them, within seconds of shaking someone's hand. He'd then use the exposed flaws and vulnerabilities for his own purposes, and his purposes most always involved money, but always power. Sam said one time, sitting on this very porch when he was much younger than you are, that the best salesmen don't try to sell something by convincing people they have to have what they're peddling. They convince them they can no longer live without what they possess. Sam came up with a version of himself that was perfect, and that's what he sold. He actually sells the idea that everyone can be like

Sam Sherwood, and that's what people buy. But he is not the person people know.

"From the first day I met him, it was almost unreal how people were drawn to him, I mean really drawn to him. I just thought that I was in that way. That made his job so easy. All people want to be happy. Sam chose the perfect product, and then sold them the idea that they could—"

"Does he actually help folks?"

She nodded. "I can't deny that he does. I've seen it over and over. I believe a lot of it is just the immense power of persuasion that he possesses. He has changed many for the better. But he destroys lives, too. Those who get too close to him, or get in his way."

"Why does he want me dead?"

Kate bent to take another drink of tea, stopped for whatever reason and put both hands in her lap. She looked at me and I could tell she was suddenly breathing fast. "We're going to have to go back a long time. A very long time to before you were born. You are not who you think you are, Benjamin."

Chapter 20

I grabbed Kate's glass of tea and downed it. Forgetting my manners, which were few and rough even on a good day, I then put down the glass and wiped my mouth on the sleeve of my robe. Kate was still breathing fast. She seemed to not like being in the pleasant skin she usually lived in.

"I'm your mother, Benjamin," she said.

I don't know what was in my look after hearing what she'd said, but it made her back up in her chair as far as she could go. I stood in a hurry and wanted to leave. I wanted to run and run like hell, but then I got dizzy and grabbed the wall behind me. I wasn't ready to hear anything like what she'd just said. If I'd known anything during all the time I'd lived, the rock amid the swirling unknown dangerous waters rest of it, it was that I at least knew who my own mother was.

At least I was sure that I knew that.

"I gave birth to you in Shady Hollow on March 28, 1942. You were born there just as your ma always told you, and she was there with you when you entered the world. She was the first person to actually hold you. But you were my baby. You were my tiny baby boy, so small and so early but so perfect. But I couldn't keep you, Ben. If I did, you wouldn't have lived to be a year old."

"I don't believe you," I said. "What kind of mess have you pulled me into…into this damn place," I said.

"Ben, your ma wanted to take care of you. She fell in love with you the first time she saw you, too."

I sat back down and looked hard at Kate. "So you had me, but gave me away to Ma. You all made some sort of deal… That's what you're telling me."

"I'm trying to tell you that—"

"I don't look a damn thing like you, Kate. I look a whole lot more like Ma than you."

"I know this is hard, and it may take time for you to accept what I'm telling you, but I am your mother."

"My ma is my mother."

Kate tried to get nearer to me and then looked around. I looked around, too, for whatever she was looking for, me being anxious of whatever may be out in the darkness. She finally settled and said, "You have to at least listen to what I have to say. I've been waiting to tell you this for a long time."

"If my ma ain't my mother, what about my brothers…"

"I'm so sorry because I know this is going to be painful to hear, but you're not actually related by blood to any of your brothers. Your youngest brother was the only child

Becca raised who was actually her own. She took in the other children, she didn't bear them. I don't have to tell you how much she loved all of you, as if all of you were her own children. You all *were* her children."

"You make it sound like Ma's place was some kind of orphanage."

Kate tried to keep her eyes on mine and then looked down. "Many women during those times ran to Shady Hollow. Women in serious trouble. Many of them, and I'm not sure if you realized this then, but I assume you'd have to now, came to have abortions." She looked back up at me. "And some of those women, once there, in such trouble with nowhere else to go, changed their minds and decided to have their babies, but they didn't have the means—or the ability to care for them—once born. Over the years, Becca took in as many of those babies as she could. She loved being a mother."

"So it sounds like you're saying I was one of those babies…."

"You were. I was carrying you and I was definitely a woman in trouble. I needed help. I needed the one person I knew I could trust, and the only person I knew I could trust was Becca."

I loved Ma and I knew how good she was to me and the rest of her boys, but I just had to say what I had to say.

"I ain't judging Ma for how she made a living. But just knowing you the little I do, it surprises me that a woman like you would leave her baby for a young prostitute black woman to raise, and especially in an outlaw place like Shady Hollow. It don't make no sense, Kate."

I felt her hands grab mine. I hadn't been looking at her. I'm not sure what I'd been looking at, as my mind went back all those years while trying to put things together, and really try to understand what she was telling me because as much as I wanted her eyes to be lying to me, they weren't. I looked at her and it looked like she'd been crying. I'd been around crying women all day, and by the lump I was getting in my throat, I'd had my complete fill of it.

"You were safe there, Benjamin. Your mother wasn't a prostitute then. She just went with me. She knew about that place, had heard about it, and I was scared then and didn't know where to go…and she went with me. But somewhere on our trip there, it was a long trip, I changed my mind. But I could not keep you. I couldn't. I felt many reasons for that but mostly, because I would be scared for you. I was weak and scared and committed a terrible sin leaving you and her. I abandoned you *and* your ma. I can never do anything to take back that. I abandoned you once you were born and fled back home, to here. But in the back of my mind, I knew you'd be loved, and that you would grow up strong with your ma raising you. I knew it. I knew what a good mother she would be to you, a mother that I couldn't see that I could be."

I let go of her hands, closed my eyes and leaned back.

There was a long pause before she said, "And you were loved, and you did grow up to be strong. Strong enough to handle anything. Strong enough to handle this."

I didn't feel too stout right then but knew what she was saying about being strong because I'd seen many men break over different things. I opened my eyes and she went to do more eye wiping when I said, "So that's how Ma ended up in that place…to do what she ended up doing for a living. Is that what you're telling me?"

"I left her, and you. As soon as I could run away from you, I just felt like I had to go. It's hurt me every day since."

Kate looked to get even more a mess all of a sudden than she had been. It hurt me a lot more for Ma. Kate stood and knocked on the window behind her. The noise of it made the men around the porch turn to look at us, before they went back to looking out into the dark. The man who brought the tea earlier walked out again, and approached her close. I watched him closer, the closer he got. I don't know if he was told to never look at me that evening or he just didn't, but he didn't.

"Could you bring me another tea, and one for the gentleman. The same as I like mine."

He nodded and left. She sat back down and fussed a little with the dress she was wearing. It was quiet except for the loud sounds of a summer night in the South, and no words were said until the man brought out the two glasses of tea. My head was still too woozy from trying to mend up, and from downing her tea earlier which now I was thinking wasn't such a good idea, so I sat mine down and waited as patient as I could for her to take a few sips. She held the glass with both hands before setting it down on the glass table. When she did, it was the first time I noticed the pretty little things she had on it, flowers and whatnot. And a lot of the whatnots had been turned over and there was water on the table leaking onto the porch floor. I guess somewhere during the last few minutes of talking about things, things had gotten messy between us and on the table, too.

"I left Becca you, but nothing else. I cannot, there is no way to forgive myself for that. The money I'd taken with me by that time had run out. It was two years before I felt able and strong enough to go back to see you and Becca. She didn't want my money then. She refused it. She told me to put it away for you to have when you became an adult. Your ma was very angry with me for a long time, the way I'd suddenly left you and her in Shady Hollow with nothing." Kate took another sip of her drink. "She was such a good mother to you… I just knew that she would be… I didn't feel like I was completely abandoning—"

"Ma always had a soft spot for runaways and stray dogs and cats that nobody wanted to feed and things like that," I said, "but it's hard to believe even though she had that nature, that she'd just take on a child of yours like you're saying she did, with the cost of it to her."

I finished what I was saying and looked at my glass, and as bad as I needed what was in it, I needed as clear a head as I could have more.

"Ben, she had more reason to raise you as a son other than her loving nature, and she and I being such close friends. Your father is Becca's older brother. His name was Augustus Lee Purdue. August also worked and lived on the plantation when we were all just kids. Growing up, I became even closer to him than I was to Becca. Our friendship developed into a romance, a dangerous one and we both knew it, he more than I, but we couldn't stop what kept building over the years. He was a very kind, very handsome man. He's the best person I have ever known. You are a lot like him."

"So when Ma was raising me as her son, I was actually her nephew."

"Yes."

"What happened to him?" I asked.

"He was murdered late that same summer you came for a visit, Benjamin. He'd been living and working under a different name since about the time you were born. By the time of his death he was married, had other children. Four boys and two girls. All of them are grown now."

"Where was he living?"

"We both knew he was in great danger when I became pregnant. He fled, and it was several years before he made contact with me. He moved around a lot then. But he eventually settled in Chicago and made a life there. He was an incredible musician. I'd arranged for him to come, to meet you that summer. For you to meet him. I was working up to telling you this then, and he was on his way to meet his youngest son, but Sam found out. It all had to be canceled quickly and you had to be taken back to Shady Hollow. August was shot and killed walking from his house a few weeks after you left. The police never solved the murder, but of course I had my suspicions…and now actually have facts that Sam was behind the murder."

Kate stopped to take another long sip. I couldn't say anything during the pause.

"Becca was so upset when you left to come here. She didn't want you to leave and learn such truths, but deep down she knew it was time, and she let you come here, to find out who you really are. Everything was so set up, I had no idea that Charles was spying for Sam. I don't know where Sam finds such men, but he finds them and then pays them very, very well."

Everything in my eyes began to fade to dark for a second, and I turned my chair so the night breeze could cool my face. I kept my eyes open even though the sick in my head was growing and growing fast and less and less light was getting in, and it now was so bad I thought I was going to fall out of the chair, which seemed to be spinning around in a tight circle.

I wondered if I was dreaming this whole story up or the whole mess of it all was part of another hallucination, but it made too much sense. For the first time for some crazy reason, I never remembered but once Ma ever looking pregnant except with little Virgil, even though new baby brothers kept coming into the house every couple years or so. We were all fairly close in age, except for little Virgil. I don't know, I guess a young boy just doesn't pay much attention to such things and I couldn't recall any talk back then that we weren't really brothers.

"I'd only been married to Sam a short time when I rekindled the affair with your father and became pregnant. I needed him."

I opened my eyes again.

"I knew that Sam would know that the baby wasn't his, even before you were to be born, because he was away during the time you were conceived. I was so scared, and I ran, and I left with the only person I could trust to help me. August had fled. I made him. I didn't know where to go, and it's a long story, but about the time the money I'd left with was gone, I ended up in Shady Hollow.

"August couldn't wait to finally meet you. You may not see much of yourself in me, but you would have in him. I actually see a lot of me in you, Benjamin, and not just in your skin color. I believe you will, too, someday."

"Why didn't you... Why didn't Ma... Why didn't Amanda... Why didn't goddamn not one of you come see me, write to me, try to help me when I was in prison all those years?"

"We didn't know where you were for a long time, but when we found out, we were all afraid."

I stood as something angry and old was about to blow out of me.

"We were afraid, mostly for you, Benjamin. Even with all of her contacts in Shady Hollow and the resources she had, it took Becca a long time to find out what happened and where you were." She reached for me and I backed away. "It was a difficult time for everyone, you especially. If your ma had such trouble finding you, we all hoped Sam would have even more difficulty finding you and finding out what had happened to you. We wanted him to think you were dead. We were afraid he was watching us and we had to act like you died that day. And as it turned out, he *was* watching all of us."

"I did die that day," I said.

I reached down for my glass, went to take a drink but instead a fury came upon me and I smashed it on the table, and then I raked a sharp edge of what was left of the glass in my hand against the back of my other one.

Kate screamed and men came running from all directions, and I soon had too many people to keep off of me, grabbing me trying to get me back into the house. I knew that that next morning, I was gonna rely on that hand, whether all I'd just heard and been through on that porch was real, or if it wasn't. That wound would speak the truth.

"Let me go, goddamn it!" I yelled as loud as I could.

I felt the pressure of fingers ease up on my arms. I turned to Kate. She was crying hard with one hand held up in the air. She walked toward me and with both hands grabbed my one that was bleeding. She looked it over, as blood dripped onto her porch floor. She then looked directly into my eyes.

"You're strong enough to handle this, Benjamin."

She didn't say anything else but kept looking deep into me. It was a look that a child only gets from a mother, and she kept that look for a long time before she turned and said something quiet to the man who'd brought us the drinks. Then she turned to me, placed a hand up under one arm and began helping me down three steps and out into the darkness of the yard. Under a tree there were two wooden chairs. I sat in one after she sat in the other. It was a comfortable chair and I was glad to be sitting again. The man who'd been standing watch under that same tree moved farther away to stand guard, and it wasn't long before a nurse came to tend to my hand. "You've gotten this far, Benjamin," Kate said, as the nurse was finishing up with the dressing. I looked over to her voice even though I could barely see her. "You're going to have to go a little farther. Do you need to rest?"

I went to speak but I could tell the words weren't going

to come out right. I did need the rest but felt like time was short and I couldn't afford it. I needed to hear whatever else she had to say. I shook my head but as slow as I could so not to lose what was left of my balance and throw up tea all over her pretty tended yard.

"You're a very wealthy young man, Benjamin Purdue. Everything as far as you can see in all directions will soon be yours, if you want it, along with much, much more. And after we accomplish what I'm about to talk to you about, so we can move on from the past and live normal lives without fear, I'd like for you to make your home here. With me. But only if you'd like, of course. I want you to know that you have a home, and you'll never have to want for things you can't have again."

I didn't know what to think about all that. It was too sudden and too unreal to even think about. I'd wanted to be rich almost all of my life, and now upon finding out that I was rich, I could care less. I had too many important questions about other things she'd said to think any more about money, and besides that, I'd come to realize money couldn't buy the things I wanted.

"Did you go to the police about the facts you said you have about Sam killing my father, or the things you know about Charles and what he did to Uncle Ray?"

"I wanted to, but, Benjamin, you have to understand, I knew that I couldn't fight this man by myself and win, or even survive. I wanted to. I needed help. I've needed you to help me."

In the dim light I looked down at the bandage on my hand as Kate talked quiet, laying out a detailed plan. It was a plan for the destruction of her husband, Sam Sherwood. It came out so easy and so easy to understand, that she had to have been working on that plan and had practiced what she was telling me for years.

I never said another word to her or anyone that night and did the best I could to take in everything she was saying. Even with a full moon, the night got darker and darker to me to where I couldn't see at all. The last thing I thought about as I found myself being carried back up the steps into the house, was whether I was even alive or not, because I didn't feel dizzy or sick or confused anymore. That strange, so peaceful feeling had started to come over me again.

But I did wake the next morning, and very early.

Amanda Lynn wasn't holding my hand this time. Sam Sherwood was. And the hand of mine he was holding had a thick bandage on it. I noted that, and as soon as I was sure of it, I grabbed him by the neck with my good hand and squeezed with all my might. What I didn't notice right then as I was staring into his eyes that were fighting to get away from me, were the other men in the room, very serious armed men approaching fast and who I'd never seen before.

Chapter 21

The biggest of the bunch resembled a walrus, and they were all big. He grabbed my free arm and pinned it to the bed, then he drove a huge thumb into a nerve on the forearm of my other arm, the same arm that was trying to crush Sam Sherwood's windpipe. My fingers flew open, Sam fell and looked half-dead as he tried to back away from me, and during that same moment, the walrus popped a hand against my right ear, which stunned me to where I couldn't move except to breathe.

Immediately there were more men around my bed and I still couldn't move but my eyes strained to see around the bodies. I saw Sam Sherwood stand back up and cough several times before he began shooing everyone away. Everyone left but the walrus. He continued to hold me down with both arms, even though the concussion from his blow had left me pretty much lifeless.

Sam took two steps back toward me, got his perfect peppered hair back in its perfect place by pushing it away from his forehead, and he kept his eyes blazing on me but nodded at the walrus. Sam looked just as Kate had described, and he'd aged extremely well from the pictures I'd seen of him from old books he'd written. He looked like a movie star. Evidently the walrus didn't see or understand the nod, because Sam then said in a booming deep voice, "Let him go."

I could tell the walrus didn't want to, because as blood was flowing back into my mind and body, he squeezed both of my arms so hard I thought they were going to splinter before he finally did as told.

He grinned quick at me with only one side of his face before he walked away. Then I turned my attention back to the man who had been trying to kill me my whole life, and was responsible for killing the only man I would ever think of as my father and, according to Kate, murdering my real father.

It may sound odd, but I wasn't scared during any of what had just happened, and I wasn't scared at that moment, either. I'd never acted like such a brave man, but I needed to look close at a man capable of such bad things. He was a man filled with bad and good. I had to study his face. The things he had done to me and those close to me and the curiosity of it all fueled my courage.

Sam sat back where he'd just been, now calm as if nothing had happened, leaned forward, used one hand to wave away the walrus, who was still at the door, and then he grabbed my bad hand again, gentle but strong the way he'd held it just moments before.

"Let's start over," he said, with eyes that never blinked and stared into mine. I went to pull away my hand again, but now he gripped it tight.

My ear was still ringing from the blow moments before, my head was pounding and I was winded from waking to such a sight and encounter, but I now had enough feeling that I could jerk my hand away hard enough that he could no longer hold it. He may have been a whole lot smarter than me, but even in my weak state, I could tell I was stronger than him. I at least had that on him.

"Where's Kate?" I asked.

"I see you're not going to play nice. That will be your loss. She's at the plantation. She's fine, a little shook up her latest ploy didn't work, but other than that, she's fine. I've summoned my doctor. Kate is not a well woman, Mr. Benjamin Purdue," he said, pointing at his head. "She's not been well for a very long time."

I looked around at the empty room and remembered the faces of the men who had just been in there. Faces I'd never seen before the struggle.

"Where are the security men who were here?" I asked.

"They were told to leave, and they did."

"They just left..."

"My name is on the deed of this property, the same as Kate's. I heard you were here, I wanted to meet you, she refused to let me in, and I have a right to enter a house that I own. I called the sheriff's office and they helped defuse a potentially very embarrassing situation. I'm very good friends with the sheriff."

"Where's Amanda?"

"She's in Chapel Hill with her family, I would think."

He had a voice that came out strong without effort, a voice with no accent. It was the kind of voice that young children to even the hardest of men would obey without thinking. It matched his face.

I kept staring at him and it became clear he was not the sort to turn away or blink first, either, or show anything at all in the eyes, if he didn't want to. He not only looked, but was just the sort of man Amanda and Kate had described to me. I sat up and then threw one leg over the bed, and the walrus must have been monitoring things through the crack in the door, because he entered and quickly walked too close to me. I drove a hand into his chest to push him back, but the blow didn't move him. I went ahead and swung my other foot over and stood to my feet. I stared up at the walrus, who was taking up too much of the room, and shoved him hard in the shoulders because he was in my way. But he didn't move then, either. Out of the corner of my eye, I saw Sam Sherwood wave him back, and he took exactly one step back.

"I've heard you're recuperating from a terrible injury. Stay in bed."

"I'm the one person in this room who doesn't take orders from you," I said, not looking at him but still gazing at the giant of a man standing in front of me.

"Out, please," Sam said in a calm voice. He then stood from his chair on the other side of the bed.

The walrus didn't linger hearing his latest order, but on leaving, he shut the door but not all of the way, same as before.

"Close it," Sam said, in a normal sort of voice, but a louder one this time. He had one of the loudest normal speaking voices I'd ever heard, even louder than Simon Fletcher's voice. It was a preaching voice.

The door closed. He then looked at me briefly before he lowered a bed table to normal level, where he poured ice water from a heavy glass pitcher into two glasses. He sat back in his chair after he moved it to one side of the table, and then he pointed at a chair on the other side.

"Sit, please sit," he said.

"I'll stand," I said.

He nodded like he was bored, worked off the tie around his neck and threw it onto the bed. "Well, don't mind my manners, but I will sit. It's been a tiring day."

"Where's Kate?"

"I told you she's at her home."

"She wouldn't just leave here."

"You're right. She wouldn't…just leave. But it was in her best interest, her only interest, to leave, so she did. It was very stupid of her to bring you here. It was the first place I thought you would surface, a place where she would feel safe and feel good about your safety. And it isn't amazing to me that there is no amazement about how simple all of that was to figure out. She has never played a game of chess, for good reason, obviously. As you have not, either, I would guess."

"Well, that shows you don't know as much as you think you do."

"I didn't know if you played or not, how could I beyond a guess? But I posed my question so you would tell me."

"Poker has always been my game," I said. "Same game you're playing right now. All you did was just take a hand."

"Poker is a tough game to play and win when the dealer is better, and cheats better than you do, yes? There is no cheating or luck in a serious game of chess. The best player always wins. Sometimes very quickly, and sometimes by a strategy that causes the slow domination and ultimately, death of his opponent."

He took a drink from his glass, and after that he took out a piece of ice and rubbed it for a moment on the back of his neck. Then he threw the ice into a trash can across the room. I wondered what he would do if it had missed, but it didn't.

He was far too steady and relaxed and it shook me. I'd almost choked him to death a minute before. A few seconds more, and he may be dead now. But he wasn't, and I wondered if it was for the same reason his ice landed exactly where he wanted it to go. He was exactly the man who'd been described to me. He never missed throwing something into a trash can.

"Where's the law now?" I asked.

"They had better things to do than stay here once it became clear to everyone that I have a right to be on my own property. I make sure every year that their department is more than adequately funded, that they have the best equipment, make plenty of overtime and so on. I help them and they help me, if a need arises. One does occasionally. It's a very simple arrangement."

"Why're you here? Amanda told me you don't like to get your own hands dirty."

"She told you that?" He smiled. "I didn't know she'd been here until you told me."

I suddenly felt fearful for her, for bringing her name up in such a way. It was a stupid thing to do.

"Well, I actually wasn't sure she was here until I posed my last statement to you, and your face confirmed it. I guess, as you'd say, I just won another hand at your best game. Your chips seem to be moving to my pile rather quickly and I'm not even trying. I'm sure Amanda and I will have a chat soon and clear things up," he said, taking a long drink. He pulled a tissue from a box on the table and wiped his mouth with it before wadding it up and dropping it on the floor. "You know...I'm sorry, but I just have to say that I can't imagine you being a very good poker player after speaking with you for such a short time."

"You harm a hair on her head and I'll kill you over it," I said. "How's that for a bet."

"You'll kill me." He nodded with a half smile. He then raised a finger, pointing at me sort of up and down, I guess me being in my robe with the bandages on my hand and still around the back of my head. "I do admire your spirit. You do have courage. But I don't admire that you speak like a fool. Only fools speak like fools. I'm actually surprised you've lived so long."

I took a step toward him and he raised a palm. I don't know why, but I listened to his hand the same way his men did, and I stopped. Whether I liked it or not, so far he was the dealer in the room.

"Suddenly, I'm not quite sure what to do with you," he

said. "I thought we would have this talk a few weeks ago, when you were to be released from prison. But due to some error, I didn't find out that your date was moved. I was waiting for you then, as was Kate. She never knew I was also waiting, however."

"You've been trying to kill me all this time because your wife had an affair with another man and I came from it."

He stood, and I saw where we were about the same height, now looking eye to eye.

"I've found it helpful over the years…that if one wants to be successful in life…to always try to put your feet into another man's shoes. You obviously haven't tried to do that, not that a man like you could ever begin to fill my shoes. But if you did, you might see where a husband may have serious issues to deal with—say any husband and not just me—if his white wife had an affair with a black man, or any man for that matter, and from that…episode…a child was produced from such sin. It's condemning behavior. Such an act at the very least could cause quite a bit of embarrassment for a man like me, and a man like me is not to be embarrassed. Or shamed. Or thought weak. No. No. No. Heaven forbid that. Do you know how many books I've written on the sacred bond of marriage, how many seminars I've—"

"You never loved her. You don't love another and they'll find love somewhere else. That ain't nothing but human nature. You're one to talk about the sacred bonds of marriage with your own breaking of those bonds, marrying for money, the whole con job you pulled to get to where you are."

"Powerful men are men of great appetites. The things I talk

about to my following, the direction I give them, do not apply
to the very powerful and—if you weren't so ignorant and
were graced with even a brief showering of wisdom, you
would know—never have. That is also a part of human nature. The strong survive, Benjamin Purdue. The strongest of
the strong conquer. That's the nature of every living thing."

He turned to walk from the room and at the door stopped.
"I do want you to know this. Amanda was wrong. I've had to
get my hands dirty my whole life to get where I am. Much
dirtier than yours have ever been, and it does make the rewards
so much sweeter. But at the end of the day, some things aren't
worth washing my hands over. Some things, like you."

"If I ain't worth you getting your hands dirty for all the
dirty you've done to get rid of me, then nothing is. Finish
this yourself like a man would."

He smiled an easy smile. "I do admire your tenacity. A man
with balls is worth a certain level of respect, so few men actually have them. If you weren't so foolish, I'd almost think
you came from me and your whore mother, not from my
pathetic wife and a whore's brother. You know, I have
changed my mind, though. Before you go, I believe I will
handle this situation to clear up any misconceptions you may
have about me."

His smile then grew sharp as a razor's blade as he suddenly
turned to the door, stuck a hand through the crack and was
saying something to the walrus on the other side.

I ran to cover the three steps between us, and threw all of
my weight against the door just as he'd turned his eyes back
to mine. The door smashed into his elbow that was caught

in it. He yelled out in a high voice that I'd guessed he didn't even think himself capable of, and something small but heavy hit the floor. It bounced in my direction.

I saw the gun between my feet, and it was the first time in a long time that I started to feel lucky.

Real lucky.

When I reached for the gun, Walrus and about five other men stormed the door from the other side, knocking me and Sam Sherwood both across the room. The gun slid on the floor, not in my direction, but his. But I scrambled for it and got it before he did, then jammed it into the side of his head and rolled his upper body on top of me for a shield.

"Back away!" I yelled. "I'll kill him for sure."

I believe the pressure of that gun barrel pressing into his temple is what made Sam forget about his elbow for a minute.

"Do as he says," he said. After his loud squeal in pain when all hell broke loose in that room, I now couldn't believe how calm his voice was.

Everybody took about a step back, cautious, and I had one gun but was looking at five or ten pointed at me.

I looked at the walrus and told him to close the door. He didn't and I yelled, "Close the goddern door!"

He didn't take an eye away from me and kicked it closed behind him.

I figured there were other of his men in the house and said in Sam Sherwood's ear, "You yell, and you yell loud, that nobody is to come through that door. Nobody opens that door."

He paused too long to do what I'd said, and I took my

one free hand and closed it around his neck hard. He struggled and I took it off.

"You tell them. Right now."

"Nobody is to open the door! Stay outside!" He yelled it so loud with his powerful voice that I wondered if the neighbors could hear it. I kept trying to get my breath and it was hard with his weight on top of me with all else going on.

"I got something to say to you and then I'm gonna let you up," I said into his ear quiet. "Me and you have some business to take care of. I hear you're a pretty good businessman. We can both die here or do business."

He nodded his head.

I talked almost in a whisper and told him, "I'd have choked the life out of you a minute ago if your men weren't here," I said. "That was just my reaction to waking with you there beside me. But make no mistake, I'd have killed you. But I don't want to kill no more, see. Even a shiny piece of garbage like you. I've had my fill of killing. I'm a changed man…or a man trying to change, and I don't want to do such a thing to even a bad man like you unless it can't be helped. You need to let me have my life, and I'll let you have yours, but under some conditions. You ain't gonna find them hospitable at first, but you will in time. You following me?"

I couldn't see his face as his upper body was pretty much on top of me, but he nodded.

"You do exactly what I say or I'm sending a bullet through that big rotten brain of yours. I know I'll soon have one through mine, but I ain't scared of dying. I've done done it and it ain't so bad. I know where I'm going and I don't think you know nothing about where you may leave from here. I don't want to kill you, but I will is what I'm saying to you."

He nodded.

"Say it," I said.

"I don't know what you want me to say," he said.

"You say your days of wanting to harm me are over. We'll start with that."

He was still, and I jammed the gun into his head to where I knew it hurt and hurt bad from past experience of having a gun jammed into the side of my head.

"I won't hurt you anymore," he said. This time his voice wasn't strong. I could tell he was in bad pain.

"And you don't hurt Kate or Amanda."

"Agreed," he said.

I pushed harder.

"Agreed!" he yelled.

"Never."

"Never!"

I let up the pressure on the gun and looked up at the walrus, and saw the sweat forming on his forehead but his gun hand was steady and little by little he was inching closer to me.

"Tell your men to slide their guns under the bed," I said loud so all could hear me.

"Do it," Sam said. "Do it now."

One at a time they did as told.

"Now you tell them to handcuff themselves together. You tell them to because I know they got handcuffs on them."

His men looked at one another when I yelled loud as I could right into Sam's ear.

"Tell them right now!"

His head jerked away from me but I held him tight.

"Do what he says!" he said.

The walrus pulled out cuffs from the back of his waist-band, then a couple of other men did, and I kept pressing the gun into Sam's head so hard I thought it was going to pop out the other side.

"Do it! Faster!" he yelled louder.

They hurried and finished with the cuffing, and then I stood, and at the same time stood up my prisoner with me.

"Cuff your free hand to that bed, big ugly," I said to the walrus.

Sam nodded, and the walrus did as told, and then I had all of them turn and face the back of the wall, including Sam, and one by one I went down the line of them with the gun at the base of their necks, jerking out their pockets and throwing whatever was in them out into one of my robe pockets, and checking them for extra weapons. I found a bunch of them, threw most out the window but shoved one small revolver I found on the ankle of one man into the robe pocket with the rest of their keys and slapjacks and money clips and mace and police sort of whatnot.

"What are you going to do now, Benjamin?" Sam said.

"You yell outside and with all your voice, that if I so much as see another man of yours, I'm gonna end this now. And you'll be the first to go. You remember, you die first. You ain't the dealer no more in this game. Me and you are taking a little trip."

Sam started to yell something and had to clear his throat

and tried again. "Warren! Freddie! Put your guns away, go into the bathroom, and close the door and stay there. Stay there until I tell you to come out."

"Warren and Freddie better be the only two men left. I see another man, and this is gonna all end quick. I took the gun and slapped Sam on the side of the head with it. "Who else is out there?"

"That's it!" he yelled.

I slapped him again.

"Who else?"

He was shaking now and looked at the men in the room and he looked to be trying to count heads. "I swear, that's it," he said.

"We're coming out!" I yelled. "I see anybody and Sam Sherwood dies!"

Chapter 22

I opened the door and kept one hand around his neck and the other hand held the gun to his temple as we went down the stairs quick, too quick, because I started to get dizzy and had to pull him to me against the wall for a few moments to get my breath.

Halfway down the stairs, I could see the half-dozen or so cars in the drive. We made it down the rest of the way, out the door, and I turned him in a circle every step or so until we made it to a car. I walked to the passenger side of the car that looked the newest and fastest, opened the door, shoved him in and then dove in behind him. I kept low in the front seat with my gun on him, gave him the handful of keys I had, and told him to start it.

"I don't know which one," he said, fumbling with the mess I'd given him.

"You find it or we're both gonna die right here. It don't matter much to me, either, it just don't, to be honest," I said. I was lying about that quite a bit, but hoped he didn't know.

He tried two or three keys, finally found the one, and the car started. I told him to go, and instead he backed up, and I yelled loud at him to get the hell out of there and he mashed the accelerator to the floor. Dirt and gravel was thrown up in the air, and that's when I jammed a foot onto the brake. More dust flew up, and once I got settled, I dug the barrel of the small revolver under his jaw, pointed that barrel north, and with my other hand, I rolled down my window and then aimed with the big gun at the tires of the other cars sitting there in the cloud of dust we'd kicked up. It took two or three tries with the pistol for each car before a tire blew, but I just kept focusing on that and not on what I wanted to hit, not paying no mind to what else was going on around me, just as Uncle Ray had taught me.

We soon drove off when I said to. Looking back I saw men running outside, some of them cuffed together like a cutout a young'un would make with a pair of scissors and a piece of paper, but I knew they'd have to change flats and find a handcuff key before they could even try to catch us. The walrus looked to be dragging half a bed frame behind him down the porch stairs.

It was quiet in the car for miles, or at least a mile, and I'd use the gun now and then to point which way to go when we'd come to an intersection or a fork. I didn't know which way to go, but I wanted to at least act like I did. I buckled my seat belt and made him keep his off, in case he decided to hit the brakes on me unexpected like I'd just done to him. I didn't know how much he knew about such things, the sort of things I'd learned in Shady growing up and then in prison, to help out in such situations, but I settled back a little bit when circumstances seemed to allow it to try and get my head together, because I feared with everything that had gone my way so far, that I was gonna pass out. I was light-headed and my hands, which weren't shaking before, were shaking so bad now I could barely hold the gun. I saw his eyes had noticed that, too.

Driving down some dirt road to somewhere, faster than a car should drive on such a road, I told him to slow down when I saw a highway sign. He hadn't said nothing in what seemed like such a long time even though it weren't that long, and asked, "Will you tell me where we're going?"

"To a place full of ghosts," I said.

"Where's that?" he asked.

I took a few more deep breaths like I'd been doing, slow as I could and deep as I could. I was covered in a slick, cold sweat, and things weren't hopeful in some ways with me being dressed in a robe and light sleeping britches and no shoes on or nothing. I wished from other times being without shoes that I'd have least found a way to get a pair on before we left, but I just hoped most that I could somehow make it to where I wanted to head to. I was thinking about all of that when I turned to look at him and his eyes were locked onto mine. He turned his head back to the road. I looked down at his feet and the fancy shoes he was wearing, and then the clothes he was wearing and I guessed then that

things may not be as bad as I thought regarding having cloth-
ing to wear. I might just borrow his.

"We got an old graveyard to visit," I said.

He turned to look at me and then quickly turned back
to the road.

"But we have one stop before then."

"I do hope you realize that you're kidnapping one of the
most well-known people in the world. How far do you
think you're going to get with all of this?" he asked. "Do you
know how many law enforcement resources are being un-
leashed right now, to find me?"

"I guess I just feel lucky," I said.

"Luck never lasts."

"It will run out eventually, I've lived long and hard enough
to know that, but you should be feeling lucky, too. You ain't
dead, yet. And as far as what you just said, I don't think you'd
make too much of a poker player with all that's just happened
and to follow that with such an empty bluff about people
out looking for you."

He looked at me with the calmest look that would seem
to speak only the truth. "I never bluff," he said. "You obviously don't know me very well."

"You're a liar because all people bluff. What you just said
was a bluff, and a stupid one. You may outwit most, but I don't
believe you'd last half a night sitting at the poker tables I've
won at. You won a couple early hands and got too cocky is
what you did. And it might be time for you to know that I
believe your chess playing could use some work, too, the way
you had me pinned in a corner, but left yourself so unpro-

tected. You know what is the dern truth right now—you're the last person who'd want any of this in the news. Any of it. You've had men killed and have tried to kill me to keep less than this sort of a thing under the rug where you can stay so clean and sparkly to people. Your men haven't called anybody, and they won't. They won't for a long time, until they figure out exactly what is to be lied about all of it."

"You talk more when you're holding a gun."

"And you talk a whole lot less when you ain't surrounded by hired guns. I'll bet right now you're thinking about how much you've been paying those men, and are wishing you've been paying them more, especially after Kate tells them what she has to say. It will take some time before anybody with a badge who's not a crook is looking for you, and that gives us plenty of time for me and you to get to where we're heading. You just keep driving."

"I'm glad I am the one driving. You're white as a ghost." He looked down at my hand that was holding the gun. I tried to steady it but it kept shaking. He turned his eyes back to the road.

"You're not a well man," he said. "Perhaps you should give me the gun so we don't have something unfortunate happen."

I took the pistol and slammed it against the side of his head. The car swerved and almost went down an embankment before he got control of it.

"You drive the car. I'll hold the gun. Let's just do that for a few miles," I said.

I blinked hard and could feel my breathing had picked up way too fast. I tried to sit up in the seat but that made me even more dizzy, so I leaned forward with my head against the glove box. But I kept my eyes and the gun aimed at him. Miles went by as the sun was high now and the car felt too hot inside. I cracked my window.

"I don't think there was a need for what you did a few minutes ago," he said. "You could've killed both of us."

"I remember reading in one of your books—I've read a couple of them—that actions speak stronger than words. You didn't use that phrase what you were talking about, but that's what you were saying. Anyway, I was talking with you through that gun when I did that."

"I didn't know you've read my books."

"I've read everything ever written that I could get my hands on."

"What did you think about them?"

I leaned over and checked the gas gauge. It was under a quarter.

"How much money do you have on you?" I asked.

"I don't carry any money, and besides, you threw what things I did have in my pockets onto the floor a few minutes ago. Remember?"

I stared at him as he looked back and forth at me and the road. He patted his front pockets, which were flat, and leaned forward showing me that he had no wallet.

It was then that I remembered the money clips and two wallets I had in my pocket, taken off of his men.

I was getting too light-headed.

I laid my head and one arm back against the dash, and pointed the gun at him with my other hand that I kept in the crook of my supported arm.

"You said we had a stop before going to the graveyard. Mind if I ask what we're going to do?"

"Be still for a while," I said.

He kept glancing at me as my eyelids and the gun both got too heavy to hold up. His face began to wash out, and just before it drifted away, he was smiling.

And then he was gone.

I was sitting in the car by myself, my gun wasn't in my hand and I wasn't wearing pajamas and a robe. I was wearing my old clothes from Shady Hollow, the ones I'd last worn as a boy. I was confused and thought I must have passed out and was now in some crazy dream. I looked down to see the bandage on my one hand and it was gone, as were the tattoos that had covered that hand and my other one. My arms and hands looked exactly the same as they had, but completely different at the same time.

I leaned to the side and pulled the rearview mirror to where I could see myself and couldn't believe what I did see. I saw me, but I wasn't almost forty years old with a face carved with a nicked-up chisel. I was still a teenager, smooth skinned and scared out of my britches looking.

My breathing had slowed about the same speed as those things became apparent to me. When the great peacefulness built up and then came on me all over, I wasn't sitting in that car at all, I was standing in the old street in Shady. It was a beautiful fall day, and as I was admiring the colors of it and looking around for people I might know, a woman's hand grabbed mine. I followed where it led me, instantly knowing her because she was a woman no man or woman would ever forget. It was Helen, and as busy as that street was, no one seemed to notice the two of us walking off to the side, stepping onto the boardwalk and then off of it heading toward the steep banks of the river.

At some point I found the courage to turn and look directly at her. Then a strange quiet suddenly came over everything. Shady had never been that quiet at any hour of the day or night. I turned back to look behind me, but Shady Hollow wasn't there anymore. I was looking at a long, sloping cornfield, and a small cemetery, and then looking back toward the river, it was gone. A lake had drowned it and its waters were now at my feet.

"You've put up an extraordinary fight. Some who pass on to their awakening, particularly those who are young and die tragically, do not want to go on."

I was back in the state where I could say whatever I wanted to without thinking or caution. "Like those old mountain songs, like the one about the little girl who got killed along some highway and every year on that date somebody sees her on the side of the highway and brings her home where she says she lives, but when they get there, she's not in the car."

"I like that song. Yes, like that, in a way. Benjamin, you almost died leaving Shady Hollow. You almost died in prison from a stab wound. And then while lost in the forest, you were so close to your awakening. You almost died several times from the wound you received to your head. Your heart actually did stop beating for a few moments. Your brain is sending signals for your heart to stop beating right now." She was now turned and facing me. "You think you're dying, but what you're going through is actually the awakening, not death."

"I ain't scared to go on, but I ain't ready to, and I ain't going to just yet unless you make me. You ain't telling me I have to go now, are you?"

"No."

"You sure?"

"Free will doesn't stop when you stop breathing. Free will is the trail that only you make, and will then be the path you have to follow."

I didn't understand all of that, turned back to look at the cornfield and then stood so I could see the graveyard hiding in it.

"Can I walk over there?"

"You can go wherever you wish."

We seemed to be at the edge of the locust fence without having taken any steps to get there. I jumped over the logs, looked back, and Helen was standing on the other side.

"You're not gonna leave me, are you?" I asked.

"I'll tell you when I'm leaving," she said.

I walked so easy through all of the brush and brambles and made it to the plot Ma had bought from the elders for all of us. I got on my knees and looked at each grave. I stared at mine for a long time, put my hand down into the dirt and felt it in my fingers.

I could feel the dirt.

I stood, knowing that I was dead in some kind of big way but not all, and went to walk out of there, and just as I got to the fence, Helen pointed back to where I'd just walked from. I saw my ma on one knee at Uncle Ray's grave. She'd aged and looked not as graceful as she'd once been, but still was beautiful and she was saying some things to him I couldn't hear, and then she left flowers where he laid. Then she walked to my brothers' graves, stopping at them to say more things, laying more flowers, and finally stopped at mine. She got down to one knee and it was more than I could bear not to rush forward and hug her for as long as I could. But I couldn't do that. Something inside me wouldn't let me. Something inside me told me I wasn't supposed to, no matter how bad I wanted to. She stood and then looked at me and I felt for her in a deep way I wasn't sure I ever had. She was smiling. It was hard being so close to her, but I knew that's as close as I could get. I wasn't sure what I was right then, but I was sure that as much as Ma looked like Ma in so many old ways, she also looked like a ghost.

After a time, she moved the bag she had slung over her back to her front, unzipped it and pulled out my old fiddle and bow. She laid both over where I wasn't actually laid yet as far as I knew, and then she waved to me and as she walked from the cemetery, she got fuzzy and fuzzier until she was gone from sight.

"She really loves you, Benjamin. She always has and always will. You were and are very lucky to have such love." Helen smiled.

I nodded. I was lucky.

Helen turned to walk away, so I jumped back over the logs to follow her, and at the lake's edge she stopped and said, "I have to go now. It's time for you to go on now, too, Ben, but only if you're ready."

I looked at her and then I looked back at my old fiddle propped up on my homemade gravestone.

"Can I take my fiddle with me?" I asked.

"No, you won't be taking anything with you. Just what makes you, you. You leave the rest for this world, including your deeds, the good you've done, the mistakes you've made. All of that stays here, and lives on...here."

"Could I play on it a while, just for a while, and then come with you? I ain't quite ready to leave this place and this world yet, ma'am. I have things left to do."

"Let's do this," she said. "You let me know when you're really ready."

I smiled and she let go of my hand and I felt her letting go of mine in an odd way I hadn't before when she'd let go of my hand. "Can I ask you some more things before you leave?" I asked. "I still have questions about so many things."

She turned and shook her head. "I can't tell you what you seek. Over time you have to answer all of your questions for yourself," she said. "Follow the light when you're ready. You'll know when you're ready. A moment will come when you won't be able to not follow it. I'll see you again, then."

And she was gone, just like that.

I looked up into the sky as it had turned dark all of a sudden. I wasn't sure which light she was talking about, but figured it was that bright one I'd seen before and I'd find it when I was ready, or it would find me. Stars filled the sky. One of them was much brighter than the others and it wasn't the North Star or a planet. I knew where those were from many a night lying on a blanket with Amanda Lynn while she showed me the heavens, where everything was. I wondered if that new bright light must be my star. My light to follow one day.

I went back to the graveyard, felt my old stone, grabbed what my ma had left for me, walked back out of there, jumped the fence and found a nice place to sit under a tree, right near the water.

I listened to the breeze in the trees and the sounds of the water lapping up against the bank. It sounded to me like music all working together, so I tuned up my old fiddle and started playing along with it.

I played every song I'd ever known. I played late into the night until there were no songs left to play, then toward sunrise, I laid back under that nice tree and closed my eyes for a rest. I went to sleep listening to the trees and the water. They weren't through playing yet and knew so many more songs than I did.

Chapter 23

When I awoke to squint at wherever the hell I was at and try to figure it all out from wherever I'd just been, if anywhere, I came to realize I was back in that car, covered in tattoos and wearing a robe. And my wrists were duct taped together. I looked quick to my left, Sam Sherwood wasn't in the driver's seat, the gun I'd been holding was gone, and I checked my pocket for the other one. It wasn't there. I looked out the windshield and saw how the car I was in was parked at a gas station, and that's when I saw Sam Sherwood standing in a telephone booth only a couple yards away. I moved myself back to the position I'd been in and closed my eyes when I saw his back and head wheel around in my direction. Five minutes passed before I heard footsteps coming, the door open, and then the weight shifted in the car. Something hard jabbed into my left cheek but I kept my eyes closed. The jab came from something about the size of a small pipe. I figured it was the barrel of the pistol.

"Wake up," he said.

I stayed quiet with eyes closed. The car started and I let my body fall against the passenger door as he took a hard turn.

It had taken all of that time for me to feel like I was actually really back in the car, and not in that wonderful lost place I'd just been. I was rattled about that, whether I was now in a dream of some kind or just coming out of one, and I needed to figure that out quick with my current predicament.

The only good thing was the feeling in my head, which had been pounding before I'd lost consciousness, and was now still. I couldn't come up with a good plan, but then I remembered something that was going to work in my favor. I was still feeling lucky and suddenly asked, "Where we going?"

I opened my eyes, turned my head in his direction and stared at the gun I'd been holding, which was now staring at me.

"Keep your hands in your lap," he said.

I looked around and then up into the sky. "Looks like we're heading back south. We're going the wrong direction."

"Be quiet," he said

"Turn the car around."

He cocked the trigger on the pistol.

"That gun's empty. I shot all the bullets out of it shooting those tires. Shot it dry. I figured I was so woozy feeling that I might be better off pointing an unloaded gun at you than a loaded one, in case you took it away from me. The other one you have somewhere is loaded, though."

His eyes went wide when I scooted over fast, raised my arms and smashed his head into the driver-side window. I heard the gun click when he squeezed the trigger, just before he dropped the gun and that same hand went to his waist where he tried to pull up the front of his shirt that he must have pulled out earlier to hide the small revolver that was secured in his belt. Since my hands were taped, one of his hands had to hold the steering wheel. He had to drive the car, and that gave me the advantage. I used all of my weight to pin him to the door and I yanked the gun from his waist.

I moved myself to the other side where I'd been as he got himself situated behind the wheel. Neither of us said anything for a short time, just the sound of both of us trying to catch our breath.

"Where were you taking me?" I asked.

He didn't respond except his face had taken on a harder look than I'd seen before.

"Back to that old farmhouse, I suspect."

"You're not going to get away with whatever it is you're going to do," he said.

"May not," I said. "I think I got a pretty good hand, though. I'm not too worried. You preach a lot on worry and the unnecessity of it, don't you?"

"There is a real time for worry," he said. "This would be one of them."

"Take your seat belt off and turn the car around. We're heading north."

He did as I said, and I leaned over and checked the gas

tank and saw where the gauge said he'd filled it. He put a hand up to his left ear, pulled his fingers down to look at the blood on them and I noted his hand was shaking.

"You look off your game," I said, as I found the edge of the duct tape and began unwinding it from my wrists.

He shook his head. "Same game. I've just gotten serious."

"You're not gonna like the game I'm going to tell you about. You don't even realize what game you're playing now. But it's the only game you have left to play."

"What are the rules?" he said.

"You're not gonna like them."

He nodded. "Let me ask you, what do you think you are going to get out of this...whatever it is that you're about to do?"

"Well, that's an easy question to answer—good things I ain't been able to do, or felt up to doing, until now."

"Like what, if you don't mind my inquiry?"

"I'm gonna be able to go visit with a young waitress, with my head high and my eyes clear. Tell her how proud I am of her and how much I love her. Tell her how sorry I am for things. And then I hope I'm gonna be able to hold a little baby that spends part of her day playing in a cardboard TV box that makes do for a playpen. Tell her how lucky I am to have ever seen such a precious angel."

"You have a family," he said.

I don't know if it was the moment, or how he'd said it, or if I still didn't have my feet all the way under me yet, but I started getting all watery eyed and tight in the throat thinking about what he'd said. It really hit me that I did have family, and in a way that it didn't when I was broken-down at that old broken-down motel. I might just be able to be a good thing to them after all.

"I didn't know you had a family," he said.

"They'll have nothing to fear from you over whatever I tell you now or after our little trip ends."

"Then I guess the plan is, at the end of our journey, you kill me. Game over?"

"That's no game. That's just killing. That's your kind of sport. You pretty much killed a big part of me a long time ago," I said. "I figured I should return you the favor."

"What does 'pretty much killed' mean?" It was quiet after a time and he turned toward me.

"You're looking dead at what 'pretty much killed' means," I said. "Take a good long look."

He took a hard look before turning back to the road.

"Kate says you used to spread the Gospel...were good at it." His look stayed hard.

"Did you ever actually believe in the words you were preaching way back in those times?"

"I still believe."

"Just for other folks, like you were saying about the things you speak about, or for people like you, too?"

"Especially for people like me."

"You're a liar," I said.

"I've been helping people with their struggles my entire life. I've helped millions, maybe even billions of people."

"You've gotten rich off their struggles is the only thing that has been important to you."

"I've been rewarded in many, many ways more than just money."

"Well, I think you may got the makings of sort of a Jesus-type feller in you. You ain't nothing like him of course but folks do listen to you and crowd around you like they did him. You've made enough money charging them for the help. You've lived a life of plenty, and I believe it's fitting for you now to give back."

"Do you have any idea how many charitable—"

"You're going to give all of it away," I said.

"All of it," he repeated. It was the first time he'd smiled since at the house. It almost looked like he was about to start laughing.

"All that preaching you've done in your early years about how people should try to live like Jesus and help one another and give your shirt to a man who don't have one. See, I think for the most part you've been pretty much just picking pockets with a slap on the back and a handshake and a good wish or prayer, taking shirts. I believe it's time for a man like you to do what he's really destined to do."

"And what's my destiny?"

"It's time for you to walk your talk, like Jesus did. Roam the earth. On foot. Spread good and help folks. You're gonna do some walking from now on. Good for a man to walk. I'm here to get you started on your journey. You're gonna take your first step in a couple of weeks."

"How will I go about…walking my talk?" he asked.

"You're gonna give all your money away is the first thing you're gonna do."

He turned toward me and laughed. Laughed loud. He then

said, "And you'll manage all of the money I've made, I would guess, distributing it where you think best."

"No. I don't need your money. Even if I did, I wouldn't have a dollar of it. Other folks could surely use it, though."

"It will actually be quite a task. Giving away several billion dollars, not easy, and all of the companies I—"

"Kate knows how," I said. "In fact, she already has a plan in place that she's acting on now to do just that, a plan she's been working on for a long time."

His face tightened.

"Even if there was any way, which there isn't, that I would agree to a scheme so stupid and frankly, naive, I believe what you don't understand is…I am a much more useful, productive, helpful human being doing what I do now, than doing what you suggest. It doesn't even make sense. Making a lot of money allows a person, like me, to give a lot of money to causes and those who do need it, who only receive such assistance from people like me. I am best to my fellow man when I am generating wealth, because I direct a substantial portion of it, as well as my time, to people and places where it is needed most."

"You ever do any of your speaking at homeless shelters or prisons, places like that?"

"No, but I've donated—"

"You're gonna start doing exactly those kinds of things."

"This walking the Earth idea would actually hurt the same people that I could be helping, doing what I do now. It's basically a noble…in a fairy-tale sort of way…and completely childish, unworkable idea."

"You're not following me," I said. "It's not the little things you'd do to help people that would be the big thing of it, though those little things are big things when folks don't have but less than little. It's the example you'd be setting for others with more than most have. Somebody like you doing something like that. Not taking so much and giving more. You're not a good man but you're a born leader for sure. People would follow and maybe do likewise…giving more, taking less, helping more. That kind of Jesus thing I'm sure you used to fire up at the end of every sermon before passing the plate back in the old days."

"So you know what Jesus would like for me to do?"

"No. But I know you're going to do exactly what I'm saying you're gonna do, and in the end, you're gonna end up more famous than you are now, which I believe would sit with you just fine. Poorer for certain, but more famous. I'm giving you a chance to do some good and have some dignity at the end of it all. 'Course if you'd rather, I could just shoot you now and be done with it."

"I'm telling you it's an insane idea, and people would think I was insane."

"No, they wouldn't. They'd think a man like me was crazy if I did it. But not a man like you. And I believe once you do it for a while, that you might actually start believing in what you're doing. You'd really see the good in it, not prospering from none of it, your hands getting dirty with things they never been dirty from…from good dirt, not bad dirt. And you might just start to feel the good in it and that might wash some of that bad out of you, see. You got a lot of bad in you. You got a whole lot more bad in you than even bad men do. It's deep in you."

"You're holding the gun," he said.

"Ain't no angels in this car, if that's what you're saying."

"And please tell me why do you think I'd ever agree to such a proposal?"

"There is no proposal for you to agree to. See, I can't just let you go, obviously, but I'm doing my best not to kill you. Now that's a problem."

"Listen to my proposal. If you let me go, I'll—"

"Your life, the one you've known and have been building all these year, the future you've dreamed for yourself. Your ambitions. It's all already gone. All of it. You just don't know or believe that yet. You're about to. You're about to meet hard times face-to-face. You're about to pay and learn from the bad you've done. I'm doing my best to give you a chance to redeem yourself for so many bad things. You don't know how lucky you are that you didn't kill me in that house."

Ten minutes later the car was parked on a dusty gravel road off of a side road somewhere in North Carolina near the Virginia border. We may have actually been in Virginia by then, but it still seemed like North Carolina to me.

I took the car keys from the ignition, got out and immediately I drew in air that was filled with water you couldn't see and it was red soaking hot once you took a breath of it. It had to be over a hundred degrees with no wind in that swamp.

I waved Sam Sherwood out of the car with the gun and he did just what it told him to do.

I let the gun point him in the direction I wanted to head, dead out into the middle of that swampy ground and far enough from the car to where we couldn't see it or any road, but not far enough where we'd both be swimming in green mud. He'd turn around occasionally and I'd motion for him to keep walking, and I wasn't surprised a man with so much to say at almost all times would have nothing to say right then. I'd seen such things before as a kid, where even the strongest get quiet. He was scared or else holding his cards tight.

"Turn around," I said.

He stopped. "This isn't quite the deal you've been speaking of," he said. "I hope you didn't change your mind." He didn't turn around.

"Turn around."

I don't know what he was saying to himself in a whisper but I figured it was a prayer of some kind. I let him finish with it. He turned around and had tears in his eyes.

I threw him the gun. He caught it.

"You can finish what you've been trying to do since I was a kid. Right here," I said. I looked all around. "Good place for it, don't think anybody'd even hear the shot. You get back in your car, go back to your business. But like I've been saying, you—"

"This gun's not loaded, either, I would guess." He suddenly pointed it at me.

"Pull the trigger."

He stared at me for a few moments, then raised it high above his head and fired it. After the boom and ringing, the sounds of the swamp got quiet for a few moments before it came to life again. Sam lowered the gun and examined it while looking at me. He used his thumb to press the button that let the cylinder fall to the side. He looked at the one empty casing and the bullets left in it before closing it back.

"Still playing poker," he said.

I shook my head. "Poker game is over. We've been playing chess for quite a while. You have the gun now, but I have checkmate."

He raised the gun and pointed it at me again. "No, the gun still makes it a poker game."

"You kill me and you're ruined. You'll be hounded by law enforcement and news people the rest of your hunted days. If that's your choosing, then I ain't afraid to die and in the end, I do win the game. This is my board we're playing on. I tossed you the gun, but I did it because you have no moves left. You shoot me, and you kill yourself, but in a much more terrible way. This is chess."

"Being not afraid to die is not an admirable quality as much as you seem to think. It makes you nothing more than a crazy man!" he suddenly yelled.

I believe the loud way that came out of him surprised him even more than it did the creatures around us, who got quiet again but for only a few moments.

"If I die here, today, right now, I will die at the least a feller who is trying to be a pretty dang good feller. And I was blessed with quite a few good years, and a few times so good others might even die to feel such things. I can die with that. And if I do, and that's your choice, you will walk out of this swamp a man who within the week will wake one morning to find that every major newspaper in the country, and news stations, and dozens of county and city and federal prosecutors are going to find packages on their desks, detailing the life and times of the real Sam Sherwood. It's one interesting story you don't want told, of course. I don't live, that story is going to be told. If I live, and you grant your wife a divorce, and you do the other things I've mentioned, you live. Those packages won't be delivered. You may even die happy and old one day, a changed man. It can happen. You will die without a nickel, though. Not one nickel. You're already a poor man and don't know it."

"That's what this is? You're trying to blackmail me?" He suddenly lowered the gun and smiled as if I were a child who'd said something funny and not on purpose.

"You're finished is what this is."

He took a step forward. "If there was evidence anywhere, for anything, to link me to anything, don't you believe that with my resources and power, I would make sure that evidence never saw the light of day?"

"I ain't educated formal, but I spent two years in prison learning to read, and afterwards read everything I could get my hands on the next nineteen years. Read a lot of books. Maybe more books than you've read. Short stories. Plays. Novels. History books. Biographies. I've read a set of encyclopedias…*A* through *Z*. You know what I figured out? And like I said I ain't got an education but it wasn't hard to figure out—the most powerful are never taken down by those less powerful than them. They always fall because they come to believe that they are all powerful and can't be taken down. That's their weakness. They ultimately kill themselves."

He looked as bone-weary battle tired as I felt standing there, but he grinned. "At times I would swear talking with you that you were my son. You even favor me in a few ways. You do know I fucked Becca on a couple of wonderful occasions before she left the plantation with Kate, don't you? It wasn't surprising when I learned of her future occupation... she was quite something."

I ran toward him in a fury and it was like my face ran into a sawed-off tree limb, but it was his shoe. I went to get myself off the ground and he kicked me again. I got up slower the second time and looked at him and he was standing half crouched down with one fist at his side and the other hand up in the air holding the gun. Then he took his back foot and lunged forward and that time, I lost a lower tooth, and on the same side of my jaw that never was in good shape from that sheriff hitting it. I laid there on my back, trying to get up but trying to do that and not swallow my own tooth, and when I got to where I was sitting, it was then I saw a shoe on a foot flying at me again. He'd kicked too slow that time, though.

I had him by the leg and he was hopping as I was trying to stand up. I got the shoe off his foot and then started swinging it, the hard sole cracking off his head and his hands that were trying to protect himself from his own shoe. The gun in one of his hands fell to the ground and we spun in a circle until I finally got to where I could kick his hopping leg out from under him, and he fell hard and even harder, when I fell on top of him with all my weight driving into his stomach. I didn't have to hold him down or nothing after that for a good spell because the wind was gone out of him, and he didn't want to fight anymore, just breathe. I stood and drilled the shoe I had in my hand at his head pretty hard, and I believe that's what kick-started him back in gear. I slapped the gun into his hand, which he took but acted like he didn't want to.

"You have nothing on me," he said.

"Why didn't you shoot just now then?" I bent down. "Your old dedicated employee, Mr. Charles, kept quite a journal," I said. "Quite the writer, he was. Dates. Names. Lot of names. Lot of interesting reading…his spy missions in World War II, and the duties he performed for Sam Sherwood after the war. And Kate has been collecting a lot more things than that over the years. The hidden loot. Women. Drugs. Blackmail. Murder."

"If Kate had anything on me she could prove, that bitch would've used it already," he said. "This is a stupid, dangerous game Kate has drawn you into, Mr. Purdue. A dangerous game that's going to end up getting a lot of people hurt, besides you."

I shook my head. "She was too terrified of you for too many years. As you can see, I ain't. She needed help to put her plan into action, and she has more help than just me. You try to harm anyone, and that plan automatically goes into motion. I don't surface tomorrow, that plan gets put into motion. Kate is harmed, that plan gets put into motion. And of course, if you actually do try to harm anyone you may think may be involved, besides the plan being put into motion, you may just force my hand to kill you outright, and then your sorry legacy will be exposed as you're lowered into the ground."

"Are you telling me that if you would have passed away or disappeared from the farmhouse, I would now be on the verge of my ultimate demise?"

"If I'd died, or disappeared, in a day you'd be the most infamous and prosecuted preacher turned self-help bag of wind who ever passed a plate or sold a book. I did myself a favor surviving your visit, and I did you a favor, surviving your visit. And now you owe and have to pay for all the bad you've done to so many, not just me."

He just kept staring into my eyes like he wanted them to catch fire.

"You had my father murdered...what should I do to a person who has done so much bad? Killing you would be too easy. Now take off your clothes. I'm giving you the car, but I'm taking your clothes. You're gonna drop me off in the closest town and I'm contacting Kate, and any of your men who may still be near there had better be long gone within an hour. Long gone. And you, and them, are never to go there again. You'll be hearing more from me tomorrow, and you'll be served divorce papers soon. You're gonna sign them. And then you're gonna do exactly what else I'm gonna tell you to do."

"You won't get away with this. You're not smart enough to get away with this."

"I already have," I said.

"You have no idea the game you are actually playing." He

stood, then he threw the revolver I'd given to him twice during the last twenty minutes deep into the swamp. He shed his shoes and socks and pants and his shirt, handing them to me in a careful way as if they were things to be taken good care of. As I handed him my robe and the rest of the thin sleeping things I'd been wearing in return, he said, "You must not have listened to your own words about the vulnerabilities of the powerful a few minutes ago."

"What?"

"The false invincibility of thought and feeling that come to those claiming huge chunks of power, believing it is rightfully theirs."

"I ain't trying to claim power," I said.

"But you are," he said. "You are." He got dressed in what I'd been dressed in, and seemed to get it all situated in a way he felt more than comfortable in than I'd been. "How does it feel, wearing a pair of four thousand dollar shoes?" He took off his watch and handed it to me. "I thought you may like to know what it feels like to wear a twenty-three thousand dollar watch."

I took the watch and threw it in the direction where he'd thrown the gun, then I tried to move my toes in the shoes I'd just put on. They were too tight. I took them off and threw them out into the swamp with the other things.

"How'd that make you feel to throw away almost thirty thousand dollars?" he asked. "Thirty thousand dollars. A lot of money. The craftsmanship, the precious metals and jewels, the animals that were bred and then raised and slaughtered and skinned to make that pair of shoes, shoes you could have donated to those without shoes or sold for a lot of money to use or give away. It made you feel powerful just tossing them away, I'd bet?"

"I have no need for a watch and the shoes didn't fit," I said. "I know what you're trying to say, but I ain't like you. I maybe could've turned out to be a man like you at one time, maybe, but my ma raised me better." I took a step closer. "You got anything else ugly to say about my ma, now's the time."

"You and I are the same nature, the same only wearing different clothes."

"Well, if either of us ever wants to wear four thousand dollar shoes or needs a good watch, we'll know where to look for them," I said.

"They're shit to me," he said.

"You must like to spend too much money on shit, then," I said.

"What are you getting nervous about?" he said.

I looked at him hard.

"You're the one with all the answers, the great plan to make me pay for all of my sins. You're wearing my clothes for Christ's sake. Throwing my jewelry and shoes away? The insult to injury of it all. Already won the chess game and all of that you've announced." He took a big breath and blew it out hard, with the same smart-ass look on his face that he'd been building. "I'm not so sure you believe that…about the chess game, being the game isn't over. One player cannot just proclaim to win. You have to win. You're wearing my clothes, but you don't look like a winner to me. You still look like a loser. It's going to be hard to cover up all of those ugly tattoos, isn't it? Even a shirt worn by the great Sam Sherwood isn't capable of that. And you know what…if you had enough 'bad stuff' on me to get me into so much trouble, you wouldn't threaten me with it, you'd bring it to the authorities. Now. You're a hack poker player who is only good enough to get in a big game, but then lose everything, and you're not a chess player, and this has been just one really dangerous bluff. You don't look well, and what's worse, you actually have nothing in your hands to make another bet with."

He was at least right about one thing. I'd bet then that I didn't look well, because I felt a long way from well and was feeling worse by the second. I took slow deep breaths and didn't look behind me, but figured in my mind how many steps it would take to get back to the car.

"Don't suddenly become shy after all we've been through," he said, taking a small step closer.

"There maybe isn't enough to send you away for the rest of your life, or to the electric chair. But we don't need that much. We just need enough, and have more than enough, to stain your name with blood all over it and destroy your reputation and everything you've built. You'll spend your fortunes fighting charges the rest of your life, and maybe can even find a way to stay out of jail, but you'll live in a courtroom and regardless of final outcomes, you'll be ruined. People will know you're nothing but a smooth-talking rattlesnake. You'll spend the rest of your days trying to explain away and deny all the terrible you've done."

I was feeling too weak to do more battle with him. I could already feel him working on me. Somehow, I felt the tide was changing. That thought sent something cold crawling up my back and I knew I had to get the hell out of that swamp and turned to leave. I walked twenty yards and looked back, and he was still standing where he'd been.

"I said I'd give you the car, but if you don't get moving I'm driving out of here," I said.

I kept walking and there was no response, and then I heard him laughing. I kept walking.

"Welcome to the real world of the survival of the fittest, the survival of the conquerors, Benjamin Purdue. We're actually very similar creatures, and only one will survive in the very end. Who do you really think that person will be?"

I turned and he was far away, but I could still make him out as I looked through the undergrowth separating us.

"In two weeks I'll be watching your last show in New York," I yelled. "It'll be your last show…"

"I can't wait to see how our game ends," he yelled, followed by more laughing.

I walked and walked as his laughing got more and more faint. I got in the car and looked in all directions but didn't see him. And that's when I remembered that the car keys were in the robe pocket, which he now wore. I continued to sit, I needed to sit, and a few minutes later he walked toward the car. He dangled the keys for me to see before opening the door.

"I believe I'd better do the driving, don't you?" he asked.

I scooted over in the seat.

He talked, not much, and it was mostly small talk things as if we were the best of friends as we made it back to the highway. I was too exhausted and too sick to say anything back. At a crossroads I spied a gas station and pointed for him to pull over. He did, I got out pretty shaky, and as I walked to a pay phone, he pulled alongside me and said, "Don't be dying on me now. I do look forward to receiving the package tomorrow."

"The package is gonna erase that smile off your face. I look forward to your last show," I said. "I'll be watching."

"I hope you enjoy it," he said, smiling. "By the way, you said that we were going to stop by an old graveyard to see some ghosts or something. Why the change of plans?"

"One day," I said.

"I'm ready to go now, if you'd like."

"Soon enough," I said.

He nodded and his face got hard. The car suddenly flew out of the parking lot. I went into the booth, picked up the phone and dialed 0. As I waited for the operator, I looked at my shaking hand. It wasn't just my head that was bothering me and making me feel so unsteady. Something that happened in the swamp and on the ride to get there and leave there had begun to shake me to the core. He was getting to me. I knew I wasn't his son, but we were too much alike.

Chapter 24

Kate had a man pick me up at the gas station and take me back to her old homeplace, where I slept much of the next week. She wanted me to stay with her at the plantation, but I liked the looks and feel of the smaller old farmhouse with the shaded porch so much better. She had people tending to me hand and foot and I had a hard time running them off. After a few days of sleep and eating all I could night and day, I actually felt normal again, and could tell my strength and balance were almost back. It took some doing, but she did finally let me be on my own, except for people coming over here and there to help clean up or bring things she thought I might need. They were all nice to me, but I didn't know what to do with all the fuss and the only person I didn't try to run off from the get-go was a nice woman named Mary.

I never saw Amanda Lynn again while staying at the

homeplace. She didn't visit, and I never brought up her name to Kate, as she didn't. I thought about her a lot while easing away evenings on the porch, but I was surprised that I didn't think about her as much as I'd always had. I still thought about her all the time, but not as much all the time, I guess. I figured I was trying to move on from her, something I never thought would happen. I still dreamed about her, though.

Mary was the one person who worked for Kate who I enjoyed most seeing every day. Sunny skies seemed to follow her around and it got to where I'd get nervous before she'd be coming over for something or another. She'd bring over meals and do various things to help me around the place. One day I convinced her to let me take her for a ride out through the pastures, by a huge oak I'd once been fond of, and down by a winding creek. She told me she'd like to go but thought she may get in trouble, but I told her I would talk to Kate and it would be fine. I did and it was.

Mary and I became pretty close during that short time, and after our one trip through the pastures we took longer ones every day to see different places. We even drove east a few hours to the Outer Banks, where I finally got to see the ocean. It was an amazing sight, and I had the best time I'd had in ages and ages. We walked miles of beach and ended up the day eating oysters and drinking ice-cold beer on a pier in a place called Kill Devil Hills. There were all kinds of stories about pirates and ghosts and shipwrecks and hurricanes and a lost colony of folks on the Outer Banks, and much of that long sandbar was still wild and not built up, and I could see why Ma would be so fond of the area. I was taken with it, and I was getting taken by Mary, too, the longer we were together. It surprised me, but I was fine with it. Way past dark, we took a ferry and found Ma's old house in Ocracoke. The windows were boarded up and there were no lights on inside. Mary and I sat on Ma's porch swing and watched the tide go out in the moonlight. It was a nice little house and a nice place to live, and Ma deserved both. It made me happy for her.

Mary didn't say much and I didn't, either, most of the time, but that didn't seem to bother us. She was younger than me but not much. Her skin was darker than mine and she was pretty in a natural and relaxed, not fixed-up way. She told me she'd been married once but said she'd married too young and that finally dawned on her and her husband, so they divorced a couple years before I came to meet her. She had a grown son named Tyler, and I got to meet him once and he seemed like a fine young feller and I believe he approved of me a little bit.

Mary didn't know much about me, and that I had very recently came into so much money. She didn't know anything at all about my past, that I was aware of. We both tended to talk about the present and not much at all about tomorrows, and especially not yesterdays. I believe we tried to let all of that be.

Kate was busy and nervous most of the time when I was with her, worried over what was coming up soon. She hadn't heard from Sam, but one of her lawyers had heard from one of his lawyers, that Sam was going to agree to the divorce, and almost all of her terms. Kate celebrated that night with her glasses of tea and she looked to lose ten years in age with such a weight lifted from her, and suddenly feeling so free. But she was still cautious…she said she couldn't celebrate to the fullest until after Sam's show in New York, where he was to make a big announcement.

Kate kept inquiring about what kind of life I'd like to have, suddenly having so much and so many opportunities to make something out of my life. The only thing I asked of her, and it was a big request, was I told her that I would like to buy the property with the monster house that over-looks where Shady used to be, the same monster house that didn't belong on the side of that mountain. I wanted to make whatever offer the owner would take, to buy it, tear it down, let the place go back wild, fix up the cemetery, and knock down all of the No Trespassing signs so anyone who wanted to come there and enjoy all of that nature, could. I figured to make it a nice spot where someone could visit their kin if they wanted to, or camp for the night and look up at the stars, untroubled that they'd be bothered by anyone for being there. She said she'd look into it for me, and she did.

As far as trying to figure out what else I was going to do with all of that money, I wanted some of it to go to a few folks I'd met and who'd helped me on that long journey from prison. And I especially wanted to visit with my daughter and granddaughter as soon as I got back from my upcoming trip to New York. I wanted them to have whatever was left.

With all that Kate had on Sam, she didn't think there was any way he would not agree to her and our terms, but at the same time, she wondered like I did if there was some way he could turn everything in his favor and escape the trap he'd actually made for himself.

She brought over a tape one evening that she wanted me to watch with her, of the last show he'd done that was on TV a couple of years before. She wanted me to have an idea of what I would soon experience for myself, things like how he could move a crowd in whatever direction he wanted them to go. We sat and watched it, and it was something.

As we began to watch, Kate pointed out things like how "he studies the audience from the darkness." I followed her finger where she pointed at the far corner of the stage. "That's where he always stands," she said. "People can't see him, but he can see them. He's back there."

"Sammy! Sammy! Sammy! Sammy!" the crowd chanted.

She said many of the people there had been sitting and waiting for him to speak for hours. The floor would shake from stomping feet and his name would echo off the ceiling.

"Sammy! Sammy! Sammy! Sammy!"

"It's almost time," Kate leaned over and said into my ear. "He's told me how important it is to wait until their hunger peaks. They're waiting for him to fix their broken lives. They'd wait all night."

"But does he really fix people?"

"The way Sam sees it, maybe he can actually help a few, maybe many, maybe only one. But what it is when it comes down to it, it's a show, a show they will never forget, and when it's over, almost everybody there will feel better than they ever have—at least for a couple of hours. I've seen it,

Benjamin. I've had to watch it happen hundreds of times now. And they'll come back again and again to feel that way, even if it's only for a few minutes."

"Feel what?"

"You'll find out soon."

"Sammy! Sammy! Sammy! Sammy!"

"Everyone who pays to hear him speak will talk about him and his message on their way home, his tapes playing in their car stereos, his just-bought books cradled in their hands. They'll try to live up to the challenges he gives them and they'll sleep with fantastic dreams of happiness and wealth. And then as their dilemmas surely creep into tomorrow, they'll wake and wonder why they all couldn't be like him."

I'd been looking at her, watching as her smile grew and then at the end faded.

"You have to admire, be amazed by the energy one person can create just with words. We're just watching it on TV, but can't you feel it?"

She turned up the volume on the set.

"Sammy! Sammy! Sammy! Sammy!"

I did feel it some and nodded.

"He's told me all about how their anticipation is about to turn to frustration. He's been watching and listening, and this is the moment he's been waiting for. He knows where the peak is, and he waits to grab it and then not let go, until he decides the show's over."

He ran to the middle of the stage for his encore and it looked like he was about to rise in the air like a magician as he spread his arms like wings and the voices of thousands roared his name, just as they had two hours before when he first took the stage. I just kept staring at him like I had been through the whole show. He was tired now or acting like it, and by his closed eyes and the expression on his face, it looked like he was at the end of the best lay in the world, or in a high that no drug or drink could ever produce. He had everyone in that place in the palm of his hand, except for one.

"Sammy! Sammy! Sammy! Sammy!"

I was no longer watching him on tape, I was sitting dead center three rows back from the stage. Kate said that she just couldn't watch it live and wasn't there with me.

His hair and shirt were now soaked with sweat under the blaring lights, and all those around me, in front of me and behind me had their hands out toward him, their faces screaming to be noticed.

He slowly held up a hand and everyone obeyed that hand and it got quiet. It was an eerie quiet, the pause before the very end, but he didn't look to be finished with them yet and they didn't want him to leave.

He reached under the podium and raised a bottle of water, drinking it down in gulps. He scanned the front row of people and they were waiting again for whatever else he had to say. It looked to me like they would wait all night. Thirty-six thousand people were there, and with a hand could become quiet as if they were sitting in church.

Looking away from the bright lights, he switched the microphone into his left hand and, with his red towel, wiped the sweat from his forehead. He asked for a few moments and they gave it to him. Looking down, he grinned what no one but someone very close to the stage could ever see, and then he glanced offstage.

I remembered Kate telling me that when he did this, his director was telling him the time he had left, and that Sam had told her one time that the thing that always amazed him was how it was all so easy. He said for the truly gifted, people are easier led than sheep. Kate said Sam believed people have always needed someone else to tell them how to live their lives for the simple reason that life is so uncertain and so full of risk and danger. The power that comes from that simple understanding of human behavior—that almost all people want to be led— is the one thing that had always amazed him. He couldn't believe there weren't many more men like him. It was so easy.

The moment was coming that she'd told me he'd raise his hands for everyone to sit, but he really doesn't want them to…and they won't.

As if Kate had seen the same movie a dozen times, what she'd just described had just happened. Sam raised his hands and pushed them down for everyone to sit, and like other times when he made what looked like pretty much the same signal, no one did. They began to chant his name again. It got louder and louder until he yelled.

"Today is your day!"

They screamed with what voices they had left and extended their hands in the air. A grin spread across his face.

"This is a great country and we are a great people!" he commanded. He sprinted across the stage, stopping to point in all directions, his actions as wired as an out-of-control water hose.

"Go from here and live your destiny. Command your fear to stay in this room! Let it die here. Here! You don't need it anymore. You are now like me. With the divine confidence that was born in you, go forth tonight with the courage God gave you!"

He made his way back to center of the floor, bowed to them, held up both arms like a battered boxing champion and began to walk from the stage, but their chants would bring him back again.

"Sammy! Sammy! Sammy! Sammy!"

He drained a fourth bottle of something that looked like water. The roar was deafening.

"Dreams are not just for children and poets to believe in!" he yelled. "It's all about you! Your world! Your day! Your hour! Being alive, now, today, this very moment, is all that you have!

"Take it! Taste it! Make love to it. We do not know the concept of failure!" He looked around quick and lowered his voice, and everyone lowered theirs likewise.

He was now at the point in the show I'd traveled almost a thousand miles to watch in person. I sat up and drilled my eyes into his. I wondered if he was actually going to do it.

"You now know what it's like to be truly alive, to feel truly alive. Give back what you can but *take* what you deserve! Take it!" He paused for a few moments and yelled his closing question with what sounded like all that was left of his strong voice.

"And what do you deserve?" he yelled.

The crowd suddenly roared "Everything!" as he began struggling to walk from the stage. His knees buckled and he leaned forward to try to grab the podium as his assistants ran onto the stage before he fell. As the lights came up, over the loudspeaker the squinting crowd was told that SherWorld products would be available in the lobby for another hour.

I leaned back. He didn't do it. He goddamned didn't do it.

I was trying to keep from being stampeded by the people leaving the arena when a slow roar turned into something that sounded like a freight train running right through the middle of Madison Square Garden.

I looked onstage and Sam was making his way back across to the very middle, where he pushed away the podium, grabbed the microphone and said, "Dim the lights for another moment."

The monster room came to a slow hush as the lights faded and at the very end it was as quiet as a mountain field. I noticed I was holding my breath, and let it out slow before taking a long deep one.

"I wanted to finish our conversation here tonight, much like I have many other times, to show the contrast in what I'm about to say now. I've recently had a…revelation…a very powerful revelation. As many of you know, I've been urged repeatedly to run for high public office to serve the great good of the American people."

The place erupted.

"Please, please," he yelled, walking back and forth across the stage. "Please let me finish."

People began to slowly sit to the motion of his hand. "I've given that very serious thought and consideration, but there is something I've been compelled to do more, to serve a greater good. I feel there is a need throughout the land for my public service, but in a much more personal way." He began to say something else, stopped and then said, "I'm sorry, I'm exhausted," and let out an exhausted easy laugh. After he looked up, I saw tears in his eyes, and for the first time he looked directly at me.

He'd known where I was the entire show.

He then looked up into the very top of the arena and said in a calm, quieter voice, "I've been so fortunate in life to have been given so much, and beginning tomorrow, I'm giving it all away. Everything. I'm going to spend the next few years on a walking tour of America, a drifter of goodwill, helping people whenever I can, and I know in return, receiving a helping hand if I should need it. I've had a great change of heart recently that we all should focus more on giving than taking, and I want to hopefully set a good example for that. There will be much in the media I'm sure over the coming days about my walk across America. I hope that we can all work together to help one another, and change this great country for the better. Everything I've said tonight still holds true, I just ask each of you now, to each day take a moment to give a little more. Help your neighbor. Help a friend. And forgive. Now the day may come in the future where I feel I can better serve my fellow man by running for the public office so many want me to seek, but for the next couple of years at least, I know my place is going to be with you, where you live, where you work, where you struggle, where I can see and experience for myself the everyday real problems and challenges you face.

"I hope to meet all of you on my journey. God bless."

He bowed, stood and looked to humbly appreciate the thunder of clapping hands. Just before putting the microphone back in its stand, he looked at me for a second, winked as he pointed one finger at me like his hand was a gun and then smiled.

The smart son-of-a-bitch, I thought. He still thinks he's gonna win the game.

As he walked back and forth on the stage with his hands and head held high, it made me wonder if someday he just might.

I couldn't wait to get out of New York City, but I couldn't wait to come back someday when I had more time to see all of it. There were so many things to see. The city was as amazing to me to stand in the middle of as it was to stand on the edge of the Atlantic Ocean and see what it must feel like to be a speck of sand. New York reminded me in a lot of ways of Shady Hollow, just a lot taller and more of everything.

But I had to make my way back south.

Kate had given me plenty of money to travel and live on for the trip, so that night I left my hotel and took a taxicab to the airport where I took the second plane ride I'd ever been on. This time I ended up landing in a bumpy small plane at a tiny airport in Wytheville, Virginia. From there I walked and enjoyed walking as I always did, thumbed a ride here and there when tired and ended up at the end of a long but fine day at Preacher Washington's house.

Trying to walk up to his porch, his chained dogs still

didn't like me and the preacher came outside. It must have been around suppertime, because he had a napkin tucked in his shirt when he opened the screen door. I could tell by his look that he didn't recognize me.

I'd gotten myself cleaned up during the two weeks I'd stayed at Kate's homeplace. I'd had a real haircut and a close shave and was wearing nice shoes. There was no way he'd remember me, unless maybe if he spotted one of my tattoos that struck a recollection chord.

"What can I do for you?" he asked.

I told him who I was and that made him uneasy at first, and then I reminded him how he'd helped me when I needed it, and told him how much I appreciated it.

"Yes, sir, I do remember you now," he said.

I told him how I'd had an account set up for him at the bank in Harlow, and that there was enough in it for him to draw on to fix up the house and church and own it all outright if he wanted to, with some to spare.

"I ain't sure what you're telling me," he said.

"I'm telling you that I came into a piece of money, and I'd like you to have some of it for the help you gave me."

He called his wife outside so loud it made me jump and she came out of the house, and she looked at me in a cautious way, scooting up beside him.

"Say what you just said again," he said.

I went through it again and he pulled the napkin from his collar and asked if this was some kind of sour joke I was pulling, and I told him it wasn't. I told him how I'd actually been worth quite a bit of money my whole life but never knew it, and now that I'd come into it, I had no need for most of it.

"I figured you might could use some," I said.

He started hollering at his dogs to hush up and they did as I approached the porch and handed him the bankbook. I watched the two of them study it careful and then heard the both of them start crying as I walked away.

"What's your name again?" he asked.

"Benjamin Purdue."

He nodded. "I believe you, because I told you a miracle was coming here one day. I told you, Mr. Purdue, and you didn't believe me then when I told you. I remember you didn't believe it…you didn't say nothing but you didn't have to because your face—"

His wife jabbed him in the ribs with an elbow. It slowed him down to take a breath.

"Ain't the workings something sometimes? Ain't they?"

I nodded.

"I told you a miracle was coming here. Do you now believe in what I believed in then? Can we pray together right here and right now… I need to give proper thanks for what's happened here today."

"I would, but I have some important things to tend to this evening that I'm running late for," I said. I waved at the both of them and was almost to the road when he hollered to ask if I'd had supper, and then if I needed another ride somewhere. I waved again. I had a full belly and a Zagnut bar in my pocket and it felt good to walk and I started out for the Groundhog Valley Motel. If I played my cards just right, and if I was lucky, I was gonna get to meet my daughter and hold my little precious angel granddaughter, named Faith.

They were my family, and I was ready to introduce myself to them if they'd let me.

The sky started to spit rain on my walk, but by that time in my travels I'd come to be pretty good pards with the weather. I put my collar up, pulled my hat down and just kept putting one foot in front of the other. One of Ma's favorite things to say growing up, and she had a bushel basket of such sayings, was that you can't fence sunshine to keep because its nature is to go wherever it wants to, whenever it wants to. I knew I wasn't bringing any rain to my daughter and granddaughter this time, even if it was starting to rain. It wasn't nothing but a little rain is all it was, anyway.

And I would have laid down a firm bet right then that the sun was gonna shine again soon, maybe even before I got there. Can't fence sunshine for sure, like Ma'd always said, but if a man kept walking to where he needed to head to, he'd probably run into it sooner or later, just not when or where he expected to, most likely.

At least that had been my experience.

I kept going over in my head the things I wanted to say to my daughter and granddaughter, and knew I'd probably have to pass inspection with the good-but-hard preacher who looked after them before any of that could happen. I kept rehearsing what I was gonna say showing up the way I was going to and it all sounded a little shaky. It never sounded right the more I went over it, so I figured I'd try to say not much at all and hoped the preacher and my daughter would do most of the talking at first.

As I got closer, I couldn't help but keep looking over one shoulder and behind me at the wilderness that had changed me like it did so many long months before, and it just felt inside like it had shown me the way to what I'd really been looking for, and didn't know it. I was finally home.

Epilogue

A long time has passed since walking that road. I'm an old man now, and as my injuries and scars from battles when I was younger started catching up to me, it got to where I couldn't walk like I used to. And I got so wore out that I figured when I only had one good walk left in me, that I knew where I needed to go, and that was back to an outlaw place that doesn't exist anymore called Shady Hollow.

Now I didn't walk all the way from North Carolina to Shady. When I got too tired I'd thumb, and I had better luck at it for some reason as an old man than I did as a young feller.

I did a lot of thinking about my life during what I felt inside of me was going to be my last walk. Mary didn't accompany me on this trek like she'd do sometimes. She wanted to, but I could tell she couldn't do the miles that we used to do together anymore, and besides that, sometimes a person just needs to walk alone, and she'd always been so good about understanding such things.

Mary and I had gotten married about a year to the day after we'd first met. Out of all of my blessings and good fortunes, she, my daughter, and my grandkids, and my great-grandkids, were my greatest blessings and kept me in good luck during the last years of my life.

It was a sad and rocky start trying to meet my daughter proper that first time. The rain did stop and it was a nice evening all the way around, and something told me when I stepped onto the porch and didn't see Preacher Fletcher in his rocker, that something was wrong. And it was. I came to learn a stroke had taken him a few weeks before I'd gotten back there to talk with him about many things, and hopefully get him to do the introduction. I was really sad about his passing in a deep way I didn't figure that I ever would be.

My daughter had a lot of hard questions about me after I'd shown up so unexpected. She was naturally suspicious and had concerns over what I was trying to tell her, so she called a friend to come over and watch Faith, and she told me to walk down to the restaurant where she worked, and that she would meet me in an hour. We sat over many cups of coffee, and I pretty much just tried to tell her about my life, the good parts and the bad parts, basically the story I've told here, and how she came to be my daughter. I asked of her to consider letting me be some part of her life because she and her daughter mattered a great deal to me, and I'd like to help her out in however I could, even though I didn't know a dang thing about being a dad. But I told her I was gonna try hard to learn and do my best at it.

I don't know why I never asked, but it suddenly hit me toward the end of our conversation that I still didn't know her name. She smiled and said, "Joy." It fit her and it made me smile. It wasn't a few days before she let me hug her, and hold my granddaughter, and I got to meet her boyfriend one evening at dinner and he seemed okay.

Joy and Faith came to live with me for a short spell a few months later down in North Carolina, until she got married to another young feller and they took off for all the things waiting for them. That left me in an empty house, but not for long.

Mary and I decided we'd build a life together out of the second halves of our lives that we wanted to put together like two sides of a cut apple, colored different on the outside but pretty much the same in the middle, and that's what we did. We made Kate's old homeplace our home, and I don't know how it happened, but I ended up being a farmer, something I never, ever thought would happen.

Just like Ma, Mary loved the sight and smell of pretty things and she tended to her flower gardens and being I loved to eat, I worked at my tomatoes and beans and corn and whatever else I could get to grow that could be put on a dinner plate. We ate and had plenty, and gave away the rest to folks that needed it.

I liked the daytime quiet of farming, and I liked seeing something good come from work. I guess for some odd reason, I ended up just enjoying work. I did end up still enjoying a game of cards or pool, too, though, and we always had music of some kind playing in the house in the evening time. I taught my grand-young'uns all I knew about things from how to grow a good tomato to how to play cards or tune a fiddle. They all turned out to be pretty good poker players.

Kate reined in my money after she noticed how fast I was making it disappear, basically just giving it away to about anybody I'd meet who I figured could use it. She put the majority of it away for my family, and I had an account I could draw on to buy things or for me and Mary to take trips to different places, which we tended to do several times a year.

Kate lived in her huge plantation home until she died just after we'd all rang in the New Year of the new century. She'd quit having her teas she liked so much several years before when she started having a good many health problems. Her last years were tough on her, but she'd turned out to be a pretty tough old gal, and a much happier one after she'd found a way to escape Sam Sherwood. Kate never did re-marry after their divorce, but she stayed busy with tending to the business of the plantation and her long lunches with friends and important cause and social engagements.

Sam Sherwood died several months after he'd began his walking tour in 1982. He'd just left a homeless shelter when he saw a man beating on a woman around the corner. Sam ran and tried to intervene, the man turned and hit him on the side of his neck with a bottle, it broke, opened up his head and skin, and he fell and quickly bled to death. Sam had a film crew with him at all times on his walk that even made him more famous than he had been, and the whole thing was caught by one of the cameramen. I didn't watch it, but I heard about it.

Sam did many good things on his walk, and he did give

away all of his money and the control over his companies, as was Kate's and my demand. But he did have an ace up his sleeve, I never was sure when or how he was gonna play it. But the way he'd went along with our demand so easily, I figured he was doing it because for some reason, it was something he decided that he was going to choose to do, not because he had to. It wouldn't take a man like him long to make all of the money back he'd given away, and I knew he knew that. I believe he actually liked the idea, and he became such a hero to folks, a regular modern-day Robin Hood type feller, and I think he was flat out getting a big kick out of the whole thing. He was constantly in the news and the cameras and the film they made about his walk across America won a big award with the movie people. Sam was still a fairly young man when he died, but he died a legend that continued to grow every year after his death, and we never released the packages. We let him pass on remembered for the good he had done, and by many accounts, he'd done quite a bit of good during his life. I don't know how the scales would tip with the good on one side and the bad on the other, but that wasn't my place to weigh such weighty things.

After his death, it didn't take long for his name to appear on hospitals, streets, schools, shelters, buildings of various kinds. All over the country, you could find his name honored on something. And he had thousands of followers, who continued on doing the good work he'd just began to do. I figured all of that would have set well with him, wherever he was at.

I thought a lot about all of those people and old times on my walk, and I also thought about Amanda. She seemed a

part of my childhood now. The very best part of my childhood, and we had such wonderful times and discoveries together that though her memory and my memory of all of
those times had faded, they would never leave me completely. I still smiled just thinking about her, and I had a feeling every now and then she thought about me and smiled.
I hoped so. I never saw her again after the time she tended
to my bedside and tried to tell me the painful things she had
to tell.

As I got closer and closer to that part of Virginia where
the mountains get so steep and time seems to slow down a
bit, the oddest thing happened. I got real tired and had to sit
for a rest, but when I stood I felt like a young man again. I
mean in my head and step and everything about me. I just
felt so young. I finally made it to the Big Walker River. I knew
exactly where I was then and figured I'd walk the train track
side awhile until I got down to Potter's Bridge, where I'd
cross over and make my way around the bottom rim of
Hellbender Mountain until I'd find an old cemetery that had
my name on one of the tombstones. It was there that I
wanted to say a few important things to Ma and also just
catch up on things that weren't so important but I just wanted
to talk with her about, and that's what I did when I got there.

Kate had bought and torn down the big ugly house up
on the side of the mountain years before, and we'd let the
whole place go back wild as was its nature to be. We took
down all the No Trespassing signs and put in picnic tables
and leveled off good places for people to camp and fish, and
I could tell they were being used. I also made sure the grave-

yard was kept up in good order, and at the end of the day went to pulling weeds around the people I'd known only as a boy. It was the oddest feeling, feeling so young again. I'd only felt like that a couple times since I was young, and those times were always when I was in a tough spot of some kind. I wasn't in a tough spot, right then, though, I didn't think. I just couldn't figure it out.

After I did my best policing up Polly Hill, I walked down to the edge of the water and decided I'd sit for a while under that big tree me and Helen had once had a talk under. I was surprised when I looked down and saw my old fiddle there. The last time I'd remembered having it was in my last strange dream when I was in that car with Sam Sherwood, and then in Shady Hollow feeling like a kid. I wondered if I was in another one of those dreams, but I suddenly couldn't stand not to pick up my fiddle and start playing tunes I hadn't played for so long. I kept playing long into the night, and at one point looked up in the sky and saw that bright light I'd seen only once before, only it was much brighter now. A blazing bright.

I believe it was calling me, I felt it calling me, but I still had a few tunes I wanted to play. I didn't figure nobody'd mind or care too much if an old feller sawed on a fiddle under a tree for just a little while longer.

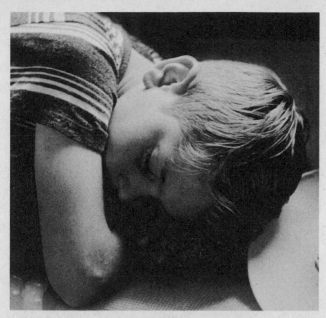

ANGEL'S REST

Charles Davis

Growing up in Virginia's Allegheny Mountains, eleven-year-old Charlie York lives at the foot of an endless peak called Angel's Rest, a place his momma told him angels rested before coming down to help folks. In 1967 his town was a poor boy's paradise... until a shotgun blast killed Charlie's father and put his mother on trial for murder.

In this remarkable debut novel Charles Davis weaves together an unforgettable melody of a mother's love, a hero's return to the living and a boy who discovers angels do exist.

"I highly recommend this beautiful story."
—*New York Times* bestselling author
Adriana Trigiani

*Available wherever trade
paperback books are sold!*

MIRA®